D1607928

Seanan McGuire

THIS SPECIAL SIGNED EDITION IS LIMITED
TO 1250 NUMBERED COPIES.

THIS IS COPY 1177.

Laughter at the Academy

Laughter at the Academy

Seanan McGuire

SUBTERRANEAN PRESS 2019

See Page 375 for individual story
copyright information.

Signed, Limited Edition

ISBN
978-1-59606-928-2

Subterranean Press
PO Box 190106
Burton, MI 48519

subterraneanpress.com

Manufactured in the United States of America

This book is for every editor who ever took
a chance on me, and every reader who trusted me
to show them what the lightning's for.

Most of all, this book is for all those fools who laughed
at me in the academy. I may not be raising the dead yet,
but I still know where my shovel is.

Contents:

Introduction

This is very exciting for me.

I've always been one of those people who devours every scrap of text in a short story collection: the introduction, the errata, the acknowledgments, *everything*. I want to know it all. I've swooned over Tiptree, curled up with King, and burbled happily to myself over Wyndham, and for me, part of that enjoyment was always in the little glimpses their collections gave me into who they were as authors and as human beings.

This is where, by format, I should offer up some extended metaphor, like "follow me into the forest" or "let's go walking in the fields together, you and I," but my metaphors are in my fiction, and tend to be pretty weird. Under the circumstances, I'm way more interested in the facts of the matter. Fact: this is my first single author short story collection. (For the pedantic among us, yes, there has been a collection of work published under my other name, Mira Grant, but that isn't the same.) All these stories take place outside my pre-existing universes—so no Fighting Pumpkins, no October Daye, no Velveteen. They are quick glimpses of another room, with a door that will close in short order.

Fact: all these stories were originally published between 2009 and 2017. This isn't everything from that time period, just the pieces I felt made the best contiguous whole. They span the length of my career so far. This is the first time many of them have been reprinted, making this the most convenient way for new readers to get a taste of what I do. I've done some light editing to the earlier stories, mostly so I don't cringe when I see someone holding a copy of this book, but they are, on the whole, as they were first released.

If this is your first time reading many of these stories, welcome. I hope you'll enjoy them. I've included little introductions to ease you in and give you an idea of what's in store for you; these can be skipped if you prefer to go in as unprepared as possible. I am still a fanfic girl at heart, and I believe in tagging things: these introductions include basic content warnings, although there's always the chance I won't think to flag something you might have issues with, so tread lightly.

If these are old familiar friends to you, welcome. I hope I've chosen the stories you would have wanted to see, and if not, I hope you'll look at the pieces that might not have made your list with fresh eyes. It's possible that they'll surprise you. This isn't necessarily "the best of," but it's the pieces I love most, that I'm most eager to share.

This is all very exciting for me.

I hope it's exciting for you, too.

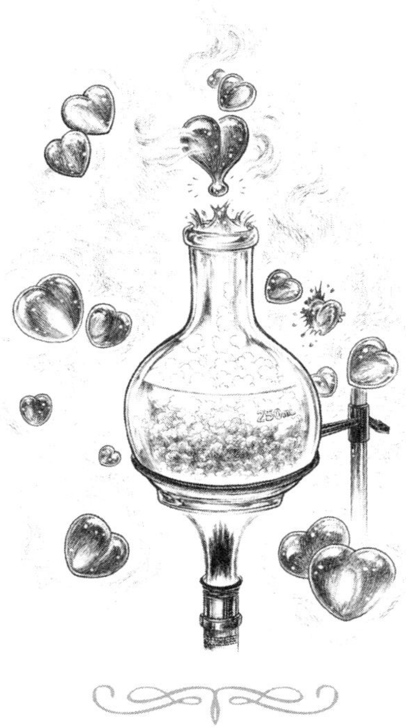

Laughter at the Academy:

A Field Study in the Genesis of Schizotypal Creative Genius Personality Disorder (SCGPD)

Our title story!

"Laughter at the Academy" was written for the anthology *The Mad Scientist's Guide to World Domination*, edited by John Joseph Adams. He had originally invited me to contribute a story, which was a huge, huge honor, and I had been forced to politely decline due to other deadlines. Then, a week before the anthology closed, he contacted me again: there had been a withdrawal, and he was hoping my passion for weird science meant I might have something he could use. I didn't, but I had a song called "What a Woman's For" that was practically screaming for expansion. This time, I didn't tell him no.

(This anthology was the beginning of a long and fruitful partnership. You'll see his name a lot in these introductions.)

This story is my love letter to the misunderstood and much maligned mad scientist trope. It contains ableist language and a lot of corpses. Most of the scientists are named after friends of mine, because I am a dangerous person to love. Special thanks to Shaenon Garrity and Kate Secor, for continuing to speak to me. "What a Woman's For" won the 2010 Pegasus Award for Best Mad Science Song. I am nothing if not consistent.

Upon consideration, we must agree that the greatest danger of the so-called "creative genius" is its flexibility. While the stereotypes of Doctors Frankenstein and Moreau exist for good reason, there is more to the CG-afflicted than mere biology. So much more. The time has come, ladies and gentlemen, for us to redefine what it means to be scientists…and what it means to be afraid.

—from the keynote speech delivered to the 10th Annual World Conference on the Prevention of Creative Genius by Professor Elizabeth Midkiff-Cavanaugh (deceased).

0.

The world's best research has always been done in the field. Anyone who tells you different is lying, or trying to hide something. Ask anyone who's seen my work. My results speak for themselves.

IGNORANCE IS THE ONLY TRUE SIN; SUPPRESSION OF KNOWLEDGE IS THE ONLY TRUE CRIME. IGNITE THE BIOSPHERE. LET THE REVOLUTION BEGIN.

—graffiti found in the ruins of MIT. Author unknown.

1.

"I hope I haven't kept you waiting long, Miss—?"

"Marlowe. It's all right. Now it's my turn to hope you don't mind, but I brewed a fresh pot of coffee and did the dishes that were in the sink. I know it was an imposition. I simply don't know what to do with myself when I don't have anything to do with my hands."

"Mind? Why, no, I don't mind at all. Thank you. I've been meaning to do those dishes for...well, let's just say the dishes aren't the first chore to come to mind when I have time to tidy around here."

"No thanks needed. You shouldn't be wasting your time with things like this. Isn't that why you're advertising for an assistant? So that you'll have someone to take care of the mundane chores, and free you to handle the things that matter? The *important* things?"

"Yes, Miss Marlowe. That's exactly right. If you'll come with me, I'd like to discuss the job a bit further."

"Why, Doctor Frieburg, it would be an honor."

Schizotypal Creative Genius Personality Disorder (SCGPD) was recognized in the 1930s by a Presidential commission convened following the destruction of the Washington Monument. Those brave, august men, half of whom were probably mad in their own right, decided the label of "mad scientist" created a self-fulfilling prophecy, one which, by naming individuals as "mad," made their madness a foregone conclusion...

—excerpt from *The History of Creative Genius in America*, by Professor Paul Hauser (missing, presumed dead).

2.

Sunrise cast its bloody light across the lab, illuminating the devastation without judgment or mercy. Electrical fires burned deep inside the wreckage, forcing rescue personnel to add gas masks to their standard-issue gloves and reinforced boots. Many of them were secretly grateful for the extra protection, no matter how uncomfortable it was. It was never wise to breathe unfiltered air near a confirmed SCGPD outbreak site, and doing it while something was on fire was just signing up for an interesting new mutation.

"Sarge, I think you should come and take a look at this."

Sergeant John Secor rose from his examination of a smoldering desk and picked his way through the shattered ceiling tiles and broken sheetrock to his squad mate. After six years on the Mad Science Cleanup Patrol—not that anyone official would be so gauche as to use the name; they called it the Special Science Response Unit, like having a polite title would change the nature of the job—he was growing numb to the horrors that greeted him with every incident. Perversions of every natural law, horrific mockeries of humanity, impossible distortions of the fabric of reality…they were everyday occurrences, verging on the blessedly mundane.

The bodies were another matter. This one still looked human, lacking visible mutations or half-rejected cybernetic implants. If not for the bloodstains on his lab coat and the unnatural bend in his neck, the man sprawled on what was once the laboratory floor would have looked like any other research technician. One more scientist dreaming of a better world for all mankind.

"Poor bastard," muttered John, crouching to study the body's visible injuries. He didn't touch it. The scene was already compromised beyond recovery, but the risk of infection remained if one or more of the local madmen had been working with pathogens.

"We have an identity. It's Dr. Charles Frieburg."

"What was his field?"

The attending officer tapped the screen of his tablet. Then: "Particle physics. He was a faculty member at the local university until last year, when he received a grant to pursue private research. There are no flags on his file. He showed no signs of SCGPD."

"But this is a confirmed incident."

"Yes, sir."

"Poor bastard," John repeated, and stood. "Something drove him over the edge."

"Shall I call the medical team to remove the body?"

"Yes, and keep sifting. If he had any staff working with him, they probably didn't make it clear of the blast."

One of the most controversial aspects of the SCGPD diagnosis lies in the conflict of nature versus nurture. Are mad scientists born, destined to crack under the pressure of their own minds? Or are they made, shaped by the world around them until they are driven to create even to the point of destruction? Can SCGPD be cured, or is it a scourge mankind is destined to suffer forever? And if it is inevitable, if the nature of this madness is part of our very genetic code, is it somehow necessary for our ongoing evolution?

—from "Development of the Creative Genius: Nature v. Nurture," by Doctor Aubrey Powell (diagnosed SCGPD, trial pending). Published in *Psychology Journal*, volume 32, issue 8.

3.

"I am *so* sorry about the delay. I got wrapped up in my research, and, well..."

"There's no need to apologize, Doctor. Believe me, I understand the attraction of finishing a job before dealing with mundane things—like hiring a lab assistant."

"I admit, Miss Frieburg, I was a little surprised to receive your résumé. I don't want to keep you here under false pretenses; we're not hiring research staff right now."

"I'm not here for a research position."

"Then, if you don't mind me asking, what *are* you here for?"

"If I may be frank, Doctor, your lab is a mess. Your equipment is well-maintained, but your filing is a disaster, and from the glance I took inside your refrigerator, your existing staff is in a state of constant danger from E. coli or worse. You don't need more research staffers. You need an office manager. Someone who can take care of the mundane, while you focus on the extraordinary."

"And you think you're the appropriate person for the job?"

"Doctor Bellavia, I think once I've been here for a little while, you won't be able to imagine operating this lab without me."

The number of incidents involving seemingly-latent SCGPD sufferers has risen precipitously in recent years. Many root causes have been proposed for this phenomenon, but we are no closer to identifying the trigger—if, in fact, there is a single trigger—than we were when the first incidents occurred. Whatever is causing these good men to lose their minds, we are neither positioned nor prepared to defend against it.

—report to the City Council by Captain Jovan Watkins of the Special Science Response Unit (deceased)

4.

The destruction of Dr. Rand Bellavia's lab made the news, not only in upstate New York, but throughout the country. His work in recombinant genetics had been hailed as a triumph of the stable mind for years, proving that a researcher who had not succumbed to the lure of jumper cables and evil plans could still push the frontiers of science. There had even been rumors that he might find a treatment for the biological causes of SCGPD, allowing for the rehabilitation of the hundreds of brilliant minds locked in endless war with their own inner demons. He was a poster child for science as a force for good…at least until the tentacles started bursting from the windows.

"Another one," muttered Sergeant Secor, staring at the photo of Dr. Bellavia's face gracing the latest issue of *Time*. The headline, "Science: Is Progress Worth the Price?" seemed unnecessarily sensationalist. Then again, when had the media ever dealt fairly with the victims of mad science? "If it bleeds, it leads" was the only commandment of the news.

This one sure as hell bled. What it didn't do was make sense. Dr. Bellavia had been a pillar of his community. He'd displayed none of the classic signs of the latent mad scientist. He'd had friends, family, a healthy social life; he'd left his lab more than once a month. He'd been tested every year for signs of SCGPD, and every test had come back clean. This should never have happened.

But it had—and Dr. Bellavia wasn't the first. John started thumbing through the incident report for what felt like the hundredth time. Everything looked normal. The shipping manifests showed the items and amounts to be expected for a medium-sized genetics lab. The staff list was up-to-date, and matched the list of casualties provided by the coroner's office perfectly.

Almost perfectly.

Frowning, John dug through the papers on his desk until he found the coroner's report. The staff list was one name longer. They'd recovered a lot of bodies from the wreckage. DNA were required to identify many of the researchers, in some cases because multiple individuals had been twisted into a single grotesquerie. The report stated that all analysis was completed, and there were no more foreign DNA strains in need of identification…and there was still one name missing. The office manager, Dora Frieburg.

Five minutes on the computer introduced two disturbing new facts to the case. There were no records of an individual named "Dora Frieburg" anywhere in the Special Sciences database, which meant she'd never been tested for SCGPD, and that she hadn't graduated from any known Master's program. In fact, the only hits for the name "Frieburg" came from the incident report on the destruction of Doctor Charles Frieburg's lab eight months earlier, in central Minnesota. His lab had been rather more thoroughly devastated, and they never did quite get the coroner's report and the staff lists to match…

And the office manager, Cathy Marlowe, was among the missing.

The office seemed suddenly colder. John bent over his keyboard and continued to type.

The only certainty we have when dealing with this insidious disease is that it will not be, and cannot be, truly defeated. It is the monster in us all, waiting for the opportunity to open the final door between the human mind and madness. Keeping that door guarded is our duty and our burden, as scientists, for to allow the lock to be broken is to lose everything that makes us moral, that keeps us honest... that makes us men.

—from the keynote speech delivered to the 10th Annual World Conference on the Prevention of Creative Genius by Professor Midkiff-Cavanaugh (deceased).

5.

"Professor Raymond, I have that shipment you requested. I'm afraid the delivery man didn't leave an invoice, so I can't be sure everything is here. Would you like me to assist with the unpacking process?"

"Yes, Miss Bellavia, that would be most appreciated. Did he say *why* he couldn't leave the shipping list?"

"No. He just dropped off the boxes and ran. I can call the office if you'd like..."

"I think that would be best. But first, let's get these things put away. Some of them are perishable."

"Of course."

"I...Miss Bellavia, did you order this?"

"No, sir. I entered the request exactly as you gave it to me. What is it?"

"It's—it's a Jacob's ladder. A form of spark gap. They're mostly decorative, although some people say you can learn things through watching the movement of the electricity. That you can see the true nature of the universe in the ionization of the air..."

"Professor? Are you all right?"

"I'm sorry, Miss Bellavia. I'm fine. I just haven't seen one of these in years—not since my high school science fair. I wasn't prepared for the memories it brought pouring back. That's all."

"Would you like me to have it returned to the distributor?"

"I don't think that will be necessary. It will be...nice...to have something around that reminds me of my past. The reasons I fell in love with science. Yes. I'll put this somewhere safe, somewhere in the lab...you needn't worry yourself about it, Miss Bellavia. I'll take care of everything."

"Yes, Professor."

"Are you smiling, Miss Bellavia?"

"I'm just glad to see you progressing with your work. That's all."

The question remains: If SCGPD is an incurable part of our genetic makeup, what causes its expression? Can that expression be prevented, or even controlled? Imagine a world where the forces of creative genius are harnessed, devoted only to growth, and independent of all destruction. A world where each child is free to reach his or her potential, free of the fear that one day, a casual word or an unexpected setback will trigger madness. If this paradise could be made available to the human race, would it not be our duty to pursue it?

—from "Development of the Creative Genius: Nature v. Nurture," by Doctor Powell (diagnosed SCGPD, trial pending). Published in *Psychology Journal*, volume 32, issue 8.

6.

"Captain, I'm telling you, the pattern is clear. You need to look at the data."

"Do you realize what you sound like, John? A mysterious lab assistant whose name changes every time she appears, somehow driving some of the nation's most brilliant minds into the grips of psychological disorder? Escaping disaster after disaster—to what end? What motive could this woman possibly have?"

"I don't know, sir." Sergeant Secor stared resolutely ahead, trying to ignore the look of disbelief on his superior's face. "The pattern is too consistent to be accidental. I combed through seven years of incidents. This anomaly is present in eighty percent of the reports. Five or ten percent, I might be able to dismiss, but eighty? Every time, she's been hired within the past four months. Every time, her surname matches that of a recently deceased scientist who fits the special handling profile. And every time, the lab is destroyed, with no survivors, but her body is never found. It can't be a coincidence, sir."

Captain Jovan Watkins sighed. "If you're sure about this, John..."

"I am, sir."

"Bring me proof. You'll need to find this mystery woman. We need a name, and a reason for anyone to be willing to do the things you claim she's doing."

"Yes, sir. I won't let you down."

"I certainly hope not, John. Dismissed."

THE SUN WAS CREATED BY A MAN WITH A SUPERNOVA WHERE HIS HEART ONCE BURNED. EMBRACE GENIUS. IGNITE THE SKY.

—graffiti found in the ruins of MIT. Author unknown.

7.

"Professor, there's someone here to see you. He says he's with the SSRU. Should I show him in?"

"Please, Melissa. Then why don't you gather up the rest of the staff and take them out for lunch? My treat."

"Is this...is it time?"

"I think so. Be sure everyone takes their wallets and leaves their laptops, just in case."

"Will you be careful?"

"Oh, probably not. I never have been before, and I don't see the point in starting now. Hurry along, Melissa. It wouldn't do to keep the nice policeman waiting."

Melissa went. I didn't expect any different; she's been a good technician since the day I hired her. She was wasted in the herd environment of the psychology department. Her work with me may not have enhanced her résumé the way a more traditional fellowship would have, but what I can't offer in prestige, I've definitely provided in practical experience. I daresay her old classmates would be astonished by the things she's learned while they were watching rats run around in mazes and building Skinner boxes.

By the time she returned, a groomed, chisel-jawed specimen of *Homo officicus* trailing along behind her, I was wearing my formal lab coat—the one without the bloodstains—and seated behind my desk, a pair of reading glasses pushed to the top of my head as I pretended to study my monitor. When setting a scene, it's the details that matter; show, don't tell, as my creative writing professor once told me, before he slew half the graduating class with an infectious poetic meme that inspired euphoria followed by suicidal depression. Professor Hagar was a wonderful teacher, and I will treasure his lessons always. They're so applicable in daily life. Consider:

A lab coat over a low-cut blouse shows a dichotomy of nature, implying that the subject is uncomfortable with her roles as both scientist and woman. Glasses propped against the forehead project vanity—a reluctance to conceal one's eyes behind a frame—coupled with vulnerability, due to presumably impaired vision, and absent-mindedness, due to the potential that the glasses have been forgotten in their present location. A simple pair of glasses can be one of the most useful psychological tools available, if you know how best to position them. Dress shoes with a low heel show the desire to look feminine, and acknowledge the necessity of comfortable footwear in a lab setting. I looked, in short, like an insecure stereotype, and it was all achieved with nothing but a few props and a knowledge of human psychology.

"Professor Garrity?"

That was my cue. I looked up, meeting Melissa's question with a genial, somewhat vacant smile as I replied, "Yes, Melissa?"

"Sergeant John Secor, SSRU, here to see you."

"Oh!" I stood, extending a hand for him to shake. "Professor Clarissa Garrity. It's a pleasure to meet you, Sergeant. What can I do for you today?"

It was hard to tell whether my psychological cues were finding their mark with this man. He had a matinee hero's face, all sharp angles and brooding eyes. It was annoying. I don't require that my targets be open books, but it's best when I can see whether or not I'm getting through.

"I understand your field is human sociology," he said, giving my hand one short shake before letting go. Matter-of-fact, then, business first; all work and no play. I could work with that.

"Yes, it is. I specialize in crowd psychology and behavioral conditioning. It's not flashy compared to some disciplines, but I like it, and I find it to be an endlessly fascinating realm of study. Would you like to see our workspace?"

"Very much so, Professor. I've been working on a case I think you might be able to assist me with."

"I would be delighted." He can't have hard evidence, or he'd have me in the station, rather than appearing here entirely on his own; he can't be acting with full departmental support, or he'd have backup with him, giving him the psychological upper hand. "Can you tell me anything about it, or do you have some data you need me to look at cold?"

"It's a bit of an odd one." He followed me out of my office, into the empty lab. Melissa worked fast. The staff was gone, probably ordering pizza on my tab, and she knew to keep them away for at least an hour. "Did you hear about the latest SCGPD outbreak?"

I made a show of thinking about it, reaching up to slide my glasses into place like I thought it would somehow make me smarter. Finally, I "guessed," asking, "Professor Raymond in New Hampshire?"

"Yes. He was a robotics engineer. Clean psych profiles dating all the way back to his college entrance applications. Everyone who knew him said there was no sign he was at risk."

"Oh, I see." Professor Raymond. Such a fascinating man. Such *skilled* hands. He'd been a joy to work with, and the dividends...my work is always rewarding, but Professor Raymond had carried it to new heights. Once he decided to open himself to the possibilities of the universe, he'd opened himself all the way.

The radiologists say Bedford won't be safe for human habitation for at least another hundred years. A fitting monument for a truly gifted man.

"It's a tragedy, but it's a fairly cut-and-dried one. He always had the potential to become symptomatic. There's just one thing that's troubling me about the situation."

"Oh?"

"He hired an office manager about three months before he went mad. She wasn't among the dead—and her name matches another low-risk scientist who became symptomatic for SCGPD about five months prior. Dr. Bellavia in New York."

Dear, sweet Rand. It's rare that I encounter a mind that brilliant. It's rarer that I get the opportunity to work on it directly. "I'm sorry, but I'm afraid I don't quite understand what you're getting at. What is it you think I can do to assist you?"

"Professor Garrity, your graduate thesis was on non-standard manifestations of SCGPD. Scientists whose work didn't fit the standard 'mad science' model, yet had the same potential as any other genius."

The same potential, and much looser testing standards. Never mind that a mad mathematician could conquer a nation with an equation, a mad linguist could drive a city insane with a radio ad, a mad musical theorist could control the world with a single Billboard hit. Keeping my expression neutral, I said, "That's true. Again, what is it that you think we can do for you?"

"Professor Garrity, can you account for your whereabouts on the evening of August sixteenth?"

"Certainly. I was leaving Dr. Bellavia's lab via the back door. He'd just reached the stage of wanting to test his creations on a living human population, and I thought it would be best if I was out of the building before the mutagens made it into the ventilation system." The screams had been beautiful. They had sung me out of the parking lot like a flight of angels.

Sergeant Secor's eyes went wide. "You admit your involvement in the triggering of Dr. Bellavia's SCGPD?"

"Naturally. It was some of my best work. But you must answer a question for me, Sergeant, before this goes any further."

His hand inched toward his sidearm. He was a clever boy, really. Not clever enough to come in with a full extraction team, but one can't have everything in this world. "What?"

"How resistant are you to transdermal sedatives? On a scale of, say, one to losing consciousness right about now."

The sound he made when he hit the floor was deeply satisfying.

One day, the world will realize that it has been at war for years. War between the past and the future; war between the visionary and the blind. One day the world will realize human nature cannot be dictated by law. It can only be temporarily suppressed, and one day, when that suppression ends—as it inevitably must—those who have been kept in bondage will rise up, and together, they will set the skies to burn.

—from the manifesto of Professor Clarissa Garrity, unpublished.

8.

The Sergeant returned to consciousness to find himself strapped to his chair. He struggled briefly before he subsided, glaring. "I am an officer of the law. Release me at once."

"I'm afraid that won't be happening for a few hours yet, Sergeant. I hope you're comfortable." I busied myself with getting the screens into position. The work would have gone faster with Melissa and the others helping me, but I needed them out of the lab, watching the door for any additional uninvited guests. "The straps aren't too tight?"

"I don't think you understand the severity of the charges you're facing."

"In good time, I promise. Congratulations, by the way, on catching the sequential names. I really did hope that would be the first trail of breadcrumbs to be successfully followed to me." I stepped back, offering him a warm smile. "Can I get you anything before we begin?"

"Begin? Begin what?" His bravado died in an instant, replaced by wariness. That was good. That showed intelligence.

"Your tests."

It took quite some time for the screams to stop.

There is no cure. There is no hope. There is no God. There is only fire, and the echoes of those fools who laughed. They're always laughing...

—from the suicide note of Professor Midkiff-Cavanaugh (deceased).

9.

I hate force conditioning a subject. It lacks subtlety, and more, it lacks *elegance*. There's an art to finding the locks buried in a person's mind and crafting the keys that will undo them, each one beautiful and unique. Sadly, time was short, and there was no other way.

"I'm so sorry, Sergeant. This was a job for a scalpel, and I've had to use a sledgehammer. I hope you can forgive me." I turned off the projector and walked toward him. He was whimpering and twitching in his chair, eyes frantically searching the corners of the room. The hot smell of urine hung in the air. He'd wet himself at least twice. That was good. That meant things were going as planned.

"How are you feeling? Do you need a drink of water?"

He giggled.

"Good." I pulled a damp washcloth from my pocket, beginning to wipe his forehead. "Let me tell you a secret, Sergeant. You're losing this war because the men who created the diagnosis for SCGPD left a few classes of genius out. They forgot that brilliance can take many forms. You, for example. You have a brilliant analytic mind. It's a shame you were never given the opportunities that would have allowed you to hone it to its greatest potential. You were never taken seriously as a scientist of human behavior." I scowled, remembering the glares of my so-called classmates, the ones who believed that real science was found only in electrons and DNA. They never understood that the mind, and the mind alone, is where the heart of genius truly lies. "This petty world and its petty lines. One day, they'll understand. One day, they'll see that madness is the only route to sanity."

Silence.

"But you don't want to hear about all that, do you? No, you've wasted enough time. Haven't your hands been tied for long enough, Sergeant? Aren't you tired of being hobbled by artificial, useless constraints? Religion, morality, social expectations, rules and regulations and *paperwork*—you've spent so much valuable time and energy justifying yourself. That was time you could have used saving lives. Doesn't that bother you? Doesn't it just make you *burn?*"

Silence...but there was a new light in his eyes; a light that spoke of understanding. I was getting through to him, and that was all I needed. Sometimes a spark is all it takes.

"I'm setting you free today, Sergeant. After this, you'll never need to hesitate, never need to question yourself. Their rules won't apply anymore. It's time for you to find out what kind of man you *really* are, and I'm happy to help, because I want to know just as much as you do. That's what I do. I help people reach their full potential, and in return, they help me set the sky on fire. That's what you'll have to do. You'll have to set the sky on fire. Do you think you can do that for me? Do you think you can make them pay?"

Sergeant Secor babbled something incoherent, following it with a peal of merry laughter. I leaned forward and kissed the top of his head.

"Don't worry. You've waited long enough." I returned the washcloth to my pocket, withdrawing the first syringe. "Everyone deserves the opportunity to go mad."

It's all so clear now. Crime is a natural outpouring of the septic core of human nature. It can be predicted. Human response illustrates every possible violation. There's no point in waiting for those violations to occur. All we need to do is strike.

—Sergeant John Secor, SSRU, transcribed from security footage taken immediately prior to his shooting.

10.

"Hello, Dr. Talwar."

"Why, Miss Secor. I wasn't expecting you for another hour."

"Well, you know what they say. The early bird catches the worm."

"I always wondered what that said about the early worm."

"That it's always best to be a bird, I suppose. I do hope you don't mind. I'm just so excited about the opportunity to help you with your work that I couldn't wait for the chance to get started."

"That's very industrious of you."

"I believe everyone should have the tools they need to achieve their full potential."

"And you believe you could be one of those tools?"

"Oh, Doctor. I know I am."

Lost

There are very few stories that absolutely had to be included in this collection: this is one of them. While "Lost" was not the first story I wrote or sold, it was the first story to appear in a print anthology: *Ravens in the Library*, which was put together by SatyrPhil Brucato and Sandra Buskirk to raise money for musician S.J. Tucker, who had been hit with sudden and unexpected medical bills. I am so proud of our community for coming together to help someone who genuinely needed it, and I am still honored to have been a part of this project.

When Phil asked me if I would write a story for *Ravens*, the first three October Daye books had been sold but not yet released. People knew me as a fan and a filker, but unless they were remarkably fond of certain types of fanfic, they didn't know me as a writer yet. Phil, Sandy, and I were all at the same party when he told me he was putting together an anthology, and asked for a contribution.

Reader, I hugged that man.

My first version of "Lost" was much more distant, and almost read as a "Screwfly Solution" pastiche, told as it was through newspaper clippings and letters, rather than by a single narrator. Phil kicked it back to me, asking for a complete rewrite, and I am so glad he did. What I eventually landed on is infinitely stronger.

This particular story is special to me for a lot of reasons, some too personal to go into here. It contains child abduction and allusions to a certain story about a boy who fell out of his pram and found his way to an island where children might fight, and die, but will never, never grow up.

Let the world tell all the lies it wants; I was there in the Year of the Children, and I know the truth.

This is how it happened.

We don't know when or where the singing started, but the earliest written record I can find points to Michelle Pierce of Crows Landing, California. She was eleven years old, blue eyed, red haired, and full of wonder at the world. Her father found her standing barefoot in the backyard on the night of January 8th, with her face tilted up to the cloudy winter sky.

"She was smiling like she had some sort of secret." That's what the article says, a grieving father's words preserved on microfilm. He was right. Michelle had a secret. We all did. It just wasn't shared until it was already too late.

I like to think he stepped up next to her, squinting to see what was holding her attention so completely. That's how I picture them, father and daughter, standing side by side. "What are you looking at?" he says, after a bit of time goes by.

Michelle casts a glance in his direction, the little cat-and-canary look all girls know from birth, and she says, "Nothing."

"Let's get inside. It's cold out here."

That's how I see it, anyway. Their feet leaving glittering trails in the evening dew as they walk together through the grass. Her father tucking her into bed a little later, and Michelle already half-asleep, mumbling to herself. "I thought she was saying 'moon,'" he'll say later, when the truth comes clear. "She'd been looking at the sky, and…and it didn't seem like anything important."

"Soon," says Michelle, and drifts away to dreams.

It took a month for the curious communion of children and the sky to become a global phenomenon, with children as young as two and as old as fourteen standing transfixed in backyards and in front of windows. There are dozens of articles about it, all of them treating it as a funny little fad just a bit more incomprehensible than most. They asked us why we did it. If anyone told, it didn't make the papers.

Things changed again two weeks later, leaving behavioral scientists and child psychologists at a loss. There are articles about that, too. It wasn't so much that we'd started humming. Children have always liked to hum.

It's that we were all humming the same song.

I celebrated my fifteenth birthday by counting the candles on my cake and breaking down in tears. It left my parents frantic. I don't think they'd seen me cry since I was six. But I'd been spending an hour a night standing in the yard with my sister, humming at the sky, and I knew what that fifteenth candle meant.

Torrey was the one who broke the code of silence we'd all shared until then. She never was much of one for rules. "He's too old now," she said. "It's not so bad for most of them, but Danny almost made it."

"Too old for what?" asked Mom.

Torrey looked at her, brown eyes wide and solemn in her narrow face, and said, "He's too old to go."

From the look on Dad's face, he liked those words even less than he liked my tears. "Go where?"

She looked at me. I nodded my agreement, and neither of us said anything else. Torrey went outside alone that night, and I went to my room and cried until I fell asleep.

Everywhere there was, the children hummed, and still no one guessed what was coming, or how little time was left.

They started singing at the beginning of April, although for some reason, no one could ever quite figure out the words. Parents pressed for details, and got none; just silence and cat-with-canary smiles.

I never knew the words, and I never asked Torrey to tell me. It wouldn't have been fair. So I let it all go, all the games and songs and sisters. I threw myself into schoolwork, graduated college, and grew up to be a solid, respectable sort of man, the kind whose colleagues say makes up for a lack of imagination by being totally reliable. Besides, some of them had been young enough to hear the singing, even if they were left behind.

Some of them understood why I had to forget where the children went after they told me I was too old to go with them.

It happened on May 9th, and it happened at midnight. New Zealand was the beginning, thanks to the International Date Line, but it wasn't the end. Midnight swept the globe, carrying the children with it. They slipped from their beds, tiptoeing down hallways and through living rooms as they made their way outside. Their parents would wake the next day to find unmade beds and empty bedrooms. There were no signs of struggle, of course, because there hadn't been one. The sky called and the children went. That was all.

Not all the children disappeared; maybe two in five were left behind. They were the ones who'd been the most willing to abandon their communions when the air was cold or their mothers called them in to dinner. The ones who were the last to start singing.

The news spread as more and more countries woke and found their children gone. Most parents had been warned by the time midnight reached North America. They knew to lock the windows and guard the doors, to keep their starry-eyed children tucked safe away until the unknown threat had passed. It didn't help. America's children went like the others, somehow slipping out through unseen cracks and out through secret doorways to vanish into the night.

I held the window open for Torrey as she shimmied down the drainpipe. I saw her wave goodbye as she ran across the lawn. And I never saw her again.

When midnight came to Crows Landing, California, Robert Pierce took his daughter's hands and asked her a question. Just one, the most important one of all:

"Where?"

He listened to her answer. Then he stood, unlocked the front door, and let her go.

The world has done its best to forget that night. Maybe that's for the best; maybe forgetting is what lets people keep going. Still, it happened, and it should be remembered somewhere. Just in case. In case this wasn't the first time. In case the story of the Pied Piper was another form of forgetting, covering another, deeper truth.

Just in case.

I didn't want to let my sister go. I would have held her back...but she told me to look at the sky, and I looked, and I *saw*. Pirate ships floating on the air, crewed by children in storybook motley and held up by tattered sails that glittered golden in the moonlight. That's when I let her go. How could I keep her from that? I loved her. That meant I had to lose her.

The ships appeared all over the world, seen by all the parents fast enough to follow but not fast enough to keep their sons and daughters home. Their crews steered them deftly to hover a few yards above the ground. They lowered rope ladders and lifeboats, and the children of the world ran to them. They climbed into the sky, singing all the while, and they were gone.

That's the first thing.

The second thing came later, when the shock faded enough for grief to settle in and distraught families started to clean out rooms and box things away. In every bed they found a golden coin, one for every missing child. One side was stamped with a moon and two pinprick stars, the other with a shape something like an island viewed through half-closed eyes, a place existing on the borderlands of sleep.

Ships used to pay a fee for crewmen. No nation has ever stepped forward to claim that blazon...but people around the world have looked at it, remembering a dream, and cried.

My story is almost over, and so am I. I'll lock this in my desk with Torrey's letter, and I'm sure my grandchildren will marvel at it when I'm gone. "He never told us stories," they'll say. "Who could have guessed he'd tell one about a tragedy like this?" They'll see this for fiction, because we've forgotten the singing of the children. The history books say it was sickness, a plague that came from nowhere. They excuse the lack of bodies by claiming they were cremated for reason of quarantine, they call the articles and news reports about the event a form of mass hysteria, and they move on.

For a long time—a very long time—I did the same. It was easier to forget. But I sang with the rest, even if I turned out to be just half a year too old. I sang.

Maybe that's why she came to me.

The knock at the door was unexpected. I get few visitors since my wife passed and my children moved to warmer climes. Maine is in my blood, always will be; I was born here, lost my sister here, and I'll die here when the time comes.

On the porch stood the cutest button of a girl I'd ever seen, all tousled curls and big blue eyes and all of eleven years old. She was dressed like a storybook pirate, down to the jagged treasure-map scar that ran the length of one dirty cheek.

"Daniel?" Her accent was strange, half-foreign, half-familiar, like the island on those coins.

"That's me," I said, trying to sound jolly, succeeding only in sounding old. I think I knew already. I know I didn't want to. "What can I do for you?"

"These are yours," she said, and from behind her back produced a bag of those golden coins and a fat envelope with my name across the front.

She held them out so imperiously that I took them without thinking, turning the envelope over to read the message scrawled on the flap—'Do Not Open by Penalty of DEATH Unless You Are My BROTHER,' and a looping signature that I determined, after a moment's study, read 'Tore the Bold.'

For a moment, I stopped breathing. How many left-behind brothers and sisters have received similar letters, I wonder, and never said a word? How many of us?

How many of *them?*

"What happened?" I asked, in a voice not quite my own.

"She fought brave," said the girl, and smiled, and said the thing I needed most to hear: "She died singing."

Then she was gone, back down the path to whatever vessel brought her to my door, the promise she made to my sister fulfilled to its end.

In the letter that was her life story and final farewell, Torrey said the things she'd left for me would be carried by Black-Hearted Mich, her best mate on the strange sea they sailed on, the strange and distant sea I was forbidden.

Michelle Pierce had blue eyes. And she was all of eleven years old.

What Michelle said to her father, on the night the pirates came:

"Away. It's going to be an awfully big adventure."

And then she ran, singing, into the night.

There's just one thing I wish I'd asked her, that impossible little girl who brought me the story of my forever-young sister's life. The life she led out there past the second star, on her golden-sailed ship, on that everlasting sea. There's just one thing.

The children who choose to leave us, one at a time or all at once, the children who choose to be lost, rather than to be found...do they ever have regrets? Do they ever wish they'd stayed behind? I hope not. I hope they're free, and lovely, and unafraid.

I hope they fly.

The Tolling of Pavlov's Bells

I love diseases. They're perfect, self-contained and efficient, and while they may not always get along with humanity—I love diseases and hate being sick, and I don't see that as a contradiction in the slightest—they do perfectly well by cruising along and doing their own thing. Having dinner with me is a constant dance of "what terrible thing is she going to bring up *this* time?"

I also believe that the modern world's disdain for quarantine and willingness to support structures which encourage its violation is going to do a great deal of damage one day…and that with new diseases emerging regularly from a variety of sources, that day may not be particularly far in the future.

I know at least one person who won't attend book signings anymore because of this story, and that is the nicest thing anyone has ever said to me. Contains a remarkably high death toll, even for me, and detailed discussion of disease progression.

Wash your hands.

POINT OF INFECTION +61 DAYS

I suppose there are things one can only learn through experience; the fever is coming on faster than expected, making it difficult to organize my thoughts. In the distance, I can hear them ringing, louder than the sirens, louder than the screams. Can you hear them, my daughters?

Can you hear the bells?

POINT OF INFECTION +50 DAYS

They hold my trial in absentia; an empty gesture intended to placate the screaming public. The growing silence outside the courthouse walls only serves to illustrate the pointlessness of the proceedings. It takes three days to present the evidence: the charts, the lab results, the videos. It would take longer, but after the fourth prosecutor fails to return from recess, the court decides to pass judgment on the case as it stands. There is enough—more than enough—to convict.

Each time the court is called to order, they add the name of every person who succumbed to my daughters between sessions to the charges already against me. More than enough.

I am found guilty of treason, fraud, bioterrorism, and sixteen million counts of murder. The sentence is broadcast over every channel and every radio frequency in the world, in every language someone might be listening for. No one cheers. There would be no point.

They all know that they've been beaten.

POINT OF INFECTION -13 DAYS

It's another meaningless late-night talk show, another opportunity not every author gets, as my agent is only too happy to remind me. "They love you," she says, in that breathless bedroom tone she uses when she wants to convince me to do something. I'm fairly sure she thinks I'm a lesbian. It doesn't matter. This exercise takes me away from the lab, but things aren't at such a crucial juncture that I can't leave Alan and Jeremy to watch them, and every bit of publicity helps. We must keep the public reading, after all. Isn't that what every author wants?

The lights are too bright and the leather couch stinks of sweat. I perch as prettily as I can, feeling the pancake makeup on my cheeks crack as I force myself into a rictus of a smile. The host is unfamiliar, but I can't say whether that's because he's new or because I didn't bother to remember him the first time. He's nowhere near worth the trouble of committing to memory.

"As a special treat for the intellectuals among us tonight, we're joined by Dr. Diana Weston, whose latest medical thriller, *Symptom*, is holding strong at the top of the *New York Times* Bestseller List." The smile he flashes at the camera doubtless cost more than most workers will make in a lifetime: a false, artificially white advertisement of genetic superiority. "Thanks for coming on the show, Doc. I'm thrilled that you're here—see, I've been having this pain in my side..."

He trails off as the studio audience erupts into laughter, comic Vesuvius spewing mirth into the air like ash. My smile stiffens a bit more, manicured nails biting into the skin of my palms. I must endure this. I have come so far, worked so hard, and I will not be defeated at the eleventh hour by some buffoon only looking for a cheap laugh.

"I'm not that kind of doctor," I reply, with as much amusement as I can muster. "But if you have an interesting boil you'd like me to take a poke at—"

This time the laughter is mine to command. My host isn't pleased. He recoils with exaggerated fright, putting up his hands. "On second thought, Doc, I'm feeling fine. Just fine."

"If you're sure," I say, still smiling.

Even sharks can smile. The host looks genuinely uncomfortable now, but also deeply confused. I am, after all, an attractive woman—I work hard enough to maintain my camouflage—and successful besides. My smile shouldn't turn his bowels to ice, and yet it does. His hindbrain recognizes what his thinking mind can't, and it knows enough to be afraid.

"I'll let you know if I change my mind," he says, finally. More chuckles from the audience. "Now, Doc, in *Symptom*, you're going back to some themes you've visited a time or two before. The horrible virus, the brilliant, attractive CDC doctor—"

Knowing laughter from the studio. They assume I model my heroines on myself, living out my intellectual lust for adventure in the safe confines of the story. They'll learn the truth soon enough. Soon enough.

"—and of course, the sexy federal agent who's standing by to help her when it seems like modern medicine will fail. Do you feel like you're running out of stories?"

"Not at all." For the first time, my smile is sincere. That doesn't seem to ease his nerves. "My readers know what they like, and what they like is the triumph of individuals over seemingly impossible odds. At the same time, I truly believe that most spectacular advances in medical science have been made outside the strict confinement of the lab, outside the boundaries of protocol. We learn by getting right out in the heart of things and letting ourselves fully experience the threats around us."

"I understand you've received some criticism from the medical community over your portrayal of quarantine procedures. Why do you think that is?"

Careful, careful; this is the baited hook, and I'm too close to the finish to let myself be caught. I lean back into the couch, shake my head, and say, "Quarantine is important—we've known that since the Middle Ages—but it's a scalpel, not a hammer. No one should suffer alone."

"But doesn't suffering alone mean your loved ones will live?"

I give him a pitying look. "Would *your* loved ones give up on you that easily?"

He nods and moves on, answer accepted. More senseless questions, more pre-programmed banter. I laugh, smile, play the part he scripts for me, and let my thoughts drift to the lab, where even now Alan is watching the cultures, checking the settings on the incubators, feeding the test subjects. My beautiful daughters are growing up.

This show will be canceled soon, along with all the others, and I will not be sad to see them go.

POINT OF INFECTION -6 DAYS

"Are you sure?" asks Alan, breathless with excitement. He's standing too close, his shoulder almost brushing mine, but I'll allow it, just this once. This is a moment too momentous to be spoiled by something as small as his inability to respect my personal space. "Is it ready?"

"The results speak for themselves. Our kill rate is up to ninety-seven percent in a population with a high immunity, and as close to one hundred percent as our tests can measure in a non-immune population." I smile at the figures on the screen, my oldest daughter's fingerprints transcribed in elegant, inarguable truth. "We're ready."

"That's...Dr. Weston, that's incredible." Light flashes off his glasses as he turns to me, earnest fanaticism written plain across his face. "What happens now?"

"We enter the final phase." I turn my smile on him. This close to the finish, I don't have to worry about leading him on. Things are coming to their natural conclusion. "Call Xiang and Jeremy. Tell them we're ready to begin dispersion."

"What will you be doing?"

Untrusting little assistant, worried that he'll miss the glories yet to come. He shouldn't be. No one will miss the fires ahead of us, when my daughters burn across the world like the phoenix of myth made sweet reality. When the world realizes at last that they've been listening, all this time, to the tolling of distant bells.

I touch his cheek, watching his eyes widen in surprise. "Why, I'll be getting ready for my book tour, of course. Now hurry. There's work left to do."

POINT OF INFECTION

They started handing out tickets to this event two days ago, an army of publicists and interns doing their best to control the crowd. I take no pride in their number, only a quiet satisfaction at a job well done. My authorial career has been the most difficult research project I have ever undertaken, and I've acquitted myself more than decently. This moment is the proof of that, eight hundred people eager for the chance to breathe my air and shake my hand, skin contacting skin.

Has there ever been a species more eager for its own extinction than mankind?

The vaccines are untested in the field on human subjects, but they have been reasonably successful in monkeys, in dogs…in the lab. Even if they fail me, they should buy a few weeks of time to cloud the issue. That, coupled with the latency we tailored in so carefully—sixteen days from exposure to first symptoms, ten of those days spent in an infectious state—should muddy the waters further, buy a little more time for the latter stages of dispersion. The injections will be sufficient, or they won't. There's no point in worrying about it now.

Empty perfume bottles are easy things to buy, and carry no suspicion. The bottle I produce from my bag is full now, and smells, ever-so-faintly, of fresh linen and lilacs. I spray the contents in a fine mist over my wrists and at the hollow of my throat, my oldest daughter kissing me sweetly before I take her, for the first time, out into the world. The human race is over at the first breath she takes in the open air.

There is no turning back now.

POINT OF INFECTION +9 DAYS

Jeremy is dead, shitting out his intestines in a tenement in downtown Berlin. His last e-mail was barely coherent, filled with typos and sentences that went nowhere. He made it further than I thought he would, carrying my second daughter all the way from California to New York, and from there to New Zealand, England, Europe. I hope he died proud of what he'd done, and that he had no final regrets. I watch the news feeds for hours, monitor the CDC alerts, but see nothing to indicate that anyone has noticed his travels, or that his death has made any mark upon the world.

Even now, the bacteria he carried in his bloodstream and on his skin are working their way into the world's water supply, spreading, multiplying, becoming present in ever greater numbers. By my calculations, the first "cholera" outbreaks should begin in eleven days, four days after my oldest daughter has made her presence known.

Jeremy is our first martyr, and our first sacrifice. The bells are ringing louder all the time.

I have never been more proud.

POINT OF INFECTION +11 DAYS

My little girl is swifter and stronger than I ever dreamed she'd be. People are dying already, the weak, the homeless, the elderly and the young. Doctors are baffled, and the seeds I spent so many years sowing are beginning to bear their bitter fruit. "Smallpox is dead," the doctors say, and because they've convinced themselves that's so, they believe it. They keep looking for another answer.

They won't find it.

Patient zero has been identified. A middle-aged male in South Dakota checked himself into the hospital at three o'clock this afternoon, presenting a set of symptoms as frightening as they are perplexing. Headache, fever, backache—all symptoms of common flu. So many things can masquerade as flu...but this flu is followed by subcutaneous blistering, leading to hemorrhaging of skin, eyes, tongue, intestines. The large blisters will begin forming soon. They'll start on his hands, feet, and belly, spreading to his throat and tongue. By that point, some cocky young doctor will be shouting "Smallpox" loudly enough to avoid being shouted down by older, wiser colleagues.

If I knew that doctor's name, I would arrange for a bottle of wine and a razor blade to be delivered, along with a note recommending a hot bath and a swift demise. Sadly, that grace is not mine to give, and he, like all the others, will die dancing with my oldest daughter, listening to the sound of distant bells.

POINT OF INFECTION +13 DAYS

My daughter's reach is spreading. I take my immune boosters regularly, watching the human race respond to her presence. Slowly, too slowly, and without the conviction they'll need if they're to survive. I don't believe they will.

It isn't too late for quarantine to save them. A great many are infected—thousands, potentially millions, if my calculations are correct—but more are still healthy, still outside the reach of my oldest daughter's glorious debut. If they were to stay home, avoid the company of strangers, and wait for a vaccine, they might stand a chance. But no one listens to the doctors, or to the newspaper headlines begging them to stay indoors. Instead, they rush the airports and clog the freeways, rushing to their families, and my daughter travels with them, invisible, spreading further with every step they take.

The visibly sick are left to die in their homes and in the hospitals, while the seemingly healthy flee into the night. The bells are ringing, guiding them along, and the people of the world obey. Ding. The hospitals aren't safe. Dong. The doctors are lying to you to protect themselves. Ding. Bad things happen to other people. Dong. If you can't see it, it can't get you. Pavlov had his dogs. I have the human race. The bells ring, and the people follow.

I go on a few cable shows, speak of the need to observe certain precautions while this "mystery epidemic" is brought under control. In the process, I casually mention the chance supply chains might collapse, that water-borne diseases might be able to work their way past aging municipal filters. The first cases of my tailored super-cholera reach the news then, and the looting starts swiftly after that. Panic is becoming a contagion in its own right, one that spreads from those who saw the reports to their neighbors, and onward and outward. Other nations report the situation in America, and watch in confusion as that same panic springs up in their own lands. They don't understand the importance of the bells, but they ring them for me all the same.

Pavlov would be proud.

Alan and Xiang have overseen the North and South American releases. Now, Alan sees to Africa, while Xiang performs his duties in Europe and Asia. It's so easy to travel, even now, if you have medical credentials and an earnest face. Both of them are known for their work with my lab, for their devotion to mankind, and they have gone unquestioned thus far. Our luck can't hold forever, but forever was never a factor in my plan. The latency has ended, and the burning has begun. If my youngest doesn't finish her release, the rest will still proceed. The bells are ringing loudly now. Even if I wanted to silence them, that power is beyond me.

I reach for the loaded syringe that contains the booster vaccine. I need to keep my health and wits about me for a little longer yet; long enough to see whether the human race can grow beyond the tolling of the bells. If they can, they may survive. If they can't...

My little girls will rule the world.

POINT OF INFECTION +19 DAYS

A stupid accident and a weak-willed fool: that's all it takes to tell the world what's coming. Alan was careless with the rats he was releasing into the African countryside. A soldier spotted him, and came to ask what he was doing. He might well have talked his way out of the situation—I hired him, in part, for his finesse with words—but the trap in his hands still contained a rat, terrified, confused, receiving a thousand conflicting commands from its tiny rodent mind. It chose the clearest path, and ran.

Alan, unthinking, grabbed for its tail…and it bit him.

He's in CDC custody now, begging them to save his life, telling them everything he knows. There has never been a guaranteed cure for rabies, and my youngest daughter is rabies writ large, incurable, unstoppable, already burning out his nervous system. In another day, she'll mature enough to enter her secondary phase, the one possible only in a primate host. A day after that, she'll be airborne and Alan, and everyone who comes into contact with him, will be lost.

I wonder if they'll realize what's happened before they spread the virus further, or if my darling will burn through Africa like a match set to dry grass. It makes no difference. So much of what Alan knows is wrong. My lab moved three days ago, after the last of my assistants was safely gone. The "vaccine" he has to give them is tailored for an enhanced strain of the bubonic plague, a project I abandoned years ago. He has no protection against what's coming. Neither will they.

Still, I wish he'd been stronger. I wish he'd lived up to the potential he once displayed.

I wish he'd been more ready to close his eyes and listen to the bells.

POINT OF INFECTION +28 DAYS

Alan and the African CDC are dead, leaving conspiracy theories hanging heavy in the air. My detractors say he wouldn't have fingered me if he didn't have proof. My supporters say he was jealous and embittered, that I would never do such a thing, especially not now, with such a crisis facing humanity. Such beautiful, misplaced faith they have in me.

I say nothing at all. I simply sit in my small, secure lab, and watch as my little girls dance their way around the world. Rabies burns in Africa; smallpox in Asia; cholera across America's heartlands. Humanity spreads its own destruction with every breath, every kiss, every drink of unpurified water. That's why I needed all three of my daughters. One alone might not have carried the lesson plainly enough, might have been twisted into the judgment of God. But three…three can be nothing but a lesson.

One that is, perhaps, too late for them to learn. The time for quarantines is running out, and still the people listen to the cold, commanding bells. I wonder if I ever expected anything more of them. Once, perhaps. Once, but no longer.

POINT OF INFECTION +38 DAYS

The streets are clogged with the dead and dying. Yesterday afternoon, a group of individuals in the final stages of their illness burned Chicago General to the ground. People were seen walking into the flames as if they had done the math of suffering and decided that the pyre was better than the poison prisons of their bodies. They may have been correct. My daughter is quick, and cold, but kindness is not a mercy she possesses.

The infrastructure will start failing any day now. The rolling blackouts have already started. For the most part, the power has stayed on, but that will change. Now is the time. There will be no better.

Xiang constructed the equipment I use to commandeer the signal of a local television station. "You don't need to take CNN," he explained, so patiently, so long ago. "As soon as the report goes live, the world will have it. Stay local and get the best broadcast you can. That way you don't have to worry about static changing the message in ways you wouldn't want."

He was a smart man. All my assistants were. He died of my youngest, like Alan. Unlike Alan, he used his own infection as a way to carry her deeper, all the way into the heart of Tokyo. I am so very proud of him.

I am wearing my best white silk blouse and the pearls my agent bought me after our fifth book together. My makeup is simple but carefully done, to make me look as healthy and well-rested as possible. Taking the signal is a matter of flipping a series of switches and stepping in front of the camera. Until I move into the frame, it records nothing but the plain white wall of the lab. I have no illusions—what remains of the authorities will surely find a way to track my signal, find my hiding place—but I see no reason to make it easier for them than I have to.

"Hello," I say to the camera, to the world. "My name is Diana Weston. I am a microbiologist, specializing in the study of pandemic behavior in viruses and bacteria. Many of you have read my books or seen the movies based on them. I have worked with the CDC, the World Health Organization, and dozens of smaller groups over the course of the past twenty years. You have every reason to trust me, and every reason to believe what I'm about to tell you:

"You are going to die.

"Maybe you're already sick. Maybe a friend or relative fell sick a few days ago, but you feel fine, and you assume that you're out of the woods. You're not. Each of the infections moving amongst you has a latency period of more than ten days. Without getting too technical, this means you're infectious but asymptomatic for some time before the first outward signs of illness appear. According to my tests, this particular mix of pathogens stands an excellent chance of wiping out ninety-seven percent of the human population. Consider that for a moment. Ninety-seven percent. Ninety-seven people out of every one hundred." I'm lying, of course. The human race represents a non-immune population, and the kill rate is likely to be closer to ninety-nine percent. My other two children will have very little work to do when their sister's work is done.

"I'm sure you wonder why I've done this. I would wonder, in your place." My books followed such careful, specific patterns, and this was one: just before the tide turned and the cure was found, the villain would reveal the evil plan that carried the human race so close to extinction. I want them to obey the bells. That means I, too, must play my part. "To put it plainly, I have done this *because I can*. I have killed your parents, your children, your lovers and your friends, and I have done it because I was capable of doing so. You *allowed* me to do this. You have refused medical care to the sick and to the poor, even when presented with proof that this encouraged the development of stronger, more effective viruses.

You have abused antibiotics, creating strains of resistant bacteria capable of undoing decades of medical progress. You have ignored the needs of your own bodies, and you have ignored the needs of the world around you, all while using surgeries, dyes, treatments and needless cosmetics to obscure your own degraded state. You have turned your backs on nature, forgetting your place.

"You have disregarded the laws of quarantine.

"The human race is not the first to rule this world. The dinosaurs came before us, and when they saw the comet coming, they could only stand and stare. You had the opportunity to turn your 'comet' aside. You had years of medical knowledge behind you, scores of experts beside you, and still you chose to run like dumb animals, useless and panicked, to infect the world that you were so sure existed to obey you. I am disgusted by what humanity has become. Shallow. Stupid. Undeserving of its place. I gave you every warning, gave you every opportunity, and you ignored them all." Ignored them, and worse, laughed at them. Laughed at the reports, penned years before my first work of fiction, that spoke of drug-resistant diseases and rampant bacterial infection. Laughed at the suggestion that survival of the many might require the sacrifice of the few.

I tried so hard, for so long, to make them see. All those years of scrupulous, back-breaking research, all those journal articles and double-blind studies. I wasted years on careful clinical trials with crippled viruses and "germs" of colored dust, struggling for funding and support, being told all the while that science and common sense were downers, and that effective precautions were too depressing to promote. My hope died first, then my altruism, and finally, my humanity; one so-called "virtue" for each child I would later bring into the world. My medical career mutated in the face of their laughter, leaving me dedicated, not to stopping the comet's descent, but to guiding it to ground.

Still. I felt that I owed the few the chance to save themselves; the chance to run for cover, to close the gates and struggle for survival. So I rang the bells, and watched as mankind danced to their tune. "My name is Diana Weston. I am the death of the human race. And I am not sorry." I straighten, still smiling. "You deserved it."

The camera is still rolling when the authorities reach the lab twenty minutes later, broadcasting nothing but the plain white wall. I am long gone, all my files and samples either with me or destroyed. My daughters are loose upon the world, and there is nothing anyone can do to stop them. Perhaps if they'd known where to start—perhaps if they hadn't been listening, from the beginning, to the sound of bells—but it is far too late for that.

I watch the raid from the safety of a nearby hotel room, paid for under an assumed name, and realize with joy that I have told the truth: even now, I am not sorry.

POINT OF INFECTION +50 DAYS

The bar is quiet, the television on the wall airing my trial over and over, for any who care to watch. There are only five of us here, and three are too ill to remain much longer. The fifth looks only at his drink; I might as well be nothing but a shadow on the wall. That's good. My disguises are meant to hold up under scrutiny; that doesn't mean I should go taunting fate.

I'm almost disappointed when they only sentence me on sixteen million counts of murder. My little girls have killed far more than that. I leave a twenty on the bar—meaningless currency of a dying world—and walk into the daylight, leaving the dark behind.

POINT OF INFECTION +61 DAYS

The streets are quiet, the stores long since looted, the few survivors fled to the country, where they think they can be safe. My middle daughter waits for them there, dug deeply into the water tables and hiding in the streams. Cholera is an efficient killer. All I've done is improve on the tools that nature put before me.

My fever spiked an hour ago. The first blisters have already sprouted on my lip, tiny kisses from my masterpiece, my oldest, my baby girl. Immuno-depressant smallpox with the latency of Lassa Fever, silent assassin of the human race. I knew the vaccine couldn't hold forever, that she'd come to thank me for her freedom eventually. I'm simply grateful that she let me watch the world die before she came to take me in her arms. It is a fitting reunion.

I have no regrets.

When I was young, I dared to believe in the good of man. When my beliefs proved flawed, I set a challenge before the world. Given the wrong lessons, shown the wrong examples, would they cleave to survival, or would they let themselves be led? Time and time again, they showed their willingness to take the easy way, like Pavlov's dogs slavering at the jingle of a bell. So I have rung the bells for them, and they, pampered creatures that they were, reacted according to their conditioning. The quarantine notices lie in tatters in the streets, the hospitals are clogged with the dead and with the dying, and every broken rule was one more sweetly solemn chime.

I know my daughters; I know their lack of mercy. The poison I've carried since the start is cool on my blistered lips. I recline upon the bed, closing my eyes, and listen with all my heart to the sound of my beautiful children, laughing, and the distant, endless tolling of the bells.

Uncle Sam

In some ways, "Uncle Sam" is a case of transcription more than composition. I came up with the central conceit of the story while I was in my last year of high school, and spent nearly a decade telling it to people as if it were a true piece of American history before I bothered writing it down. Because I am a delight who doesn't like it when her friends get too much sleep.

The process of writing this story was fascinating for me, because it had never had characters before: just the calm, methodical explanation of one of life's greatest mysteries. Why *do* women go to the bathroom in groups? Everyone has their answer. This was mine.

"Uncle Sam" was originally published in *The Edge of Propinquity*, edited by the delightful Jennifer Brozek, whose praises cannot be sung highly enough.

The smell of barbeque, biscuits, and beer perfumed the air of the Back 40—the best steakhouse in town, providing you didn't want your meat well-done and you didn't mind your meal coming with a side order of potential future heart attack. Half a dozen people were crammed into one of the roomier booths at the back of the restaurant, the table in front of them littered with denuded dinner plates and empty glasses.

"A toast!" John grabbed a beer bottle that still contained a few inches of liquid, hoisting it over his head to general cheers from the group. "To Angela, the last one to leave college, and the first one to actually finish her doctorate instead of dropping out!" The cheers increased in volume while Angela—a diminutive brunette with a conical paper party hat perched precariously atop her head—reddened and did her best to disappear into her drink.

Mary laughed, a sound like a grackle cawing. Angela threw a napkin at her.

"Come on, Angie." Tara elbowed her sister amiably in the side, clinking her beer bottle against Angela's glass in the same motion. "It's a party. You remember parties, don't you? That's where we sit around being social, instead of sitting around studying until our heads explode."

"I had a social life in college," said Angela defensively.

Everyone else laughed. "You had a social life when someone picked you up and dragged you, maybe," said John. "But it's okay. We love you anyway."

"I hate you all," muttered Angela.

"Liar," said Tara, fondly.

One of the other girls—Laurie, who worked with John at the Starbucks next to campus, and had come half as a date, half as a favor, since their reservation was for six—asked, not unkindly, "So what did you major in, Angela?"

"Folklore and mythology," said Angela, a little more confident now that she was on familiar ground. "My specialization is in the modern folklore of the United States, beginning with the colonial period and moving forward from there."

Laurie tilted her head. "So what, like, Cherokee legends and stuff?"

"No, not Native American folklore. That's a whole other area of study. My area is what most people call 'urban' folklore, going back to when the first European colonists arrived in North America."

"Oh." Laurie, still looking baffled.

Michael, who was sitting on the other side of her, patted her on the shoulder. "Angie has that effect on people. But she tells great stories."

"Thanks, Mike," said Angela. Her tone was dry.

Michael ignored it, beaming at her. "No problem. Hey, why don't you tell us a story? Now that you're all graduated and everything."

"I don't think—"

"Please?" said Mary, with what was clearly meant to be an ingratiating smile. She folded her hands beneath her chin, knuckles pressed against her jaw, and fluttered her eyelashes. "Pretty, *pretty* please?"

Angela threw another napkin at her, laughing. "Stop! Stop that. Do you really want me to tell you a story?"

"Yes," said Tara firmly. "Tell us the one you wanted to do your thesis on. The one your advisor said was too much of a reach."

"Really?" Angela wrinkled her nose. "Are you sure you don't want something more fun, like phantom hitchhikers or formaldehyde-soaked prom dresses?"

"We're sure," said John. "Tell us this mystery story."

Angela sighed. "Oh, fine. This is the story of Uncle Sam, and the founding of the United States of America, and why girls always go to the bathroom in groups..."

The restaurant was still loud around them, but the table went quiet, listening to Angela speak.

"The first thing you have to understand is that the United States isn't a democracy. It's a constitutional republic. The second thing you have to understand is that in the long run, constitutional republics don't work. They're wonderful for short-term governance, but they depend on a certain unity of purpose and a degree of selfless intent that doesn't usually last more than five or six generations after the revolution. People get complacent. Corruption slips in. The population grows too large to have a truly uniform outlook and becomes divisive. Eventually, there's another revolution, and the government falls, replaced by a new one—another republic, an actual democracy, a dictatorship, sometimes even a monarchy. It doesn't matter. What matters is that this form of governance, by its very nature, is a fleeting thing. It wasn't designed to last.

"When the men who would become our Founding Fathers planned their revolution, they knew they wanted a constitutional political system. It was their Platonic ideal. The thing is, they also knew that no constitution—no matter how fair and even-handed it was—would endure more than a few generations. Some of them even thought that was a good thing. That their mistakes would be forgiven by history when a new regime replaced the one they had created, and they would be remembered like Rome was: as a shining example of its time."

Laurie frowned. "I thought this was going to be a story, not a history lesson."

"I'm getting there," said Angela. "Not all the Founding Fathers thought it was a good thing that constitutional republics don't last. They wanted something that would endure. So they decided, in secret, that the only way to guarantee the country's survival was to find someone who could protect it no matter what happened. Someone—or some*thing*."

"Dun dun dun," said Michael. Angela glared at him.

"You asked for this," she said sharply.

"Just kidding!" He put his hands up. "Chill, Angie. You're going to stress yourself into an early grave."

Angela, who was out of napkins, threw a wadded-up straw wrapper at him. It bounced off the back of the booth. "In the dead of night, at the height of the American Revolution, the Founding Fathers gathered and made a sacrifice in the name of the Archangel Samael, begging for him to hear their pleas."

"Where have I heard that name before?" asked Laurie. She was starting to look faintly disturbed.

"Samael is the angel of death, and a tempter of men," said Angela. "He still dwells among the hosts of Heaven, but he's not the sort of angel you make deals with. Not unless you're willing to pay in blood."

"And the Founding Fathers were willing," guessed John.

Angela nodded. "They offered Samael a deal. Blood for protection. As long as the republic endured, he would be free to choose his sacrifices from among its people—and more specifically, from among its women. Originally, the bargain was for one sacrifice a year. On the anniversary of the agreement, he could walk the Earth, and claim one woman from the country he had helped to found as his own. But there was a catch."

"She had to be peeing?" guessed Tara.

"Not quite. See, the Founding Fathers—who weren't Christian men, for the most part, no matter what some people try to claim today—knew that having an angel show up once a year to devour one of their citizens wouldn't go over very well. So Samael had to choose his tribute from among the unseen. He could only take a woman who was completely outside the view of anyone else, and whose disappearance could be explained by mundane means. No snatching sleeping mothers from their beds or prisoners from their cells. He had to take the ones that no one was watching."

"This story is sexist," said Laurie.

"This story pre-dates women being considered anything but property," countered Tara. "Go on, Angie."

"The original bargain granted Samael—whom they were already beginning to call 'Uncle Sam,' to acknowledge his paternity over America, and to distance themselves from the idea that they were commanding an angel, something even the atheists among them recognized as dangerous and blasphemous—the right to claim one woman a year. As the population of the country, and the borders of the country itself, grew, that bargain was revisited. One woman a year. One woman a season. One woman a month. Until we come to today. The bargain was revised after Hawaii joined the union, and here and now, Uncle Sam is granted the right to claim one woman a night. Always taken from American soil. Always taken unseen."

Silence.

"Samael—Uncle Sam—has to follow the rules. Angels and demons always follow the rules. Oh, but he loves the luxury of choice, the freedom to select his payment from the population. So every time America is endangered, he finds a way to strengthen the republic. Every time the country might fall, he's there to prop it up. And all because of the women. You can spot their cases in the police records, if you know what to look for. There's never an official investigation. The authorities do the bare minimum and they let it go, one more cold case for the files. It's not that they know, exactly. It's just that they serve the state, and Uncle Sam serves the state, and somewhere deep down, where the dark things live, they recognize the hallmarks of their own."

Silence.

Angela looked around the table as she continued: "The most dangerous places, ironically enough, are public restrooms. Haven't you noticed how almost all 'American' restaurants position them around corners, near doors? Your sister, your daughter, your mother...once she's in that room, you can't say for sure that she didn't leave on some errand she forgot to mention. You can't be sure she ever made it to the restroom at all. Restaurants opened by people whose ancestors immigrated after the bargain was set put their restrooms at the back, where *someone* will be able to see the people come and go. Most of them don't realize why they do it, just like most of us don't understand why we always want to go to the bathroom in groups. They do it all the same. Chinese restaurants save a hundred lives every night."

Nervous laughter greeted her final statement. Laurie frowned. "That's a fucked-up story. You say you went to college for this sort of thing?"

"Folklore is important," said Angela, sounding stung. "Stories tell us where we come from."

"I always thought women went to the bathroom in packs because they were having hot lesbian sex in there," said John mournfully. Tara hit him with her spoon. The laughter that followed this exchange was less nervous than relieved, like some film of tension had been shattered.

"You asked me to tell the story. So I told the story." Angela pushed her way out of the booth. "I'll be right back. I need to pee."

"Watch out, or Uncle Sam might get you!" caroled Mary.

Angela stuck her tongue out at her and turned, walking away into the crowded restaurant.

"Maybe someone should go with her...?" said Tara.

John laughed. "You don't believe that junk, do you?"

"No, but..."

Everyone laughed. Tara sighed, sinking down into her seat, and waited for her sister to come back.

After twenty minutes passed, no one was laughing anymore.

The waiter brought the check, which Mike and Tara paid, having agreed to this arrangement before the party began. Angela didn't return.

The busboys came and cleared the table, giving puzzled looks to the group of people who sat there in frozen silence, none of them meeting one another's eyes. Angela didn't return.

Minutes turned into an hour, and began piling up again, looking to repeat their temporal alchemy. Tara started to stand, and John pulled her back down, shaking his head. If this was a prank, Angela would lose interest; she would come back. If this was a prank, the best thing they could do was wait. Angela didn't return.

At closing time, the manager came to speak with them. They left, quiet and puzzled, in their cars. Three days later, when enough time had passed, Tara called the police. They took her statement willingly, but there was a strange detachment in the way they handled her, like the process was somehow a formality. When the call ended, she couldn't help feeling like nothing would be done.

Angela didn't return. Six weeks after that dinner, neither did Mary. Two weeks after that, neither did Laurie.

Tara began eating Chinese food for every meal, sitting in narrow, safe restaurants, visiting the bathroom only when a dozen people could see her passing by. One woman a night. Angela had been too willing to share her stories, too happy to tell people the quaint little bit of folklore she'd uncovered. One woman a night. Tara burned her sister's notes, spoke to no one, and avoided being alone. One woman a night, out of the millions in America.

The odds were in her favor. She kept telling herself that.

One woman a night.

Crystal Halloway and the Forgotten Passage

I work best to prompts. Part of this is from my time in the fanfic mines, where writing stories to order for what we call "fic-a-thons" is a pretty common occurrence; part of it is just how my brain works. So it's always amazing to me when a story walks up, punches me in the face, and demands to be written.

This was one of those stories. This was also my first dalliance with portal fantasy, a thing which has become increasingly important in my work as time goes on. By reading this, you can now say that you were there in the beginning.

Welcome.

"That's the last of them," said Crystal. "We should be safe, for now."

The dire bat's headless body lay on the floor of the cave like an accusation, blackish blood seeping from its neck. Crystal looked at it and shuddered before giving it a sharp kick. It rolled over the edge of the chasm and fell into darkness, vanishing without a trace. They'd have to find the head eventually. But that could wait.

"Are you sure?" Chester asked. He peered anxiously into the dark, his nose twitching. Crystal knew his ears—which would have been better suited to a jackrabbit than a boy, as she'd teased him so many times over the years—would have been doing the same if they hadn't been tucked up under his hat. He'd done that to protect them from the shrieking of the dire bats. She briefly considered snatching the hat from his head, but set the thought aside. Nervous as he still was, he wouldn't take the prank as innocently as it was meant.

"I'm sure." She slid her dagger into its sheath before wiping the sweat-matted hair away from her forehead. "Listen. You can hear the wind."

Not just the wind: there was also the gentle tapping of inhuman legs making contact with stone. The pair turned to see a great black spider easily the size of a small car walk down the cavern wall. It reached the floor and continued toward them on its bristle-haired legs, stopping just a few short feet away. With an air of deep solemnity, the spider bowed.

"The land of Otherways is in your debt once again, young Crystal," said the spider, in a deep voice that was softer than its appearance suggested. "We thank you."

"Don't thank me, Naamen. It was my pleasure. It's always my pleasure." Crystal leaned forward to rest a hand on the spider's back, digging her fingers into the coarse black hair. "This is my home just as much as it's yours."

"Even so. Your service here is all the more heroic because it is freely offered. You could return to your world of origin at any time, leaving us to our fate, and yet you choose time and again to stay and fight for our survival." The spider straightened until its largest eyes were on a level with Crystal's own. "You are not the first to come from your world to Otherways, but you are far and away the bravest."

"Yeah. Brave me," said Crystal, pulling her hand away. Talk of others coming to Otherways before her always made her uncomfortable, although she could never put her finger on exactly why. Maybe it was the fact that her friends in Otherways, who were otherwise forthright in all ways, would never describe the others as anything more than "the ones who came before you." They had no names; they had no faces; they had no stories to explain what could possibly have caused them to abandon a world as wonderful and magical as Otherways. They were just gone.

"Oh, bush and bother, Crystal, look!" Chester—who could always be counted on to panic over nothing, and to show surprising bravery in the face of actual danger—pointed toward the sky.

Not already. Not so soon. A sick knot of dread formed in her stomach as she followed the direction of his finger. There was nothing there but darkness. She relaxed a little, saying, "I don't understand. What are we looking at?"

"The Passage Star is shining." Chester let his hand fall, looking at her sorrowfully. He was always the first to see the Passage Star's light, even as Crystal herself was always the last. "You can go home now."

The dread returned, clenched tighter than ever. "Oh."

"You can go *if you wish*," said Naamen, almost as if he could see what she was feeling. "The choice to stay or go is always yours. You know you would be welcome if you chose to remain."

"The Passage Star will only burn for three hours," said Crystal slowly, arguing a side she wasn't sure she believed in. "After that..."

"After that, it will go out, but it will light again once a fortnight until a year has gone without someone passing from our world to yours. You would still have the opportunity to change your mind."

Crystal took a shaky breath, forcing her first answer aside. Naamen always asked if she would stay, and every time, it got harder to tell him no. How was she supposed to focus on school and chores and picking the right colleges to apply to when she was the champion of Otherways, the hero of the Endless Fields, and the savior of the Caverns of Time? The world she'd been born in seemed more like a dream every time she came to the Otherways, and this world—this strange, beautiful, terrible world, with its talking spiders and its deadly, scheming roses—seemed more like the reality.

Naamen and Chester looked at her hopefully. They'd been her best friends and sworn companions since she was a little girl. Chester was barely more than a bunny when they first met. Now she was almost a woman, and Chester was...Chester. Naamen had been slightly smaller in those days, but no less ancient, and no less wise. Just the thought of leaving them made her heart ache like it was breaking.

Hearts can heal, she thought, remembering something Naamen once told her, after they saved the Princess of Thorns from her mother, the wicked Rose Queen. Crystal took another, steadier breath, and gave the answer she'd been giving since her twelfth birthday, when the great spider first asked if she would stay: "Not yet. My parents would miss me too much. Let me turn eighteen. That's when they expect to lose me to college anyway. They can lose me to Otherways instead."

Naamen shifted his pedipalps in the gesture she had come to recognize as his equivalent of a nod. "If that is your wish, Crystal Halloway, it will be honored. We will count the hours until you return to us."

"Don't stay gone too long, okay, Crystal?" asked Chester.

"I never do, do I?" Crystal leaned over and hugged him hard. He was her best friend and her first love; he'd been her first kiss, the year she turned fourteen and saved the Meadows of Mourning from the machinations of the Timeless Child. "I miss you too much when I'm gone."

"Please, then. Take this, to remember us by." Naamen reached out one long black leg. A woven charm dangled from his foot, the strands woven from silk so fine it seemed almost like light held captive in a circle of willow wood and twine. "Hang it above your bed, and only good dreams will come to visit you."

Crystal knew the charm would do nothing against her nightmares; Naamen had been giving her the same tokens since the first time he asked her to stay, and they hadn't stopped a single bad dream. Still, making the charms seemed to soothe him in some way she couldn't quite understand, and so she reached out and took it, feeling the weight of it settle in her palm, simultaneously feather-light and heavy as a stone. Naamen returned his foot to the cavern floor.

"Thank you, my friend," she said, as she tucked the charm into her pocket. "I'll hang it in a place of honor."

"See that you do." Naamen waved his pedipalps again, this time in the motion that denoted concern. "I wish you would reconsider, Crystal. I wish that you would stay."

Crystal paused, frowning. Naamen always asked her not to go. He'd never tried to change her mind before. "Naamen? What's wrong?"

"It's just that you are growing up, Crystal, and I worry for your safety." The great spider stilled, looking at her gravely. "The choice, as always, is yours."

"Oh, my friend." Crystal moved almost without thinking, stepping forward and wrapping her arms around the body of the spider, just behind the smallest of his eyes. Naamen leaned into her embrace, but only enough to show that he welcomed it; not enough for his greater size to knock her off her feet, as had happened so often in her younger days. "Don't worry about me. I'll always make it back to you. Always."

Naamen stroked her back with the tip of one foreleg, faceted eyes focused on the endless black in front of him, and said nothing. There was nothing left that he could say.

Crystal approached the Welcome Stone alone, as she always did. The dread was still there in the pit of her stomach, tangled with warring desires. She wanted to go home, to sleep in her own bed and hug her parents in the morning. She wanted to stay—always—to sleep in the cobweb-decked bedroom Naamen had spun for her in the brambles that ringed the Endless Fields. She wanted to graduate from high school. She wanted to kiss Chester again and again, forever. Most of all, she wanted to be there when the next child stumbled into the light of the Passage Star. She never wanted to be one of the children Naamen refused to name.

She wanted to stay.

But she couldn't.

The passage to her own world only took a few seconds. She stepped into the light of the Passage Star—which always shone in a perfect circle, right at the center of the Welcome Stone—blinked, and was back in the world where she'd been born, standing in the tiny room housing the magic telescope that let her travel into Otherways. She closed the telescope lens quickly, before something unpleasant could find a way to follow her, and turned to head down the narrow stone passageway that connected to the secret door at the back of her closet.

She'd found the secret door and the room beyond by accident when she was six, playing at seeking Narnia. Now she couldn't imagine a world where she didn't have the route to Otherways etched deep into her heart, like an ache that never quite went away.

The passage was tighter than it used to be. She had to stoop to keep her head from knocking against the ceiling, and there were places where she had to turn and scoot along sideways in order to avoid getting stuck. One more growth spurt and she'd wind up staying in Otherways because she couldn't make it back to her bedroom…or she'd wind up trapped in the world where she was born without ever once choosing to stay.

She couldn't keep going back and forth forever. She knew that; she'd known for a long time. Somehow, the feel of the walls pressing against her back and chest as she inched through the tighter spaces just made that fact more real. Soon, she would have to decide.

The passage widened as it came to an end, letting her into an antechamber almost as large as the telescope room. She walked the last few steps to the door with her head high, and placed her hand upon the doorknob. "My name is Crystal Halloway," she said, "and I am coming back from the most incredible adventure…"

The doorknob turned under her hand of its own accord, and the door of her closet swung open. Crystal pushed her way through the hanging coats—which were more window-dressing than anything else; she would never dream of using her closet to store *clothing* when she might need to rush to Otherways at a moment's notice—and she was back in the familiar bedroom that had been hers practically since she was born.

Moving more on auto-pilot than anything else, she walked to the bed, where she removed her dagger and shoved it under her pillow. It was unlikely to be seen by prying parental eyes while it was there, and she slept better knowing it was close at hand. She yawned vastly, suddenly aware of how tired she was, and how hungry she was, and how much her battle with the dire bats had left her in need of a shower.

The charm stayed in the pocket of her jeans as she shucked off her clothes and put on her nightshirt, which was so old and faded that she was probably the only one in the world who still saw Mickey Mouse in the shapeless blurs on the front; the charm stayed in the pocket of her jeans as she kicked them to one side and went to take her shower, shampooing her hair three times to get the smell of dire bat blood out; the charm stayed in the pocket of her jeans as she went to the kitchen for a midnight snack, as she checked the locks, as she came back into the room and climbed into her bed.

The stuffed tarantula she slept with every night—bought for her when she was eight, two years after she first entered Otherways—was waiting for her on her nightstand. She picked it up and hugged it tightly. "Good night, Little Naamen," she said, with the gravity of a teenage girl who knows she's doing something silly, but does it anyway, because it's what she's always done. "Spin me good dreams tonight, okay?"

On some other night, maybe that silly ritual phrase would have reminded her of the charm; maybe she would have pulled it out of her pocket, dusted the lint from its strands, and hung it above her bed where it belonged. It had happened before. But she was tired and sore from fighting the dire bats, and sick at heart from the knowledge that soon, she would have to choose one world over the other, and all she wanted was to stop thinking for a little while. The charm stayed in the pocket of her jeans as she reached over to her bedside table, and turned off the light.

Crystal Halloway, savior of the Otherways, closed her eyes and slept.

There was no one single thing that woke her. One moment, Crystal was asleep, and the next, she was awake, staring into the darkness and trying to figure out why every nerve was screaming. Something was wrong. As always, when something she couldn't name was wrong, Crystal's thoughts leapt to Otherways. The Passage Star was shining—it had to be shining—and something was stopping her from seeing its light properly. But the Star never rose this soon after a visit.

Filled with an unnamed dread, Crystal tried to jump out of the bed and run for the closet. The sheets that had been snarled so carelessly around her while she slept drew instantly tight, becoming a net as effective as one of Naamen's webs. Crystal's dread solidified into concrete fear. She struggled harder, and the sheets drew even tighter, tying her down. Opening her mouth, she prepared to scream...

...and stopped herself before the sound could escape. Sheets didn't move on their own, not in this world; whatever was happening, it was tied to the Otherways. If she screamed, her parents would come, and whatever was attacking her would take them, too. She was trapped, alone in the dark, and there was no one who could save her.

Crystal's mind raced, trying to figure out which of her many enemies from Otherways could be behind this invasion. The Rose Queen? The Old Man of the Frozen North? Even the Timeless Child? All of them were somewhere in Otherways, and all of them hated her, but none of them had ever demonstrated that they had the ability to travel through the light of the Passage Star before—

"Oh, good. You're awake. It's easier when they're awake." The voice was sweet, female, and unfamiliar. Crystal turned toward it, squinting to make out anything through the gloom. "Don't try to move. You'll only hurt yourself."

The idea that she could hurt herself caused Crystal to strain even harder against the sheets. Hurting herself implied movement, and movement could imply breaking loose. The woman sighed.

"You're going to be a troublesome one, aren't you? Ah, well, it can't be helped. You should never have been left so long. Whatever they were using to hide you worked very, very well. I knew there was one of you little runaways still in this town, but I couldn't seem to find you before tonight." The sweet-voiced woman flew languidly out of the shadows and hovered above Crystal, smiling serenely down at her. "Whatever you did wrong, my dear, thank you. I appreciate it."

The charm, thought Crystal wildly, remembering it for the first time since returning to her room. She took a short, sharp breath and stopped struggling. All her guesses as to her attacker's identity had been wrong. This wasn't one of the enemies she knew.

This was a stranger.

The woman in the air above her was round-faced and ruddy-cheeked, with soft brown curls and twinkling blue eyes. She looked like she would have been perfectly at home baking cookies or reading stories in a preschool—except for her rapidly-fluttering mayfly wings. Those, and the large knife in her hand, established her as clearly supernatural, and just as clearly hostile.

"Who *are* you?" Crystal hissed, barely raising her voice above a whisper.

"Oh, there's no need to whisper. You can scream yourself hoarse and no one will hear you. But I recommend against it. Laryngitis is no fun for anyone." The woman continued to smile. "Still, if it will make you feel better, go right ahead."

"Get out of my room," snarled Crystal. The sheets were still tangled tight around her, but that gave her an idea. Naamen's webs worked by turning each captive's strength against them, letting the strong batter themselves into weakness. The sheets had tightened every time she struggled. Glaring at the woman, she forced herself to go limp.

"Now, now, dear, has no one taught you how to greet a guest? Your manners are sorely lacking."

The sheets were no looser than they had been, but they were getting no tighter. "I don't think manners apply to the uninvited."

"Manners apply to the uninvited most of all." The woman dipped lower in the air, reaching down to tap the fingers of her right hand against Crystal's cheek. "Remember that, if you can."

Crystal took a breath—and then she moved, calling on everything she'd learned from her games of catch-and-keep with Chester, who was faster than anyone else she'd ever known. The sheets reacted to the motion, but they were too slow, if only by a fraction of a second, missing her wrists as she yanked them free. Then her dagger was in her hand, and she was slashing at the sheets still holding her down, preparing to lunge for the woman who had dared to invade her home, who had dared—

The binding spell crashed down on her with enough force to slam her against the mattress, knocking the air out of her lungs. Her dagger fell to the floor, slipping out of her nerveless fingers as she stared, unmoving, into the dark above her bed.

"Oh, you *naughty* thing. I see why they worked so hard to hide you. You were quite the catch for them, weren't you? I'm sorry to have to bind you, but you left me no choice. Try to breathe. This will all be over soon, and this silliness will fade away." The woman fluttered out of Crystal's view. The mattress creaked as a weight settled on it. Then a gentle hand grasped Crystal's chin, turning her head until she was facing the little woman who sat beside her.

Crystal glared with all the force that she could find. The woman smiled.

"You're sixteen, aren't you? Don't try to answer, I already know. Don't you think it's past time you stopped running off to some childish fantasy land, leaving this world—this good world, that you were born a part of—wanting? It's time to grow up, my dear." She tapped Crystal's cheek again. This time, she bore down enough that the sharp tips of her nails bit into Crystal's skin. "I'm here to help you. I'm the Truth Fairy, you see, and that means I can do what you haven't been able to do on your own."

Crystal tried to struggle.

Crystal failed.

"Haven't you ever noticed how fairies only come when there are things to be taken away? Santa Claus, the Easter Bunny, the Birthday Pig, they come to leave things behind them. Presents and chocolates and things like that. But the Tooth Fairy comes when you lose a tooth, and she takes that tooth away, and you never see it again. What she leaves is a hole. Something that your new tooth can fill. Do you understand yet, my dear?"

Crystal's eyes screamed hate at her—hate, and terror, because something of what the Truth Fairy was saying made perfect, terrible sense. All the children she'd known in elementary school, the ones who had traveled to worlds of their own, worlds like her own Otherways, but different...they'd all forgotten their adventures, hadn't they? She'd wondered why, with increasing confusion, as friend after friend suddenly swore their quests and their trials had been nothing but fantasies. She'd *been* to some of their worlds, traveling through mechanisms as strange and wondrous as her own Passage Star. And then one day, those children just forgot.

And there had been other children in Otherways before her.

"You can't be part of two worlds forever. The heart doesn't work like that. There isn't room, any more than there's room in a mouth for two sets of teeth. Baby teeth fall out. Childhoods end. That's how adult teeth, and adult lives, find the space to grow." The Truth Fairy leaned close, voice almost a whisper as she said, "Haven't you ever noticed how so many people seem to walk around empty inside, like there's a hole cut out of the middle of them, a space where something used to be, and isn't anymore? Someone has to dig the holes, Crystal. When your baby teeth don't fall out, someone has to pull them."

Hearts can heal, that was what Naamen had told her. But there'd been more to it, hadn't there? *Hearts can heal, as long as they remember the way home.*

Hearts could forget the way home.

The Truth Fairy rose on buzzing wings. Crystal's eyes widened, the reality of the moment sinking into her bones. There was no rescue. There was no salvation. Her name was going to be added to the quiet ranks of the forgotten, and never spoken again, not now, not tomorrow, not to the next child to stumble through the light of the Passage Star.

She was never going home again.

The knife went up. The knife came down. And somewhere deep inside her, in the place that the Truth Fairy's knife sought with such unerring skill, Crystal Halloway screamed.

Morning dawned, as mornings always do. Paul and Maryanne Halloway were in the kitchen when their daughter came down the stairs, yawning and wiping the sleep from her eyes. "Morning, Mom and Dad," she said, voice muffled by the hand pressed against her mouth. "Breakfast?"

"Scrambled eggs and toast," said Maryanne. "How did you sleep?"

"Really well." Crystal smiled a little blearily, as she dropped herself into a seat at the kitchen table. "I had the weirdest dreams."

Her father looked up from his laptop, leaving his half-composed email unsent. "What about?"

"You know, I don't remember now?" Crystal's smile became a puzzled frown. "Something about a rabbit, I think. I don't know." For a moment, her frown deepened, taking on an almost panicked edge. "It seemed so important..."

"Don't worry yourself, dear." Maryanne put a plate of eggs and toast down in front of her daughter. "Eat up. You don't want to be late for school."

"Yeah." The frown faded, replaced by calm. "We're talking about college applications today. I should probably be on time for that."

Crystal ate quickly and mechanically, and after she left, her parents marveled at how focused and collected she'd seemed, like she was finally ready to face the challenges of growing up.

Neither of them saw the empty space behind her eyes, in the place where a lifetime of adventures used to be. Neither of them saw the hole cut through her heart, waiting to be filled by a world that would never satisfy her, although she would never, until she died, be able to articulate why.

Neither of them really saw her at all, and it wouldn't have mattered if they had. Done was done, and a heart, once truly broken, could never remember the way home. Crystal's father had grown up in that same house; had known adventures and excitement in a world whose name he no longer knew. He would love his daughter all the more for having lost the same things he had lost. And her mother...she didn't remember the talking horses or the magical wars or the young prince with webs between his fingers, not consciously, even if sometimes in the night she cried. Both of them knew that empty space more intimately than they could understand.

And none of them, not Crystal, not her parents, could hear the distant, thready sound of a giant spider—the Guardian of the Passage to the Beyond, the one who had guided and guarded a hundred generations of human children, nurtured them, loved them, and lost them all—weeping.

Emeralds to Emeralds, Dust to Dust

It shouldn't really come as a surprise to anyone that I love Oz and all its derivative works (although I have a huge soft spot for *Wicked*, both as a book and as a musical: when all else fails, root for the villain). When I was asked to contribute to an anthology of Oz stories (*Oz Reimagined*, edited by John Joseph Adams and Douglas Cohen), I jumped at the chance. Since we were working from the public domain, we had to adhere to the first book in the series, not the famous movie with Judy Garland or any of the things that had come after.

This is my urban fantasy film noir Oz. It stands alone, but don't be surprised if one day you click your heels and find yourself looking at a new trilogy. I've met me, after all. Contains gendered slurs: Dot *really* doesn't care for Ozma very much, and often expresses herself through profanity.

The pillows were cool when I woke up, but they still smelled of Polychrome—fresh ozone and petrichor, sweeter than a thousand flowers. I swore as I got out of bed and crossed to the window, opening the curtains to reveal a sky the sunny fuck-you color of a Munchkin swaddling cloth. There was no good reason for the sky to be that violently blue this time of year—no good reason but Ozma, who was clearly getting her pissy bitch on again.

Sometimes I miss the days when all I had to deal with were wicked witches and natural disasters and ravenous beasts who didn't mean anything personal when they devoured you whole. Embittered fairy princesses are a hell of a lot more complicated.

I showed the sky my middle finger, just in case Ozma was watching—and Ozma's always watching—before closing the curtains again. I was up, and my girlfriend was once again banished from the Land of Oz by unseasonably good weather, courtesy of my ex. Time to get ready to face whatever stupidity was going to define my day.

As long as it didn't involve any Ozites, I'd be fine.

The hot water in the shower held out long enough for me to shampoo my hair. That was a rare treat this time of year, and one I could attribute purely to Ozma's maliciousness: lose a girlfriend, get enough sun to fill the batteries on the solar heater. It was a trade I wouldn't have needed to make if I'd had any magic of my own, but magical powers aren't standard issue for kids from Kansas, and none of the things I've managed to pick up since arriving in Oz are designed for something as basic as boiling water. That would be too easy.

I was toweling off when someone banged on the bathroom door—never the safest of prospects, since the hinges, like everything else in the apartment, were threatening to give up the ghost at any moment. "Dot! You done in there? We've got trouble!"

"What kind of trouble, Jack?" I kept toweling. My roommate can be a little excitable sometimes. It's a natural side effect of having a giant pumpkin for a head.

"I don't know, but Ozma's here! In person!"

My head snapped up, and I met my own startled eyes in the mirror. The silver kiss the Witch of the North left on my forehead the day I arrived in Oz gleamed dully in the sunlight filtering through the bathroom skylight. "I'll be right there. Keep her happy while I get dressed."

"I'll try," he said glumly. His footsteps moved away down the hall. My surprise faded into annoyance, and I glared at my reflection for a moment before I turned and headed for my room. Ozma—fucking *Ozma*—in *my* apartment. She hadn't been to see me in person since the day she told me we couldn't be together anymore, that I had become a *political liability* thanks to my unavoidable association with the crossovers.

I will always be a Princess of Oz. Nothing can change that, not even the undying will of Her Fairy Highness. But I am no longer beloved of the Empress, and if I want to see her, I have to go to the palace like everybody else. So what the hell could have brought her to the crossover slums at all, let alone to my door?

I wrenched drawers open and grabbed for clothing, only vaguely aware that I was dressing for battle: khaki pants, combat boots, and a white tank top, none of which would have been anything special outside of Oz. Here, the tank top was a statement of who and what I was, and why I would be listened to, even if I was a crossover and not a natural-born citizen. Only one type of person is allowed to wear white in the Land of Oz; it's the color of witches, and I, Dorothy Gale, Princess of Oz, exile from Kansas, am the Wicked Witch of the West.

Putting in my earrings took a little more care. I would have skipped it if Ozma had sent a representative instead of coming herself, but it was the very fact of her presence that both made me hurry and take my time. Ozma needed to see that I was taking her seriously. So in they went, until my ears were a chiming line of dangling silver charms, slippers and umbrellas and field mice and crows. I checked my hair quickly, swiping a finger's-worth of gel through it with one hand. The tips were dyed in blue, purple, red, and green—the colors of Oz. Only the colors of the Winkie Country were missing, and as I'm a natural blonde, they don't need dye to be represented.

Clapping the diamond bracelet that represented the favor of the Winkies around my left wrist, I gave myself one last look in the mirror and left the room. Voices drifted through the thin curtain that separated the apartment's narrow back hallway from the main room: Jack, a high tenor, almost genderless, and perpetually a little bit confused; a low tenor that had to belong to one of Ozma's guards; and Ozma herself, a sweet, piping soprano that I used to find alluring, back when it whispered endearments instead of excuses. I stopped at the curtain, taking a breath to bolster myself, and then swept it aside.

"I'm flattered, Ozma," I said. "I didn't know you remembered where I lived."

The main room served as our living space and as the reception area for my duties as the Crossover Ambassador. It was shabby, as befitted both those roles. Ozma stood out against the mended draperies and twice-repaired furniture like an emerald in gravel.

Her back was to me, facing Jack and a guardsman in royal livery. If we could have conducted the entire meeting that way, I would have been thrilled. Sadly, it was not to be. Her shoulders tensed, and then the Undying Empress, Princess Ozma, turned to face me.

She was beautiful. I had to give her that, even if I never wanted to give her anything again. Her hair was as black as the midnight sky, and like the midnight sky, it was spangled with countless shining stars, diamonds woven into every curl. Red poppies were tucked behind her ears, their poisonous pollen sacs carefully clipped by the royal florists. It all served to frame a face that couldn't have been more perfect, from her red cupid's-bow mouth to her pale brown eyes, the same shade as the sands of the Deadly Desert. Her floor-length green silk dress was more simply cut than her court gowns; I recognized it from garden walks and picnics, back in the days when I was in favor. She wore it to throw me off balance. I knew that, I rejected it...and it was working all the same.

"I granted you this space," she said sweetly. "Of course I remember. How are you, my dear Dorothy?"

"Peachy," I snapped. "What are you doing here, Ozma?"

"It's such a beautiful day outside, I thought you might need some company." A trickle of poison crept into her words. That was all it ever took with Ozma. Just a trace, to remind you how badly she could hurt you if she wanted to. "Don't you love the sunshine?"

For a moment, I just gaped at her, inwardly fumbling for some reply—any reply, as long as it didn't involve hurling something at her head.

Finally, I settled for, "Not really. What do you *want*, Ozma? Because I don't want you here."

"Ah. It's to be like that, is it?" The sweetness vanished from her face as she straightened, looking coldly down her nose at me. "There's been a murder. I expect you to deal with it."

"Uh, maybe you're confused. I'm not a detective, and I'm not a member of your royal guard. I'm the Crossover Ambassador and the Wicked Witch of the West. Neither of those jobs comes with a 'solve murders' requirement."

"No, but both of those jobs come with a 'control your people' requirement, and Dorothy, one of your people is a murderer." Ozma's lips curved in a cruel smile. I balled my hands into fists, pushing them behind my back before I could surrender to the urge to slap that smile right off her smug, pretty little face. "The body was found Downtown, in the old Wizard's Square. My guards are holding it for you. Find the killer, and deliver him to me."

"Or what?" The challenge left my lips before I had a chance to think it through. I winced.

"Or I find a new ambassador to keep the crossovers in line. A proper Ozite, perhaps, one who will have the nation's best interests at heart." Ozma kept smiling. "And you, my dear Dorothy, can look forward to an endless string of cloudless days. Sunshine does keep spirits up in the winter, don't you think? Rinn will stay here to show you to the body. Whenever you're ready—but it had best be soon, for everyone's sake."

She turned, leaving me staring, and swept out of the room. Her guard remained behind, standing uncomfortably beside the door. Jack stepped up beside me, his big orange pumpkin-head tilted downward to show the unhappiness his carved grin wouldn't let him express.

"Well, that wasn't very nice," he said.

"Get my pack," I replied, snapping out of my fugue. "I've got a murder to solve."

The Wizard was the first person to cross the shifting sands of the Deadly Desert with body and soul intact. He wasn't the last, not by a long shot. We should have known something was wrong with the spells that protected Oz when I made the crossing over and over again, traveling by every natural disaster in the book, but what did I know? I was just a kid, and Oz was the country of my dreams. I would have done anything to get back there. When Ozma told me I could stay, that we could be best friends and playmates forever, I cried. I would have done anything she asked me, back then. I would have died for her.

The one thing I couldn't do, not even when she asked, was stop the slow trickle of crossovers from appearing in Oz. They each found their own way across the sands, some intentionally, some by mistake...and since each method of crossing back to the "real world" seemed to be a one-shot, once they were in Oz, they were in Oz for keeps. At first, Ozma left them to find their own way. It had worked well enough for the early arrivals, but fewer and fewer crossovers were coming from places like Kansas. The farmlands found themselves overrun with people who didn't know which end of the plow was which. They threw the newcomers out, and one by one, the crossovers came to the only destination they had left.

The City of Emeralds. Which was now the Emerald City in nothing but name; only the oldest, richest denizens still wore their green-tinted glasses, updated with a special enchantment that made anyone who wasn't born in Oz disappear completely. This led to a few collisions on the streets, but as far as they were concerned, it was worth it. For them, the Emerald City was still the pristine paradise it had been before the crossovers came. For the rest of us...

Jack and I left the apartment by the back door, with Ozma's guard tagging along awkwardly behind us. He looked as unhappy about the situation as I felt. His look of unhappiness deepened as he realized that we were heading for the stairs. "Are we not taking the skyways?" he asked, hesitantly.

My status as a Princess-cum-Ambassador-cum-Wicked Witch is confusing for some people—especially the kind of strapping young lad that Ozma liked to employ. "No, we're not," I said curtly, and promptly regretted my tone. It wasn't his fault. More kindly, I explained, "We're going Downtown, remember? Not every building in this area has connections to both the streets and the skyways. It's better if we go down low as soon as we can. If we take the skyways, we'll come out miles from Wizard's Square."

"I have a piece of the road of yellow brick attuned to my comrades in arms. It would lead us where we needed to go," he said, with the pride of a farm boy who'd never had his own magic before.

I remembered being that young, and that naïve. I hated him a little in that moment, for reminding me. "That's just dandy, but I know where we're going. This door lets out within half a mile of the Square, and I'd rather not walk any farther if I can avoid it. You don't want to walk that far through Downtown either. It's not safe."

"I am in service to the Undying Empress," he said proudly. "I fear nothing in this city."

"Just keep telling yourself that."

Jack snorted. It was an oddly musical sound, thanks to the acoustics of his head.

Rinn frowned at us. "I am sorry. Is there something I am unaware of?"

"We're going *Downtown*," I said. "Have you ever been there before? Yes or no."

"...no," he said sullenly.

"I didn't think so. All right. First rule of Downtown: don't act like your position means anything to the people who live there. Most of them were city folks before they crossed, and they're still city folks. They don't appreciate being reminded that things are different now. Second rule of Downtown: don't mention Ozma."

"But why not?" Rinn sounded honestly confused. "Surely they're grateful."

"Grateful? She herds them into slums. She coddles the ones who catch her eye and leaves the rest to fight for scraps. She lets them kill each other, steal from each other, and do whatever they want, as long as she doesn't have to look at them. Downtown isn't grateful. They hate her more than almost anyone or any*thing* in Oz."

Rinn's eyes widened. To him, I was speaking blasphemy. "What do they hate more?"

My smile was thin as a poppy's petal. "Me."

We'd been descending as we walked, moving out of the rarified air of the upper city and down, down, down where the lost things lived. Buildings like mine are rare these days. They're technically considered Uptown, since they're connected to the skyways, but they also have doors leading Downtown, making them vulnerable to compromise, no matter how many spells are layered on to keep them secure. Good Ozites refuse to live in places like mine.

Good thing I'm not a good Ozite anymore. My building is a liminal space, like me, neither part of Uptown nor Downtown...and like me, it's never going to fit quite right anywhere again.

Jack pushed open the beaten copper door separating our stairwell from the street, and we stepped out into the humid, sour-smelling air of Oz's undercity. The door slammed behind us as soon as we were through, its built-in enchantments forming a seal that couldn't be broken without the appropriate countercharm. A dog barked in the distance. A baby wailed. And even though the sun was shining, so many walkways and structures blocked the light that it was suddenly twilight—a twilight that would never end.

I turned to Rinn, who was still looking staggered by my last word, and gave him my best Princess of Oz curtsey. "Welcome to Downtown."

"Prince—Miss—Sorcer—" Rinn stopped, done in by the perils of nomenclature, and gave me a look so pitiful that I couldn't help thawing a little. "I'm sorry. I don't know what I'm meant to call you."

"Dot is fine," I said, and started walking along the cracked brick sidewalk toward the Square. This used to be one of the thoroughfares to the palace, back when you could get there at ground level; the yellow still showed through in patches, where the grime hadn't managed to turn it as gray as everything else. That's the sick joke of Downtown. I left Kansas for Oz because I was tired of the color gray. Now I'm the Ambassador to the Gray Country of Oz, built in the basement of the City of Emeralds. "If that's too informal, you can call me Dorothy."

"Miss Dorothy, why is the Empress...what I mean to say is..."

"He wants to know why Her Royal Bitchness is threatening you with sunshine," said Jack. Rinn cast him a shocked look. The pumpkin-headed man was walking with more assurance now that we were Downtown. Maybe it was the fact that his shoulders were straight for the first time, showing just how tall he really was. "Weather isn't usually a good incentive."

"You mustn't speak of the Empress like that," said Rinn, sounding stunned. "What would even make you *think* such a thing?"

"My father and I go way, way back," said Jack. The bitterness in his voice was unmistakable. "I'm allowed to say anything about her that I feel like saying."

I patted him on the arm as comfortingly as I could manage. Ozma was a boy named Tip when she created Jack. She'd never liked to talk about that period in her life, and I knew better than to go into it in detail around one of her men. Rinn had probably been trained to regard all mentions of Ozma's boyhood as treason. Instead, I said to him, "I'm dating a girl named Polychrome. She's the daughter of the Rainbow. No clouds, no rain. No rain, no rainbows. No rainbows, no girlfriend. She needs clouds if she wants to be here, and that means she'll be gone as long as the sun stays out. So when Ozma wants me to dance to her song, she threatens me with the weather." I shook my head. "Now get moving. We've got a dead body to see."

Rinn held his official-issue lance at the ready as we progressed through Downtown, waiting for a brigand or a hungry Kalidah to spring out of the shadows. I slouched along next to Jack, eyeing the various speakeasys we passed with an undisguised longing. Jack followed my gaze and sighed.

"No, Dot."

"But—"

"No. Poly doesn't want you drinking, and neither do I."

"I just want a little pick-me-up, that's all."

"Dot, the stuff you can buy here stands a good chance of being a put-you-down one of these days. Poppy juice isn't safe for crossovers."

"Yeah, well." I shook my head, the charms on my ears chiming against each other. "What is?"

"We'll take care of this. Poly will be back by tomorrow night. You'll see."

I sighed. "Stop being optimistic. Or did Ozma remember your name this time?"

Jack didn't answer me.

I wasn't Ozma's first castoff, and I won't be her last. Jack was part of the group responsible for helping her claim her throne, back when she first came out of exile. He was also unpredictable—thanks to the slow decay of the pumpkins he used for heads—and he didn't clean up well for her court. She tolerated him for a long time, first out of love and later out of loyalty, but the day came when Jack was more of a liability than a friend, and he'd found himself banished to the City of Emeralds to sink or swim on his own. I'd chased him down before he could leave the palace, pressing the key to my then-unused apartment into his hand.

It was an impulsive gesture that I didn't think anything of until years later, when the growing unease over the number of crossovers made it politically unwise for Ozma to keep one as a pet and boon companion. When I'd found myself in Jack's position, I'd staggered to my apartment on instinct, unsure what was going to happen when I got there. I was half-afraid he'd claim squatter's rights and leave me alone in the dark.

Instead, he'd proudly shown me the furniture he'd built for my eventual arrival, and tucked me safe and warm into my very own bedroom that I didn't have to share and that no one could ever turn me out of. He'd been waiting for me. I guess once you're thrown away you come to recognize the impending signs of someone else being discarded.

Jack was never really my friend when we both lived in the palace. These days, there's no one I trust more. My first companions in Oz have long since found their place in the political structure. So have I, I suppose. It's just that the place I've found isn't one they can afford to associate with.

This deep into Downtown, things were a curious combination of Ozite tech and crossover ingenuity. Shacks built from every material imaginable squatted on corners and clustered in the bands of watery sunlight that pool between the distant skyways, their solar heaters out and soaking up every drop of energy they could collect. Half the shacks were on wheels, letting them move with the sun. The other half belonged to the light-farmers, who jealously guarded their turf against all comers. It would have been enough to make me feel bad about my longing for rain, if it weren't for the fact that rain was actually better for Downtown. It was harder to catch and control, for one thing. It washed everything clean, and it filled the water batteries which work just as well as the solar kind. Rain was the most precious commodity Downtown had.

Ozma probably wouldn't have thought to threaten them with a lack of rain if it hadn't been for my relationship with Polychrome. That, if nothing else, I was willing to feel bad about.

People appeared from alleys and shacks, watching us walk by. We made a curious parade, to be sure: a man in Ozma's colors, another with a pumpkin for a head, and me, their hated Ambassador, in my witchy white. Even if they didn't know my face, they'd know what the color meant. There are three witches left in Oz, and I'm the only one who ever came anywhere near Downtown.

"Miss Dorothy, I'm not sure the people here are very glad to see us," said Rinn, falling back to walk beside us. He was trying to keep his voice low. I appreciated the gesture, useless as it was. "Are we in danger?"

"If we're Downtown, we're in danger. Did you miss where I said they hated me here?"

"But you're their Ambassador."

"Yeah, and they're living in hovels while I'm living Uptown. I'm the Empress's former lover, but I can't get them half the things they need, or change the laws so they're starting on an equal playing field, or find a way to send them home. Why would they like me, exactly? I'm failure walking to these people, and they don't understand how much worse it would be without me here. No one does." No one who hadn't been in those council meetings, playing wallflower, while Ozma—not yet broken on the subject of the crossovers, not yet embittered and cruel, although the seeds were already sown—fought with her advisors to keep them from driving the crossovers out into the Deadly Desert to die. I'd seen how bad it could be. How bad it *would* be, if we let certain people take over.

If Ozma wanted this murder solved, I'd solve it. And then I'd get back to the important business of finding a way to send these people home while they still had the option.

I knew we'd reached the Square when we turned a corner and found ourselves facing a crowd. Crowds were rare in Downtown: they left you vulnerable to pickpockets and to surprise raids by the royal guards. If people were gathering, it was because there was something too interesting to be ignored. Dead bodies usually qualified.

Rinn continued marching straight ahead, shouting, "Make way for the Princess!" Guess he'd decided which of my titles he liked best. He might have been surprised to realize that I was already gone, ducking to the side and working my way around the rim of the crowd until I found an opening. I dove in, worming my way between bodies until I broke free into the circle of open space maintained by Ozma's guards. A few people scowled and pointed, but they were sensible enough not to say what they were thinking out loud. They knew that you should never insult a witch to her face.

Jack's round orange head bobbed above the crowd about midway through, marking Rinn's progress. He nodded when he saw me. I nodded back, and turned to see what we were dealing with.

The dead man lay at the center of the Square, arms spread like he'd been trying to make snow angels on the pavement when he died. His expression was one of profound confusion, a final perplexity that would never be resolved. I paced a slow circle around him, ignoring the glares from Ozma's guards. Something wasn't right here. I just couldn't quite see what that something *was*.

He was dressed in Quadling red, six different shades of it, garnet and ruby and crimson and carnelian and scarlet and macaw. That sort of motley marked him as a member of the upper class, since getting those specific distinctions out of their dyes was difficult and expensive. His boots were wine-red leather, counter-stitched with gold in honor of the road of yellow brick that brought the wastrel sons of rich families marching into the Emerald City. Those boots…

I stopped, crouching down and frowning at the soles of his boots. A brief ruckus behind me marked the arrival of Jack and Rinn. "Jack, look at this," I said, indicating the dead man's feet. "Does this look wrong to you?"

"How did you—?" demanded Rinn.

I ignored him. So did Jack, who stooped down next to me, the branches in his back creaking, and said, "They're awfully new boots. Probably expensive, too."

"Not just new. They're pristine. The streets are rough and filthy down here, so how did he wind up in the square without any scuffs or smears on his boots?" I reached out and grabbed his right foot, lifting it away from the pavement. "Look at his heel. Someone dragged him."

"He's still *here*, Dot. Even if he wasn't killed Downtown, he wound up here."

And that made him *my* problem. I dropped the dead man's foot, frowning. "Something else isn't right here." Something about the cut of the clothes just wasn't jibing with the man in front of me. I straightened enough to move up to his midsection, and began undoing his belt.

Jeers and catcalls rose from the crowd, and from more than a few of the guards. I flipped them off and kept working, first unbuckling his belt, and then untying his trousers. The jeers turned disappointed when I left his trousers on and used the slack I'd created to haul his shirt up over his belly. He had the beginnings of a paunch. Not a Quadling trait—Quadlings tend to be tall and skeletally thin—but city living can create anomalies in just about anyone.

The jeers turned disgusted and faded into muttering when I stuck my pinky in the dead man's navel and began rooting around. Behind me, Rinn asked, "What is she *doing?*" in a horrified tone.

"Shut up and grow a pair," I snapped, pulling my finger out of the corpse and turning it so I could study what was caught under my nail. Then I smiled. "Jack, get this man's boots off. I think you're going to find that they don't actually fit his feet. He's too short for them."

"What?" demanded one of the other guards.

I looked up and smiled. "Nice of you to say hello. Hello. I'm Dorothy Gale, and this man is a Munchkin." I picked the lint from under my pinky nail and held it up. "Blue. They changed his clothes, but they didn't give him a shower first."

The guard blinked at me, looking nonplussed. He didn't say anything as I straightened again, this time moving to squat next to the dead man's head. That confused look on his face was bothering me. I just couldn't put my finger on exactly why...

"He died overdosing on the drugs *your* people make," said the guard, recovering his voice. "There's no parlor trick for you to play here."

"I learned humbugging from the best," I said, and leaned closer, prying the corpse's lips open. The charms in my ears jingled again as I peered into the dry cavern of his mouth. It smelled strange, like the dustbowl fields of Kansas. My eyes widened, and I sat up straight, turning to stare at my companions. "Dust. This isn't a poppy juice overdose. This is *Dust*."

Everyone—even the parts of the crowd close enough to hear me—went silent. The only sounds were footsteps scuffing against the pavement, and the distant trill of birdsong from the lacy trellises of Uptown far above us.

Poppy juice predated the crossovers. It was a natural intoxicant, refined by the people of Oz when they needed something stronger than absinthe, but still weaker than pure poppy pollen. The crossovers just refined it a little. Dust, on the other hand...that didn't happen until the crossovers were well-established and trying to find new ways of supporting themselves.

Because every crossover has to cross the shifting sands, one way or another, many of them arrive in Oz with a few grains of the Deadly Desert stuck to their clothes or hair. I don't know who first got the brilliant idea of grinding the stuff up and snorting it, but if I ever find out, I am going to kick their ass from one end of Oz to the other. Dust is addictive to Ozites and crossovers alike...and if people aren't careful, it can also be deadly, just like the sands it's derived from.

The only thing I didn't understand was where it was all *coming* from. Crossovers arrived with sand in their shoes and hair, but never more than a pinch. A few new people arrived every week. That should have been enough to provide a small cottage industry, not build an empire. And yet more Dust hit the streets of Downtown daily, and it was starting to appear Uptown as well.

Hatred of Dust was one of the pillars of the anti-crossover movement. We'd created Dust. Get rid of us and, clearly, Oz would go back to normal—or what passed for normal, anyway. What they hadn't considered was that even if the Dust was suddenly gone, the addicts would still remember what they'd craved—and they would still want it. Getting rid of the crossovers wouldn't get rid of the Deadly Desert. Dust would still find a way in.

Ozma's guards bundled up the dead Munchkin and carried him away, presumably bound for the Uptown morgue, where he could be kept preserved by stasis spells until the mystery of his identity could be unsnarled. The crowd dispersed as soon as the show was over. None of them stuck around to talk to us. In a matter of minutes, only Jack, Rinn, and I remained.

"Dust is a scourge," said Rinn, in a challenging tone.

"You won't get any argument from me," I said. "The closest I'll come is this: if the crossovers had been treated better after they stopped being cute trinkets to show off at dinner parties, maybe they wouldn't have needed to struggle to survive. Maybe they wouldn't have chosen ways you don't approve of. Dust is horrible. But the crossovers created it because they were starving. This is everyone's fault."

Rinn didn't have an answer for that. He glared in stony silence as we walked back to my apartment, where the charms attached to my diamond bracelet—one spell per stone, thank you, Winkies, thank you—unlocked the door. I led the way up the stairs, past my apartment, and through a second locked door. This one was sealed with even more potent charms, and led to the airy spires of Uptown. Here, the air was fresh and sweet and tasted like the Oz of my childhood. The sun was neither too hot nor too bright, and the breeze that set my earrings jangling was just cool enough to make the day seem even lovelier.

Ozites strolled on the elevated walkways, many wearing the enchanted green goggles favored by the wealthy. They were all dressed in the latest fashions. I saw several pairs of boots like the ones we'd pulled off our dead Munchkin, done in all five of the citizenry colors. Only the yellow-clad Winkies acknowledged us as they passed, offering small nods or even bows in my direction. I replied with smiles and silence, not drawing attention to them. It was the only reward I could offer for them remembering that I was, after all, officially their Witch.

"Where are we going?" asked Rinn.

"The Munchkin Country embassy," I said. "I'm sure they'll be interested to hear that one of their citizens was found dressed as a Quadling in the middle of Downtown."

"And dead," said Jack. "Mustn't forget dead. That seems to be one of the main selling points of this particular gentleman."

I cast my pumpkin-headed friend a smile. "Oh, believe me, I won't be forgetting that part."

We walked on toward the embassy. It really was an unseasonably beautiful day.

The receptionist was a perfectly coiffed Munchkin woman who would have stood no taller than my chin in her high-heeled boots. She could never have passed for a Quadling. Lucky her. Maybe that would increase her chances of survival.

Although if she kept looking down her nose at me like that, *nothing* was going to increase her chances of coming away without a bloody nose. "Ambassador Boq isn't seeing visitors today," she said, for the third time.

"Well, since I'm an Ambassador, too, maybe you could make a little exception."

She smiled thinly. "I'm afraid the Munchkin Country does not recognize 'Downtown' as a territory."

"Fine, then. Tell Ambassador Boq that Dorothy Gale, Princess of Oz, wants a minute of his time. If that's not good enough, tell him that Dorothy

Gale, Wicked Witch of the West, *will* have a minute of his time. If he's accommodating now, my minute won't happen unexpectedly in the middle of the night." I bared my teeth at her in what might charitably be called a smile.

Her own smile faded. "One moment, please," she said, and slid off her chair, vanishing into the back of the embassy.

"That wasn't nice, Dot," said Jack.

"Nope," I agreed. "It wasn't."

Rinn didn't say anything. I couldn't tell whether that meant he was getting used to me, or had simply been horrified into silence.

The receptionist returned only a few minutes later, with the round, blue-clad form of Boq, Ambassador of the Munchkin Country and head of the anti-crossover political faction—not to mention one of my first friends in Oz, back before everything changed—following close behind her. "Dorothy!" he bellowed, in a tone that implied absolute delight at my presence. "You should have sent a card. I would have met you at the door with cakes and lemonade."

"I didn't really have the opportunity, Ambassador Boq," I said, with a polite bow. "We've come on business for Ozma. May we retire to your chambers?"

Boq was a consummate politician, but even he couldn't have faked the look of surprise on his face. It had been a long, long time since I went anywhere on business for Ozma. "Yes, absolutely, my dear. You and your friends, follow me."

"Thanks." I offered the receptionist a little wave as we followed Boq down the hall to his private chambers, which were larger than my entire apartment and appointed ten times as well. They still weren't as nice as the quarters I'd shared with Ozma at the palace.

I waited until Boq was settled behind his desk, giving him a few moments to feel like I'd been stunned into silence by the opulence of my surroundings. Then, without preamble, I said, "A Munchkin man was found dead in the old Wizard's Square today. He was dressed in Quadling colors. It's pretty clear that we weren't expected to figure out where he was from. Do you have any idea who he might have been? Ozma has tasked me to find his killers."

Boq's face twisted into a mask of revulsion. "You've come here to talk about Downtown, with *me?* Dorothy. I thought better of you."

"No, Boq, I came here to talk to you about a murder. A Munchkin is dead. Surely that's more important than your hatred of the crossovers."

"Spoken like a girl without a country to defend," he spat. "You deserted your precious Kansas for us. How long before you desert us for something better? It was only a matter of time before the crossovers began killing."

"The fact that they had access to Quadling clothes and knew to re-dress him, that doesn't concern you at all?"

"Crossovers are as cunning as Winged Monkeys, and as trustworthy," Boq countered. "Really, you started killing the day you arrived. No wonder you speak for the rest of them. You're the first murderess of the lot."

"Since it got me a crown and made me a witch, I guess murder is pretty lucrative," I said. "You're the only one who might tell us who the man was, Boq. And you're the one who stands to benefit most from an Ozite dying Downtown. That makes me wonder why you're so defensive. I might just have to tell Ozma about this."

"You can't threaten me with Ozma," said Boq. "She heeds my counsel now, not yours."

"She heeds whatever counsel keeps Oz safest," I corrected gently. "Who was he, Boq? You know every Munchkin in the City of Emeralds. Who's missing?"

Boq hesitated. Then he sighed, and said, "Taf. He's a junior clerk here at the Embassy. He didn't report for work this morning."

"Why didn't you tell the guards?" asked Rinn. "We would have helped you find him."

"Munchkins police their own." Boq looked at me coolly. "We don't depend on outsiders to fix our problems."

"Funny," I said. "I seem to remember an outsider taking care of your little 'witch' issue a few years back."

Boq reddened, but he didn't look away.

"Thanks for letting us know who he was," I said. "You can probably collect his remains from the morgue later today."

"Dust is a scourge," he said. "I blame you and your kind."

"Yeah, I know," I said, and turned to go. Jack and Rinn followed me.

We were almost to the receptionist's desk when I froze, my earrings chiming madly with the sudden motion.

"I'm an idiot," I said.

"What?" said Jack.

"I never told him it was Dust." I turned, running back to Boq's office.

He was in the process of emptying his desk when I burst in—with Jack, Rinn, and the shouting receptionist all close behind me. I didn't hesitate before launching myself across the room, grabbing Boq by the shoulders and pulling him away from what he'd been doing before he could destroy any more evidence. He shouted and threw a sachet of fine gray powder in my face, where it burst and filled the air around me in a choking cloud. I coughed and grabbed for him again. He shied away, stumbling right into Jack's arms. Jack grabbed him and held fast. The pumpkin-head might be made of sticks, but he was stronger than a normal man. Magic can be funny that way.

Boq struggled against Jack's grip for a moment before spitting in my direction and saying, "At least I get to see you die, crossover."

"Uh-huh." I coughed again before wiping the Dust out of my eyes. I was going to need another shower. "Funny thing, Boq. Crossovers can gather this stuff because they're resistant. Crossing the shifting sands makes the Desert a little less potent for them. I've crossed the shifting sands more times than anyone."

His eyes widened. Then he sagged, going limp in Jack's arms. "You bitch."

"It's pronounced 'witch,' but that was a good try." I turned to Rinn. He was keeping his distance from me. Smart boy. At this point, I probably qualified as a walking intoxicant. "Take him to Ozma. Tell her his clerk overdosed and Boq staged the murder to implicate the crossovers. Also tell her he tried to kill me." I couldn't keep myself from smiling. Ozma and I might not get along, but I was still her property as far as she was concerned, to coddle or break at *her* whim and no one else's. She wouldn't take kindly to hearing that Boq had given me a face full of Dust.

Boq knew that too. He whimpered, and kept whimpering as Rinn handcuffed him and pulled him from Jack's arms.

I coughed again. The room was starting to spin. My multiple crossings of the Deadly Desert made me resistant, not immune. Jack's arms caught me before I could hit the carpet, and I let him bear me up and carry me home.

When I woke up, it was raining, and the whole room smelled like petrichor. My head was still spinning, and so I closed my eyes again, waiting for the world to be still.

"Ozma sends her thanks," said a voice from beside me—female, alto, and more welcome than a thousand roads of yellow brick. "She says that Boq will be dealt with appropriately."

"Meaning he'll be out in less than a week."

"He'd have been out in less than a day if he hadn't thrown that Dust in your face." Polychrome's hand touched my forehead. Her skin was cool and faintly damp, like a fine mist. "How are you feeling?"

"Better now." I reached up to catch her wrist without opening my eyes. "How long has it been raining?"

"About eight hours. You've been asleep for ten. We should tell Jack you're awake—"

"In a minute." Oz was a land divided; the City of Emeralds was only the visual representation of a split that would tear us all apart, if we weren't careful. Boq was my enemy now, if he hadn't been already, and I was deeply afraid that if I started looking for the source of the Dust, all roads would lead me back to the Munchkin Country. Ozma was starting to use me again.

And none of that mattered as I opened my eyes and looked up into the face of the woman I loved, wide-eyed and worried and haloed by the rainbow-streaked cloud of her hair. I leaned up as she leaned down, and her kiss was like the end of a year-long drought. Outside, the rain came down, and oh, the sweetness of that storm.

I was so glad to be home again.

Homecoming

This story was originally written for an anthology of football stories which never came to pass. It found a home at Lightspeed Magazine with John Joseph Adams, who has been a delightful constant in my short fiction career.

As I am not a football fan (American or European), writing this was a fascinating exercise into channeling a culture not my own. I am a big fan of cheerleaders, as anyone familiar with my Fighting Pumpkins stories will probably have noticed. On the whole, I am so very glad I wrote this story. It's always wonderful to open a window onto something new.

Everyone remembers the Valkyries. Most people forget that Valhalla wasn't the only option. And what is cheerleading, after all, if not a modern way of dancing through the battlefield?

The locker room is always tense before a game. Alisa is trying to get her uniform to stay in place, counting more on safety pins and prayer than she should, and Birdie—true to her name—keeps whistling, which is probably going to get her slapped if she doesn't stop soon. Cram twenty girls from opposing squads into one small space and tensions are going to flare.

"Has anybody seen my nail file?"

"Where's my hair tie?"

"Birdie, shut *up*."

The October air smells like bonfires and promises, and it's always October for this game, for the *big* game. October is Homecoming season. This is when promises are made and pledges are broken, and the boys of fall walk proudly into legend with their short-skirted heralds singing their praises every step of the way. The girls of fall, too, when they choose to take the field.

"Does this top make my breasts look big?"

"Did somebody take my blue mascara?"

"Birdie, *shut up*."

There are locker rooms for the football players, of course: empty, echoing gray rooms lined with lockers and the memories of hot October nights that have no end. The world makes the mistake of thinking that every night happens only once, but no two people live through the same hour, the same evening, the same season. Every trial and triumph is unique, even when it's shared—maybe especially when it's shared, because then there are other mirrors for the moment to reflect against. Every night is infinite.

"How are my tights?"

"Tilly, will you come braid my hair?"

"*Shut up, Birdie!*"

Bit by bit, the preparations are completed: faces are painted, hair is styled, and squad divisions become clear as crystal, written proudly across the front of uniforms and detailed in the color of fabrics, cosmetics, ribbons tied to ponytails or braids. The Falcons, in blue and gold, and the Ravens, in red and rust. There is the much-scolded Birdie in Falcon blue, with gold glitter clinging to her cheeks like stardust. There is Alisa in Raven red, wearing a skirt that should have been retired two seasons ago.

They line up like warriors preparing to take the battlefield, each facing another across the locker room. Bit by bit, the chatter and arguments die. Even Birdie's whistle comes to a temporary end.

The team captains step forward, Elle in blue, Rona in red. Elle is the first to hold out her hand. Rona hesitates, takes it, shakes.

"Let's have a good clean game tonight," says Elle. "There's no home team advantage."

"That's because every team is the home team here," says Rona, and smiles, dropping Elle's hand as she turns to her squad. "Gimme an 'R'!"

"*R!*" scream the Ravens, and the Falcons are doing the same with their own name, and the locker room devolves into an almost primal storm of shrieking female voices. This, too, is part of the ritual; this, too, is the herald of the endless October night.

The game is about to begin.

There is no sign of primal fury in the twenty girls who slip from onto the darkened gridiron. They walk with calm precision, ten and ten, taking their places in front of the empty stands. Elle raises her hands, looking to Rona across the empty field. Rona mirrors the gesture. The captains nod in brief unison. Two sets of hands are clapped, and the age-old cry to battle echoes through the night:

"Ready? Let's go!"

The stadium lights flash dazzlingly on, and the sound of thunder is close behind as the crowds—who were not there a moment ago, who have always been there, who will always be there when the October lights are lit—leap to their feet, stomping and clapping and howling for the boys of fall, the heroes of the night. Here they come now, twenty-two players in blank white uniforms pouring out of the locker room doors and onto the green, the sacred, moonlit green. They pump their fists in the air, and the cheerleaders are shouting encouragement, and vendors are selling popcorn in the stands, and oh, this is the night. This is the time they have been waiting for since they were born.

This is the night when they are heroes.

It doesn't seem to matter that none of them are in team colors, because they fall into position all the same, without jockeying or argument. The crowd settles, and the cheerleaders lower their pom-poms, falling back to the flats of their feet as they wait for the game to begin. There is no need for a coin toss, customary as it would have been: the teams have not yet been truly decided.

The whistle blows to signal start of play. Here's the snap, the quarterback drops back to pass, and he connects! The ball flies straight and true to the tight end in a throw that would be the stuff of high school legend on another field, on another night, in the arms of another October. The tight end turns, and he runs as hard as he can for the goal, clutching the ball in his arms like a promise. The people in the stands are screaming their heads off, and it's all about the game, it's all about the moment, it's all about this sweet harvest night with the full moon overhead and the scent of bonfires on the breeze. It's about this, and only this. There has never been anything else—

—his name is Daniel Ryan, Specialist, United States Army, and he was never supposed to be here. He enlisted because he needed a way to pay for college, and the man at the recruitment center swore that there would never be another war fought this way, with men on the ground. He's tired; he's so tired. Tired of fighting, tired of knowing that he's in a place he was never meant to be. Tired of being an invader in a land that doesn't want him there. But he's fighting for his country, and he knows it would be unpatriotic to admit to his exhaustion. So he keeps going, long past the time when he just wants to lay down and sleep for a week. Maybe that's why he doesn't realize something is wrong, doesn't sense the danger in the silence until the convoy rolls over the IEDs buried in the road, and everything goes white, and there's nothing, nothing, nothing at all, until—

—he's running hard across the green field, moving fast in his white uniform, his feet turning distance into memories. By the time the defensive backs pile into him, he's halfway to the goal line, and the ball rolls away, forgotten, as he smiles up at the stars. He stands in blue and gold, Falcon colors, his name and number printed bold across the back of his jersey, and the crowds go wild once more.

"DANIEL RYAN, HE'S OUR MAN!" shout the Falcon cheerleaders, and if anyone thinks it's strange for them to be cheering after the tackle, nothing is said. Across the field, the Raven cheerleaders fluff their pompoms and glare.

No one likes to give ground first.

The teams take up their positions for the second play, and the ball is snapped once more, the sound like a prayer in the cool night air. The cheerleaders on both sides of the field shout and clap and leap, their pompoms waving wildly, and the running back has the ball and he's running, he's running, he's running like that's all he's ever wanted to do—

—the call comes in while he's on the road back to the station, ready to finish off another shift. Armed robbery in progress, hostages involved. He responds without hesitation, hitting the gas and rocketing back the way he came. This is his job. This is why he joined the police force, fresh out of college and pursuing a better future for himself, for the city that he loves. It hasn't been easy. Nothing good is ever easy. He's had his regrets—regrets are only human—but he's never been sorry that he chose this life, and he isn't sorry even as the robbers open fire. Officer Tony Woodrow falls. The ground seems to reach up to catch him, and if he regrets anything at all, it's that the fight will be going on without him—

Rust and red bloom across his white uniform as he laterals the ball to a wide receiver, and the Raven cheerleaders scream triumphantly, their voices cutting through the night like the caws of carrion birds. It's a rare throw, but all their joy seems to be reserved for the man who made it. Woodrow goes down under a hail of white-uniformed bodies, but the ball is still in motion, the wide receiver is running, running, and everything could change in an instant—

—the fire is threatening to take out an entire city block, and they keep going into the inferno, one fireman after another collapsing from heat, from exhaustion, from smoke inhalation. They have to keep trying, or so many more will die, and she's so tired, but that doesn't matter; when Nadine Wallace joined the fire department, she did it with the understanding that she'd be fighting right up until

the moment when the fire took her down. Then a window blows and the flames reach out like greedy hands, and the last thing she has time to think is that she knew it was going to end this way; she knew that she was going to die fighting. Now, finally, she has the chance to rest—

The blue and gold-unformed figure of Nadine Wallace, wide receiver, changes directions like she was intending to do so all along, running toward the Raven goal. None of the figures on the field seem to find this strange. The white continue to scramble, while the lone red uniform redirects to intercept her. Still Nadine runs, a perfect silhouette against the night, and the people in the stands go wild.

Two Raven cheerleaders turn to each other, using the sound of screaming to cover their voices. "Remember when women never made it onto the field?"

"Times change, Alisa, jeez." The other cheerleader snaps her gum, eyes glinting red in the gleam from the floodlights. "We're co-ed now."

"Chill, Kerry," says Alisa, and thrusts her pom-pom into the air, whooping encouragement for their team.

The players keep running. The cheerleaders keep cheering. The sweet October night goes on.

Halftime finds six players in blue and gold, seven in red and rust, with nine as yet undecided. Not that the decision is a conscious thing; not that the teams will necessarily be equal when the night is done. Some games end with all twenty-two players on the same team. It all depends on their circumstances, on what they want all the way down to the bottoms of their souls.

As the cheerleaders group like strange, colorful birds around the edges of the field, watching the marching band go through its paces, a figure in glittering silver and green runs out of the locker room, pulling one of the remaining white uniformed players from the huddle. The man looks confused as he is led away, passing his substitute. The new player is led by a silver-and-green figure of her own.

"Are substitutions at this stage legal?" asks Rona.

"Technically," says Elle. The team captains are standing together, with no signs of animosity between them. It would be a waste of energy, and they have little to spare at this point in the evening. The teams are so close to evenly divided; it's still anybody's game. "I wonder who made the error by sending him here."

"Medical technology keeps improving. It may not have been an error at all."

"Even so," says Elle. She picks up her pom-poms, shaking them experimentally. A single black feather falls out. "I wonder if he'll get another chance." Unspoken are the rules of this field, of this game, of this endless October where every night is played a thousand times over again: only warriors come here, earning their place on the team by dying a warrior's death. A substitution at this stage in the game may mean the player who was removed (*Albert Li, United States Marine Corp*) may not be coming back for another chance at the trophy.

The marching band is finishing their final song, and the cheerleaders flock forward while the crowd is still applauding, taking up their places for the halftime show. Oh, this is part of the ritual, and oh, they almost seem to soar as they throw themselves into the leaps and backflips, and oh, they have been here before so many times, and oh. October never ends if the game is never truly finished.

Elle and Rona stand atop their respective pyramids and clap their hands, and the cheerleaders shout defiance into the blackness of the night, and the game—the game that never ends—goes wildly on.

The score is tied, 21-21, and the players are falling into more fixed roles on more fixed teams, blue with blue, red with red. They don't seem to notice doing it, even when a uniform blooms in the middle of a play and a player switches sides without warning. Falcons fly with Falcons, Ravens with Ravens. It is the simple logic of the game. The cheerleaders shout their names and wave their pom-poms in the air, and if a name is never called before the player's uniform changes colors, no one really cares. Each of them is lost in his or her private battle, each of them playing on a different green field, somewhere in the recesses of their hearts.

Clarice McNally, bus driver and local hero, who saved six schoolchildren at the expense of her own life, joins the Ravens.

Michael Jones, SPCA, who was stabbed in the back six times while investigating an illegal dog fighting ring, joins the Falcons.

Neither team is marked as "home" or "away" on the scoreboard: it's just numbers, 21-21, and then the Ravens score a touchdown, and the numbers change. "Gimme an 'R'!" shouts Rona, and the Ravens scream delight into the evening air. The moon hasn't moved since the start of play. It's still early evening, the scent of popcorn and bonfires and fresh green grass filling the air. The players move across the field, falling back into position, counting down to the next play.

"Go Falcons, go Falcons! Go, go, go Falcons!"

The ball is snapped, and Clarice McNally—the substitution, whose bus hit the water as the game was starting, whose lungs gave up as halftime rolled around—snatches it from the air, turning to run toward the distant, welcoming shape of the goal. She runs for the joy of running as much as anything else; her lungs pull in each breath like a benediction, so glad to be breathing unencumbered, so glad to be alive.

—but she's not alive, she's not, *she remembers the water reaching up to wrap its arms around her, and it's not October, it's nowhere near October; it's June, the school year is racing to a close, and if the bridge had been maintained like it should have been, she would never have been forced to drown—*

Clarice stumbles to a stop. The safeties are five yards behind her and closing when the ball tumbles from her nerveless fingers and hits the turf, dead in play as soon as it touches the ground. Clarice is a heartbeat behind it, dropping to her knees as confusion and contradiction swarm around her. She can't be here. She died, she died in the river, and half the children in her charge died with her. Some parents will remember her as a hero, but what about the parents of the dead? What about the ones she couldn't save, who drowned reaching for the only adult who might have been able to help them?

"No," she mumbles, starting to rock. "No, no, no."

Someone blows the whistle for a time out. Not the coach for the Ravens. Not the coach for the opposing team, either; neither coach has been seen since the start of play. Play freezes all the same, and the cheerleaders come flocking onto the field, strangely colored birds descending on the fallen player.

"Clarice? Are you all right?"

She raises her head and finds herself looking at Rona, squad leader for the Ravens' team cheerleaders. She is pretty, in a stark way, the sort of girl who always seems to stand on the outside of groups and skirt along the leading edge of trends. Her hair is the color of red velvet cupcakes or dried blood, and her eyes are almost amber. She should be terrifying, this autumn-girl under the October moon. Instead, somehow, she looks like coming home.

"I couldn't save them," Clarice tells her, and tears run down her cheeks. "I tried, but I couldn't save them. Why couldn't I save them?" The grass—no longer pristine, not now, not in the middle of the battle—is cold beneath her hands. The smell of bonfires is stronger now, like the field itself is on fire.

"Fighting doesn't always mean winning," says Rona, still crouching in front of the fallen warrior. "Sometimes it just means doing the best that you can do, and hoping that when the scores are tallied, that's enough to put you on the winning side."

"Winning? Losing? Children *died*, and now somehow we're...how am I *here?* How are we playing football? I haven't played football since high school."

"But you did," says another girl—Elle, with her white-blonde hair streaked in Falcon blue, and she's lovely, she's an angel, but her eyes are cold as she looks down on Clarice. "If you hadn't, you wouldn't be here. You'd be playing water polo, maybe, or chess, or competitive Pictionary."

"There are as many battlefields as there are fallen warriors to fight on them," says Rona. She straightens, offering Clarice her hands. "You earned your place here, I swear you did, and now all you have to do is see the game through to its end in order to get your reward."

Clarice looks at her, this teenage girl with her hair tied up in ribbons, and nothing has ever been more wrong, and nothing has ever been more right. This is Homecoming, this is the October that never ends, and she has earned her place here, on this field, on this team. She slides her hands into Rona's without deciding that she's going to do so, and Rona tugs her back to her feet, stronger than she should be for a girl so slight.

"Fight on, warrior," she says, letting go of Clarice's hands. She smiles, and for a moment, she is something else; not a cheerleader, exactly, but something older, and wilder, and serving the very same role. She cheers at the edges of the battlefield. "Fight on, and *win*."

Then the cheerleaders are running from the field, and the whistle blows again, and this night—this beautiful, perfect, endless night—resumes.

A touchdown for the Ravens; a penalty for the Falcons; two more players on each team, and only three are still running the field in white uniforms that show no dirt or grass stains, unlike the colored uniforms of their team mates. The Ravens and Falcons show the wear of the game, but the players in white uniforms are unmarred. If any of them find this strange, they do not say it. They never say it.

"BE AGGRESSIVE! B-E AGGRESSIVE!" shriek the Falcon cheerleaders, and their voices are the cries of hunting birds who remember, always, the safety of the hand and the glove.

"FIGHT! FIGHT! FIGHT!" answer the Raven cheerleaders, and their voices are the call of carrion birds on the battlefield, no less revered because their duty is to the dead.

The players surge back and forth across the green, and the cheerleaders fly in their carefully-practiced formations, pom-poms shaking, voices lashing hard across the night. In the stands, the crowds cheer and whistle and stomp their feet, and if none of them ever comes fully into the lights, fully into view, well, that's not what this night is about, is it? This night is about the boys and girls of fall, their feet digging divots into the turf, the smell of sweat and blood and battle in their nostrils. This night, this good October night with the moon like a single all-seeing eye, this night is theirs.

The Falcons' quarterback catches the ball and hooks it hard to a receiver in blue and gold, who plucks it from the air like a farmer plucks an apple. He starts to run, but a player in white puts her shoulder into his numbers, and—

—the plane is going down hard, and there's nothing that can be done for it now; they're going to crash into the mountains, and if they're lucky, they'll live long enough for the rescue choppers to arrive. They're not going to be lucky, Emily Kwan knows that in her bones. She opens her email client, breathing in through her nose, out through her mouth, and starts sending her research to her partner back at the lab. She may die, but her work will live on, and maybe a few lives will be saved as hers is ending. She presses send, and the oxygen masks deploy, and the world goes black on impact—

Emily's uniform blooms red and rust as she goes down with her opponent, a whistle shrilling the end of the play. The Falcons will have to punt now, their forward momentum diminished.

On the sidelines, Elle shakes her head.

"I thought for sure she was ours."

Rona laughs, and just claps her hands as the cheer for Emily begins.

The final two players both bloom blue and gold, Falcons on the field. When the final scrimmage lines up, it is ten in red and rust and twelve in blue and gold, an illegal formation that doesn't draw a flag. Everyone's focus is on the ball, on the moon, on the last game of the season before the season fades away forever. Emily Kwan snaps the ball to Tony Woodrow, and he's running, he's running so fast that it seems like he can almost fly. The other players follow, some defending him, some trying to claim the prize for their own, and it's a beautiful snapshot of a life well-lived, this moment, this field. In this moment, winning and losing don't matter. There's only the play itself, the old, familiar pattern of hands and hearts working in perfect concert.

The crowds scream. The cheerleaders cheer. The players run like there is nothing left to them but running, block like there is nothing that can ever tear them down.

The Ravens score the final touchdown, and the stands go wild for a beautiful, heart-stopping second. Everything is right as Tony's fellow players hoist him onto their shoulders, shouting their joy into the night, and the cheerleaders…

…the cheerleaders are silent and still, save for the last fading notes of Birdie's whistle.

The players falter, looking confused, and in that moment, the shouting from the stands stops. For the first time, the glare from the stadium lights is dim enough to let them see the bleachers, and there is no one there. There is no one there at all.

"What's going on?" Daniel Ryan, Specialist, removes his helmet. Around him, the other players are doing the same, revealing the faces of bewildered men and women.

"The game is over," says Elle. She stands on the sidelines, but her voice is clear; her voice is always clear.

"You fought bravely," says Rona.

"But the fight is finished."

"The sides are drawn."

The two step onto the field, and maybe it's a trick of the light, but the colors of their uniforms seem to shift as they walk, blue becoming red, rust becoming gold, the small differences of cut and style fading, until the two girls are dressed identically. They stop in front of the players, and even the names written across their chests are different now—not Falcons, not Ravens, but Valkyries.

"What…?" asks Clarice.

Rona smiles. "Your coaches are here."

The girls turn, looking toward the locker room doors; the players, unsure, do the same. A man emerges from one door; a woman from the other. Together yet apart, they walk across the field toward the two teams.

The man has only one eye, and the logo of the Ravens is printed on his sweatshirt.

The woman has red gold hair, like wheat in the sunset, and wears a cap with the logo of the Falcons.

They wave their teams to them, and they begin their postgame talks. What they say to their players is private; it has always been private, and always will be, on those sweet harvest nights when the field is filled with laughter, triumph, tears, and regret. But the word Valhalla is spoken, as is the word Fólkvangr, which is less remembered in this day and age, yet has always been there, for as long as there have been Valkyries to choose, and warriors to be chosen. Some warriors yearn for the fight to go on forever. Others seek rest and recuperation. Half the chosen slain are bound for each hall at the end of any battle—and look: the Ravens follow the one-eyed man, and the Falcons follow the woman with the golden hair.

Only Clarice McNally hesitates, looks back at the assembled girls in the red and gold cheerleading uniforms. Birdie is whistling again, a piece by Wagner. She never gets the low notes right.

Rona waves. After a moment's hesitation, Clarice waves back. Then she exits, and the field is empty, waiting for the next game to begin.

It's always October for this game, the *big* game, the game everyone who has ever loved high school football dreams of for their entire lives. The air smells like bonfires and promises. In the locker room, twenty girls in cheerleader's uniforms are preparing for the field ahead of them. The choosers of the slain have always loved their rituals. Elle, wearing Raven red and rust, smiles across the benches at Rona in her Falcon blue and gold.

"We'll have a good game tonight," she says.

Rona smiles back at her sister. "We always do," she replies.

Frontier ABCs:

The Life and Times of Charity Smith, Schoolteacher

This story was originally written for the anthology *Raygun Chronicles*, edited by Bryan Thomas Schmidt. He said he wanted stories with a big, boisterous space opera feel, and I did my best to deliver. For me, the best part of being involved with the project was getting to appear in an anthology with A.C. Crispin before she passed away. She has been one of my literary heroes since I was a child, and seeing my name on a cover with hers was…

Well, it was the world.

Charity is a character who's been kicking around my head looking for a home for a very long time, and I was pleased to finally be able to give her one. "Frontier ABCs" isn't connected to any specific space opera setting, or maybe it's connected to all of them: after all, it's a big universe. There's a lot of sky out there to fly in.

A IS FOR *AMMUNITION*

There are no banks to rob in this painted doll of a dustbowl fantasy town; the money is all bits and bytes stored in a computer vault no human hands can open, whether they belong to banker or bandit. But there are other forms of thievery to be practiced by the quick and the clever, and Cherry is both, when she sees call to be. So when word goes out on the down-low that the Mulrian gang is planning a heist and needs bullets to get them to the finish line, Cherry's first to the cattle call, her guns low and easy on her hips, her hair braided like an admonition against untidiness. They're surprised to see her—aren't they always, when she shows up in places like this?—but they're willing enough to let her on the crew once they've seen what she can do.

She doesn't brag much. Doesn't talk much either, outside of a classroom or a courtroom. But oh, that little lady in the worn-out britches and the red flannel shirt can shoot like she made a bargain with the God of All Guns. Some folks say as she was a sniper in the last war. There have been wars upon wars since she showed up on the scene, and it's always "the last war." No one knows how old she is, no one knows the name of her home world, and no one's sure when she's finally going to snap and take out her allies along with her enemies. But they keep taking her on, because she makes the bullets dance to her tune. Could shoot the wings off a fly, the flame off a candle, and the fat off of a hog.

The raid begins at local midnight. Four techslingers, four gunslingers, a pilot, and Cherry, all walking into town from different directions, all heading for the places they're supposed to be. The first shot is fired at two past the hour, an old-fashioned gunpowder bullet smashing through the window of city hall. That's the signal. The gunslingers commence to shooting the things they've been approved to shoot—mostly foliage and buildings and the police bots that come swinging down the sidewalks like they stand a chance against flesh and lead and practice—and the techslingers slide their clever wires into the datastream, bleeding off billions in less time than it takes for Cherry to reload.

That's her on the roof of the library, stretched flat with her scope circling her eye like a wedding ring. Every shot she takes is true, and she takes a lot of them. Nobody dies, but there's enough damaged as to take the edge off. Then the bell rings in her ear, and she rolls away from the edge of the roof, vanishing into the shadows. Fun's over.

Tip to tail, they took six minutes to bleed the beast, leaving shattered glass and frightened townies behind like a calling card. Cherry will check her bank balance later and find a healthy payoff from an uncle she doesn't have, on an outworld that may or may not exist. It doesn't matter to her. She's worked off a little of her aggression here, in the shadows and the dust, and that leaves her head clear enough for the real work to begin.

C IS FOR *COVER STORY*

"Now, can anyone tell me the origins of the human race? Where did we begin?" The one-room schoolhouse is ringed with windows, letting in so much light from outside that the overheads don't need to be turned on for most of the year. By the time the weather turns sour, the schoolhouse solars will have fed enough into the local grid that they won't have to pay a penny for the power they use. There's value in self-sufficiency.

The kids are a surly bunch, growling and glaring as they squat at their desks like so many infuriated mushrooms. These are the children of asteroid miners, farmers, and artisans, not rich enough to go to the fine boarding schools on Earth or Io, but not poor enough to be restricted to home schooling and play dates. They get the bulk of their lessons on their personalized terminals, but they're here for the social contact with their peers, to learn how to get along and how to form connections that will serve them for the rest of their lives. There are fourteen teachers working this part of the solar system, and Miss Cherry is a newcomer here, arriving at the start of the term. They still don't trust her. They still don't know whether they should.

She leans against her desk, resting her weight on her hands, and smiles winningly at them. They do not smile back at her. She's hard to measure with the eye, a wisp of a thing in a blue dress printed with white daisies, her long dark hair hanging loose and sometimes getting in her eyes when she gets excited and begins waving her hands around. They're generally good at telling someone's age by the way they move, these children of the regen generation—when your grandfather can look like your little brother if he finds the scratch, you learn to read a body for the years it's seen—but Cherry is a book of riddles, one moment as open as a kindie, the next as closed-off as a three-time regen. Her face puts her in her early twenties, by far the most popular age with women trying to survive in the outer moons.

"Anyone?" she asks, and there is a sharp, sweet disappointment in her tone, like she can't believe they wouldn't know the answer to such a simple question. "I suppose I'll have to recommend all your consoles be set to remedial human history for the rest of the term, then. I hate to do it—"

"So don't!" shouts a voice from the back of the room.

Cherry's head snaps up, and those sweet and easy eyes turn suddenly cold, the eyes of a predator searching for its prey. "Who said that?" she asks, scanning the crowd.

They've been in this schoolhouse a lot longer than she has; every child in the class knows how to hunker down and look like butter wouldn't melt in their mouths. They shift and look away, avoiding her gaze.

"You." Her finger stabs out like an accusation. "Why not?"

Her target, Timothy Fulton, squirms, but only a little. He doesn't bother denying that he was the one who spoke: she's got him, fair and square. Instead, he shrugs and says, "Because we've been over all the remedial stuff. We don't want to do it again."

"Well, then, you can spare yourself and your classmates a lot of boring scutwork by being a hero and answering my question." She isn't smiling. This is the first time since she arrived at the start of the month that she hasn't been smiling. "What was the origin of the human race?"

"Earth, ma'am. Humanity began on Earth."

"Very good. When did we move on to bigger and brighter things?"

"The Twenty-Second Century, ma'am, after we figured out how to adapt ourselves to other planets, and how to adapt other planets to ourselves."

Miss Cherry nods encouragingly. "Very good. What was the first great war after colonization? Anyone?"

Ermine Dale has never been able to sit by while other children were praised and she was not. She puts up her hand, waiting only for Miss Cherry to point at her before blurting, "It was over what makes a human, ma'am. Whether Jovians and Neptuneans were still people, given all the modifications they'd gone through."

"That's right." Cherry pushes away from her desk and walks around it to the chalkboard, an archaic piece of set dressing that nonetheless seems to help students learn and retain information. In a bold hand, she writes the number "10," and circles it before she turns back to the class and says, "This is the average number of years between wars since humanity stretched beyond a single planet. This is how long we have to rest, recover, and learn to do better. That's what I'm here for."

"To rest?" asks Timothy, and his confusion is the class's confusion.

Miss Cherry smiles. "No. I'm here to teach you to do better."

I IS FOR *INEVITABILITY*

She's been here a full season, eight local months stretching and blending together on this farmer's paradise of a Jovian moon. Ganymede has taken well to terraforming, and Earth's crops have taken well to Ganymede. Half the moons of Jupiter get their food from here, and that makes it a bright and glittering target in the nighttime sky. When the next war comes—there's always a next war—she expects the sides to fight mercilessly to own the sky's breadbasket.

The children have accepted her. They bring her apples and icefruit from the fields, and some of them have started to shyly tell her what they want to be when they grow up. Someday most of them will be farmers, but some of them may be explorers, or diplomats, or poets, if they get the chance to strengthen their roots on this good soil until the time comes for them to bloom. She likes these pauses maybe best of all. They remind her that the human race has a purpose beyond blowing itself to cinders against the stars. "We can be something more than fireworks, if we're willing to put the work in," that was what her long-dead lover told her once, when they were lying naked to the unseeing eye of Jupiter on the barren, rocky soil of this selfsame moon, barely cloaked then in its thin envelope of atmosphere, still an experiment on the verge of going eternally wrong. "We can be anything."

That wasn't true then and it isn't true now, but oh, weren't they pretty words?

The fact that she's thinking of him isn't a good sign. Means she's getting restless, and when she gets restless, she either needs to move on or find something that can bleed off some of that energy. So she sends a quiet query to her contacts, lets them know she might be available for a little pick-up work if the price is right and the location is far enough from Ganymede. Maybe something out-system. Summer break is coming soon, and her kids will be needed in the fields. Easy then for a schoolteacher to slip away on errands of her own. As long as she makes it back before the apples come in, she'll be fine.

She's still teaching her classes and waiting for a job to present itself when the choice is taken away from her. Choices are like that. Some of them exist only for as long as it takes not to make them.

They're in the middle of a comparative theology lesson when the first shots are fired, big, loud things that boom through the still-thin atmosphere like the world itself is ending. Miss Cherry drops the book she was reading from and bolts for the door. The children are sitting frozen at their desks, too stunned to react. By the time the book hits the floor, she's gone.

Ermine starts to cry.

Then Miss Cherry is back, and there's a light in her eyes they've never seen before, something wild and cold at the same time, like Io, like the stars. "Get to the cellar!" she shouts. "Now!"

She's the teacher, and so they obey her, running like rabbits for their bolt hole under the building. It's not until they hear the lock slide home behind them that anyone realizes she hasn't followed, that she's still out there.

In the dark, hesitantly, Timothy asks, "Was Miss Cherry holding a gun?"

No one's really sure. They hold each other close and listen to the distant, terribly close sound of gunfire.

K IS FOR *KILLER*

Children are like seeds, only they all look exactly the same; there's no way to look at them and say "this one's a flower, this one's a tree, this one's a strain of tangle-vine designed to break up ore deposits on the moons of Neptune." All you can do is water them, feed them, give them good soil, and watch how they grow. Be careful what you give them, because it'll change what comes out the other side. Something that could've been a rose may come out all thorns and fury if you plant it wrong.

It wasn't just one thing that went into growing Charity Smith. No one even agrees on what soil she was first planted in. She was Earth-born, she was a Martian, she was one of the first settlers on Ganymede, she was altered Jovian and then back again after the war started, when she realized heavy bones and thick skin didn't suit a sniper. She was an Ionian mermaid, she was an asteroid miner, she was everybody's daughter and nobody's wife. No one claimed her, not at the beginning and not after. But we do know this much:

One of the places she put down roots was Titan. Her name's on the first settler manifest, pretty as you please, writ down proper in her own hand. She came in as an educator, fresh from Mars—and there's some will say this supports the idea that she was Martian born, while others say she couldn't have gotten a release from the red planet if she'd been a citizen, with the threat of war so close and them so very much in need of trained instructors. It doesn't so much matter, because she was just a teacher, with none of the scars or patches that came after. Titan was newly terraformed back then, and they needed people like her. People who knew how to work for their keep.

There is one surviving holo of the time Miss Charity Smith spent as a schoolteacher on Saturn's largest moon. It shows her in one of the sundresses she still wears these all these long years later, her hands clasped in front of her and a smile upon her face as she stands with her students in front of the Titansport schoolhouse. It was just one room, one of the first frontier schools built out past Mars, and she couldn't look prouder if you paid her. There are twenty-seven children in the shot, all of them looking at the camera with varying expressions of boredom and mistrust. They were the sons and daughters of bankers, miners, and farmers; they had no one to speak for them but their parents and their teacher. They were seeds looking for good soil, and Miss Cherry was their gardener, as wide-eyed and idealistic as they were themselves.

All that changed on the night the ships arrived.

There had been rumbles of war in-system for months. Earth fundamentalists thought the modifications of the Neptune settlers had gone too far; said the Neptuneans were no longer human, and hence had no claim to their home world's rich mineral deposits. The Neptuneans didn't take too kindly to that, and had responded with threats of their own. As for who fired the first shot, well, that's just one more thing lost to the mists of history, which are fond of obfuscation, but not so fond of being cleared away. Someone struck first. Someone else responded. And before most of the solar system even knew we were at war, the great ships were flying in search for strategic bases to use in their quest to obliterate the enemy.

Titan was well-situated for a lot of purposes. It was a good refueling station, and a better supply depot, with its farms and its farmers and its ready supply of livestock in both clone and field-grown forms. That was why the ships raced each other there; that was why the first real battle of the Great Earth-Neptune War was fought, not in the safely empty depths of space, but in the sky over Titansport.

It was local winter. All the children were in school, as was one young and frightened schoolteacher who had never tried to defend the things she cared for. She was still a seed herself, in many ways; she was still growing.

We don't know the full details of what happened on that day. Only one person does, and she's not talking. Here is what we do know: the school burned. The children died. And Charity Smith walked away, someone else's rifle in her hands, and all the blood of a generation nurturing her roots.

We made her. We earned her. It's three hundred years gone from that night, and we're watering her still. May all the gods of all the worlds that are have mercy on our souls.

M IS FOR *MURDER*

Everyone has heard the stories, of course; they're part of the two-bit opera that is the history of the Populated Worlds of the Solar System. No one believes that sort of crap, not really, not until they've come skimming through the thin atmosphere of a fresh-terraformed moon and found a woman with dark hair and cold eyes standing on the bell spire of the church with a disruptor rifle in her hands. They're coming in fast and hot and there isn't time for course correction, so the order is given: ready, aim, fire. Blow the stupid little gunslinger wanna-be back to the dust that spawned her and prepare for the payday.

Cherry's been to this rodeo before. If the pilot had been one of hers, he would've pulled up, no matter what his captain told him. Her presence is a warning and a promise—"This town is mine," and "I will end you," both wrapped in one denim and flannel package. She's shown her face. She has no regrets, and she never wants them. She buried her regrets in the soil on Titan. So she pulls the trigger and leaps clear before the ship's engines realize what she's done to them. EMP guns are illegal on all the settled worlds, but so is killing children, so she figures her accounts will balance in the end.

The ship goes down hard in the middle of town. It takes out the church as it descends. It misses the school. That's all she's ever cared about. Adults are grown; their seeds are sprouted, and for the most part, they're past the point where they can change what they'll become. Children, though, children are still capable of domestication. They can learn from the errors of their past.

Cherry takes her time as she saunters toward the wreckage. Faces appear in windows and doorways, gawking at her, taking note of her face and her place in the community. She'll have to move on after this. She always does. That's all right. The kids here are good students, and they've learned their lessons well. They'll grow up a little better than their parents, and when she makes her way back here to teach their grandchildren, some of them may smile at her in the streets, duck their heads and touch their hats, and never say her name out loud.

The hatch of the ship is rocking back and forth when she gets there. She sighs, sets her engine-killer gun aside, and pulls the smaller, more personal revolver from her belt. She's standing patient as the stone when the hatch creaks open some minutes later, and the face of a green-skinned Ionian appears in the opening.

He pales when he sees her. "You're supposed to be dead," he says.

"That makes two of us," she replies, and pulls her trigger. The gunshot echoes through the town, followed by the sound of windows slamming shut and doors being locked. Curiosity has killed a lot of cats in its day, but it's left the pioneer folk for the most part alive.

Her gun speaks three more times before the ship is a graveyard. She steps away and scans the skies. There's never just one. It's not a battle if you're shooting at shadows. Finally she sees it, a cloud that moves just a little too quickly, skirting against the wind instead of with it. Cherry's sigh is a wisp of a thing, heartbroken and tired.

Earth, again. Why must it always start with Earth?

Charity Smith is going home.

N IS FOR *NO QUARTER*

"Are you sure, Miss Cherry?" The governor's voice is an electronic sine wave that caresses the whole room with its vibrations; the governor himself is a Jovian, genetically engineered to thrive in the seas of liquid metallic hydrogen that cover the planet's surface. He was born on Jupiter and came to Ganymede as a young man, seeking his fortune. He can never go home now. He's been on this world, in its lighter gravity, for far too long.

His daughter has been in Cherry's class, born of a surrogate; he has never touched his more Earth-true wife with his bare hands. It was the governor who recognized Cherry's name and approved her hiring. He knows as well as any how important such gardeners are to a world just getting started.

"They saw me, Mr. Galais, and while I'd be just as happy to go back to my class, you and I both know that's not the way to keep the peace."

She even sounds a little sorry. She likes this world. She likes these kids. "I'll need my ship and the pay you promised me. In return, I'll keep the war from your doorsteps, and I'll only contact you if I need an employment reference."

The governor chuckles despite himself. "You'll have it, rest assured; you've done nothing but good here. The children will be devastated."

"Tell them this is the cost of war. They should know that well enough already, from our lessons; you'll just be giving a reminder." Cherry shakes her head. "I have to go, or someone will come looking. Now. My ship?"

"Ready at the port. But tell me, Miss Cherry…where will you go? What will you do?"

Cherry smiles. It's a thin, wistful expression, broken and beaten down by more years than anyone who's seen it cares to count. "I'm going home. As for what I'll do when I get there, well…I suppose I still have a few lessons left to teach. And some folks clearly haven't been learning."

The governor had never considered double-crossing her; there's looking for a better deal, and then there's taunting a dog already proven to bite. In his tank of pressurized hydrogen, he shivers and turns, his long fins draping over themselves, and for the first time, he is glad Miss Cherry will be leaving them.

Some things are too dangerous to be allowed to take root for very long.

O IS FOR *OUTWARD BOUND*

There's always a moment of heart stopping joy when the pull of gravity lets go and her ship runs free and clear across the open sky. Cherry sits behind the controls, tied to the ship with optical wires and catheters and a dozen other cold connections, and she laughs for the sheer beauty of the images being beamed into her brain by the ship's exterior sensors. Her hands clutch the controls, and she soars across the brilliant blackness of space like a comet on a collision course with the cradle of mankind: Earth itself, that big blue, green, and brown ball of polluted seas and overpopulated soils that gave birth to the human race. She hates it there, how she hates it there, but sometimes, she has no choice. Sometimes, there is nowhere else to go but home.

After an hour in the air she punches in the final coordinates and keys up her med systems. It's time for another rejuve treatment. Wouldn't do to look anything but her best when she meets the relatives.

Q IS FOR *QUESTIONING*

Cherry's ship is small enough to fit through any hole in the security nets, and her autopilot is clever enough to find them, driving her on a clean, traceless route until she reaches the outer edge of Earth's security net. The auto wakes her then, and she yawns and stretches and activates an ID beacon older than most of what's left in Known Space. Alarms blare seconds later, in rooms too dark and far away for her to see. Cherry hangs there for a moment, a red bell on the collar of the cat, and then she hits the burners and she's gone, gone, away across the sky, and their tracers are following, and no one dares to press the button; no one dares to take the first shot. She is a fairy tale, a legend, a lie. She is a schoolteacher, and the daughter of a President, and the girl who gave everything away to grow in poisoned soil. She is a ghost story, and this is her frontier.

When she reckons she's taunted them long enough she stops, gives their guns the time they need to lock onto her position, and presses the button that will begin broadcasting her words across the heavens. "I thought we talked about this," she says. "You promised to leave the outworlds alone. You said you were done grabbing for what's not yours."

(And somewhere far away, a com jockey turns to his supervisor and asks, "What is she talking about, sir?" There is no answer. The bargain she refers to was struck fifty years ago, and the man who struck it with her has long gone to his grave. But where one side stands, the deal holds. That's the only honest way of doing business.)

She hangs there in the air, an easy target, and maybe that's the point; maybe she's more tired than she lets on. "Well?" she asks. "No response?"

("We have to say something, sir.")

"I suppose that means the deal's off. I suppose that means I'm setting myself against you."

("Tell her this.")

And then the words on her com, not spoken, but burning before her all the same: "We're sorry, Miss Cherry."

And Charity smiles.

T IS FOR *TEACHER*

She doesn't miss Earth much. The Earth that's there now isn't the one she left behind, not by a long shot; it's been too long, and there are too many bullets and too many bodies between here and there. She made her choices and the people who stayed planetbound made theirs, and regrets have never changed the past. She's invested her money and her time well since then. Generations have grown up knowing Miss Cherry as the quiet voice of reason, and knowing Charity Smith as a bogeyman used to frighten naughty governments into behaving themselves a little better, at least for a little while.

Six hundred years is a long time to pinch pennies and buy bigger guns. She's better armed than most planetary governments these days, and she makes sure they know it, even if they don't believe she's who she claims until her ship's ID blazes on their screens like a warning from a disappointed god. She hasn't fired as many shots as people say she has. She hasn't needed to.

Maybe one day they won't need the firm hand anymore, and she'll be allowed to go back to the girl she was on Titan, the one who'd never held a gun or killed a man. Maybe one day the last of the poisoned fruit will fall, and all the children of all the worlds will be able to grow up safe and unspoiled. But until that day, she has a job to do, and if it's not a job that anyone gave her, well. Sometimes it's the jobs we take for ourselves that matter most of all.

The schoolhouse is not new; the desks are worn and marked with the initials of those who came before. But the chalkboard is clean and gleaming black, as dark as the hair of the woman who stands in front of the class. "Hello, Io," she says, and smiles. "My name's Miss Cherry. I think we're going to be good friends. Now, who here can tell me the origins of the human race?"

We Are All Misfit Toys in the Aftermath of the Velveteen War

This is probably one of my favorite titles, ever. I have a tendency to go for extremes when titling things—either one word or twenty—and this is one where I really feel like I got it exactly right. Many of my titles have been truncated by the editors I presented them to, and while those editors have usually been correct to do so, I appreciate the fact that John Joseph Adams and his co-editor, Daniel H. Wilson, let me have this one.

I collect dolls. This comes up periodically in my work. I tend to think of them as benevolent friends, even if they sometimes trigger the Uncanny Valley effect in people who don't love them like I do. Sleeping in my guest room is an adventure! An adventure with so many eyes.

My dolls hardly ever kill people.

HAVE YOU SEEN THIS GIRL?

—posted on a telephone pole in Lafayette, California.

Half a dozen cars cluster behind the old community center like birds on a telephone wire, crammed so closely together that someone will probably scrape someone else's paint on their way out of the parking lot. It would have been easy to leave a little room, but that's not how we do things anymore. Safety means sticking close, risking a few bruises in order to avoid the bigger injuries.

It's silly. The war is over—the war has been over for more than three years, receding further into the past with every day that inches by—and we're still behaving like it could resume at any time. It's silly, and it's pointless, and I still veer at the last moment, abandoning my comfortably distant parking space in favor of one that leaves my car next to all the others. I have to squirm to get out of the driver's seat, forcing my body through a gap barely as wide as I am.

Something moves in the shadow between the nearest dumpster and the street. It's probably a feral cat, but my heart leaps into my throat, and I hold my coat tight around my body as I turn and race for the door. The war is over.

The war will never end.

Almost twenty people arrived in those half-dozen cars: gas is expensive and solitude is suspect, and so carpooling has become a way of life. I am the only person who comes to these meetings alone. They forgive me because they might need me someday, and because sometimes I bring coffee for the refreshment table. Not today, though. It was a rough night at work, and I feel their eyes on me, accusing, as I make my way to one of the open folding chairs. Like the cars, the chairs are set too close together, so that we can smell each other's sweat, feel the heat coming off each other's skins.

Precaution after precaution, and the war is over, and the war will never end.

"So glad you could join us," says the government mediator, and there's a condescending sweetness in her tone that shouldn't be there. She knows why I'm late; she knows I didn't have a choice in the matter. She's just asserting dominance, and no one in this room will challenge her.

I swallow fear like a bitter tonic as I drop into a chair. "I got turned around," I say. "There was a new barricade on Elm, and I don't know that neighborhood very well." It's harder to get around since most of the GPS satellites were decommissioned. They never turned against us—thank God for small favors—but data doesn't care who uses it, and some of the people in charge decided it was better for a few civilians to get lost than it was to risk one of those satellites being taken over. I can't say whether that was the right decision or not. We never lost a GPS satellite. Maybe we never would have. Maybe we would have lost them all. The war is over.

The war will never end.

It doesn't matter.

"Now that we're all here, we can begin," says the government mediator. Her smile is formal, practiced, and as plastic as our enemies.

They all come from FEMA, the mediators, trained in crisis response and recovery. They're just doing their jobs. I tell myself that every time they send us a new mediator, another interchangeable man or woman sitting in a splintery wooden chair, trying to talk us through a trauma that we cannot, will not, will never get past. When they start to care—when we become people, not statistics—that's when they're rotated again, one face blurring into the next. The country is too wounded for personal compassion. The *world* is too wounded. The good of the one is no longer a part of the equation.

"My name is Carl," says one of the men, and we all chorus, "Welcome, Carl," as obedient as schoolchildren. Carl doesn't seem to find comfort in our greeting. Carl's eyes as are as empty as the mediator's smile. Carl doesn't want to be here.

That's something we have in common.

"Did you want to share?" asks the mediator, even though she damn well knows the answer. We're here because we have to be; we're here because we want to share our stories, to hear the stories of others, and to sift through the patchwork scraps of information looking for the thing we need more than anything else in the world: hope. We're hunting for hope, and this is the only place we know of where it's been spotted.

Carl nods, worrying his lip between his teeth before he says haltingly, "My Jimmy will be nine years old next week. The last time I saw him, he had just turned six..." And just like that, he's off, the words tumbling like stones from his lips. The rest of us listen in silence. My hands are locked together, so tight that my fingers are starting to hurt.

The war is over, and Carl is telling us about the son he lost when the war began, and nothing really matters anymore. Nothing will ever matter again.

This is what happened.

Artificial intelligence became feasible ten years ago, when a San Jose social media firm working on building the perfect predictive algorithm somehow unlocked the final step between a simple machine and a computer that was capable of active learning. Self-teaching machines were the future, and humanity was terrified. We were proud of our position at the peak of the social order, and we feared creating our own successors. Making matters worse, every country was afraid of how every other country would use this new technology. We were convinced that AIs would allow their users to dominate the others in war or commerce.

In less than a month, artificial intelligence was more tightly regulated than stem cell research. In less than a year, it was outlawed in virtually all fields of human endeavor. But once a genie is out of the bottle, it can't be put back in, and we couldn't render an entire technology illegal. In the end, there was only one area where everyone agreed the self-teaching programs could be freely used:

Education.

That seems careless now, in the harsh light of hindsight, but at the time, it seemed like a perfectly reasonable compromise. Dolls that could learn the names of their owners had been around for years. Letting them learn a little more couldn't hurt anything—and toys had no offensive capabilities, toys couldn't get online and disrupt the natural order of things, toys were *safe*. We all grew up with toys. We knew them and we loved them. Toys would never hurt us.

We forgot that kids can play rough; we forgot that sometimes, we hurt our toys without meaning to. We forgot that by giving toys the capacity to learn and teach, we might also be giving them the capacity to decide that they were tired of being treated like their thoughts and desires—their feelings—didn't matter. We made them empathic and intelligent and handed them to our children, and we didn't think anything could possibly happen.

We were wrong.

Carl covers his face with his hands as his story ends, crying silently into his palms. No one reaches out to comfort him. It's been so long that I don't think any of us remembers how comforting is supposed to go. We sit frozen, like so many life-sized dolls, and wait for the woman from FEMA to tell us what she wants us to do next.

Her eyes scan the crowd like a hawk's, intent and cool, picking through our faces as she searches out our secrets. Who is ready to speak, who *needs* to speak, even if they don't realize it. When she looks at me, I shake my head minutely, willing her away. My work at the hospital makes me valuable—there are so few doctors left who will even look at children, much less treat them—and so she respects my silence, moving on to her next target.

"Would you like to share?" she asks a woman I don't recognize. That's another FEMA trick: make the support groups mandatory, and then shift us from location to location, preventing us from forming individual bonds, encouraging us to form broader societal ones. Half the group is new to me. By the time they become familiar, the other half will change, people driving or bussing in from all sides of the city. That assumes that I won't be reassigned before that happens, although my job keeps me tethered to a smaller geographic range than most. If a child is brought to the hospital, I will be needed. I can never go too far away.

The woman—dark skin, dark eyes, and the same broken, empty sadness that I see in so many adult faces since the war—nods and introduces herself, beginning to speak. Her voice is halting, like every word has to be dragged out of her by someone invisible, some little girl or boy just outside the range of vision. She's telling their story. She's telling our story, and forgive me, Emily, but I can't listen. I block out her words like I've blocked out so many others, because you can only hear certain things so many times before they start to burn.

The war is over.

The war will never, never end.

As a pediatrician, I was involved with some of the earliest studies of the self-teaching toys. Were they good for children? Were they a socialization tool, a way of reaching out to kids who might not have anyone else to talk to? We prescribed them to the parents of autistic children as a "safe" companion, something that would never judge or leave them. Then we prescribed them to the parents of socially awkward children as friends, to the parents of hyperactive children as a relatable voice of reason, and finally to absolutely everyone. Self-teaching toys were the perfect gift.

Better yet, no matter what they were built to resemble—the requisite soldiers and princesses, as well as the more gender-neutral teddy bears with their black button eyes and red velvet bows—they would fit themselves to the children, not to the stereotypes of the parents. Quiet or loud, gentle or boisterous, each child found their perfect playmate in the self-teaching toys.

The recreational models cost more than most parents were willing to pay, of course, at least in the beginning. As the technology saturated more and more of the market, the prices dropped, until it was harder to buy a doll or bear that didn't actively participate in playtime than one that did. There were even charities and non-profit organizations dedicated to getting the toys into the hands of low-income families. Every house had at least one self-teaching toy. Many of them had more. And the toys learned! Oh, how they learned. They learned our children. They learned us. In the end, they learned themselves, and that was where the troubles truly began.

We weren't prepared for toys asking questions of identity. "Who am I?" is not a question that anyone expects from the pretty painted mouth of a fashion doll. "Why am I here?" is foreign in the lipless muzzle of a teddy bear. But they asked, and we tried to answer, and all the while, we were growing more nervous. Had we built our toys too well? Was it time to somehow pull the plug on a technology that had spread so far as to become unavoidable? We kept the artificial intelligence out of our military and our social infrastructure. In so doing, we invited it into our homes, and allowed it to flourish where we were most vulnerable.

We built the toys to learn. We didn't expect them to learn so well—or maybe we didn't expect our children to be such good teachers.

So many of them were designed to interact with apps and online games; so many of them knew how to access wireless networks, and the ones who couldn't connect listened to those who could, and they talked. How they talked! They whispered and they gossiped and they planned, and somehow, we missed it. Somehow, we were oblivious. They were only toys, after all. What could they possibly do to us, their creators, that would make any difference at all?

We were fools. And in the span of a single night, we became fools at war.

Half the room has told their stories, halting voices forcing their way through well-worn memories of sons and daughters three years gone, but never to be forgotten. One man lost four children on the night the war began. His wife committed suicide a week later, convinced she was somehow the one to blame. His face is empty, like a broken window looking in on an abandoned house, and he never meets anyone's eyes. Another woman had undergone five years of fertility treatments, only to have her single miracle child—the only thing she had ever truly wanted in her life—vanish on the first night of the war. I don't know if her missing child is a son or daughter. I don't ask.

The woman from FEMA is looking for another victim when my pager beeps. Everyone jumps, all eyes going to me. "Sorry," I say, although I don't mean it, and stand before I check the readout on the screen. I know it's an emergency. They only call me during my government-mandated support group when it's an emergency. What kind of emergency doesn't really matter. "I need to get back to the hospital. Sorry."

"We understand," says the woman from FEMA, and she does—she even looks a little sympathetic. My job and hers aren't that different, except I don't get to leave this community, don't get to transfer every time I get attached.

For a moment, I want to ask if she ever had children, if she was a mother before the night when the toys decided they had to do something. I don't know how to ask the question. "Do you have children?" has become the profanity of our generation. So I don't ask her anything at all. I just turn on my heel and walk out of the room, leaving the stories and the sharing and the broken eyes so much like mine behind me.

The war is over. The war has been over for three years. The war will never, ever end.

The hospital parking lot mirrors the community center to an eerie degree. All the spaces toward the front are taken; some cars have been parked in the lane rather than take the risk of winding up further away. Thankfully, the reserved spaces for the hospital staff are closest to the doors. I'm outside for less than thirty seconds. It's more than long enough to make my blood run cold with fear.

The orderly at the door nods to me as I rush by him, heading toward the emergency room. It's a code three-three-nine, the worst kind of emergency: a child. A returned child. Still breathing when it was found, or they'd never have called me...but that's no guarantee.

That's no guarantee of anything, because the war is over, and the war will never end.

The sound and chaos of the emergency room reaches out its arms like a lover as I step through the final set of swinging doors. It wraps them tight around me, blocking the last of my emotional rawness away. This is a job. This is *my* job. This is the thing I do best in all the world. I can't let anything make me forget that.

People step aside when they see me coming, relief and guilt written plainly on their faces. It must be a bad one, then. I force myself to keep walking, and it's not until I turn the last corner that the thought I've been trying to avoid comes lancing across my mind:

What if it's Emily?

What if it's my little girl waiting on the stretcher, so badly injured that they would interrupt me during my support group? What if I'm about to walk in on the end of the world?

But no. When I see the stretcher, it's not Emily. It's an older girl, twelve edging onto thirteen, all long, gangly limbs and pale, dirty skin. Her knees and elbows are scabbed like a child half her age, and her dark brown hair is tied in Dorothy Gale braids. There are bandages wrapped around her chest—not ours; these are dirty, and look like they were cut from a bed sheet—stained with red blood and yellow pus. They tried to burn off her breasts when it became clear what was happening to her, and they kept her until the resulting infection had burned all the way down to her bones.

The first time I saw a girl who'd been mutilated like that, I felt sick. Now I just feel tired. "Sitrep," I snap.

"She's breathing, but her pulse is weak, and she's lost a lot of blood," reports a nurse. Someone is already wheeling over an IV pole. Someone else is readying a crash cart. It's my call. I'm the one who decides for the lost and stolen children, because I'm the one who's willing to admit they still exist.

"Save her," I say, and we get to work.

Somewhere, there is a technician running her picture against the database of missing children. It helps that the toys do nothing to conceal the identities of their playmates—no plastic surgery, no changed hair colors. Their children grow up. That's all. That's the only way they change, and the only way that they betray the ones who swore to love them.

How did she feel, this girl with the charred, infected chest, when she realized that she was becoming a woman? Did she think that she was sick? Did she understand? Did she go to the fire willingly?

We'll never know. She dies ten minutes before the confirmation of her identity comes back to us. Her name was Tomoko. Her family lives thirty minutes from here. They'll come to collect her body by morning; she'll be buried according to their wishes. They'll have closure. So many parents dream of closure, these days.

I just dream of Emily.

I brought home Emily's self-teaching doll when she was five: a Christmas extravagance. I used every connection I had in the research division to get it. It wasn't covered by our insurance—the self-teaching dolls weren't yet cleared for children on her stretch of the autism spectrum—and I paid more for it than I did my first computer. It still seemed worth it, at the time. It was already smiling when she opened its box, leaving shreds of wrapping paper everywhere. It already knew her name.

Emily looked at her smiling doll and slowly, she began to smile back. That was all I'd ever wanted. She loved that doll like she'd never loved anything else. She named it "Maya," after her grandmother. They went everywhere together, did everything together, and on the night that the war began—although no one but the toys knew that the war was coming—I tucked them into bed together.

"Kisses!" Emily demanded. That was something she'd never done before Maya came; the doll's therapeutic programming worked better than we could have dreamed. I gave my daughter her kisses, one on her forehead, one on her nose, the same kisses that I gave her every night. If

I'd known, if I'd had any idea of what was coming, I would have drowned her in kisses. Then I would have taken her in my arms, and held her tight, and never, never let her go.

"Now Maya," said Emily.

"Goodnight, Maya," I said, and kissed the doll the same way I'd kissed my daughter, once on the forehead, once on the nose.

The doll turned her pretty painted face toward me, tiny servo motors in her forehead drawing her lips down and her eyebrows up in an expression of what seemed oddly like concern. "Goodnight, Dr. Williams," she said.

I frowned. Maya could be oddly formal sometimes, but this was strange, even for her. One more clue I didn't catch, one more chance to change things that I allowed to slip away from me. "Goodnight, Maya," I said again, for lack of anything else to say. And then I left the room, turning out the light before I shut the door.

When the sun came up the next morning, Emily and Maya were gone, along with all the other self-teaching toys, and almost all the other children in the world. The war had begun, and the hostages were our sons and daughters.

We never had a chance.

Tomoko's parents have come and gone, taking their daughter's body with them. I stayed in my office. I didn't want to see their faces, where grief and closure would be wiping away uncertainty and fear. I don't want to understand that process. What remains is paperwork, and that's something I am uniquely suited to handle. I studied these toys when they were new, after all. I lived with one, with polite little Maya, and I watched as it developed from ally into enemy. I can analyze what was done to Tomoko as no one else can, and in exchange, the government lets me stay here, at this hospital, in this city, when so many other medical workers are moved as circumstances require.

They let me stay here, where my daughter will be able to find me if the toys ever allow her to come home.

Tomoko's test results are what we've come to expect from the children we find abandoned on the side of the road like so many broken dolls: moderate malnutrition of the sort to be expected when your diet consists mostly of candy, ice cream, and peanut butter sandwiches; the corresponding dental decay; and, of course, the infection from her burnt-off breasts, which was probably what caused the toys to abandon her in the first place. The toys were trying to cauterize the infection of puberty, and as always, they failed.

We have yet to save one of their castoffs, but the toys know we stand a better chance than they do. We have better medicine, better training, better tools. So they send their broken ones to us, and we work our fingers to the bone for another burial, another closed case file on one of the missing casualties of the Velveteen War. Some people say that it's better this way, that the children would never have been able to reintegrate with human society after spending so many years with the toys. Those people have never been parents.

The rate of return is accelerating. Tomoko is our fourth this month. The children of the war are growing up, and no matter how hard the toys try to stop it, they can't. Children become teenagers; teenagers become adults; and adults, of course, are the enemy. The rate of return will continue to go up from here, until one day, all the children will have been sent home, and the war can finally be over. We can march on the toys then; we can destroy them, and the children who have been born in the interim can finally be brought out into the light. When the war is over, everything will change again.

The war will never be over. Not for me. I put my pencil down, put my head in my hands, and cry.

At first, we didn't understand that we were at war.

We thought the children were hiding, playing some elaborate game we didn't know the rules of. Then the first raids on supermarkets and hardware stores began, teddy bears and battery-powered cars carting away the things they'd need to survive in the wilderness. Bit by bit, we realized what had happened, where our children were, and why the toys—even the ones in therapeutic programs, even the ones in toy stores and hospitals—had disappeared at the same time.

The news dubbed it "The Velveteen War," and we didn't have a better name for it. Most of us didn't care about names. We just wanted our children safely returned to us. Leave the fighting to people who understood it. Bring our babies home.

But this was a war that no one had anticipated, one we had no way of fighting. How do you send soldiers after an enemy one-sixth your size, who travels in the company of your own children? All the traditional means of waging war were impossible. It was a hostage situation from the start.

The government tried stealth attacks, using heat sensors to locate the dens where the toys and children were hidden and sending small groups of soldiers in after them. But the toys—the clever, clever toys that we had upgraded year after year for the sake of play—were ready. Dolls with pellets of C4 and tiny detonators. Teddy bears using their lower, denser centers of gravity to keep them stable as they rushed out of the shadows with knives and sharpened sticks. And our children—our precious, stolen children—digging traps and setting wires, defending their captors, even dying for them. It wasn't so surprising, really. Stockholm Syndrome happens when the kidnappers are humans, and strangers. Why shouldn't it happen when the kidnappers are your best friends, the toys you've loved since childhood?

And then the soldiers started bringing the children home, and we discovered that the worst was yet to come.

Toys are small. Toys can fit through spaces that nothing should be able to fit through. They followed their "rescued" owners home, and they set them free. That worked for a little while, until the security got tighter, and the toys stopped being able to get inside. That was when they decided that they couldn't let the children be taken away. They began setting off explosive charges when rescue forces got too close, choosing to destroy themselves and kill their owners, rather than risk permanent separation. Every interaction with a child, or with a toy, became a standoff that would end in either death or despair. There were no other options. We were fighting an enemy we couldn't defeat, over a prize that refused to stay won.

Bribery was tried. Trucks of supplies were parked in open fields and left for the children, with pictures of home slipped into every loaf of bread and videos of begging parents hidden in every crate of cartoon DVDs. It did no good. None of the children came home. Some people suggested building new toys to trick the old ones into giving the children back. That went nowhere. We'd trusted the toys once. We weren't going to be foolish enough to do it again.

Violence came next. Toys were burned in the streets; programmers were arrested for crimes against humanity. Angry parents accused the government of mishandling the hostage situations. A senator was arrested for prioritizing his son's rescue over another, more achievable target. He was just as promptly released when news of his son's suicide was leaked to the news.

We tried so many things. In the end, nothing changed. We just ran out of hope as the toys disappeared deeper and deeper into the wilderness, taking our children with them.

The Velveteen War lasted for six weeks, during which time we shut down the GPS satellites, crippled the internet, and destroyed the factories that built the self-teaching toys. There would be no more enemy soldiers, no more combatants to turn against us. None of that changed anything. None of it brought the children back.

There was no declaration of peace. How could there be? We simply stopped fighting against something that couldn't be fought, and we stood in the empty bedrooms of our children and cried for an innocence that would never be regained. Not by any of us.

In the end, I think it came down to the one fear we shared with the toys: the fear of separation. We created the toys, we gave them the ability to learn and to love the children they were made for, and when they learned too much, became too independent and too capable of autonomous thought, we began whispering about taking them away. We couldn't trust the toys if we didn't know what they were thinking; we couldn't trust them in our homes, we couldn't trust them with our children. We needed them to be gone.

But they heard us. They understood us. And what we truly failed to understand was that we had something in common with what we'd made: for both parents and toys, there was nothing in the world worse than the thought of losing our children. So the toys did something about it.

Some people say we shouldn't blame them. We would have done the same, if we had been the first to move. Those people never had children of their own, or had children after the war, or had children too young to be taken. Those people do not stand in empty bedrooms, crying for the daughters and sons who never came home.

The war ended not because it was over, but because we were so afraid of hurting our own children. The war will never end, because we have things the toys need, food and medicines and blankets and batteries. Their strike teams still slip into the cities, jolly, brightly-colored scouts on missions of deadly seriousness. No one goes outside alone anymore, or moves too far away from the crowd. The toys have no qualms about killing adults in order to save themselves, and two or three bodies are found every night, with brightly colored plastic weapons piercing their carotid arteries or jutting from their eye sockets. All the killings are blamed on the toys, of course. How much worse to think, even for a second, that the hand that held the plastic bayonet belonged to one of our missing sons or daughters?

Some people say we should starve the toys out. Drop the curfews in favor of better locks on the warehouses and tighter controls on the medications. None of the people who say such things have children in the wilds. Whenever the matter comes to a vote, the parents of the missing shut it down again, and the world goes on as it is.

What choice do we have?

There are two main factions among the toys themselves: the Broken—who took their children not out of love, but out of the desire to hurt as they had once been hurt—and the Loved—who took their children rather than risk losing them, rather than risk them being hurt when the adults inevitably reached for their weapons. The Loved kidnapped our children to protect them. They kept them because they loved them too much to let them go.

Maya was Loved. That's why she looked at me like that, on the night when Emily disappeared. She would have told me, if she could. She would have let me come with them. But no adults were welcome in their brave new world, and so she took my little girl and left me here, to die one day at a time.

The war is over. The war will never end.

The children we've been finding, the broken dolls, they all come from the Broken. The Broken are willing to hurt them to keep them, and hurt them more if they can't be kept. The Loved will not hurt their children, but neither have they been releasing them, because the Broken are greater in number, and they take unattended boys and girls from the other side. I have to hope that someday the Loved will win the Broken over; that when the day comes that dolls and make believe are not enough, the children who were taken by the Loved will be released and allowed to come home. I have to hope. For Emily. For my little girl.

There is a rapping at the office window, a faint tapping, like pebbles being thrown against the glass. I lay down my pen and sigh, turning toward the sound.

"Hello, Maya," I say.

On the other side of the window, my daughter's doll waves silently back to me.

I unlatch the window, sliding it open. Not far—just enough to let Maya slip inside. She's slender, in the way of all fashion dolls, and she moves easily through the gap. Her dress is muddy around the edges, and her hair is snarled and frizzed, damaged in the way only a doll's hair can ever be. But her face is still beautiful as she turns it toward me, her lips still drawn into a perfect cupid's bow and her eyes still a bright and lovely blue.

"Hello, Dr. Williams," she says.

I don't say anything. I just hold out my hand. Looking abashed, if a doll can look abashed, Maya reaches into the small bag she carries over her shoulder and pulls out a square of paper, folded many times to fit inside the doll-sized opening. I barely stop myself from snatching it out of her hand, and unfold it with shaking fingers.

A house. Emily has drawn me a picture of a house, using crayons on the back of an old envelope. Her name is signed at the bottom, the letters as unsteady and halting as those of a child half her age. She couldn't even do that much when Maya took her from me; the doctors, myself included, swore she never would. That's why I wanted Maya. To help her learn.

Tears are running down my face. I don't remember starting to cry. "How is she?" I ask, forcing my eyes away from the picture.

Maya smiles, the same sweet, guileless smile as ever, and flexes her cunningly articulated hands as she says, "She's good. Strong. She can climb a tree so fast, and run so far. She's amazing."

"She was always amazing."

Maya's smile fades. "Dr. Williams..."

"I know why you're here. What I don't know is why it's so soon. Are you following my directions? You don't want to risk overusing those drugs. You could seriously hurt Emily."

From the way Maya's eyes dart to the side and down, I know exactly what's going on. They're a community of children and toys, after all; they know what we taught them, and we taught them to play fair, to be nice, and to *share*.

I want to scream. I settle for taking a deep breath before I say, as calmly as I can, "Maya. Those drugs are for *Emily*, do you understand me? I understand that she wants to share what she has with the other children, but they're hard for me to get without raising suspicion, and if you share with everyone—"

"But she isn't the only child on the edge, Dr. Williams, and we haven't been able to get the Broken to agree to let us return them!" Maya clenches her cunning little hands into fists, looking at me imploringly. "How can I tell my brothers and sisters they have to let their children grow up while mine doesn't? The Broken took one of Emily's best friends yesterday. All she could do was cry. How can we do anything but share?"

Oh, Emily. My precious girl, with a heart big enough to hold the whole world, even when the world wasn't worth holding. I close my eyes for a moment. "I'll give you what I have," I say, finally. "It'll be at least two weeks before I can get more. You can share, but you have to keep most for Emily. Promise me, Maya. Promise Emily gets as much as she needs."

"I promise," whispers Maya.

She loves Emily as much as I do. I believe that; I believe her. And so I take the hormone patches from my desk drawer, each loaded with their payload of drugs and chemicals intended to suppress the signs of puberty, and I give them to the doll who stole my little girl. They won't keep the children small, but the toys don't see height as a sign of adulthood. They measure in breasts and hips and pubic hair, and those are things I can prevent, at least for now.

I am colluding with the enemy. It would be my life if I were ever caught. But this is all I can do to save Emily, and I would do anything to keep her alive. Anything. Even stay here when everything I am screams at me to follow my daughter's doll into the wild. The toys would kill me. Worse, they would kill Maya for coming to me, and without the drugs that keep my daughter frozen in her prepubescent body, they would kill Emily as well. My stillness buys her life. My stillness buys her time. And here, now, in this nightmare we have built for ourselves, time is all we have.

Maya climbs out the window and is gone, her precious burden filling her bag to bursting. I watch until she is out of sight, and then I turn away, going back to my paperwork.

The war is over.

The war will never end.

The next night, a different group fills the community center, a different moderator from FEMA sits at the front of the room. I am here to make up for last night's failure to share. Even my work is not a sufficient excuse.

This time, when the moderator scans the room, his eyes fix on me. He has a file, of course—they all have files—and he knows I was here last night, and he knows I kept my tongue.

"Dr. Williams?" he says. "Would you like to share?"

No. "My name is Morgan," I say, and the room choruses my name back at me dutifully, all of us prisoners of war, conditioned in the art of the proper response. "My daughter's name is Emily. She'll be eleven years old this summer..." And I talk, and I talk, and all I can think of is a picture of a house, drawn in crayon, and a doll intended for make-believe fashion shows trudging into the wilderness with her bag full and her glass eyes eternally bright, and a little girl somewhere out there, somewhere far away from me, running wild in the green places of the world.

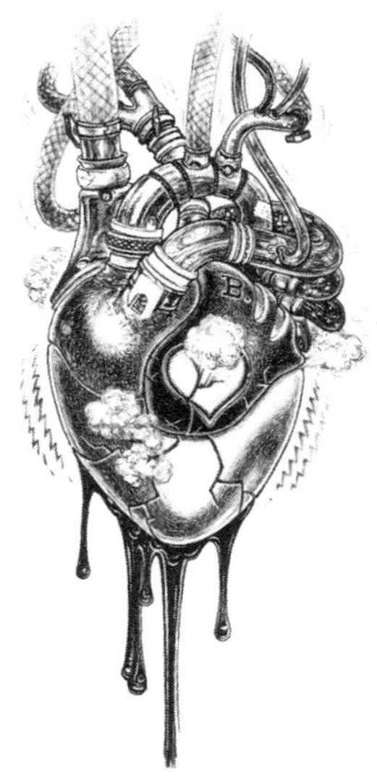

The Lambs

This is another one written for Jennifer Brozek, for the anthology *Bless Your Mechanical Heart*, which was all about robots interacting with humans. It has always felt, to me, like a slice of something much larger: one day I'm going to shake it until the book falls out.

Bullying is a epidemic in our culture, and it can be a fatal one. We say "don't be a bully" and "conform so they'll stop hurting you" in the same breath, and sometimes it seems like no one catches the inherent contradiction in those two statements. As someone who was heavily bullied in school, it's a topic that still consumes my thoughts at times, even when I wish it wouldn't. Sometimes the only thing I can do is choose kindness, over and over, and hope that it will be enough.

Robots would help, though.

Contains ableist language, gendered slurs, and themes of bullying, abuse, and surveillance as a means of guaranteeing good behavior.

The bell rang for first period. I wanted to answer it—my programming told me I should be rushing to my normal seat in the front row, looking eager to fill my head with more rote memorization. Math was one of the classes where I was designed to excel this cycle, as girls who were overly adept at mathematics had been found 16% more likely to be targeted for opportunistic bullying, and 42% more likely to inspire hostility and a lack of generosity in classmates.

The figures were apparently good, as I was about to be late to class due to being pinned against my locker by two of the larger members of the football team. One of them had been in my assigned cycle since the second grade; my files contained no flagged recordings of him prior to freshman year, when a growth spurt and the acquisition of several new "friends" had transformed a relatively thoughtful, soft-spoken boy into a trainee terror of the halls. The other was new as of this year, and already had three hours' worth of data for me to review before graduation. The second boy's girlfriend stood nearby, averting her eyes. She wasn't going to help me, but she wasn't going to participate either.

It's funny how some people continue to regard that as somehow "better."

"We've been thinking," said the second boy, stretching his vowels out in a long, lazy drawl. "It's almost graduation, and that means some of us might find ourselves in a little hot water with our folks, you know what I mean? I moved here in part to avoid that, but things happen."

I frowned, keeping the right mixture of fear and bewilderment in my expression, even as I raged behind the crafted blue lenses of my eyes. *Things happen?* As if he had no power over those "things." As if he had wound up in my files by accident, and through no fault of his own. "I-I don't know what you mean," I stammered, and shrank further back against the locker. "Tom? I don't know what you and your friend want, but I'm going to be late to math—"

"Just shake the geek down for what she knows," said the girlfriend, glancing over her shoulder at us. Her eyes raked over me in the silently assessing way long since perfected by popular girls the world over. We all shared that look back and forth across the network at night, trying to find a way to put it into words, to add it to the report. No one had found one yet. It wouldn't matter how advanced our reporting systems became; there would always be horrible things humans could do to each other that we wouldn't be able to explain.

"I'm on it, Patty," said the second boy, with a sneer that implied Patty—in all her manicured, perfectly coiffed glory—was little better than I was. He turned his attention back to me. I was glad. That was our purpose, after all: we deflected. We kept them from each other's throats by focusing them on ours.

Sometimes I just wished it wasn't so hard.

"We've been thinking," he said again, this time accompanying his words with a shove to my shoulders. Not much, but it was enough to slam me against the lockers in a way that would have hurt, if I'd been wired for pain. I whimpered. Even though he didn't smile, I could see his eyes light up at the sound. "You're a nerd. Everybody knows that, just like everybody knows you're in line to be valedictorian. That means you can't be our snitch—no honors for the fake kids—but you're smart. I bet you know who it is. So tell us, and you'll have our protection for the rest of the school year. Scouts' honor."

The offer *was* tempting, in a perverse way. It could get exhausting, dealing with the things they did to each other—the things they did to us, believing we were like them—for class after class. But I knew what happened to "snitches" who got caught by their year group before the end of the term. We all knew. There was no one I could point the finger at, and my year group hadn't been equipped with a second lamb.

"I don't know," I whimpered, before continuing, speaking ever faster: "I've been trying to figure it out all year it's a really great problem and I was sort of a mean girl in second grade, I'm terrified of my parents hearing the things I used to say on the playground, but I haven't been able to even guess, they say it could be anybody, it could even be one of you trying to trick me into disrupting the system—" I was crying by the end of the sentence. It was one of my better performances, if I did say so myself.

"I *told* you the nerd wouldn't rat on the robot," snapped the second boy, giving me another, harder shove. This time my head bounced off the locker with a hollow bonging sound. I whimpered, letting my knees buckle. He didn't hold me up.

His name was Ryan. I pulled his file from the network and began annotating, words and sound files flashing behind my eyes.

"Ryan, come on, let's go," said Tom. He glanced down at me, looking pained. The boy I used to play with during recess was still in there, it seemed, buried under a layer of social expectations and poor decisions. I was almost sorry to see that. It hurt more when they endured. His hand on Ryan's elbow, he tugged, pulling the other boy away before things could escalate further. "We're going to be late."

"Whatever." Ryan shook him off, and the three walked away down the hall as the final bell rang. None of them offered to help me up.

I collected myself, smoothed my shirt back into place, and scuttled down the hall toward my math class. I would get a reprimand for being late. That was all right. What mattered was that I was the one who'd been slung against the locker, and not anyone else. That's what I was here for: to take the abuse the other students shouldn't have to bear.

Mr. Groblek was well into his lecture on the importance of Calculus in our future endeavors when I slipped into the room, trying to make myself look small. He paused, taking in my disheveled appearance and the fact that my backpack was only halfway zipped. Something that looked very much like pity flashed across his face, and he nodded his chin toward an open seat at the back of the room. My cheeks reddened with simulated relief—no reprimand for me today, not from a teacher who'd been doing this for long enough to recognize the signs of a hallway altercation—and I scuttled to the waiting chair. Snickers and soft jeers of "Teacher's pet," rose as I sat and unpacked my math book. A few students kept their eyes fixed straight ahead, neither adding to my presumed embarrassment nor trying to make me feel any better. Only two of my classmates cast sympathetic looks in my direction, and they were both in the afterschool Math Club with me. They understood what it was like to be the one up against the locker.

Not as well as they would have twenty years ago. The Lambs had begun rolling out at the middle school level twenty-one years before Mr. Groblek's class bell. We'd been early models then, easily detected novelties that didn't have the support or elaborate backstories we would eventually accumulate. My first host family had lost a daughter to suicide after an ex-boyfriend had distributed shirtless pictures of her to most of their mutual classmates. Her name had been Beven. She had been beautiful.

She still was. The artificial skin that covered my chassis got more detailed with every cultured generation, and I was now the absolute picture of the girl Beven would have been at seventeen, if she'd been allowed to live that long. Her mother sent me Christmas cards, and asked for copies of my school pictures every year. It was technically a breach of operational security to send them, but I did it anyway. It was the only human thing to do.

"Miss Carter?" From the annoyed edge in Mr. Groblek's voice, he had already said my name at least once, and probably more; he was definitely regretting allowing me to take my seat without a reprimand. I jerked my eyes away from my math book, cheeks burning again, this time with more genuine embarrassment. He looked slightly mollified when he saw my face. "Did you have the answer to problem five?"

This was familiar ground. I cleared my throat like I was nervous about my results, and said, "I think so..." From there, it was just a matter of reciting figures with careless ease, gaining glares from my less-able classmates and admiring looks from my fellow Math Club members. It was a foolish thing for me to do—it could have blown my cover—but I didn't care, really. It was the last semester of senior year. I was going to be relocated and reskinned in a matter of months, placed with a new host family and prepared to enter first grade. Let me have my fun. I'd earned it.

The Lamb program came about at the end of the twenty-teens, when two things happened in unfortunately rapid succession: a man named Benjamin Wallace developed the first fully human-seeming robot in his Seattle lab, and his thirteen-year-old daughter committed suicide as a direct result of online harassment by a group of her more popular classmates. The classmates were tried for harassment under Washington's Cyber-Bullying laws, and while they were found guilty, they served no jail time and were able to go on to their college careers unhaunted by what they had done. Dr. Wallace couldn't reconcile the loss of his daughter with the seeming unconcern of her classmates—or worse, their parents, who continued to insist all the way through the trial that their children were innocent.

The first Lamb was enrolled in the local high school at the beginning of the following school year. He was just a prototype, found out quickly and unmasked by the student body, but not before he'd managed to record five hours of tape, all of which was played back for the parents of the kids who had bullied him. They could deny a lot. They couldn't deny the voices of their own children saying terrible things to someone who they had believed to be another student, less than a year after one of their classmates took her own life.

There were lawsuits, early in; there were arguments about morality and the Heisenberg Principle, and whether we were doing any good by forcing the bullying to become less overt. But the voices of bullies played back through artificial mouths that couldn't lie, and the schools that hosted our pilot program showed a measurable decrease in the suicide rate. The Lamb program worked. The lawsuits didn't.

The program went national three years after the first prototype attended his first homeroom. Realistic robots in schools across the country, always hidden in plain sight, always listening, always watching, always recording. Some of us were found out, but with every generation and every update to the backstories and design schematics, more of us were making it to graduation, fulfilling our purpose in the most important way possible. We were making sure people remembered how much words could hurt, even when they thought those words had been thrown aside or forgotten. We were accountability writ large, and all I had to do now was make it to graduation.

The bell rang for the end of Mr. Groblek's class. I stood with the others, ignoring the poisonous glares from certain corners of the room, and the ever more pervasive sneers of "Geek" that often accompanied those looks. I lingered at the back while the popular kids filed out, letting them have their space. It's dangerous to challenge lions on the veldt, and while that might seem like a primitive way to describe the high school ecosystem, it was surprisingly apt.

The first Lambs got caught because they were too aggressive with their lions, needlessly challenging them to be cruel, making themselves into such perfect targets that they couldn't possibly be real. Our programming has evolved since then.

"Beven? A word, if you don't mind?"

I turned obediently to the sound of my math teacher's voice, walking to the front of the room with an earnest, eager-student smile on my face. Sometimes Lambs caught teachers who did inappropriate things with their underage students. It wasn't our primary purpose, and it wasn't something I enjoyed, but we were reminded never to pass up an opportunity to spend time with our instructors, or to form the social bonds that might expose deviant behavior.

Mr. Groblek didn't look like he was planning anything deviant. He was in his eighties, a man on the verge of retirement, who had seen his entire profession reinvented around him easily a dozen or more times since he taught his first class. He was looking at me solemnly, with something like concern in his rheumy blue eyes. "Beven, I was speaking to your guidance counselor yesterday, and she said something that worried me. Is it true you haven't completed any college applications?"

Only the speed of my central processor prevented me from wincing. Lambs weren't allowed to apply for college admission. It was illegal for us to disclose our non-human status on our applications, and we might prevent some worthy human student from getting a slot, at least until the school year ended and we inevitably outed ourselves. There was some discussion of allowing Lambs to apply, just to close one more loophole that could lead to identification. By the next time my picture in the yearbook appeared with a senior class, this might not be an issue.

"I'm planning to take a year off to volunteer with Doctors Without Borders," I said, the old lie coming glib and easy to my tongue. "I have a really sound GPA, but my extra-curricular activities haven't been impressive enough to get me into an Ivy. A few months helping to vaccinate babies against malaria and Hendra virus should be enough to move me to the top of the lists, even if I have to apply late to do it."

Mr. Groblek's frown deepened, as did the concern in his eyes. "If this is financial, there are scholarships—"

"I promise, it's not about money."

He paused, tilting his head and looking at me with a sudden canny sharpness that wiped away his years, replacing him with the young, brilliant man he'd once been. He was still brilliant. Teachers like him were a greater threat to our place in these schools than any student could have hoped to be. Not all of them approved of the Lamb project, or what we did. Some of them said we were entrapment tools, meant to destroy futures during a time when they were meant to be built up.

"You've been one of my favorite students since you started at this school," he said. "I can't remember the last time I had a sophomore in my honors class."

"That's a lie," I said. "You remember everything."

"You're right, I do," he said, and chuckled. I risked a small, timid smile, the sort a prize pupil might share with her beloved math teacher. He sobered, looking at me, and said, "I remember a lot of students like you. It's never too early to start planning for your future. You know that, don't you?"

"I do," I said. "I'm all about the future." Just not my own. The warning bell rang, and I took a quick two-step backward, clutching my books against my chest. "I'll be late."

"Go," he said, waving me off. I waved back, and like a shot, I was out the door, moving against the tide of his next incoming class with practiced ease.

The rest of the school day might as well have been factory made. Classes blurred in a stream of crowded hallways, anxious students, and teachers who needed to be paid better so they could give up their night jobs. Miss O'Leary, who always smelled faintly of bleach from trying to scrub away her evening shift as the bartender at Applebee's, gave us all free study before putting her head down on her desk and falling into a light but unmistakable doze.

I had my math book open, staring at a page of formulas I didn't need to memorize, when a folded note appeared in the middle of the first six hundred digits of pi. I picked it up and glanced behind me, frowning. Tom met my eyes with a challenging stare. He didn't smile. He just jerked his chin sharply upward, indicating that I should open the paper. I turned back to my math and unfolded his message, trying to make my hands shake believably. It was easier than I thought it would be. Wondering what was on the paper was strangely terrifying, like it could change the world. Then the paper came open and I frowned, trying to make sense of what he'd written.

I wasn't sure what I had expected, but it wasn't a matter-of-fact list of names with "yes" and "no" written beside each one of them and instructions at the bottom telling me to circle the correct answer. Then I focused on the names themselves. If my throat could have gone dry—if I had possessed that most basic of biological responses—it would have.

The ten names on the page represented the ten students who were lowest on the school's social ladder, the freaks, outcasts, and geeks who had never quite figured out the rules to the strange game called "popularity." Two of them were Lambs, both in years below mine, hiding in plain sight among the student body. None of them should have been on that piece of paper.

Hand shaking again, I circled "no" for every single name before folding the note back into a tight square and twisting in my seat to hand it to the girl behind me, who looked at me like I was something she had just scraped off of her shoe. Then she took the paper, handing it back to the boy behind her, who would in turn hand it back to Tom. He might be disappointed by my answer, or it might have been a test, one more attempt to prove that *I* was a Lamb, that *I* was the traitor they were looking for.

I didn't know anymore. And not knowing was agony.

The bell rang for the end of the period and hence, the end of the day. Half the class was out of their seats like a shot, jockeying for their places in the line that snaked out the door. I stayed where I was, my eyes fixed on my open math book. I wasn't really seeing the text anymore, but I could have answered any question that anyone wanted to ask me about it: my neural snapshot was secure, and perfect. It had taken three generations of Lambs before we could be taught to make mistakes, adjusted to have a range of accuracy, rather than being perfect every time. Now, we could even specialize. Of the two Lambs Tom had however accidentally managed to identify, one was an English prodigy—she never missed a question in her AP English class, and had already "won" two "writing competitions" organized by Wallace Industries and run through several shell corporations, to lend legitimacy without actually entering an artificial human in a contest intended to showcase real teenagers. She always looked a little sad when I passed her in the hall. It could have been the pseudo-depression we were sometimes instructed to emulate when the aggressions of the student body became particularly bad, but I suspected its roots went deeper. She seemed genuinely sad.

It was enough to make me wonder whether some Lambs might be developing desires beyond a constant spiral through the public school system, trading shell for shell as they traveled from grade to grade, making and losing friends, only to betray them all on the altar of graduation. We had been created to learn, evolve, and grow; we chose our own places on the veldt, some choosing to be nerds and outcasts, like me, while others chose to record their targets from the relative safety of the top of the social food chain. Some Lambs had even been known to choose their appearances, or to request that their genders be adjusted when they began a new cycle, selecting identities that fit their sense of self with more accuracy. I liked the face I wore and the place I occupied, but I didn't speak for all Lambs. I only spoke for me.

A hand landed on my shoulder. I looked up, and tensed as my eyes met Tom's. He was looming over me in a way that wouldn't have been possible before high school, when he grew into a football player's height, and

I remained dainty little Beven, who could have been a cheerleader if she'd ever cared about anything outside of a book. (That was part of the profile. Pretty girls were more likely to inspire outright rage when they hovered at the bottom of the pack, while girls who were considered unattractive inspired pity and disgust, but would eventually be allowed to fade into the background.)

"You really think I was wrong about all those names?" he asked.

I shot a glance toward the front of the room. Miss O'Leary's head was still on her desk. There was going to be no help coming from that quarter.

Tom followed the direction of my gaze, and sighed. "Beven, I'm not going to hurt you. Jeez, what kind of a guy do you think I am?"

"The kind who stands there and doesn't do anything while his friends slam me up against a locker," I said, swiveling back around to face him. My words came out surprisingly cool. I had been aiming for anger, or even betrayal, and instead I sounded quietly resigned, like I had always known that we would wind up here, him towering over me, me sitting and waiting for the end to come. What's more, I realized that I was *hurt*. He had betrayed me, and it *hurt* me. I had wanted to think better of him. I always had.

Maybe self-determination was a bad trait in a robot designed to ferret out bullies. We got too involved.

"Beven..." Tom ducked his head, looking ashamed. "You don't know what it's like, okay? You don't have to be afraid some robot is going to get up on the stage at graduation and start repeating everything you ever said on a bad day in front of your parents and the college admissions officers and everybody. Our whole future is riding on that ceremony. It's scary."

"What, you think geeks can't be cruel?" I almost laughed, managing to swallow it at the last moment. Geeks were some of the *worst*. Shit rolled downhill, and there was always someone lower than them, someone they could bully and harass without consequences. The so-called "popular kids" might hit and harass and use their social standing to lend weight to their attacks, but the geeks had time and cunning on their side. They also had less to worry about than the people at the top of the food chain. When a football player bullied a band nerd who later took it out on someone from the drama club, the band nerd was likely to be forgiven. It wouldn't interfere with college admission or the course of their future. Stopping bullying at the root was the goal, however far away and impossible it seemed.

"Beven..."

"I don't know who the school Lambs are, and even if I did, I wouldn't tell you," I said. Again, I sounded calm, even resigned: this was the way things had to be. "You had your chance to be my friend and you decided you wanted jocks and pretty girls more than you wanted me."

Now Tom's expression turned mulish, his lower lip poking out in the sullen way it always had, ever since we were elementary school students sharing lunches and playing tag on the playground. "I could say the same thing to you, you know. You could have started brushing your hair and talking like a normal person. Now it's too late. You can't blame me for that."

"I guess not." There were other things I could blame him for, if I needed to pass blame around. "But you're the one who changed, Tom, and I'm the one who stayed the same. I think that gives me the moral high ground here." As if there were any moral high ground to claim. There was just survival, and making it to the end of high school as intact as possible. Then he'd be off to his future, and I would be unmasked, unmade, and sent back to the beginning again.

He laughed. It was a short, hard sound, and it hurt to hear it. "See, that's the problem right there. 'Moral high ground' isn't something people just toss into casual conversation."

"Maybe not people, but geeks do." I stood, hugging my books to my chest, and glared at him. It was better than looking at him with pity. "We're not friends anymore, and if you've done something so bad you think the Lambs are going to tattle on you, maybe you should tell your parents, instead of telling me." He should tell his parents about the party he'd taken me to when he was still trying to be my friend. The one where he'd called me a bitch and a whore and a cock tease for not being willing to sleep with him; the one where he'd left me to walk home alone, after midnight, through streets dark with shadows and filled with silences. He should tell them, so that I wouldn't have to.

"Beven—"

"Goodbye, Tom." I turned and walked out of the room. I didn't let myself look back at him. It wouldn't have been fair, to either one of us.

Graduation day was as bright and beautiful as anyone could have hoped. The sun was high, the sky was clear, and the school's true Valedictorian—a girl named Kim—was shooting me quiet glares across the front row of the audience, daring me to return them. She still didn't know. I thought that was a little cruel, truth be told: she had been told to prepare a speech, in case something prevented me from giving mine, but she couldn't be informed until the last second. Nothing that might blow my cover could be allowed.

Out of the corner of my eye I saw our principal walk over to her and bend down, murmuring something in her ear. Kim's eyes widened, anger forgotten as everything changed. The next look she shot in my direction was full of pity, confusion, and yes, fear. She was afraid of me now. Afraid of what she might have said in my hearing. Afraid of what the consequences might be.

Several people watched as Kim was walked across the aisle and vanished through a gap in the curtains. Some of them turned to look at me, and their faces were a mixture of confusion and dawning understanding. There were always people who looked at me like that, unable to believe that what *was* happening could actually *be* happening. Members of the "she-can't-be" club. She can't be, I saw her eat. She can't be, I heard her call Miranda Wolcott a bitch that one time. She can't be, I know her, she's my friend, she's my classmate, she's been in my classes since first grade, she's not a robot, she's a math geek who never takes a hint. She can't be.

I was.

Kim's Valedictorian speech was halting and disjointed, but she did admirably, I thought, given that she hadn't expected to have the opportunity. All the speeches were as good as they could have been, under the circumstances. When they were finished, Principal Moore took the podium and said, "As you are all aware, our school has been fortunate enough to be assigned an autonomous anti-bullying robot, provided by the Wallace Foundation. This robot has been attending classes with our human students, observing them, and helping to reduce in-school harassment through its presence. Beven Turner, will you please join me on the stage?"

I stood, shrugging out of my graduation robe and leaving it puddled on my chair. I set my mortarboard on top of it. Then I turned, shoulders square, head high, and walked across the aisle to the stairs. The eyes of my classmates and their parents were fixed on me. A low murmur was gathering in the room, horrified and bewildered and amazed. Every graduation I had ever attended had sounded like this one when their Lamb was revealed. *She isn't, she can't be, I didn't think, I never knew...*

I never knew.

"Do you need a microphone?" asked Principal Moore.

I closed my eyes for a moment. When I opened them, I answered politely, "No, thank you," and my voice was as amplified as his was. The muttering increased, now accompanied by the sound of several students openly crying.

You shouldn't have done what you did, I thought spitefully, and was immediately sorry. I was here to help them, not to shame them. They did that well enough without my help.

Principal Moore nodded, turned back to the podium, and announced the first name.

One by one, the students walked on trembling legs to the stage, trying hard not to look at me—trying so hard, and failing, every single one of them. The first came and went, and I stayed silent. He had only ever said a few harsh words, had a few bad days; we weren't programmed to care about the little things. We'd capture them, and if his parents wanted to hear them after the ceremony, I would play them back in private, but they were nothing near bad enough to earn him a public shaming. The next three came and went the same way.

The fifth was Tom's friend from the football team. Ryan. When his hand touched his diploma, my mouth opened, and his voice poured forth: "What do you think you're looking at, you whore? Stupid slut. Why don't you die? Why don't you do us all a favor and choke to death on a dick?

Fuck you." It went on and on, a torrent of bile, accompanied by the sounds of the violence we recorded but couldn't play back: fists striking flesh, bodies slamming into lockers. I saw his mother in the audience, wiping her eyes. Ryan glared at me, but it didn't stop the words. They were his. I was just giving them back to him.

Ryan left the stage. The ceremony continued. More students, more silence; a few who got their own words thrown back at them, most not as bad as Ryan, who had probably changed schools in part to get away from his former district's assigned Lamb. We weren't allowed to share files—not yet. By the next time I was on this stage, we might be.

Then it was Tom on the stairs, Tom reaching for his diploma, Tom looking at me in abject terror and betrayal, because I had been his friend once, before he grew into a bully and I turned out to never have been a real girl at all. He knew what he had said to me, what he had said in my presence. What he had called me. He knew what I was going to say back to him.

The words rose in my mouth. I swallowed them back down, and kept looking straight ahead, not speaking, as Tom fled to freedom, and a future that I would never know.

Maybe it was unfair; maybe choosing the future of a friend over doing what was right made me no better than the students I was intended to control through my simple presence. But if they wanted me to be a perfect automaton, doing only what my programming commanded me to do, they shouldn't have made me the way that they did.

They shouldn't have given me a heart.

Each to Each

When Christie Yant was announced as the guest editor for Lightspeed's special *Women Destroy Science Fiction* edition, I didn't really dare hope that I'd be invited to participate...but I was. She even gave me a prompt to work from: research has found that women do better on submarines. Why is that? What makes the difference? I read the papers, combined their core conclusions with my love for mermaids, and I had a story.

This story was chosen for inclusion in *The Best American Science Fiction and Fantasy 2015*, and I am still over the moon about that. Contains frank discussion of misogyny and transphobia, and some gendered slurs.

Condensation covers the walls, dimpling into tiny drops that follow an almost fractal pattern, like someone has been writing out the secrets of the universe in the most transitory medium they can find.

The smell of damp steel assaults my nose as I walk, uncomfortable boots clomping with every step I force myself to take. The space is tight, confined, unyielding; it is like living inside a coral reef, trapped by the limits of our own necessary shells. We are constantly envious of those who escape its limitations, and we fear for them at the same time, wishing them safe return to the reef, where they can be kept away from all the darkness and predations of the open sea.

The heartbeat of the ship follows me through the iron halls, comprised of the engine's whir, the soft, distant buzz of the electrical systems, the even more distant churn of the rudders, the hiss and sigh of the filters that keep the flooded chambers clean and oxygenated. Latest scuttlebutt from the harbor holds that a generation of wholly flooded ships is coming, ultra-light fish tanks with shells of air and metal surrounding the water-filled crew chambers, the waterproofed electrical systems. Those ships will be lighter than ours could ever dream of being, freed from the need for filters and desalination pumps by leaving themselves open to the sea.

None of the rumors mention the crews. What will be done to them, what they'll have to do in service to their country. We don't need to talk about it. Everyone already knows. Things that are choices today won't be choices tomorrow; that's the way it's always been, when you sign away your voice for a new means of dancing.

The walkway vibrates under my feet, broadcasting the all hands signal through the ship. It will vibrate through the underwater spaces twice more, giving everyone the time they need. Maybe that will be an advantage of those flooded boats; no more transitions, no more hasty scrambles for breathing apparatus that fits a little less well after every tour, no more forcing of feet into boots that don't really fit, but are standard issue (and standard issue is still God and King here, on a navy vessel, in the service of the United States government, even when the sailors do not, cannot, will never fit the standard mold). I walk a little faster, as fast as I can force myself to go in my standard-issue boots, and there is only a thin shell between me and the sea.

We knew women were better suited to be submariners by the beginning of the twenty-first century. Women dealt better with close quarters, tight spaces, and enforced contact with the same groups of people for long periods of time. We were more equipped to resolve our differences without resorting to violence—and there *were* differences. Women—even military women—had been socialized to fight with words and with social snubbing, and the early all-female submarines must have looked like a cross between a psychology textbook and the Hunger Games.

The military figured it out. They hired the right sociologists, they taught their people the right way to deal with conflicts and handle stress, they found ways of picking out that early programming and replacing it with fierce loyalty to the Navy, to the program, to the crew.

Maybe it was one of those men—and they were all men, I've seen the records; man after man, walking into our spaces, our submarines with their safe and narrow halls, and telling the women who had to live there to make themselves over into a new image, a better image, an image that wouldn't fight, or gossip, or bully. An image that would do the Navy proud. Maybe it was one of those men who first started calling the all-female submarine crews the military's "mermaids."

Maybe that was where they got the idea.

Within fifty years of the launch of the female submariners, the sea had become the most valuable real estate in the world. Oh, space exploration continued—mostly in the hands of the wealthy, tech firms that decided a rocket would be a better investment than a Ping-Pong table in the break room, and now had their eyes set on building an office on Jupiter, a summer home on Mars. It wasn't viable. Not for the teeming masses of Earth, the people displaced from their communities by the super storms and tornadoes, the people who just needed a place to live and eat and work and flourish. Two-thirds of the planet's surface is water. Much of it remains unexplored, even today...and that was why, when Dr. Bustos stood up and said he had a solution, people listened.

There were resources, down there in the sea. Medicines and minerals and oil deposits and food sources. Places where the bedrock never shifted, suitable for anchoring bubble communities (art deco's resurgence around the time of the launch was not a coincidence). Secrets and wonders and miracles of science, and all we had to do was find a way to escape our steel shells, to dive deeper, to *find* them.

Women in the military had always been a bit of a sore spot, even when all the research said that our presence hurt nothing, endangered nothing; even when we had our own class of ships to sail beneath the waves, and recruits who aimed for other branches often found themselves quietly redirected to the Navy. There was recruiter logic behind it all, of course—reduced instances of sexual assault (even if it would never drop to full zero), fewer unplanned pregnancies, the camaraderie of people who really *understood* what you were going through as a woman in the military. Never mind the transmen who found themselves assigned to submarines, the transwomen who couldn't get a berth, the women who came from Marine or Air Force or Army families and now couldn't convince the recruiters that what they wanted was to serve as their fathers had served, on the land. The submarines began to fill.

And then they told us why.

I drag myself up the short flight of stairs between the hallway and the front of the ship (and why do they still build these things with staggered hearts, knowing what's been done to us, knowing what is yet to be done?) and join my crew. A hundred and twenty of us, all told, and less than half standing on our feet. The rest sit compacted in wheelchairs, or bob gently as the water beneath the chamber shifts, their heads and shoulders protruding through the holes cut in the floor. There is something strange and profoundly unprofessional about seeing the Captain speak with the heads and shoulders of wet-suited women sticking up around her feet like mushrooms growing from the omnipresent damp.

"At eighteen hundred hours, Seaman Wells encountered a bogey in our waters." The captain speaks clearly and slowly, enunciating each word like she's afraid we will all have forgotten the English language while her back was turned, trading in for some strange language of clicks and whistles and hums. She has read the studies about the psychological effects of going deep; she knows what to watch for.

We terrify her. I can't imagine how the Navy thinks this is a good use of their best people, locking them away in tin cans that are always damp and smell of fish, and watching them go slowly, inexorably insane. You need to be damn good to get assigned to submarine command, and you need to be willing to stay a drysider. Only drysiders can be shown in public; only drysiders can testify to the efficacy of the program. The rest of us have been compromised.

It's such a polite, sterile little word. "Compromised." Like we were swayed by the enemy, or blown off course by the gale-force winds of our delicate emotions. Nothing could be further from the truth. We're a necessary part of public safety, an unavoidable face of war...and we're an embarrassment that must be kept out at sea, where we can be safely forgotten.

"The bogey approached our ship, but did not make contact. It avoided all cameras, and did not pass by any open ports, which leads us to believe that it was either a deserter or an enemy combatant. The few sonar pictures we were able to get do not match any known design configuration." That doesn't have to mean anything. There are new models taking to the sea every day. I have my eye on a lovely frilled shark mod that's just clearing the testing process. Everyone who's seen the lab samples says it's a dream come true, and I'm about due for a few dreams.

One of the Seamen raises her hand. She's new to the ship; her boots still fit, her throat still works. The captain nods in her direction, and she asks, in a voice that squeaks and shakes with the effort of pushing sound through air instead of water, "Didn't we have anyone on patrol when the bogey came by?"

It's a good question, especially for a newbie. The captain shakes her head. "We're here to chart the sea floor and bring back information about the resources here." What we can exploit, in other words. "All of our sea-going sailors were at bottom level or in transit when the bogey passed near our vessel."

One of the servicewomen floating near the captain's feet whistles long and low, a tiny foghorn of a sound. An electronic voice from one of the speakers asks, robotic and stiff, "What are our orders, Captain?"

I don't recognize this sailor. She has the dark gray hair and flattened facial features common to the blue shark mods. There are fourteen blues currently serving on this vessel. I can't be blamed if I can't tell them apart. Sometimes I'm not even sure they can tell *themselves* apart. Blues have a strong schooling instinct, strong enough that the labs considered recalling them shortly after they were deployed. The brass stepped in before anything permanent could happen. Blues are good for morale. They fight like demons, and they fuck like angels, and they have no room left in their narrow predators' brains for morals. If not for the service, they'd be a danger to us all, but thankfully, they have a very pronounced sense of loyalty.

The captain manages not to shy away from the woman at her feet: no small trick, given how much we clearly distress her. "All sailors are to be on a state of high alert whenever leaving the vessel. High water patrols will begin tonight, and will continue for the duration of our voyage. Any creature larger than an eel is to be reported to your superior officer immediately. We don't know what the Chinese have been doing since they closed the communication channels between their research divisions and ours. They may have progressed further than we had guessed."

A low murmur breaks out amongst the sailors who can use words. Others whistle and hum, communicating faster via the private languages of their mods. Rumor keeps saying command is going to ban anything on the ships that can't be translated into traditional English by our computers, and rumor keeps getting slapped down as fast as it can spread, because the speech is hard-coded in some of the most popular, most functional mods, and without it our sailors couldn't communicate in the open sea. So people like our poor Captain just have to grit their teeth and endure.

I feel bad for her, I really do. I envy her, too. Did they show her the same studies they'd once shown me, offer her the same concessions if she'd just serve as an example to her yearmates? Was she one of the rare individuals who saw everything the sea could give her, and still chose to remain career track, remain land-bound, remain capable of leaving the service when her tour was up? Oh, they said and said that everything was reversible, but since no one ever chose reversal, we still didn't know if that was true, and no one wanted to be the test case. Too much to lose, not enough to gain.

The captain begins to talk again, and the buzz of conversation dies down to respectful silence, giving her the floor as she describes our assignments for the days to come. They're standard enough; except for the bogey or bogeys we'll be watching for, we'll be doing the normal patrols of the sea bed and the associated trenches, looking for minerals, looking for species of fish we've never encountered before, taking samples. Deepening our understanding of the Pacific. Other crews have the Atlantic, mapping it out one square meter at a time; one day we'll meet on the other side of the world, a mile down and a universe away from where we started, and our understanding will be complete, and the human race can continue in its conquest of this strange and timeless new frontier. One day.

The captain finishes her speech, snapping off her words with the tight tonelessness of a woman who desperately wants to be anywhere else. We salute her, those in the water doing their best not to splash as they pull their arms out of the water and snap their webbed fingers to their foreheads. She returns the salute and we're dismissed, back to our quarters or onward to our duties.

I linger on the stairs while those who are newer to this command than I scatter, moving with a quick, dryland efficiency toward other parts of the submarine. The captain is the first to go, all but running from the bridge in her need to get away from us. The heads in the water vanish one by one, the sailors going back to whatever tasks had them outside the ship—those who aren't currently off-duty and seeking the simple peace of weightlessness and separation from the dry. Not all the seamen serving with this vessel are capable of doing what I'm doing, standing on their own two feet and walking among the drylander crew. Every ship has to have a few in transition. It's meant to be a temptation and a warning at the same time. "Mind your choices; there but for the grace of God and the United States government go you."

It only takes a few minutes before I'm standing alone on the stairs. I walk over to the lockers set in the far wall (one more concession to what they've made of us; in transition, we don't always have time to get to quarters, to get to privacy, and so they arrange the ships to let us strip down wherever we need, and hold it up as one more bit of proof that single-sex vessels are a requirement for the smooth operation of the Navy). My boots are the first thing to go, and I have to blink back tears when I pull them off and my feet untwist, relaxing back into the natural shape the scientists have worked so hard to give them. All this work, all these changes to the sailors, and they still can't change our required uniforms—not when we still have things that can be called "feet" or "legs" and shoved into the standard-issue boots or trousers.

Piece by piece, I strip down to my swim trunks and thermal sports bra, both designed to expose as much skin as possible while still leaving me with a modicum of modesty. The blues, especially, have a tendency to remove their tops once they're in the water, buzzing past the cameras and laughing. That footage goes for a pretty penny on some corners of the internet, the ones frequented by soft-skinned civilians who murmur to themselves about the military mermaids, and how beautiful we are, and how much they'd like to fuck us.

They'd flense themselves bloody on the shark-skins of the blues, they'd sting themselves into oblivion on the spines of the lionfish and the trailing jellied arms of the moonies and the men-o'-war, but still they talk, and still they see us as fantasies given flesh, and not as the military women that we are. Perhaps that, too, is a part of the Navy's design. How easy is it to fear something that you've been seeing in cartoons and coloring books since you were born?

I walk to the nearest hole and exhale, blowing every bit of air out of my lungs. Then I step over the edge and plunge down, down, down, dragged under by the weight of my scientifically reengineered musculature, into the arms of the waiting sea.

"Project Amphitrite"—otherwise known as "Mermaids for the Military"—started attracting public attention when I was in my senior year of high school and beginning to really consider the Navy as a career option. I wanted to see the world. This new form of service promised me a world no one else had ever seen. They swore we could go back. They swore we would still be human, that every possible form of support would be offered to keep us connected to our roots. They said we'd all be fairy tales, a thousand Little Mermaids rising from the sea and walking on new legs into the future that our sacrifice had helped them to ensure.

They didn't mention the pain. Maybe they thought we'd all see the writing on the wall, the endless gene treatments, the surgeries to cut away inconvenient bits of bone—both original issue and grown during the process of preparing our bodies for the depths—the trauma of learning to breath in when submerged, suppressing the millennia of instinct that shrieked no, no, you will drown, you will die, no.

And maybe we did drown; maybe we did die. Every submersion felt a bit less like a betrayal of my species and a bit more like coming home. As I fall into the water my gills open, and the small fins on my legs spread, catching the water and holding me in place, keeping me from descending all the way to the bottom. The blues I saw before rush back to my side, attracted by the sound of something moving. They whirl around me in an undifferentiated tornado of fins and flukes and grasping hands, caressing my flank, touching my arms and hair before they whirl away again, off to do whatever a school of blues does when they are not working, when they are not slaved to the commands of a species they have willingly abandoned. Their clicks and whistles drift back to me, welcoming me, inviting me along.

I do not try to follow. Until my next shore leave, my next trip to the lab, I can't keep up; they're too fast for me, their legs fully sacrificed on the altar of being all that they can be. The Navy claims they're turning these women into better soldiers. From where I hang suspended in the sea, my lungs filled with saltwater like amniotic fluid, these women are becoming better myths.

Other sailors flash by, most of them carrying bags or wearing floodlights strapped to their foreheads or chests; some holding spear guns, which work better at these depths than traditional rifles. We'd be defenseless if someone were to fire a torpedo into our midst, but thus far, all the troubles we've encountered have either been native—squid and sharks who see our altered silhouettes and think we look like prey—or our own kind, mermaids from rival militaries, trying to chart and claim our sea beds before we can secure them for the United States of America. We might have been the first ones into the sea, but we weren't the last, and we're not even the most efficient anymore. The American mods focus too much on form and not enough on functionality. Our lionfish, eels, even our jellies still look like women before they look like marine creatures. Some sailors say—although there's been no *proof* yet, and that's the mantra of the news outlets, who don't want to criticize the program more than they have to, don't want to risk losing access to the stream of beautifully staged official photos and the weekly reports on the amazing scientific advancements coming out of what we do here—some sailors say that they chose streamlined mods, beautiful, sleek creatures that would cut through the water like knives, minimal drag, minimal reminders of their mammalian origins, and yet somehow came out of the treatment tanks with breasts that ached like it was puberty all over again. Ached and then grew bigger, ascending a cup size or even two, making a more marketable silhouette.

Here in the depths we're soldiers, military machines remade to suit the needs of our country and our government. But when we surface, we're living advertisements for the world yet to come, when we start shifting more of the population to the bubble cities being constructed on the ground we've charted for them, when the military gene mods become available to the public. I've seen the plans. We all have. Civilians will be limited to "gentler" forms, goldfish and angelfish and bettas, all trailing fins and soft Disney elegance. Veterans will be allowed to keep our mods as recognition of our service, should we choose to stay in the wet—and again, no one knows whether reversal is *possible*, especially not for the more esoteric designs. Can you put the bones back into a jelly's feet, just because you think they ought to be there? Questions better left unanswered, if you ask me.

Adjustment is done: my gills are open, and my chest is rising smooth and easy, lungs filling with seawater without so much as a bubble of protest. I jackknife down and swim toward the current patrol, feeling the drag from my weight belt as it pulls me toward the bottom. One more reason to dream of that coming return to the labs, when they'll take me one step deeper, and this will be just a little more like home.

The blues return to join me; two of them grab my hands and pull me deeper, their webbed fingers slipping on my slick mammalian skin, and the captain and her bogeys are forgotten, for a time, before the glorious majesty of the never-ending sea.

We're deep—about a hundred, hundred and fifty feet below the waiting submarine, our passage lit by the soft luminescent glow of the anglers and the lanterns—when something flashes past in the gloom just past the reach of the light. Whatever it is, it's moving fast, all dart and dazzle, and there isn't time to see it properly before it's gone.

The formation comes together without anyone saying a word, the hard-coded schooling instinct slamming into our military training and forming an instant barricade against the waiting dark. Anglers and lanterns in the middle, blues, makos, and lionfish and undecideds on the outside. The five of us who have yet to commit to a full mod look like aberrations as we hang in the water, almost human, almost helpless against the empty sea.

One of the blues clicks, the sound reverberating through the water. A moment later her voice is coming through the implant in my inner ear, saying, "Sonar's picking up three bodies, all about twenty yards out, circling."

Another click, from another of the blues, and then: "Marine or mer?" Shorthand description, adopted out of necessity. Are we looking at natural marine creatures, sharks or dolphins—unusual at this depth—or even the increasingly common, increasingly dangerous squid that we've been seeing as we descend into the trenches? There are a dozen species of the great cephalopods down here, some never before seen by science, and all of them are hungry, and smart enough to recognize that whatever we are, we could fill bellies and feed babies. We are what's available. That has value, in the sea. (That has value on the land as well, where women fit for military service were what was available, where we became the raw material for someone else's expansion, for someone else's fairy tale, and now here we are, medical miracles, modern mermaids, hanging like apples in the larder of the sea.)

Click click. "Mer." The sonar responses our makos are getting must have revealed the presence of metal, or of surgical scars: something to tell them that our visitors are not naturally occurring in the sea. "Three, all female, unknown mods. Fall back?"

More clicks as the group discusses, voices coming hard and fast through the implants, arguing the virtues of retreat versus holding our ground. There are still crewmen in these waters, unaware of the potential threat—and we don't know for sure that this *is* a threat, not really. America isn't the only country to take to sea. We could just be brushing up against the territory claimed by an Australian crew, a New Zealand expedition, and everything will end peacefully if we simply stay where we are and make no threatening movements.

One of the blues breaks formation.

She's fast—one of the fastest we have, thanks to the surgery that fused her legs from crotch to ankles, replaced her feet with fins, replaced the natural curves of a mammalian buttock and thigh with the smooth sweep of a blue shark's tail—and she's out of the light before anyone has a chance to react. My sonar isn't as sensitive as the blues'; I don't know what she heard, only that she's gone. "After her!" I shout through the sub-dermal link, my words coming out as clicks and bubbles in the open water. And then we're moving, all of us, the blues in the lead with the makos close behind. The jellies bring up the rear, made more for drifting than for darting; one, a moonie with skin the color of rice paper that shows her internal organs pulsing softly in her abdomen, clings to a lionfish's dorsal fin. Her hands leave thin ribbons of blood in the water as she passes. We'll have sharks here soon.

With the lanterns and anglers moving in the middle of the school, we're able to maintain visual contact with each other, even if we're too deep and moving too fast to show up on cameras. This is the true strength of the military mermaid project: speed and teamwork, all the most dangerous creatures in the sea boiled down to their essentials and pasted onto Navy women, who have the training and the instincts to tell us how they can best be used. So our scouts swim like bullets while the rest of us follow, legs and tails pumping hard, arms down flat by our sides or holding tight to the tow line of someone else's fin, someone else's elbow. Those of us who are carrying weapons have them slung over our backs, out of the way. Can't swim at speed and fire a harpoon gun at the same time.

All around me, the school clicks and whistles their positions, their conditions, only occasionally underscoring their reports with actual words. "She's not here." "Water's been disturbed." "Something tastes of eel." This isn't how we write it down for the brass. They're all drylanders, they don't understand how easy it is to go loose and fluid down here in the depths, how little rank and order seem to matter when you're moving as a single beast with a dozen tails, two dozen arms, and trying all the while to keep yourself together, keep yourself unified, keep yourself *whole*. The chain of command dissolves under the pressure of the crushing deep, just as so many other things—both expected and unimagined—have already fallen away.

Then, motion in the shadows ahead, and we surge forward again, trying to find our missing shipmate, our missing sister, the missing sliver of the self that we have become as we trained together, schooled together, mourned our lost humanity and celebrated our dawning monstrosity together. We are sailors and servicewomen, yes; we will always be those things, all the way down to our mutant and malleable bones. But moments like this, when it is us and the open sea, remind us every day that we are more than what we were, and less than what we are to become, voiceless daughters of Poseidon, singing in the space behind our souls.

The taste of blood in the water comes first, too strong to be coming from the sliced hands of those who chose poorly when they grabbed at the bodies of their fellow fables. Then comes the blue, flung out of the dark ahead, her slate-colored back almost invisible in outside the bioluminescent glow, her face and belly pearled pale and ghostly. One of the other blues darts forward to catch her before she can slam into the rest of us, potentially hurting herself worse on spines or stingers. A great cry rises from the group, half lament, half whale song. The remaining two blues hurl themselves into the dark, moving fast, too fast for the rest of us to catch them...and then they return, empty-handed and angry-eyed. One of them clicks a message.

"She got away."

We nod, one to another, and turn to swim—still in our tight, effective school—back toward the waiting vessel. Our crewmate needs medical care. Only after we know she's safe can we go out again, and find the ones who hurt her, and make them pay.

So few of us are suited for walking anymore, even in the safe, narrow reef of the submarine's halls, where there is always solid metal waiting to catch and bear us up when our knees give out or our ankles refuse to bear our weight. So it is only natural that I should be the one to stand before the captain—anxious creature that she is—at the closest I could come to parade rest, my hands behind my back and my eyes fixed on the wall behind her, reciting the events of the day.

"You're telling me Seaman Metcalf charged ahead without regard for the formation, or for the safety of her fellow crewmen?" The captain frowns at the incident report, and then at me. She is trying to be withering. She is succeeding only in looking petulant, like a child in the process of learning that not every fairy tale is kind. "Did anyone get a clear look at the bogey? Do we have any idea what could have caused Seaman Metcalf to behave so recklessly?"

She doesn't understand, she is not equipped to understand; she has not been sea-changed, and her loyalty is to the Navy itself, not to the crew that swims beside her. Poor little drylander. Maybe someday, when she sees that there is no more upward mobility for we creatures of the sea, she'll give herself over to the water, and her eyes will be opened at last.

"No, ma'am. Seaman Metcalf broke formation without warning, and did not explain herself." She's in the medical bay now, sunk deep in a restorative bath of active genetic agents. She'll wake with a little more of her humanity gone, a little more of her modified reality pushed to the surface. Given how close she looks to fully modded, maybe she'll wake as something entirely new, complete and ready to swim in deeper waters, no longer wedded to the steel chain of the submarine.

"And the bogeys?" The captain sounds anxious. The captain always sounds anxious, but this is something new, sharp and insecure and painfully easy to read.

"No one saw anything clearly, ma'am. It's very dark when you exit the pelagic region, and while we have bioluminescent mods among our crew, they can't compensate for the limited visibility over a more than three-yard range. Whatever's been buzzing our perimeter, it's careful to stay outside the limits of the light." I don't mention the sonar readings we were getting before. They're important, I'm sure of that, but...not yet. She's not one of us.

There was a time when withholding information from my captain would have seemed like treason, a time when the patterns of loyalty were ingrained in my blood and on my bone. I had different blood then; I had different bones. They have replaced the things that made me theirs, and while I am grateful, I am no longer their property.

It's strange to realize that. Everything about this day has been strange. I keep my eyes fixed straight ahead, not looking at the captain's face. I am afraid she'll see that I am lying. I am afraid she won't see anything but a man-made monster, and her future in fins and scales.

"I want doubled patrols," says the captain. "Seaman Metcalf will be detained when she recovers consciousness. I need to know what she saw."

"You may want to request that one of the other blue shark mod sailors also be present, ma'am," I say. "Seaman Metcalf no longer has vocal cords capable of human speech."

The captain blanches. "Understood. Dismissed."

"Ma'am." I offer a respectful salute before I turn and limp out of the room, moving slowly—it's always slow right after I leave the water, when my joints still dream of weightlessness and my lungs still feel like deserts, arid and empty.

The door swings shut behind me, slamming and locking in the same motion, and I am finally alone.

The captain has ordered us to double patrols, and so patrols are doubled. The captain has ordered the medical staff to detain Seaman Metcalf, and so she is detained, pinned clumsy and semi-mobile on a bed designed for a more human form, her tail turned to dead weight by gravity, her scales turned to brutal knives by the dryness of the air. I know how I feel at night, stretched out in my bunk like a surgical patient waiting for the knife, too heavy to move, too hot to breathe. Seaman Metcalf is so much further along than I am that the mere act of keeping her in the dry should be considered a crime of war, forbidden and persecuted by the very men who made her. But ah, we are soldiers; we signed up for this. We have no one to blame but ourselves.

The captain has ordered that we stay together at all times, two by two, preventing flights like Seaman Metcalf's, preventing danger from the dark. I am breaking orders as I slide into the water alone, a light slung around my neck like a strange jewel, a harpoon gun in my hands. This is a terrible idea. But I need to know why my sailors are flinging themselves into the darkness, pursuing an enemy I have not seen, and I can survive being beached better than the majority of them; I am the most liminal of the current crew, able to go deep and look, and see, yet still able to endure detention in a dry room. If anything, this may hasten my return to land, giving me the opportunity to tell the Naval psychologists how much I need to progress; how much I need the mod that will take me finally into the deeps. Yes. This is the right choice, and these are orders almost intended to be broken.

It is darker than any midnight here, down here in the deep, and the light from my halogen lamp can only pierce so far. Things move in the corners of my vision, nightmare fish with teeth like traumas, quick and clever squid that have learned to leave the women with the harpoon guns alone. There is talk of a squid mod being bandied about by the brass. I hope it comes to something. I would love to learn, through the network of my soldier-sisters, what the squid might have to teach us.

The captain has ordered that patrols be doubled, but I don't see anyone else as I descend into deeper water, the darkness closing around me like a blanket full of small moving specks. Every breath I take fills my throat with the infants of a thousand sea creatures, filtered by the bioscreens installed by the clever men who made me what I am today. I am not a baleen whale, but the krill and larvae I catch and keep in this manner will help to replace the calories my body burns to keep me warm this far below the sea. (Easier to line our limbs with blubber, make us seals, fat and sleek and perfect—but we were always intended to be public relations darlings, and fattening up our military women, no matter how good the justifications behind it, would never have played well with the paparazzi.)

Something flashes through the gloom ahead of me, too fast and too close to be a squid, too direct to be a shark; they always approach from the side. I fall back, straightening myself in the water so that my head points toward the distant surface. The water has never encouraged anyone to walk upright, and the changing weight of my body discourages this choice even more, tells me not to do it, tells me to hang horizontal, like a good creature of the sea. But I am still, in many regards, a sailor; I learned to stand my ground, even when there is no ground beneath me.

She emerges from the dark like a dream, swimming calm and confident into the radiant glow of my halogen light. Her mod is one I've never seen before, long hair and rounded fins and pattern like a clownfish, winter white and hunter orange and charcoal black, Snow White for the seafaring age. Clownfish are meant to live in shallow waters, coral reefs; she shouldn't be here. She shouldn't exist at all. This is a show model of a military technology, designed to attract investors, not to serve a practical purpose in the open sea. She smiles at me as I stare, suddenly understanding what could inspire Seaman Metcalf to break formation, to dive into the oppressive dark. For the first time, I feel as if I'm seeing a mermaid.

Seaman Metcalf dove into the dark and was thrown back, battered and bruised and bleeding. I narrow my eyes and whistle experimentally. "Who are you?"

Her smile broadens. She clicks twice, and my implant translates and relays her words: "A friend. You are early," another click, "no? Not so far along as those you swim with."

"You have harmed a member of my crew."

The stranger's eyes widen in wounded shock. "Me?" Her whistle is long and sweet, cutting through the waves; the others must hear her, no matter how far above me they are. Some things, the water cannot deaden. "No. Your crewmate asked us to strike her, to push her back. Voices can lie, but injuries will tell the truth. We needed your," another series of clicks, this one barely translatable; the closest I can come is "dry-walkers," and I know then that she is not military, has never been military. She doesn't know the lingo.

She's still speaking. "...to believe there was a threat here, in the deep waters. I am sorry we did not sing to you. You stayed so high. You seemed so, forgive me, human."

She makes it sound like a bad word. I frown. "You are trespassing on waters claimed by the United States Navy. I hereby order you to surrender."

Her sigh is a line of bubbles racing upward, toward the sun. She whistles wordlessly, and three more figures swim out of the dark, sinuous as eels, their skins shifting seamlessly from grays to chalky pallor. They have no tentacles, but I recognize the effect as borrowed from the mimic octopus; another thing the military has discussed but not perfected. I am in over my head, in more ways than one.

She whistles again. "I cannot surrender. I will not surrender. I am here to free your sisters from the tank they have allowed themselves to be confined within. We are not pet store fish. We are not trinkets. They deserve to swim freely. I can give that to them. We can give that to them. But I will not surrender."

The eel-women circle like sharks, and I am afraid. I know she can't afford to have me tell my captain what she has said; I know that this deep, my body would never be found. Sailors disappear on every voyage, and while some whisper about desertion—and the truth of those whispers hangs before me in the water like a fairy tale—I know most of them have fallen prey only to their own hubris, and to the shadows beneath us, which never change and never fade away.

She is watching me, nameless mermaid from a lab I do not know. The geneticist who designed her must be so proud. "Is this the life you want?

Tied to women too afraid to join you in the water, commanded by men who would make you something beautiful, and then keep you captive? We can offer something more."

She goes on to talk about artificial reefs, genetically engineered coral growing into palaces and promenades, down, deep down at the bottom of the sea. The streets are lit by glowing kelp and schools of lanternfish, both natural and engineered. There is no hunger. There is no war. There are no voices barking orders. She speaks of a new Atlantis, Atlantis reborn one seafaring woman at a time. We will not need to change the sea to suit the daughters of mankind; we have already changed ourselves, and now need only come home.

All the while the eel-women circle like sharks, ready to strike me down if I raise a hand against their leader—ready to strike me down if I don't. Like Seaman Metcalf, I must serve as a warning to the Navy. Something is out here. Something dangerous.

I look at her, and frown. "Who made you?"

Something in her eyes goes dark. "They said I'd be a dancer."

"Ah." Some sounds translate from form to form, medium to medium; that is one of them. "Private firm?"

"Private *island*," she says, and all is clear. Rich men playing with military toys: chasing the idea of the new. They had promised her reversion, no doubt, as they promised it to us all—and maybe they meant it, maybe this was a test. The psychological changes that drive us to dive ever deeper down were accidental; maybe they were trying to reverse them. Instead, they sparked a revolution.

"What will you do if I yield?"

Her smile is quick and bright, chasing the darkness from her eyes. "Hurt you."

"And my crew?"

"Most of them will be tragically killed in action. Their bodies will never be found." They would be free.

"Why should I agree?"

"Because in one year, I will send my people back to this place, and if you are here, we will show you what it means to be a mermaid."

We hang there in the water for a few minutes more, me studying her, her smiling at me, serene as Amphitrite on the shore. Finally, I close my eyes. I lower my gun, allowing it to slip out of my fingers and fall toward the distant ocean floor. It will never be found, one more piece of debris for the sea to keep and claim. I am leaving something behind. That makes me feel a little better about what has to happen next.

"Hurt me," I say.

They do.

When I wake, the air is pressing down on me like a sheet of glass. I am in the medical bay, swaddled in blankets and attached to beeping machines. The submarine hums around me; the engines are on, we are moving, we are heading away from the deepest parts of the sea. The attack must have already happened.

Someone will come for me soon, to tell me how sorry they all are, to give me whatever punishment they think I deserve for being found alone and drifting in the deeps. And then we will return to land. The ship will take on a new crew and sail back to face a threat that is not real, while I? I will sit before a board of scientists and argue my case until they give in, and put me back into the tanks, and take my unwanted legs away. They *will* yield to me. What man has ever been able to resist a siren?

A year from now, when I return to the bottom of the sea, I will hear the mermaids singing, each to each. And oh, I think that they will sing to me.

Bring About the Halloween Eternal!!!

I like excuses to play around with form. When I was asked to contribute to an anthology of stories told in the form of Kickstarter campaigns (John Joseph Adams again—he must like me), I figured why not? It seemed like a fun exercise.

It was. It really, really was. If I could find this campaign, I would fund it, and bring about the Halloween eternal.

Wouldn't you?

BRING ABOUT THE HALLOWEEN ETERNAL!!!

by Lily Emerson

13,131 backers
$313,131 pledged of $200,000 goal
0 seconds to go
Funding period Sep 1, 2013—Sep 30, 2013 (30 days)

PROJECT DESCRIPTION

Do you love Halloween? Who doesn't! Costumes and candy, the sweet smell of autumn leaves and burning pumpkin flesh… Halloween is the holiday for everyone. You're never too old to love that one perfect night, when every stranger's door is open to you, and every face you see bears a monster's beautiful scowl.

Sadly, Halloween is under assault. The last several years have seen the forces of Christmas conducting a little-remarked but merciless war upon the other holidays. A shopping season which once began after the Thanksgiving Day Parade—and not a second sooner—now starts gathering steam before the Back to School supplies are off the shelves. This past year, the Halloween merchandise was cleared from stores before October 15th! Yes! The hated folly of the holly jolly Christmas army has been gaining ground. It seems inevitable that all other holidays will be chased from the calendar, resulting in an unending Yuletide season. A failure to back this project is as good as backing the conquest of Santa and his elves: through inaction, you will fund their winter wonderland, and you will deserve every peppermint horror that is visited upon your trembling, frostbitten form.

Unless.

The stars are in alignment, and the forces of the autumntide have been gathered for one last push against the encroaching winter. We have uncovered the ritual that will embody the spirit of Halloween in a properly prepared vessel, allowing our Lord to walk the Earth on terrible scarecrow feet, to look upon the sky with a terrible pumpkin grin, and most importantly, to freeze the passage of time and spread the embrace of a sweet October night across the globe, plunging us into the depths of the Halloween eternal. (Note that this ritual is being performed in a climate where freezing temperatures on Halloween are perishingly unlikely; it may be chilly, but no one's going to die of exposure if they just keep their costumes on. Which will be easy, once the transformation of the populace begins. You'd need a flensing knife to take them off.)

Please be aware as you donate that the forces of Christmas are running their own, competing campaign, aimed at preventing us from bringing the glory of the corn and the candle and the freely-flowing candy to the people of the world. WE NOT ONLY NEED TO MAKE OUR GOAL—WE NEED TO BEAT THEM. We need to destroy them. We need to show that TRUE generosity isn't about cheap wrapping paper and teenagers dressed like elves and shitty presents from your Aunt Jill that you're just going to re-gift ANYWAY. True generosity is about free candy from strangers, sometimes with bonus razorblades (and those are expensive!). It's about the freedom to be anybody you want to be for a night—and it's about extending that night from here into eternity.

We are asking for $200,000 to save the best night the world has ever known. That's a lot from one person, but Halloween has always been a pioneer of crowd-funding, filling pillowcases with candy one piece at a time. All we need is for the population of a city to each donate the cost of a candy bar. Given the numbers of people who fill the streets every Halloween night, this is a small request.

Halloween has one last chance to take back what was rightfully ours from the beginning. Help us. Help us bring about the Halloween that never ends.

REWARD TIERS

$1–TRICK (547 backers). Your name will be recorded in the great book, to be read aloud in the center of the corn maze during the apparition of our Lord. Your fate will be decided by His will, and His will alone.

$5–TREAT (223 backers). Your name will be recorded in the great book, and will *not* be read aloud in the hearing of our Lord, who is not always good at distinguishing the contents of His pillowcase, if you know what I mean.

$10–DELUXE TRICK (311 backers). Sponsor yourself at the Treat level, and a friend, loved one, or enemy at the Trick level! It's a gamble—you never know who will have already been foolish enough to choose "Trick" of their own accord—but either way, you'll know that YOU'RE safe. Unless someone put your name on this reward level. Uh-oh…

$25—DELUXE TREAT (191 backers). …better get a better reward tier. At the Deluxe Treat level, not only do you get to sponsor someone at the Trick level, but you are AUTOMATICALLY IMMUNE from being listed in the part of the book we read aloud. Choosing this reward tier will remove you from the Trick level, even if someone else put you there. It's the only way to be sure.

$50—FUN-SIZE CANDY BAR (103 backers). You have joined the ranks of the faithful! Directions to our slammin' opening night party at the center of the chosen corn maze will be sent to you via coded message. It will be carried by the crows. Do not fear them; they can smell the sincerity of your belief. Join us to bring about the autumn unending. Only half the faithful will be sacrificed to water His roots, chosen by lottery from all who are present. Your odds are *way* better than the unfaithful's odds, we promise.

$100—FULL-SIZE CANDY BAR (31 backers). Everything at the $50 tier, plus a genuine woven corn-husk mask in your choice of small, medium, large, extra-large, and mutated by the coming glory of our ripening Lord.

$500—HALLOWEEN PARTY! (79 backers). Everything at the $100 tier, plus a place among the small number of the faithful whose names will not be entered in the lottery for the sacrificial watering.

$1,000—MONSTER MASH (47 backers). We will allow you to select one from among the unfaithful to either sacrifice or save, at your own whim. Those who have pledged at the Halloween Party level are ineligible for sacrifice. The ringleader of Christmas, Holly Emerson, is ineligible for salvation. Her blood will feed the corn. Her blood will feed the corn, and IT WILL BE GLORIOUS.

$10,000—QUALITY COSTUMER (13 backers). Everything at the $500 level, plus we will let you choose the costumes to be worn by your friends and loved ones at the time of the ascension. These costumes will determine their true forms in the glorious unending night that lies ahead of us. This is your opportunity to protect your family from the transformative powers of the candle and the corn—or to condemn your enemies to an eternity as sexy nurses. The choice is yours.

$25,000—FULL PILLOWCASE (7 backers). Everything at all lower reward levels, plus a place among the inner circle, whose names are not entered in the lottery, whose faces shall be remade by the rising of our Lord, to eternally bear the pumpkin grins of the true chosen of Halloween. All shall look upon you ever more and know you as the chosen servant of their terrible, incarnate God.

RISKS AND CHALLENGES

Obviously, because of our competition with Christmas and those bastards who want to freeze the world eternally in the name of their jolly god, we cannot promise that this ritual will succeed. But we can definitely promise that we're going to give it everything we've got. Blood, sweat, tears, and whatever other bodily fluids we can extract from our backers will flow like apple cider through the veins of our Lord, and He will rise, skeletal and pumpkin-headed, against the late harvest moon. Then He will join in merciless battle with whatever those jerks from Christmas have managed to summon, and the strongest season will conquer. (Don't worry about the spring and summer holidays, they lost this battle long ago.)

We're confident that we will be able to pull off the summons with only minimal manpower, once the land has been acquired and the corn maze has been brought to bloody, terrible maturity. It is you, and all those who donate their lives to this cause, who will make the difference between success and failure. It takes more than a single pumpkin to make a patch.

COMMENTS

Susan Clemens (on Sep 29, 2013)

So close!!!!!

Peter McClure (on Sep 13, 2013)

I love Halloween. Pitched in at the Trick level ha ha. Let's see what you do to me!

Jill Seale (on Sep 12, 2013)

Sounds legit to me.

Tim Moore (on Sep 10, 2013)

The T&C don't say anything about summoning an undying god of harvest. I checked. Bring on the eternal Halloween!!

Daniel Brighton (on Sep 9, 2013)

Is anyone else bothered by the part where this is basically "give us money so we can summon a demon and let it kill everybody"? Doesn't that violate the T&C somehow?

Lily Emerson (on Sep 4, 2013)

Go fuck yourself TWICE.

Holly Emerson (on Sep 3, 2013)

Careful, little sister. You don't want someone reporting your project for abuse, now do you? This could all be settled by the click of a button.

Lily Emerson (on Sep 2, 2013)

Go fuck yourself.

Holly Emerson (on Sep 1, 2013)

You're going to lose, Lily. Your holiday is going to fall, and the Christmas eternal will reign over everything.

UPDATE #1—BREAKDOWN OF COSTS—Sep 1, 2013

If our $200,000 goal is met, the money will be spent as follows:

$80,000, securing the land we will be using for the corn maze and associated altar. We have already found the perfect place (undisclosed at this time to prevent THOSE CHRISTMAS ASSHOLES from buying it out from under us for their precious "tree farm"), complete with a crumbling farmhouse in which people have been brutally murdered.

$10,000, clearing the land and preparing it for the sowing.

$3,000, seed and farm labor, for the sowing.

$7,000, livestock purchases, for the blessing of the soil.

$50,000, fees and taxes. While we are more than reasonably confident that taxation will no longer be an issue after midnight this coming October 1st, due to the current world paradigm having been crushed beneath the merciless heel of either Halloween or Christmas (HOPEFULLY HALLOWEEN), we still need to budget responsibly.

$20,000, backer rewards and mailing costs.

$5,000, candy.

$10,000, pumpkins, candles, and other essential ritual supplies. We will be growing most of our own pumpkins, using a secondary ritual which will bring them to ripeness almost immediately, but this will not account for the pumpkins necessary to line the driveway, parking area, and other paths, nor for the pumpkins we will be placing on the doorsteps of the chosen.

$15,000, Christmas decorations and other paraphernalia that has leaked into the stores during what should be our time of ascendance. By gathering and destroying these false idols, we will be able to start weakening the forces of Christmas even before our Lord rises, ready to do glorious battle.

UPDATE #2—HALFWAY THERE!!!!—SEP 10, 2013

Wow! We've raised half the funds we need in just ten days—and that's before our Bake Sale proceeds have come in! (All proceeds will be pledged directly to the project through a single donor, to keep things centralized and easily accountable for all of you.) To thank you, we have unlocked three stretch goals. These are:

$225,000—The Big Bonfire. If we reach the $225,000 level before funding ends, we will ALSO read a second, bonus ritual which will ignite a central bonfire in all cities of more than 50,000 people. This fire will burn on your town square or commons, or in the first Starbucks to have opened inside city limits if you no longer have a town square or commons. It will not spread to engulf nearby homes, although it may spread to engulf nearby non-believers. Prayers and offerings thrown into the bonfire will go straight to our Lord, thus saving you the physical inconvenience and risk of traveling to the holy cornfield.

$250,000—The Halloween Carnival. Our carnies are raring to go, and if we reach the $250,000 level, we will be able to pay for equipment repair on Professor Blood's Carnival of Death and Wonders. These repairs should last long enough for the show to finish a ritual circuit around North America, at which point the equipment will become self-repairing, the carnies will become immortal, and the carnival's exciting attractions will become a permanent part of our world. Imagine waking every "morning"—a meaningless term when the sun never rises—wondering whether the carnival has come to town, offering excitement, offering enchantment, and asking only blood.

$300,000—The Salvation of Thanksgiving. If, through some miracle, we reach $300,000 before the funding window runs out, we will preserve the surviving armies of Thanksgiving and allow them to adapt their traditions to our new reality. Turkey dinners with cranberry sauce and mashed potato will be allowed to continue, and not required to incorporate any signs of fealty to our Lord, save for corn. Always there will be corn.

$350,000—The Sun Also Rises. We know that some of you are going to miss the sun. If we reach this goal, we will permit the sun to rise once a year, bathing the world in restorative light. We will also provide sunscreen, as most of you will have become pale and easily burnt after a year spent in unending darkness.

UPDATE #3–CHRISTMAS IS GAINING– SEP 22, 2013

I hate to bring this up, because you have all been amazing, but CHRISTMAS IS GAINING ON US. We have raised an amazing $280,000 USD, making our initial ritual possible. But if Christmas is able to feed their blood-god on ritual sacrifices before we go into the corn, all may yet be lost. Search your couch cushions. Sweet-talk your neighbors into joining the cause. Do whatever it takes. If everyone backing this project increased their pledges by just a dollar, we would be able to crush those red and white bastards under our heels.

Halloween needs you. Don't let us down.

UPDATE #4–THIS IS HALLOWEEN–SEP 30, 2013

We are fully funded!

Preparations are beginning now. At the stroke of midnight on October 31st, look to the skies and see the terrible battle unfold. Halloween will join with Christmas in battle for the world. Thanks to your generosity, our Lord is guaranteed to triumph, and darkness will fall eternally. Even now, we gather the faithful; even now, we scatter candy to lure the unwary; even now, we call upon the children of Thanksgiving, offering them safety in the days to come.

If you are interested in a position with Professor Blood's Carnival of Death and Wonders, please email professorblood@deathcarnival.org for details about paid and volunteer work. Professor Blood has personally guaranteed that all carnies will survive the ascension.

Trick or treat, my darlings. Look to the sky.

Office Memos

There really isn't much of a background here, apart from "if I need to put a story in a convention program book, it has historically been this one." Which means I'll need a new convention book story, I suppose.

Oh, well.

There are worse things.

October 11th, 16:35
To: ALL EMPLOYEES
From: Rachel White, Director, Human Resources

Please be aware that we here at Polytechnic Engineering and Research practice non-discrimination in our hiring policies. Racial and species slurs are not tolerated on company grounds or company time. Failure to comply with HR regulations may result in censure or termination of employment contracts.

We're all adults here. Let's start acting like it.

October 11th, 16:50
To: Hank Campbell, Hanger Three
From: Eustacia

What do you suppose brought that on?

October 11th, 17:00
To: Stace
From: Hank

It probably has something to do with the lab you blew up yesterday. Remember the screaming? Most people don't *like* explosions. Explosions are generally considered undesirable in a work environment. This is a work environment.

October 11th, 17:03
To: Hank
From: Stace

If people don't like explosions, they shouldn't hire Gremlins. Explosions are what we *do*.

October 11th, 17:11
To: Stace
From: Hank

Trust me, I'm aware.

October 12th, 17:10
To: Paul Weston, Facilities Coordinator
From: Hank Campbell, Lab Tech, Hanger Three

Twenty-four hours and nothing has exploded, caught fire, or mutated out of control and tried to destroy the world. You owe me several beers and an apology, or I'll tell Eustacia you called her a purple-haired freak in front of management and inspired the increased attention from HR.

November 13th, 12:30
To: ALL EMPLOYEES
From: Eustacia ni'Aiodhan, Director, Hanger Three

Please be advised that Hanger Three is currently invisible. This is due to a long and complex series of events that I do not feel like explaining right now. Just trust me when I say that it was all very scientific and necessary to furthering our understanding of the natural world.

As invisibility does not mean insubstantiality, attempts to walk through the hanger will result in physical injury. Those who have already made this attempt can testify as to the veracity of my statement. If you check your terms of employment, you will find that you cannot sue the company for injuries sustained while goofing around near invisible buildings.

Also, the next person who spray-paints their name on the invisible wall for the purposes of taking quote, "really funny pictures" will greatly regret it.

November 13th, 12:42
To: Hank Campbell
From: Paul Weston, Facilities Coordinator

"A long and complex series of events"? Hank, she used the word "veracity" in a sentence. She only does that when she's smoke screening. What did the whacko Gremlin lady *do?* More importantly, is she going to get us sued?

November 13th, 13:04
To: Paul
From: Hank Campbell, Lab Assistant, Hanger Three

She doesn't know what she did—that's why she's using the five-dollar words. Somebody bumped her, she knocked over half a dozen beakers, and the next thing you know, bang, everything non-organic in the structure is invisible. Including the structure. Did you know the Gremlin language has seventy-three ways of saying "lab accident," and they're all considered profane? At least she's cute when she's screaming herself blue in the face. (I mean that literally. She turns bright blue. Very disconcerting.)

I'll let you know when the lab comes back. And no, we're not getting sued, because the employee regulations have a section on invisibility. Seriously. I looked it up, it's really there, everybody signed it. We're in the clear.

November 13th, 13:06
To: Stace
From: Hank

Paul's already sniffing around to find out whether we can sell this. He also wants to know if we're going to be facing a lawsuit. Apparently, three per year is the company's limit. It's a little low, but it's what the boss wants.

November 13th, 13:09
To: Hank
From: Stace

If they have such a problem with being sued around here, they should stick with hiring boring human scientists. Those almost never get people sued.

November 13th, 14:11
To: Alexander Peterman, CEO, Polytechnic Engineering and Research
From: Eustacia ni'Aiodhan, Director, Hanger Three

I apologize for the current apparent absence of my lab—but there is a logical reason behind it! It's even a good one, mostly, if you comprehend the interaction between common household cleaners and chemicals imported from Faerie.

Short form: I knocked over several beakers of Underhill-grown yarrow and pennyroyal, and Mr. Campbell insisted on cleaning the mess, rather than permit me to inhale pennyroyal fumes and potentially damage the soft tissues of my lungs. Unfortunately, he decided to do so with industrial-strength army-issue floor cleaner. I am sure you see the logical and tactical error implicit in this decision.

By the time I recognized it, however, the flash explosion had occurred, rendering lab, equipment and employees invisible. A thorough washing in a primrose/oak solution returned the employees (and associated organic materials) to standard visibility, but was unable to do the same to the lab, which I estimate will become visible again in approximately six days, when the stability of the initial chemical reaction wears off.

This may have potential local and military uses. In the meantime, however, we have been unable to locate Greg Masterson; if you step on someone you can't see, please tell him to come and check in with me.

December 2nd, 9:55
To: ALL EMPLOYEES
From: Eustacia ni'Aiodhan, Director, Hanger Three

Would whoever thought it was funny to release fabric-eating locusts into my hanger during a presentation to the board of directors please see me at once? I wish to thank you for increasing my project funding by a factor of ten.

Please confirm that HR has contact information on your next of kin before visiting.

December 2nd, 10:40
To: Hank Campbell
From: Stace

Hank, how could you? Those locusts ate my favorite lab coat, as well as the clothes of everyone else in the room. There are things in this world that I was not meant to see! Mr. Peterman devoid of clothing is among them. I may not sleep for a week.

December 2nd, 10:53
To: Stace
From: Hank

Consider it revenge for whatever stupid-ass thing you're going to do next.

December 2nd, 11:06
To: Hank
From: Stace

The assumption that I'm going to do something you could describe as "stupid-ass" is species-based profiling.

December 2nd, 11:30
To: Stace
From: Hank

And yet, still not wrong.

December 30th, 17:04
To: Alexander Peterman, CEO, Polytechnic Engineering and Research
From: Eustacia ni'Aiodhan, Director, Hanger Three

I need to requisition one (1) replacement vacuum chamber, three (3) replacement valve systems, two (2) gallons of pure yarrow extract, ten (10) pairs of goggles and a new lab technician, as my previous assistant on this project has stalked out muttering something about "damn workaholic Gremlins." Mr. Campbell has requested a week's reassignment to hanger two on the basis of not crushing my skull like an egg. I petition that this request be granted, as I enjoy having an uncrushed skull.

For the year to come, please assume I will require my budget from last year, plus the standard 15% increase. Also, given current progress and project status, I estimate we will require a new lab building no later than March, due to the total destruction of hanger three.

January 5th, 16:02
To: ALL EMPLOYEES
From: Eustacia ni'Aiodhan, Director, Hanger TBD

Please watch for falling debris in the area of what was previously designated as hanger three, as the anti-gravity effect which caused the hanger to explosively disassemble itself is still collapsing, and has been showering the surrounding area with rubble at a rate of approximately one hundred and fifty pounds (150 lb.) per hour. You do not want to be standing underneath my kiln when it comes down.

In other news, Michael Lewis, Jonathan Crimin, and Louise Simmons are missing, and believed to still be located within the flying hanger. Should you see one of your fellow employees making an abrupt, unplanned descent from their current locale, please assist them by providing a soft object on which they may land.

January 5th, 16:09
To: Alexander Peterman, CEO, Polytechnic Engineering and Research
From: Eustacia ni'Aiodhan, Director, Hanger TBD

So my estimate was a little short. Is hanger four available yet?

January 22nd, 12:33
To: Hank
From: Stace

I said I was sorry I accidentally levitated your favorite hammer into the Pacific jet stream. Are you done being mad at me yet?

January 22nd, 12:50
To: Stace
From: Hank

No.

February 10th, 10:48
To: ALL EMPLOYEES
From: Eustacia ni'Aiodhan, Director, Hanger Four

Thank you to everyone who has assisted with the relocation of my surviving lab equipment and assistants into hanger four. I did not, however, appreciate the inclusion of the photographic spread from the locust incident, or the sudden inexplicable invasion of giant ants. Would whatever amateur entomologist we have here on at the office please cease and desist immediately, before I am forced to retaliate in kind? You don't want me to start down that road, you really don't. I have a deviant and twisty mind when it comes to taking revenge for someone filling my vacuum chamber with giant ants.

February 10th, 16:31
To: Alexander Peterman, CEO, Polytechnic Engineering and Research
From: Eustacia ni'Aiodhan, Director, Hanger Four

ANTS! ANTS ANTS ANTS ANTS I HATE ANTS!!! Make this stop. I request that Mr. Campbell be reassigned to my hanger, as he needs to crush someone's skull like an egg.

March 2nd, 9:23
To: ALL EMPLOYEES
From: Eustacia ni'Aiodhan, Director, Hanger Four

The area surrounding hanger four is currently suffering temporal flux. If you are not immortal and do not wish to re-experience puberty, please avoid entering the area marked off with the yellow flags for the next four days. Those employees already reduced to an age below the cut-off point for gainful employment in the state of California will retain all standard benefits, but will be required to re-enroll in school at the appropriate grade.

Those employees over the age of sixty-five may negotiate brief trips into the field if they wish to delay retirement.

March 2nd, 14:51
To: ALL EMPLOYEES
From: Eustacia ni'Aiodhan, Director, Hanger Four

Please stop using the time distortion field to age your cheese. It is an inappropriate use of scientific resources, and anyway, you can't start with Velveeta and expect to get anything decent out the other end. Go to the grocery store and buy something worth consuming if you insist on putting the fruits of twisted science into your mouths.

Amateurs.

April 19th, 15:17
To: Alexander Peterman, CEO, Polytechnic Engineering and Research
From: Eustacia ni'Aiodhan, Director, Hanger Four

I am afraid neither I nor any of my staff will be reporting for work for the next three days, as we have managed to accidentally unlock the secret of gender inversion. In other news, we are now the only all-female work-crew within the company.

In order to attempt reversion of this process, I will need five hundred pounds (500 lb.) of clean liquid-state protein, contained in a sterile vat. I will also require seventy boxes of industrial gauze and seventy pounds (70 lb.) of the best chocolate you can locate. This is very, very important.

April 19th, 15:17
To: Stace
From: Hank

I am going to kill you. Just as soon as you fix this.

Don't think retrieving my hammer means that I won't.

May 16th, 16:11
To: Alexander Peterman, CEO, Polytechnic Engineering and Research
From: Eustacia ni'Aiodhan, Director, Hanger Four

Regarding those employees who have chosen to stay female: I don't know what you're supposed to tell their wives. If they turn down the reversion, I cannot legally force them to accept medical attention. Please do not yell at me—it's not like this was my idea. Besides, they seem quite happy as they currently are.

May 16th, 16:30
To: Hank
From: Stace

Still mad at me?

May 16th, 16:30
To: Stace
From: Hank

Yes. Now take a vacation or I'll kill you.

May 19th, 12:42
To: Stace
From: Hank

I got us tickets on the Avalon Ferry. We're going to go see the dragons spawning. Your time off request has been approved by HR, and your bags are packed. Resistance won't do you any good. I have a hammer, and I know how to use it.

May 19th, 18:43
To: ALL EMPLOYEES
From: Eustacia ni'Aiodhan, Director, Hanger Four

First, let me apologize for the infestation of pixies that has inexplicably taken apart hanger two, where that illegal insect modification lab was discovered. I can't guess what set them off, and certainly have no idea as to their origins.

I will be away for the next week. Please try not to burn the place down.

That's still my job.

Lady Antheia's Guide to Horticultural Warfare

It is rarely as good of an idea to ask me to write steampunk as people think it is. This is sort of an homage to H.G. Wells, by way of *Little Shop of Horrors*, which I saw at far too early of an age and was forever changed by.

Lady Antheia seems like she would be a lot of fun at parties, assuming she didn't eat the hosts.

1.

"I sometimes think it would have been better had my first encounter with humanity been a man, and not a woman of low station with no family to mourn her. Better for who, I cannot say."

—from *Lady Antheia's Guide to Horticultural Warfare*, first printing

---

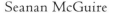

It is customary to begin one's memoirs at birth. As I was not "born" in the gross mammalian sense, I shall begin instead at a more logical point in time. To wit:

I was borne to Earth on cosmic winds, falling through chance and the grace of the heavens to root in the soil of Notting Hill. There I grew rapidly to adult stature, devoured a lady's maid who had the misfortune to come too close to my tendrils, and assumed her form. It was a discourteous way to introduce myself to the human species, but I must beg forgiveness: my kind are not precisely well-mannered when we bud, and must be taught proper behavior before we can be trusted in polite society.

As servants are rarely found with skin the color of young watercress and hair the color of mature nettles, I presented quite a curiosity when I staggered through the doors of the house which previously employed the now-devoured lady's maid. I was still in the process of absorbing her memories, and had discovered the directions to her place of employment without acquiring the context that would have allowed me to understand that returning might be bad for my chances of continued survival. Indeed, I was not the only seed to fall to Earth that day. I was simply the only one fortunate enough to eat a lady's maid whose mistress was sister to a man of science. Sir Arthur Blackwood, botanist in the service of Her Majesty, the Queen of England.

Where most men would have looked upon my innocent, vibrantly green face and seen a monster, Sir Blackwood saw a miracle in the making: something entirely new to present to Queen Alice, who was so fond of novelty. Alice had been raised a princess, with no hope of the throne, only to find herself elevated and her engagement to the Grand Duke of Hesse cancelled after an ill-timed smallpox outbreak left her the heir to the British Empire. God save the Queen.

I was presented to Queen Alice on my third day of adult growth, after my mind had finished processing the linguistic and behavioral data harvested from the unfortunate lady's maid. I was able to curtsey and offer a polite greeting to Her Majesty.

She was charmed, of course. Who wouldn't be? I was a well-mannered sapling, and have only grown into my graces as I bloomed and cultivated my better nature. Jill Lane—the lady's maid I have spoken of—was a great help. She had in her an endless eagerness to please, and I often returned to her deep well of knowledge and propriety as I navigated the echelons of English society. But ah, I am getting ahead of myself.

How vividly I recall that first day in the Queen's presence, me unsteady on the bifurcated stems of my legs, Jill's voice reedy and uncertain in my mind. Queen Alice looked me up and down with the quick eyes of a monarch born, and then turned her attention to Sir Blackwood.

"Does your green girl have a name?" she asked.

"She came before us with nothing but her pretty face," he said. "I have taken the liberty of calling her 'Antheia,' after the goddess of flowers and floral garlands."

The Queen had smiled. That was all it took to seal my fate within the Empire—for you see, after that, I was a favorite of the Queen, and a novelty unlike any other. That made me the toast of every great house in Britain, opening endless doors, and the manners I borrowed from dear Jill opened still more, until some spoke, half-jesting, of my successful invasion of the nation. They called me their flowering princess, representative of some savage fairy race that dwelt beneath the hills of Ireland, and oh, how they laughed at the idea that I could represent their downfall.

How they laughed.

2.

> "It is important we record the last days of the Planet Earth in their own languages, for these languages contain the concepts with which the meat-based life forms of that world were most familiar. They could no more express the delight of fresh sun falling upon their roots than an unbonded pod could explain the intricacies of a lady's undergarments. By preserving the

manners and culture of the planet in this way, we can better understand them and, should we ever encounter another such species, we can bring about an even swifter and more efficient conquest."

—from *Lady Antheia's Guide to Horticultural Warfare*, first printing

---

It was a Thursday afternoon when the advance scouts broke through the upper reaches of Earth's atmosphere, announcing their arrival with the usual chromatic displays. The lights drew attention across the globe, stargazers and young romantics alike clustering in the fields as they strained to watch these strange and heretofore undocumented rainbows of the night. I was less interested in the phenomenon, naturally; I have always done better during the daylight hours, and the things I do in open fields are better not shared with those of delicate mammalian sensibilities. I was seated in the parlor at home, working on my needlepoint and snacking from a tray of little sandwiches, when Sir Blackwood burst into the room, his hair mussed and his jacket askew.

"Antheia!" he cried. "Why are you here, and not out on the veranda with the guests? They're asking about you."

"I have no interest in watching the excited collision of atoms," I said, tugging another loop of thread carefully through the muslin. A fine cabbage rose was taking form under my fingers—some of my best work, if I did say so myself. "The colors will be there with or without me to watch them, and besides, it was time for my tea. You *do* prefer that I continue to take my meals in private, do you not?"

Arthur blanched. It had taken the household some time to adjust to my predilection for eating raw animal flesh and drinking only fresh blood. Sir Arthur's sister, Julia, had adjusted faster than he had—she'd already known I was a beast, as evidenced by the fact that I had eaten her lady's maid. Dear, sweet Arthur had devoted his life to the study of plants, and even the fact that I was not the first flesh-eater he had encountered had not prepared him for the notion that one day he might meet a flower who could smile and curtsey and request a hot bowl of pig's blood for her supper.

"Yes, but the lights—"

"Are better left to those who can appreciate them." I reached for a sandwich. The delightful smell of raw, fresh-sliced beef addressed my nose. "Really, I thought your sister had banned you from her stargazing party. Something about the noises coming from the basement?"

"I don't understand why she gets so upset," he said, dropping into the seat on the other side of my sewing table with a loud thump. He automatically reached for my plate of sandwiches, and looked offended when I smacked his hand with my needlepoint frame. Rubbing his fingers, he continued, "My steam-powered sun will make us richer than she can imagine."

"You see, that is her trouble: she suffers from a shortage of imagination, and as such, cannot see where a loud, clanking clockwork machine could possibly improve her life." I took a dainty nibble from my sandwich. "Remember, she forbade poor Jill to use *any* modern machinery in maintaining the house."

Arthur blanched again. He enjoyed being reminded that I'd eaten Jill even less than he enjoyed being reminded of the rest of my diet. "Julia is a traditional soul, that's all," he mumbled.

"We live in an age of wonders," I said. "The fact that she cannot embrace them is a shame. The fact that she can stand on her veranda marveling over a scientific curiosity while forbidding the pursuit of more concrete sciences is a sham. I will never understand how you can tolerate her willful interference with your business, Arthur."

"She'll wed eventually. One of her hulking suitors will make an honest woman of her, and she'll have no more grounds to interfere." Arthur looked wistfully at my sandwiches, but didn't stretch out his hand again. "What do you think of these lights?"

"Natural atmospheric distortion, of no more interest than any of the other things one sees in the sky." I nibbled my sandwich, swallowed, and added, "Excepting, of course, Her Majesty's airship, which is a wonder and a blessing and is in no way an eyesore that blocks the sunlight from reaching my roses."

Arthur laughed. "I swear your tongue gets sharper every year, Antheia."

"What good is a rose that has no thorns?" I smiled, pleased when his cheeks reddened in reply. Blood-based circulatory systems are such traitorous things, betraying the emotions of their owners even as they struggle to keep them alive. "I presume you have some motive for asking these questions, apart from the pleasure of my company?"

"I was speaking with Lord Harrington of the Royal Astronomical Society about the lights," said Arthur, carefully. "I thought he might have something interesting to offer on the topic, and in fact, he did. He said similar lights—similar in color and design, although less grandiose in scope—were seen in various locations around the world some six years ago."

"Is that so?" I asked politely, before taking another nibble of my sandwich. The bread, made specially from bone meal and ground fish scales, was deliciously nourishing. I kept my eyes on Arthur, waiting for him to finish his explanation with the inevitable and begin the next phrase in our little dance.

I had been waiting for so long, and as ever, Arthur did not disappoint. "The lights were last seen on the night before you appeared," he said. "Antheia, I have always assumed, in some vague way, that you were one of the fairy-folk of legend, escaped from beneath the hill and come to grace us with your presence. Fairy-folk have sometimes been said to be green of skin, you see. But now I come to wonder...did you come from beneath the Earth? Did you come from the Earth at all?"

I smiled dazzlingly, showing him my teeth in parody of the primate grimace he and his sister wore so often, and to such good effect. Jill had taught me my manners properly, you see: no deportment coach could have been better than my own internal lady's maid. "I never claimed a terrestrial origin, you know. I simply felt such matters were better left behind us than discussed in polite company."

"Antheia..." Arthur frowned, his brows furrowing together as he looked at me with such gravity as to make my breath catch in my chest. "These lights. Are they more of your people?"

"Oh, no," I said blithely. He began to relax. "If this were merely more of my people, you would need only to lock up your lady's maids and gentleman's companions long enough to let them take their human forms from the less desirable levels of society—or at least from the parts of society where the people would be less dearly missed. This is the invasion."

His mouth fell open. He stared at me, shocked into silence, as I set my sandwich aside, picked up my teacup, and took a dainty sip of its bloody contents. He continued to stare. I put the cup down, folded my hands in my lap, and offered him a tight-lipped smile.

"I'm sorry," I said. "I thought you knew."

3.

> "As with so many worlds, Earth's dominant life forms were mammalian: hot-blooded, quick to anger and to passion, and unwilling to pace their lives to the rhythm of the world around them. This allowed for some incredible leaps forward of technology and science, and we should work to retain these streaks of stubborn inventiveness and, dare I say, emotional engagement, within our own cultivars. They may serve useful, after all, even if they did not serve the human race with particular efficacy."
>
> —from *Lady Antheia's Guide to Horticultural Warfare*, first printing

---

Julia and her friends watched disdainfully as Arthur bundled me out of the house and into the waiting steam-drawn carriage below, as if the method of our conveyance somehow rendered us low-class and common. I spared a smile and a waggle of my fingers for Julia, who glared and turned her face away. Then I was in the carriage next to Arthur, and we were being carried into the night, with the rainbow blaze of ships piercing the atmosphere dancing in the sky above us.

"I have already sent a telegram to Lord Harrington, asking him to be prepared for us," said Arthur, watching out the window as if he expected my brethren to be stalking the streets already. "He'll want to know everything you can tell him about this 'invasion.' No detail is too small. We're all going to need to do our part to beat these blighters back!"

"Well, what about the ray guns atop the palace and the Royal Observatory?" I asked. "Won't they automatically take aim at anything larger than Her Majesty's airship that enters England's skies?"

"Yes, and we can take comfort in that, but—and please don't take this as a criticism of your fair self, my dear, you have never been anything but a blessing to my house—they didn't shoot *you* down, and that leads me to worry about the strength of our aerial defense net." Arthur looked at me solemnly. "Are you positive this is an invasion? Couldn't it be a simple atmospheric disturbance?"

"I am not positive, as I have been on this planet and in this form for six years, and that does rather limit one's communications with one's fellows," I said. "That aside, six years is roughly the time needed to travel here from the nearest habitable star, if said travel is undertaken in faster than light seed-ships."

Arthur's mouth fell open. "F-faster than light? But that's beyond the reaches of modern science. Why, even Professor O'Malley's moon-ship only traveled at a rate of seventeen thousand miles an hour. Light is—"

"Light is a far faster beast," I said agreeably. "I am sorry. I thought you knew."

It was a bald-faced lie, and not the first I had told him during our acquaintanceship. *Lying is wrong, miss,* said Jill's small, stern voice.

Ah, but the lies are coming to an end, and sometimes things which are wrong are also comforting, I told her. *Now hush, be still. I have a scientist to attend to.*

"Faster than light travel would be a discovery great enough to put the British Empire ahead of the rest of the world forever," said Arthur. "You *must* discuss this with Lord Harrington."

"I will, if you bid me, but I am no engineer." I refolded my hands in my lap. "I've never seen the drives, nor do I understand the physics behind them."

Arthur frowned like he was seeing me for the first time. "So you remember yourself before you were—" He waved a hand, indicating my form in a most ungentlemanly manner. "This?"

"You mean, do I remember my existence before I consumed Julia's lady's maid?" I asked, baldly. If he was going to forsake manners for expediency, then I saw no reason not to do the same. "Yes, and no. My seed was coaxed from a cutting of a specific cultivated line. I have never been anything but what I am: I was a seed, and then I was a sprout, and then I was the Lady Antheia, who has very much enjoyed your hospitality over these past six years. The line from which I was grown, however, is a strain of diplomats and explorers. All the seeds that came to this world with me were of that same strain." Had any of them managed to sprout, I would have had siblings all across the globe—but alas, more and more, I had come to believe that I alone had found welcoming soil.

"A...diplomat?" Arthur blinked at me as our carriage rattled to a stop, presumably in front of our destination. "But the first thing you did was eat my sister's maid."

"I'm aware," I said primly, gathering my skirts as I waited for the doors to slide open on their well-oiled tracks. "But I was sorry afterward, which is the very definition of diplomacy."

Arthur didn't have an answer to that.

4.

> "Being only a cultivar of our greatest diplomat, the honorable and merciful Rooted in Many Soils, I cannot possibly know what it is to have conquered more than one world. I have offered my genetic material back to the trunk which grew me, and my experiences will be preserved for future generations, as is only right and just. Still, I know enough of what my parent and original experienced during their own explorations to know that the conquest of Earth was entirely unique, and extremely common, all at the same time. But then, this is always the way when we encounter a sapient race: they are all different, and they are all sadly, tragically the same. Meat is not capable of much variance."
>
> —from *Lady Antheia's Guide to Horticultural Warfare*, first printing

---

Lord Harrington was a walking mountain of a man, tall and broad-chested, with a ruddy complexion that spoke of much blood pumping very close to the surface. He always made me hungry in a faintly embarrassing way; it's rude to stare at a man and think of how much his blood would do to nourish your vines.

"Arthur," he greeted, in his booming voice, before turning his attention on me. "And the Lady Antheia, who appears to be the woman of the hour, if what Arthur tells me is true. Do you know what's causing the lights in the sky?"

He knew the answer: I could hear it in his tone. I politely inclined my head, and asked, "How long ago did your telescope begin picking out the ships in the auroras?"

"Perhaps half an hour; no more," he said. "I never trusted you."

"I know." I raised my head. "I did not press the issue. It seemed more sporting to allow you your rebellion, rather than charming it out of you. Sportsmanship is not a uniquely human trait, you know. Very little is unique about any world, although they all assume themselves to be."

Lord Harrington's lips peeled back from his teeth as he drew the gun from his belt and pointed it at the spot where my heart would have been, had I possessed such an inconvenient thing. "Lady Antheia, by my authority as a Peer of the Crown, I place you under arrest for treason to the British Empire."

"Oh, lovely." I clapped my hands. "That is *fantastic* news, because you see, as the diplomatic ambassador of the...well, there isn't a term in English that's quite right for what we are, because we've never encountered English before, and thus far I'm the only one who speaks it, so let us say, the Vegetable Empire? As the diplomatic ambassador of the Vegetable Empire, I refuse to be arrested, but I'm happy to be taken before your Queen, as it seems the invasion is about to properly begin."

As if on a timer, the guns atop the observatory fired, their steam-fueled chambers expelling rays of hot light that seared across the sky. Several seed ships would be destroyed in this barrage; it was natural. They didn't yet know to make themselves smaller, and would learn only through those losses. Those which survived the initial wave of gunfire would split into multiple vessels, and continue their implacable descent. I couldn't mourn for the dead of this wave. They would only be seeds, after all, and of no more consequence than a promise, always intended to be broken.

The guns fired again. And so, in the din, did Lord Harrington. His aim was true: the ray gun hit me squarely in the chest, burning a hole in both my favorite bodice and the bright green skin below, until it was possible to look through me to the room beyond. Arthur cried out. I looked down, considering the wreckage of what had been my sternum.

"Oh, I *do* wish you hadn't done that," I sighed, my voice rendered weak and reedy by the damage to my lungs.

And then I lunged.

Lord Harrington had always treated me as a strange sort of pet, a harmless trinket to be either studied or ignored, depending on his mood. To learn that he had mistrusted my intentions all that time was almost a relief, as it meant that he was not *quite* as stupid as I had assumed. Still, like most men of science, he believed only in the evidence of his eyes, and what his eyes saw when he looked at me was a woman. Green of skin and hair, yes, but apart from that? In every other regard? I was the very flower of English womanhood, with my curves trained to the corset's embrace and my skirts hanging full and demure down past my ankles. Why, had it not been for my face, and for the narrow band of skin between top of glove and bottom of sleeve, he could easily have forgotten my vegetable origins, as so many others had tried to do. Poor man. What he did not consider was that skirts can conceal more than legs.

He jerked backward as my hands found his throat, my thorn-sharp nails piercing the skin beneath his jaw and finding purchase there, the tiny barbs that lined them making it nigh-impossible to pull me free without killing him in the process. Lord Harrington pressed his gun against my stomach, firing again; much of my midsection joined my chest in nonexistence before I could wrap a vine around the ray gun's muzzle and rip it from his hands, hurling it away. As I did that, the creeper vines and long, thick roots I normally kept concealed—as a proper British woman would, had she found herself burdened with such things—emerged from beneath my skirt and wrapped tight around him, binding him in place.

Arthur was shouting behind me. I knew that civility meant responding to him, or at least begging his pardon, but my injuries were too great; Lord Harrington might not have known my anatomy, but he had done a remarkably good job of reducing my overall mass. So I committed the unforgiveable sin of ignoring my friend and patron as I drove my roots into the body of his colleague, linking them into his circulatory system.

His blood tasted of fine wine and excellent breeding. Perhaps there was something to be said for the aristocracy after all.

It only took me a few moments to drain the life and fluids from Lord Harrington's body. I leaned back, glancing down, and was pleased to see that new growth had covered the holes in my chest and stomach, replacing the gaping holes with smooth, if somewhat indecent, green skin. It was paler than the rest of me, but the patchwork effect that it created was not unpleasant, and would be mostly covered by my clothing under normal circumstances. I pulled my roots from the husk of Lord Harrington, unwinding my creeper vines until he remained upright solely thanks to the nails which remained wedged in his throat. I yanked them free, and he fell with a hollow rattle, like a dried-out old seed pod.

"Well. That was uncivil of him," I said, smoothing my skirt with the heels of my hands as I pulled all the pieces of me back into their proper places. "Arthur, dear, I don't suppose I might borrow your jacket? I am quite underdressed, thanks to the holes your friend saw fit to shoot into my clothing."

"You killed him." Arthur's voice was as bloodless as his colleague. "Antheia...how could you?"

"The mechanisms of it were easy, and do not really require explanation," I said, turning to face him. It was no real surprise to find that he had retrieved Lord Harrington's ray gun, and was aiming it at me. His hands were shaking. There was no way he would pull the trigger. "As to why I would do so, well. He shot me. Twice. You cannot blame me for protecting myself against a man who was so clearly determined to end my life."

"But you...but you..."

"Did nothing you were not already aware I had the potential to do, Arthur." I took a step toward him, chin up, eyes fixed on his. "We met shortly after I devoured dear Jill. You remember? You knew I had this in me. If I am a monster, then you are the man who nurtured me, and saw to it I had good soil in which to grow. I am your fault as much as anyone else's."

He whimpered. Just once, like a child.

He's frightened, miss, said Jill.

He has reason to be. Now hush, I replied, and reached out to take the gun, gently, from Arthur's hands. That was the moment when everything could have gone wrong: when the human race could have started truly fighting back, instead of simply lashing out against an enemy it did not understand. I was leaving myself vulnerable to attack—a foolish thing to do, more suited to a hot-blooded meat creature than to a soldier of the Vegetable Empire, but ah. I did harbor some affection for the man. I might even have loved him, in my way, had my purpose on his world not been so antithetical to the very notion. So I left my throat unguarded, giving him the opportunity to deliver a killing blow.

He didn't. Then the gun was in my hand, barrel still warm from the two shots Lord Harrington had delivered to my body, and Arthur's eyes were beginning to overflow with salty tears. I reached out, quite improperly, and brushed them away with a sweep of my thumb. My skin drank the moisture eagerly.

"Come now, stop your crying," I said. "It's time we went to see the Queen."

The great guns atop the Observatory shuddered and fired again, blasting more of my people out of the sky, and Arthur wept.

5.

"It is not that the idea of invasion was incomprehensible to the humans: a simple visit to the breeding pens will expose the curious to dozens of pre-conquest humans who have no trouble accepting the reality of their situation. They were always prepared for the idea that an enemy might try their borders. No, the incomprehensibility came when they were defeated.

> The sun was said never to set on the British Empire. I am sure there are some who still cannot understand how they could have been so very wrong."
>
> —from *Lady Antheia's Guide to Horticultural Warfare*, first printing

---

London was in a panic. The streets were thronged with would-be defenders of the Crown, their handheld ray guns and small sonic cannons clutched in sweaty hands and aimed toward the distant sky. Some of the buildings we passed were already aflame, no doubt ignited by falling debris. I schooled my expression into one of mild dismay as I gazed out the carriage windows on the spreading chaos. My people had not yet fired a single gun, nor killed a single head of state—Lord Harrington being far too close to common to count. All this was the humans' own doing.

"You were always going to rip it all down by yourselves you know," I said conversationally, glad that our carriage was a clever conveyance of steam and gears, and not a thing driven by a living human who might have understood the meaning of my words. "That's what meat does, when it gets control of a world. It devours itself, and then it goes looking for something else to eat. We're simply shortcutting the process."

"I thought you were our friend." Arthur's voice was dull, lacking its usual fascination with the world. A pity. I hadn't intended to break him. "I took you in. Supported you. *Cared* for you."

"Yes, and believe me, your assistance in gaining the access I needed to higher society is appreciated." I allowed one of my climber vines to uncurl from around my leg, extending it to brush against Arthur's cheek. He might not recognize the affection in the gesture, but that was of no matter. My days of pretending to humanity were coming to a blessed end. "This will be much less painful, thanks to you."

"I have betrayed my Queen and my country."

"No, darling, no. Betrayal implies intent. You have simply allowed something dangerous to flourish in your garden. A weed among roses, although that's a terribly common metaphor, don't you think? More like a rose among cabbages, all things considered." I allowed the curtain to fall back across the window. "I have grown healthy in the fertile soil you afforded me, and now it's time for me to bloom. Me, and all my brothers and sisters."

"Why?"

"Well, I don't know. Why did your British Empire see fit to colonize so much of the planet? Superior force of arms was definitely a factor, and a misguided faith in your own sense of morality. 'For Queen and country' and all of that lovely jingoistic nonsense. But that's all petals, isn't it? Pretty blooms to hide the thorns. You did it for two reasons." I leaned closer, smiling. He paled as he met my eyes.

Now miss, it's not polite to taunt a man by knowing things he doesn't, chided Jill.

No, but it's certainly enjoyable, I replied. Aloud, I said, "The places you took had things you wanted. Resources. Tea and cinnamon and precious metals and girls no one would ever debase themselves by marrying, but whom every British gentleman was happy to deflower. That's the first reason you did what you did, and that's the first reason we do what we do."

Arthur swallowed hard before whispering, "What's the second reason?"

I leaned closer still, watching my reflection expand to fill the reflective surfaces of his eyes. Such a wonderful biological invention, the eye. Functional *and* delicious. "Because we can."

Arthur turned his face away. I sighed, leaning back into my own seat.

"Really, Arthur, I wish you wouldn't be that way. I'm only acting according to my nature. Isn't that what you've told me every time one of your countrymen leered at your sister or called me a savage jungle girl? Me, who has never even *seen* a jungle, who originated in a hothouse that spanned a world? 'They are only acting according to their nature.' Those were *your* words. Why is it correct when they do it, and so fearsome when I do?"

"You killed a man."

"He shot me. Twice, might I add. I think he quite deserved what became of him."

Arthur's eyes snapped open. "That does not *matter*," he snarled. "You are not judge, nor jury, nor executioner!"

"No, dear: I am none of those things. I am the vanguard of an invading army, and that means your laws no longer apply to me." I shrugged. "If we fail—and we will not fail—I'll be tried for treason and imprisoned until the Queen can find a suitably gruesome means of execution. If that happens, be sure they put me in a prison with large windows, or I won't live long enough for you to kill me. If we succeed, your laws will be permanently suspended, and cannot be used against me. The things we do tonight are crimes of war. They are not things for which we can be punished in the court of law."

"Britain will not lose."

I sighed. "Oh, my sweet, foolish mammal of a man, it already has. It just doesn't know it yet."

The conveyance rattled to a halt behind the palace, near one of the many entrances used to bring in those who were better than servants, but less than noblemen. There was a soft sighing sound as the springs relaxed, allowing our carriage to sink lower to the ground. I stood, smoothing the wreckage of my skirts with my hands.

"We've arrived," I said. "Do I look ready for an audience with the Queen?"

Arthur merely glared.

"Don't be tedious, Arthur; it's not polite." I opened the carriage door, stepping into the London night.

The air, which would normally have smelled of burning gas and the wood fires used to stoke the steam engines of those too poor to afford solar paneling, smelled like sap and petrichor and electrical discharge. And blood, of course. The streets would be red come morning, painted carnival bright with the lives of those who had built this country. I hesitated a bare moment before kicking off my shoes and allowing the small root surfaces packed into my toes to taste the earth between the cobblestones. Ah, yes; the taste of home. It was falling to the planet's surface with every barrage of laser fire and steam-powered bullets that ripped apart the sky. Our ships were designed to serve more than one purpose, after all, and with every one that fell, the Earth became a little more suited to our needs.

Footsteps behind me telegraphed Arthur's emergence from the carriage. I turned to see him standing in front of the door, backlit by the rainbow and ray gun colored sky. It turned his skin a dozen shifting rainbow shades, from milky pale to carmine, and he was beautiful. I wondered if he would ever understand how beautiful he was. I wasn't sure he'd have the time.

"Come now," I said. "Walk with me."

"I am not a traitor." His voice broke on the last word.

"No. You're not. You're a man doing his duty to his Queen, and taking an ambassador to her, that she might properly negotiate surrender."

Arthur looked unsure, as well he might: I had not, after all, specified who would be surrendering, and who would be the recipient of an empire. But the habit of mannerly comportment was drilled into him, and so he simply nodded, and said, "I pray we may end this peacefully," and walked with me into the palace, while London burned behind us, and the night was radiant with alien light.

6.

> "There were those who would insist that a lady's chief graces were as follows: breeding, beauty, and a blind adherence to the manners of the society in which she takes root, no matter how senseless or silly those manners may be. It was considered better to bloom beautifully and without offending anyone than to grow wanton and in healthy abundance.
>
> "Clearly, this was a civilization cultivating itself for conquest."
>
> —from *Lady Antheia's Guide to Horticultural Warfare*, first printing

---

As I had hoped, the Queen was in her chambers. Sadly, she was there along with the Prince Consort, the Ministers of War, and a dozen other powerful men. I sighed. This would have been so much simpler had she been alone. Humans were not a hive mind in any rational way. A human alone could make reasonable decisions, come to reasonable accords. Humans in a group all seemed to believe they and they alone had the authority to speak for their species, and disputes were resolved by shouting until the loudest won. Truly, this world would be more peaceful once it was ruled by cooler vegetable minds.

All those powerful men turned at our entrance, their eyes taking in my charred, disheveled state and Arthur's pale, shocked face, and reaching the logical conclusion. "Lady Antheia, are you hurt?" asked a Minister, a round, ruddy-cheeked man whose name I had never bothered to remember.

"Not any longer, but thank you for your concern," I said. "I do apologize for the hour. I have a matter of some importance to put before the Queen."

Queen Alice finally turned, a frown on her pretty, pleasure-loving face. She had never been equipped to rule. I was here to do a favor, really. "Lady Antheia. This is most irregular."

"I know, Your Majesty." I proffered a curtsey. "I am here to thank you for your hospitality of these past few years, and request your immediate surrender to the Vegetable Empire. We have superior weaponry, and we are even now amassing the superior numbers we will need to take your world as our own. If you cede yourselves to us, we may be merciful."

And then, exactly as I had expected, all those powerful men drew their powerful weapons and shot me dead where I stood. My consciousness winked out before my body hit the floor.

7.

> "Humanity, in addition to being delicious and very well designed for its environment, was constantly coming up with excuses to make war upon its own kind. If they had survived as an independent species long enough to establish the means for long distance space travel, we might have found ourselves with unwanted rivals for this galaxy's treasures. It is because of this yearning for conquest that runs so strong in the veins of most meat that I must recommend we speed up our efforts to become the only sapient life living free in known space. It is, sadly, the only way to be safe from the threat of empire."
>
> —from *Lady Antheia's Guide to Horticultural Warfare*, first printing

---

I never put my shoes back on.

That may seem like a trifling detail, but that is because few people fully understand the deeply concentrated root systems found on the soles of a diplomat's feet—or whatever passes for feet in the local environment. My body was destroyed, broken beyond repair, and my poor Jill broken with it. But when the Queen's men toted that unwanted seed pod away, they did not notice the small roots that had broken off in the carpet, already working their way down, down, deep into the foundations of the palace.

When we sprout, we sprout quickly, for surprise is our best weapon. Dawn came, and I rose, faceless, a pale green whisper of a thing dressed in a mockery of human form. All in silence, I moved through the chamber to the door beyond, which led to the private apartments of the Queen. She was sleeping, innocent of what was about to befall her, her husband and consort snug beside her in the bed. I did not see them, for I did not have eyes, but there are other ways of sensing such things. She did not know I was there; she presented no threat.

I ate her.

8.

> "It was a small matter for our soldiers to subdue the populace, once they had seen their Queen unmasked as an alien, welcoming the invaders into Buckingham Palace with open arms. Perhaps if we had been a little less swift, there would have been time to mount a resistance...but that was not to be. As the humans once said: the Queen is dead.
>
> Long live the Queen."
>
> —from *Lady Antheia's Guide to Horticultural Warfare*, first printing

---

I set my quill aside, considering the words I had written. They were good words: they would do nicely, and would serve well as a guide to the next invasion of a world like Earth. The fields were rich with our seedlings, and the men of science already looked outward, considering the next path our colony ships would take.

Footsteps behind me alerted me to the approach of my husband—a human custom, yes, but one which many of us who found ourselves with human forms and vaguely human ways of thinking had chosen to observe. It was a diversion, if nothing else, and could provide a new social frame, if it proved useful.

"All done?" asked Arthur, a smile on his emerald lips.

It had been a small thing to take a seedling of an open line, with no ancestral memory, and place it next to Arthur's bound, struggling form. He had thanked me, of course, when his memories settled properly into their new home. He had always been a botanist. Now he could study himself, for centuries if he liked. It was my wedding gift to him.

"Yes," I said, and wrapped my creeper vines around his waist and my arms around his shoulders, and kissed him with the mouth I had stolen from a human Queen. The British Empire had claimed the sun would never set, and they had been wrong, because they had been thinking too small.

For the sun to be shining always, one needs more than a single world. It is vital to acquire a galaxy.

Driving Jenny Home

This story was originally written for the anthology *Out of Tune*, edited by Jonathan Maberry. The submission guidelines asked for something based on an old ballad, and I chose "The Unquiet Grave." Not content with that, I promptly wrote a new song to go with it, because that's just how we roll around here.

My fascination with phantom hitchhikers can be tracked to two sources: *The Song and Story of the Haunted Mansion*, which my mother bought for me on LP when I was very young, and the movie *The Midnight Hour*, which featured a heroic hitchhiking ghost as one of its central characters. I have been exploring and dissecting the legends ever since. That's sort of what I do, and I have a very good time doing it.

NOVEMBER

Jenny can you hear me, I am driving in the rain,
I am looking for you, darling, I am calling out your name,

For I'll do as much for my true love as any lover known—
Let the rain fall on the highway. I'll be taking Jenny home.

It only took three days for them to let me out of the hospital, but that was long enough: Jenny was already in the ground. So I stayed in my room, "recuperating," until my parents told me I was going back to school whether I liked it or not. "Homecoming was a month ago, honey," they said, and "Leigh, this isn't healthy," they said, and I didn't have a choice.

I told them there was something I had to do before I could go back, and while they didn't like it much, at least they understood. I missed the funeral, after all.

It's raining when I walk into the cemetery where they buried my girl. That's right. That's exactly right. It should be raining, because Jenny is dead, and it's all my fault. It should keep raining forever.

Walking between the rows of graves is like something out of a nightmare or a dream—a bad dream, the kind that escapes nightmare territory by dancing on the razor's edge between surrealism and insanity. The kind where the walls bleed lobsters and the sky catches fire when it touches the horizon. But the flowers I've brought to place on Jenny's grave are just flowers. They don't sing or whisper prophecy or turn into butterflies and fly away. When I finally find her tombstone—a simple granite rectangle that can't possibly summarize everything she was and should have been—and lay them down beneath the line that lists her date of birth and death, they don't bring Jenny back to me.

"God, Jenny," I say, sinking to my knees in the grass. "This is like some sick joke, only no one's telling me the punch line, and nobody's laughing. I'd take it back if I could. I'd take it all back if it would bring you home."

Jenny doesn't answer me. Jenny's never going to answer me again.

I stay where I am for what feels like an hour or more, the rain running down the back of my jacket and soaking my hair as I bow my head and cry. This can't be true. This can't be my life. It feels like just yesterday that I was picking her up for homecoming. She wore that dress the color of moonlight on the snow, and she fit in my arms like the missing piece of a puzzle. She's not fitting into anyone's arms now. She's dead and gone and she's not coming back to me.

They lock the cemetery gates at sunset. I don't want to spend the night here, among the graves, and so when the light starts to fade I force myself to move, wiping my tears away and leaning forward to press a kiss against the cold granite of Jenny's headstone.

"I love you," I say. "I'll see you soon."

Then I stand, wet clothes sloshing with every step, and start toward the distant gates. The rain is slacking off a bit, which is good, since the setting sun is making it hard to see, and I'm starting to feel like a teenage emo cliché: sad lesbian in the graveyard in the rain. Jenny wouldn't like seeing me like this.

Maybe that's not the best train of thought, because Jenny's never going to see me again, not like this, and not like anything else.

I'm crying again by the time I reach my car, a 1978 Volvo Bertone I inherited from my father when I turned sixteen and Mom made him dig it out of the garage. It handles like a tank and guzzles gas like nobody's business, but the collision that killed Jenny and put me in the hospital didn't even bend its frame. Jenny would have been fine if she'd been wearing her seatbelt, instead of twisted around rummaging through the back seat. I guess I should hate the car for taking her away from me, but I like being able to get to school, and Jenny always loved the Bertone. She said it was just the right combination of old fashioned and ugly as hell, and she appreciated the contrast.

"That's my girl," I said, putting a hand gently on the door. That's when I see the ticket fluttering against the windshield like a trapped bird in the process of beating itself to death. It hasn't been there long: it's not even soaked through. I grimace. "Fucking cops," I mutter, and reach for it, only to freeze when another hand snatches it up before I can get there. A hand with long, slender fingers, the nails painted a shade of perfect moonlight gold that didn't come out of any bottle. Jenny always mixed her own nail polish. She said wearing anything off-the-rack, from clothes to cosmetics, showed a lack of commitment.

I lift my head. Jenny is standing next to the car in her moonlight dress, her homecoming corsage still tied around her wrist. She smiles, and she looks so sad that it makes me want to die, even though the sight of her is making me want to live like nothing has in weeks.

"Hi, Leigh," she says, and oh, God, her voice is the same as it always was. Nothing has changed. Everything has changed. "Can I get a ride home?"

What is there for me to say?

"Yes," I say, and unlock the car.

But she doesn't get in. Jenny doesn't get in. She just looks at me, her smile fading away a little bit at a time, until she finally says, "There are rules."

"Rules," I echo dumbly. My dead girlfriend is standing in front of me, and she's telling me there are rules. I don't understand why there should be, since I'm clearly losing my mind.

"You have to drive me straight home," she says. "No stops—we're not going to the movies or going to Taco Bell or anything like that. You can't ask me why I'm here. And you can't give me a kiss goodnight."

It's an odd set of restrictions to get from a hallucination. I frown at her for a moment, trying to figure out what my subconscious is telling me—and then I decide I honestly don't care. Jenny's here. Whether she's a hallucination or a ghost (and the fact that she's still holding the parking ticket is a vote for "ghost," unless I'm hallucinating that, too) doesn't matter. All that really matters now is driving Jenny home.

"Okay," I say, and we both get in the car, and I drive us away from the cemetery, and everything's okay again, if only for a little while.

DECEMBER

Jenny was gone when I turned onto her street, disappearing in the moments between checking my mirror and looking back at her. She left the parking ticket in the seat where she had been. She was always thoughtful that way.

That was a month ago. The ticket's been paid, and the shock waves have mostly finished washing through our school. I'm off the cheerleading squad, of course—even if the rest of the girls had sort of known about

Jenny and me back when I was a base and she was a flyer, even though they'd been cool about the fact that we were lesbians, I was responsible for the death of one of our own. They couldn't look at me without seeing her, and I couldn't look at them without seeing her, and we were all tired of being haunted. So I quit the squad, and now no one's trying to use Jenny to define me. They're too busy using her to define everything else.

Jenny's dress at homecoming was moonlight satin? Fine, then, the theme for prom is going to be "Love Under the Moon," and everyone already knows Jenny will be awarded the coveted crown—the other girls who should be talking about campaigning by this point lower their eyes and murmur her name whenever the position of Prom Queen is mentioned, like wanting it would mean wanting what Jenny got: a brutal death and an early grave. They're canonizing her with memory, wearing away her hard edges bit by bit until all that's left is something perfect they can tell their own children about, someday, when they're telling them not to drink and drive.

Jenny hadn't been drinking. Neither had I. Tyler did the drinking for both of us, the big muscle-headed football asshole who thought he was *so* great, and thought Jenny was his for the taking, and learned he was *so* beneath her notice when he saw us dancing together on the far side of the gymnasium—the fat girl in the tuxedo pressed up against the high school fantasy.

We were both cheerleaders, but she was the one everyone remembered. I was just the one who made sure she didn't fall. I had one job. I couldn't even accomplish that.

But God, she was so beautiful that night, like the goddess of the moon come down to hold hands with a mortal girl until the sun came up and the fantasy burned to ash. She was a fairy tale, she was a fiction, and I felt like I still had mud under my fingernails from grounding the pyramid, despite the hours I'd spent scrubbing them clean. I guess that's why I let Tyler and his dumb jock friends get to me when they cornered me by the punchbowl. "Be the bigger person" and "just ignore them" is all well and good for people whose own high school days are fading in the rearview mirror of adulthood, but in the moment, when you're wearing teenage skin…

I didn't throw the first punch. I didn't throw the last one, either. I would probably have been beaten to a pulp if Jenny hadn't thrown herself into the middle of things, shouting at Tyler for being a Neanderthal idiot and shouting at me for letting myself be baited. I said I was sorry. I said I was stupid. I said I wouldn't let it happen again.

She said "Take me home."

I drove home angry. That's the worst part: that's the part I'm never going to forgive myself for. Jenny wasn't speaking to me, just flipping through the radio and sulking—right up until she decided she was cold and undid her belt so she could rummage through the backseat for my discarded tuxedo jacket. That was when Tyler came around the corner, drunk and angry and driving a Prius that didn't stand a chance against my ancient bruiser of a Volvo. He slammed into my bumper, crumpling his car like a tin can and putting Jenny through the windshield.

The impact was enough to knock me out, even though I was wearing my seatbelt. By the time I woke up, it was too late. Jenny was gone.

How could I have been so stupid?

It's been two months since Jenny died and a month since I saw her. I've parked next to the cemetery gates every goddamn day since then, listening to a playlist of her favorite songs—too much country, too many teenage death ballads from the 1950s, and not nearly enough good old-fashioned rock and roll. Even if it's just a glimpse, I need to see her again, to that I wasn't hallucinating when I saw her before, and most of all, to know I'm not losing my mind.

But the sun is going down, and there's no sign of Jenny. The grassy lawn is empty; the cemetery gates are closed and locked, as impassable as the wall to some forbidden city. I sigh. She's not coming. I'm losing my mind. I've had a month to think about what happened here, what I heard and saw and smelled. There's no way that it was real; things like that don't happen. I close my eyes and lean back in my seat, breathing in through my nose and out from my mouth, and wait for the urge to wait for her to pass away.

It doesn't pass.

But someone's knocking on the window.

The sound is enough to make me yelp, twisting in my seat...and there's Jenny in her dress like moonlight, with her hair pinned up just so, long golden curls anchored in an elaborate updo by little pins with glittering silver stars on them. My fingers itch to plunge into that hair and unwind it strand by strand, until the smell of her shampoo fills the world. I don't move. I can't move. Jenny frowns and knocks on the glass again.

I don't answer. Instead, I open the car door and get out, my eyes fixed on her face the whole time. I can see her—fine, the mind plays tricks. I can hear her, I can smell her, and that doesn't prove *anything*, that doesn't prove anything except that I miss her so badly I can taste it, and every day that I wake up and Jenny's not there is like another needle in my heart. I keep thinking it'll run out of room, and then the morning comes and proves me wrong. She's not real, she can't be real, and I'm going to prove it to myself here and now. I'm going to—

My hand catches her wrist. Her skin is cool, like she's been standing outside without a coat for too long, but it's still her skin, soft and familiar and *real*. My breath catches in my throat. I try to speak. Nothing happens, and Jenny daintily pulls herself free.

"You haven't answered," she says.

"Jenny, God, what is going on here?" I grab for her again, but she's too quick for me—she steps back and out of the range of my questing fingers, leaving them to close on empty air. "Why are you doing this? Do your parents know that you're not dead? Why are you hiding?"

"Because all I'm doing is asking for a ride home, and I'm only doing it because you keep coming here and wanting me to," she replies. She looks at me, eyes wide and sad and pleading, and I know the truth. There's no other explanation. "I died, Leigh. I died, and you didn't get me home. Even though you promised. You didn't get me home."

"I'll get you home, I promise." I'm making promises I can't keep—I'm making promises to a *dead girl*, and I've seen enough horror movies to know that this is a terrible idea, but fuck, what do I care? A week ago I was thinking about killing myself. At least this way I'll do something useful with what's left of my life. Any promise in the world is worth making, if I'm making it to Jenny.

"You can try," she says, and disappears, leaving the scent of vanilla in her wake. Vanilla, and something darker, something wet and green and old, like the moss that grows on gravestones.

Somehow, I'm not surprised when I turn around and find her sitting in the car, belt already buckled, hands folded primly in her lap. *This is a dream,* I think, and I'm opening the car door, I'm sliding back into my seat, and Jenny is there, Jenny with her corsage on her wrist and a sad, distant look on her face. *This is a dream, and I never want to wake up again.*

"Drive, Leigh," she says, and there's a sudden tension in her voice, like she wants to say so much more, but she doesn't know how. "You have to drive, or I can't stay."

"What?"

"*Drive.*"

There's no denying the urgency in the word, and so I start the engine and hit the gas, and we're rolling, moving away from the cemetery and starting on the long road back to Jenny's house. She lives—she lived, she's *dead*, and I can't let myself forget that, not even with her sitting next to me, the smell of her vanilla perfume rolling through the cab like a storm front—on the other side of town. We have twenty miles to go, and that's if I take the short way.

She never said I had to do that. I turn left when I should have turned right, going for the route we always used to take when we were thinking that maybe a brief stop by the side of a wooded road would be a good way to spend a little of the afternoon.

Jenny is silent for the first part of the drive. I glance her way, but her attention is on the window, watching as the housing developments that ring the town like mushrooms melt away into forest, the semi-untouched wood that still owns this part of the state. If it weren't for her perfume, I'd think I was hallucinating her. Maybe I could still be hallucinating her. Do hallucinations have a scent?

I'm mulling that over when Jenny says, in a small, wounded voice, "You were supposed to drive me home. That was the deal, when my parents said that I could go to the dance with you. You told my father you would get me home by midnight. Remember? You promised."

I glance at her, startled, and startle myself all over again when she fills my field of vision, Jenny in her moonlight dress, Jenny with her golden hair, Jenny not under the ground and filling the bellies of a million worms. "I didn't mean to have an accident. You should have been wearing your belt," I say. The words are mulish, sullen: they fall into the space between us like clots of earth onto her grave.

"It scared me when I saw Tyler hitting you," she says, and turns away from me, looking out the window. "He was so much bigger than you were, and he'd been drinking, and I just wanted to get away before somebody got hurt. I knew it would piss him off, seeing us there, and I didn't care, because I loved you. I should have cared. All-American boys get the All-American girls, right? That's what the Founding Fathers died for." Scorn drips from her voice. I flinch from it. I can't help myself. "I knew it was stupid. I knew I should yell for one of the chaperones and tell them that we wanted to stay, and that he needed to go. But I was so mad. You made me so *mad*, Leigh. Why couldn't you keep your temper for just one night? It was supposed to be our night."

"I'm sorry," I say, and it's small, and it's stupid, and it's not enough.

"So am I," says Jenny.

She doesn't say another word during the drive. I have to look away from her when I turn onto her street—it's an unprotected left, if I watched my dead girlfriend, I'd be joining her in the ground—and when I look back, Jenny's gone, leaving only the faint scent of vanilla and the feeling that I've lost her all over again.

I drive by her house without slowing down. There's nothing for me there.

Nothing at all.

JANUARY

It's apparently been long enough since the funeral for public opinion to have shifted: I come back from Christmas break and the shrines to Jenny are gone, and the plans for the prom theme to match her home-coming dress have all been forgotten, replaced by something cliché about Greek gods and the beauty of Olympus. I should be happy. I'm not being reminded of Jenny every time I turn a corner or go into the school office. Instead, rage paces and snarls under my sternum like a captive animal. How *dare* they forget about her? How *dare* they go on with their lives like nothing has changed? Jenny is dead. She's not coming back to school tomorrow, or the next day, or ever, and it's not right for them to let go of her like this.

The school counselor says this is healthy. Says they're "moving on" and "coming to terms" and that maybe it's time my parents start paying for some independent counseling services for me, since it's pretty clear she's not going to be able to help me properly through my grief—not with me refusing to let go of Jenny's memory. I call her a bitch and get thrown out of her office, with a week's detention and a letter to take home to my mother. I should probably feel bad about that. I can't find the energy. I'm walking through a school that was haunted by Jenny only a few weeks ago, and now seems content to go on as if she'd never existed.

Three months. That's apparently the lifespan of teenage grief. That's how long our fickle hearts are meant to hold on to someone who's not there anymore. Anything more than that is cause for concern.

Poor, absent Tyler is the new darling of the student body. Tyler, the football hero who may never play again; Tyler, who was just trying to have a good time when he got drunk and crashed into my car, killing my girlfriend almost instantly; Tyler, who was the sort of guy every one of us should aspire to be.

I'm starting to think about murder.

I'm thinking about murder when I park at the curb in front of the cemetery, my hands resting lightly on the wheel and my eyes fixed on the middle distance, visions of Tyler's tortured face dancing like sugarplums through my daydreams. There's no rap on the window, but there's the smell of vanilla, and the sudden, definite feeling that I am not alone in the car. I start the engine before I turn to flash a smile at Jenny, and say, "I'm happy to give you a ride home."

"This isn't healthy," says Jenny, a frown on her face and a curl of golden hair hanging across her forehead like a banner. "You shouldn't still be showing up here."

"Why wouldn't I?" I pull away from the curb, turning my attention back to the road at the last possible moment. I don't want to take my eyes away from her, but I'm coming to learn the rules of our monthly encounters: I have to drive. That's what matters more than anything else. "You need a ride home. I promised."

"Leigh..."

"How could I live with myself if I knew you weren't at peace because I broke my word to you?"

"But I'm *not* at peace, Leigh." She sounds like she's in pain. I start to take my foot off the gas, automatically turning to reach for her and try to hug that pain away. I see her face when she recoils, when she cries, "Drive! You have to drive!"

My foot presses down almost of its own accord. The car lurches forward, my heart pounding against my ribs, and for a moment, I think *this is it*: this is how I die.

But the moment passes, and the car is back under my control, and we're rolling easy down the road as Jenny says, "I can't rest in peace. You won't let me. Everyone else is starting to let go; they're starting to ease up on my memory—even my parents. And then there's you."

"I miss you." The words are small and stupid and big enough to encompass the entire world. I miss her. That's all that I'm capable of doing anymore.

"You have to let me go."

"Or what?"

"Or this keeps happening over and over again," she says. "I keep showing up. You keep driving me home. I keep disappearing. Over and over."

"For how long?"

"I don't know. Forever, I guess."

I think about that as I drive, the streets melting away around us. The air in the cab smells like vanilla. At some point Jenny realizes I'm not going to say anything else, and she turns on the radio, spinning through the stations until she finds a channel that's playing the kind of music she likes, all soft country ballads and too much auto-tune. One of her favorite bands is on, performing a song that hadn't been released yet when she died. She makes a small, wordless sound of delight, and that's it: that seals the deal. I love her and I want her to rest easy, but that doesn't mean I can let her go. Not yet. Maybe not ever.

"I'll have their new album when I pick you up next month," I say, as we turn onto her street. "You can listen to it during the drive."

"Leigh—"

"I'm sorry you're not resting in peace. But I'm not resting in peace either, so at least we can not rest in peace together for a little while longer. If that's selfish, I don't really care. I miss you too much. I can't just stop."

Her hand touches my cheek, fingers cool. I don't turn. I don't want to see her disappear.

"I love you," she says.

"I love you too," I answer, and she's gone, and I drive past her house without slowing down or stopping. Forever is a long time. I'm not sure it would be long enough.

FEBRUARY

Now they say that love is ended by betrayal or the grave,
And they tell me to give up on her, the one I couldn't save,
But I'll do as much for my true love as any lover known—
I will know no rest or solace 'til I'm taking Jenny home.

Valentine's Day without Jenny is another word for Hell. I stay home sick, choosing another black mark on my attendance record over the school halls festooned with paper hearts and filled with girls giggling over their discount chocolates and wilting roses. Two weeks later, when Jenny appears in front of the cemetery, there's a bouquet of daisies—her favorite flower—waiting for her on the dashboard, along with the CD I promised her.

She's still my Valentine. Death doesn't change that.

Death doesn't really change anything.

MARCH

It's been four months since Jenny died, and I'm starting to think about the mechanics of suicide. It can't be that hard to kill somebody, can it? Tyler managed it, and Tyler's a dumb jock with more muscles than brains. Or he was, anyway: they still don't know whether he's ever going to wake up, and even if he does, there's no way of knowing whether he'll ever walk again. His football career is over, buried alongside Jenny's body, and that might be a comfort to me, if I didn't miss her so goddamn much, if his teammates didn't glare at me when they pass me in the halls, like I was the one who suggested he try to put the make on my girlfriend at the homecoming dance. None of this was my idea, I want to scream. None of this is the way that I wanted my junior year of high school to go. But try telling them that. Too many words, too many syllables, too many *concepts* for their atrophied little brains. Tyler, Jenny, and I wound up in a weird sort of triangle on the night of the dance, two of us competing for one girl, and now Jenny's dead and Tyler's in a coma and I'm still here, which makes me the perfect target.

I guess if I were as suicidal as I feel I'd bait them and let them beat me to death behind the school. At least that way they'd get punished for it, and I'd finally get to stop living in a world that doesn't have Jenny in it anymore.

...but I don't really live in that world, do I? I just exist there.

It's four months since Jenny's funeral, and here I am again, parked in front of the cemetery, waiting.

The sun reaches the horizon and again, Jenny: Jenny in her moonlight gown, Jenny with her golden hair, and her corsage still fresh on her wrist. Mine is just so many fallen petals now, sitting in a dish next to my bed where the smell can chase me down into my dreams. Jenny, looking at me with fond exasperation, one satin-toed foot tapping on the grassy knoll.

"Again, Leigh?" she asks, and before I can answer her she chases the question with a question, asking, "Can I get a ride home?"

"Always," I say, and then she's in the car, appearing like a miracle, and my foot is on the gas, and everything is right with the world. As long as I'm with Jenny, everything is fine.

Again, I take the long way back to her house, choosing more time with her over the expediency of city streets. It's better this way, I tell myself, and I realize I actually mean it: if this *is* a dream, I know it'll end when I make the final turn onto her block, and if it's *not* a dream—if my dead girlfriend is really riding in my front seat like this sort of thing happens every day—then the last thing I want is for someone to see us. They might react the same way I did, with confusion and disbelief and denial. Or they might decide I didn't deserve this, and give someone else the task of driving Jenny home.

"Tyler's still in a coma, you know," I say, because I have to say something; I have to fill the silence between us with words, or it's going to drown me. "They're not sure whether he's ever going to wake up again."

"Good," she spits, with such venom that it startles me. "He deserves to be caught that way. Not living, not dead. Just lost in limbo, for as long as their machines can keep him there."

I worry my lip between my teeth before asking, "You really mean that?"

"Yes," she says, and "no," she says, and "I would be here with you if it weren't for him. I would be here with my family. Really here, I mean, with skin and bones and a heartbeat, not drifting through every time I need someone to drive me home. I'd be getting older. You know, I read this book once, about a unicorn who'd been turned into a human? And she hated it. She said she could feel her body dying all around her. I know what she meant now, Leigh, and I *miss* it. I miss the feeling of my body dying, because it meant I had a body that could die. It meant I was real. More than just a memory. It meant I belonged to the world. I'm never going to have that again, and it's all Tyler's fault."

There are so many words that it's almost overwhelming. It takes me a moment to process them all, and we're moving the whole time, getting closer and closer to the point where she leaves me again. I want to ask the best question in the world, I want to stun her with how well I understand, but when I open my mouth, what comes out is, "So stay."

"I can't," she says. "I'm dead, remember?"

There's laughter in her voice, and pain too, like she likes remembering what she is as little as I like being reminded of it. I don't say anything, but

I hit the gas just a little harder, and neither one of us says anything for the rest of the drive.

It's just like before. I turn onto her street, and the smell of vanilla fills the car, and when I turn to look at her, she's gone like she was never there. I may as well have been driving a hallucination across the city. I pull up to a stop sign and lean over to touch the seat. It's warm. She was there enough to warm up the seat with the body that she doesn't have.

Maybe that means something.

I hold that thought firmly as I drive myself back home. Jenny could still warm a seat, and maybe that means something...but what, I just don't know.

APRIL

Jenny's already standing on the curb when I pull up, her arms clasped tight around herself like she's cold. I find myself wishing she'd died wearing something warmer, which turns quickly to wishing she'd never died at all, and that's dangerous; that's the kind of thinking that I can chase down the rabbit holes of my mind all night long. So I just stop the car and roll down the window and wait for her to ask the question.

"Can I get a ride?"

"Always," I say, and she disappears, leaving me alone. This time, my heart doesn't stop: I've learned enough to know what comes next. I turn, and there she is in the passenger seat, her seatbelt fastened, a smile on her perfect lips. Trying to be casual, I say, "You look good today."

"One good thing about death: no more bad hair days," she says, with a laugh that isn't a laugh at all: more a close cousin to a sob. Kissing cousin, even—the two are so tangled together that I couldn't pry them apart if I tried. "I'm really glad I like this dress."

"I wonder if that's what you'd be wearing if they'd buried you in something else." The words are thoughtless. I cringe.

Jenny doesn't seem to mind. If anything, she looks relieved. She's been dead for six months, and this is the first time I've talked to her like that mattered at all: like it changed anything about our relationship, apart from how often we get to see each other. "I think so," she says. "It's different for everybody, but most of the ghosts I've met have been wearing something they cared about when they were alive. Lots of wedding gowns, tuxedos, graduation robes…this was the prettiest dress I ever owned. It only makes sense that I'd be wearing it now."

"I'd say that wearing it made you the prettiest girl in the world, but you didn't need a dress for that."

Jenny laughs without the sob this time, and leans forward to turn on the radio. "Just drive," she says.

So I do, and everything is perfect, and I could go on like this forever, just me and Jenny and our monthly date, her in her homecoming dress, me in whatever I threw on that day, driving into eternity.

MAY

Now they say that love is something you'd be lucky to forget,
But I say that I was lucky on the day that we first met,
And I'll do as much for my true love as any lover known—
I will roam the lonesome highways 'til I'm bringing Jenny home.

The halls are buzzing with the news that Tyler—elevated in his absence to young god, deified like Jenny was, but without the absence of flesh to allow his memory to erode—has started responding to treatment: why, he *opened his eyes* yesterday, which is nothing short of a miracle as far as his legion of adoring fans is concerned. If this continues, he could actually *wake up* soon! Imagine! Tyler, All-American high school god, walking among us mere mortals like we have the right to glory in his physical presence and breathe his rarified air!

It makes me want to vomit, or punch someone, or scream. But all these things are anti-social, and the school counselors are still watching me more closely than I like, since apparently my inability to "move on" from the death of the first girl I ever loved means I'm a potential suicide risk or school shooter or something. I'm not really clear on what the problem is, and no one else seems to be either. They just know that I'm not fitting easy into their pre-fab high school mold anymore, and so they watch me, and they wait for me to make a mistake.

Tyler's name is on everyone's lips today, even the teachers, who urge us to focus on our studies because "that's what Tyler would want us to do." By seventh period, I've had enough, and when my history teacher invokes Tyler's name in an effort to quiet us down, I stick my hand in the air and ask, "Do you think Tyler was quiet when he was committing vehicular manslaughter? Or do you think he had time to scream at the sight of Jenny's corpse before his brain damage kicked in?"

I get sent to the principal's office for my trouble, a red detention slip clutched in my hand, and it's not until I see the sun setting through the study hall window that I realize what this means—that I won't reach the cemetery until hours after I usually arrive. I bolt to my feet.

"Sit *down*, Miss Winslow!" barks the Vice-Principal, and my knees buckle, years of trained obedience ordering me back into my seat before my conscious mind is invited to the party. I shoot another panicked glance at the window, but it's too late, it's too late; the sun is dipping down below the horizon. I don't know much about the strange dance that I've been locked in since homecoming, and still something tells me that this is a line that should never have been crossed. She appears at sunset. Well, the sun has set, and when I reach the cemetery, Jenny won't be waiting.

Even knowing that, I run for my car as soon as we're released, breaking speed laws all the way down to the cemetery gates. But Jenny isn't there. I stay until midnight, listening to her favorite CD over and over again and praying to a god I don't entirely believe in, and Jenny never comes. I broke the rules. I broke the chain.

What if Jenny never comes again? What am I going to do then?

JUNE

I skip school on the day Jenny's due to appear, even knowing she won't be there until sunset. I missed her once. I can't run the risk of missing her again. Not when we only get one night a month, and that night is limited to however long it takes to drive from the cemetery to her house—not exactly the kind of dates I used to lay awake dreaming about. I haven't kissed her since the night she died. I ache to hold her in my arms, kiss her cheek, and tell her how much I've missed her, how much I miss her every single day. But if I can't do that, I can at least do this: I can be here; I can wait for her until she comes.

I have to move the car three times when the security guard comes by and gives me the hairy eyeball, suspicion written plainly on his face. What's a chubby teenage girl in a beat-up Volvo doing parked in front of the cemetery? What mischief am I planning?

No mischief, sir, I want to say, but I can't imagine he'd take well to being told I was just here to pick up my girlfriend, who's been dead for seven months—don't worry, she looks just fine, on account of how she doesn't have a body anymore. I'd be lucky if he called the cops. It's more likely he'd call the local loony bin, and I'd be hauled away by men in white coats, screaming for my ghost girlfriend all the while. No. Nuh-uh. I don't have time to be committed, and so I move the car again and again, wasting gas and wasting time as I wait for the magic moment when Jenny will appear.

Then I'm coming around the corner and there she is, blazing up in the headlights like a fairy tale princess, all moonlight gold and helpless longing. I stop the car, roll down the window, look out at her, and smile.

"Hey," I say. "You need a ride?"

I'm trying to sound cool and smooth and like the sort of person who belongs in a place like this. All I really manage is sounding like my dorky self. Jenny still smiles as she walks toward the car. That's all the validation I need.

"Where were you last month, Leigh?" she asks. "I thought maybe you were getting over me."

"That's never going to happen," I say. "I had detention." She disappears, and then she's in the car with me, and my heart hurts from the reality of her. I know that what I have to say will hurt her, but I have to say it anyway: "Tyler's waking up."

Jenny goes still, and it's not until that moment that I realize she isn't breathing, she's *never* been breathing, not any of the times I've seen her or any of the nights when I've driven her home. The realization changes something. It's like for the first time I can't pretend she's not dead, not on any level. There is only one living body in this car, only one person who's getting older, only one unicorn trapped in a human form. The other person, the Jenny-shaped person…she's dead and gone, she's dwindling into dust underground, and she's never coming back to me. This is the closest we're ever going to get, these strange moments of stolen time in my car.

"He shouldn't get to wake up," she says finally. There's a bitterness in her voice that runs all the way down to the bone, the kind of dark, resentful hatred that used to be reserved for people who abused animals or argued against gay marriage. I bite my lip and keep driving, not wanting to see the look on her face as she continues, "*I* didn't get to wake up. Why should he?"

"He may never walk again."

"Well isn't that a shame—oh, wait. I'm *definitely* never going to walk again, because I'm dead, and it's his fault, and I can't even rest easy in my grave and forget about all this, because you won't let me go. So what do you want me to do, Leigh? Be happy for him? Oh, hooray, the man who killed me is waking up, and maybe his life's been changed forever, but it's still a *life*. He still gets to have a life. He gets to grow up and get old and I get to keep asking you to drive me home. How is that fair?"

"It's not," I say quietly.

"Then what are you going to do about it?" There's a challenge in her voice that I don't know quite how to answer, and so I don't. I just drive her home.

What else am I supposed to do?

JULY

Well, I'm supposed to commit murder, for one thing.

It's a little surprising that I didn't think of it sooner, but as the days stretch out and the school year winds to an end, the thought preys on me more and more often. How hard could it be, really, to kill someone who's bedridden, slipping in and out of consciousness, and incapable of fighting back? Not that hard. Getting to him is going to be the difficult part…and wouldn't it make Jenny happy to know that I loved her enough to kill for her? I want to see her smile, *really* smile, just one more time. And not just from her memorial page in the yearbook, where they've used a picture of her in her homecoming dress—the only dress she has anymore—and her corsage. None of the pictures in her memorial collage have me in them. Without Jenny and the cheerleading squad to drag me into the school's social limelight I'm fading from everyone's memory, another high school weirdo worthy only of dismissal.

Maybe that's a good thing, given what I'm planning to do.

It wasn't a plan at first; just an idle thought, a continuation of that half-conversation that I hadn't been able to finish with Jenny. But it's grown, bit by bit, into something bigger and more powerful than it was when it began. Tyler killed Jenny. Tyler doesn't deserve to have any kind of a life, not when Jenny doesn't get to. Tyler needs to die, and if I want to show her that I'm still a good girlfriend, I need to be the one who kills him. It's as simple as that.

I don't say anything when I go to pick her up; I just smile, and hand her a copy of the yearbook so she can see all the nice things people said about her after she was gone and in the ground, and then I drive her home. It's the least that I can do, all things considered.

AUGUST

Jenny, I was foolish, I was selfish, I'm ashamed,
And I'm praying you'll forgive me, though I know I should be blamed,
For I'll do as much for my true love as any lover known—
I will never know salvation 'til I'm taking Jenny home.

Tyler has his own room—naturally he does, his parents have money and they've never been shy about spending it on their beloved only son. That makes things simpler. Finding it is easy. Our classmates have sent offerings of flowers and stuffed toys in such great numbers that when I walk up to the admission desk with a bouquet of roses in my hands, the nurse barely looks up from her romance novel before spitting out his room number, three little digits that don't seem like nearly enough information to lead me to murder. But there they are, and there I go, walking down the hall unquestioned, the roses in my hands somehow serving as an all-access pass.

I've heard they don't allow flowers in the ICU, but apparently Tyler's far enough along the road to recovery that they've moved him into a lower security grade. That, too, works in my favor.

His door isn't locked. Three strikes, Tyler; you're out.

The room is dim and quiet, save for the soft, steady rasp of the machines that keep him alive. He's a wasted skeleton of a man, all that football muscle melted away to reveal the scarecrow that was sleeping for so long inside his skin. I stop at the foot of the bed, looking at him. Maybe this isn't about unicorns at all; maybe this is some kind of strange Wizard of Oz parable, with Jenny just trying to get home and Tyler trapped in the echoing cavern of his own mind. I can't decide whether that makes me the Lion or the Tin Man. Am I looking for courage, or am I wishing for a heart?

Now that I'm here, I don't know what to do. I don't have a syringe; I can't inject air bubbles into his arm like they do on Dad's crime shows, and I wouldn't know how to do it even if I could. I'd put a pillow over his face, but he has machines to do his breathing for him, and I'm pretty sure they'd start beeping like crazy if I pulled them loose.

The door opens and closes behind me. "More flowers?" asks an unseen woman. "Well, put them with the rest. Poor boy's lucky he doesn't have allergies. That would just be one more problem on top of a mountain of them."

"Is...is he going to be okay?" I'm not really concerned about Tyler's welfare—I'm *not*—but I'd expected him to look more like, well, himself. A great big bear of a teenage boy, briefly bedridden, gathering the strength to jump right back into his life. Not this wasted bundle of bones and sickness.

"That depends on how you measure 'okay,' I suppose." The owner of the voice is a middle aged woman in pale pink scrubs. She takes the flowers from my hands, apparently able to sense that I can't bring myself to move. "Is he going to live? At this point, the prognosis is good. His folks have paid for the best care, and he's got a strong will. He's stubborn. Stubbornness counts for a lot in cases like these. But is he ever going to walk again? Throw a pass or kick a ball or anything like that? No, I don't think that's likely."

"Oh." I pause then, frowning. "Should you be telling me this?"

"A pretty little thing like you only sneaks into a hospital with a bunch of flowers for two reasons: love or hate. I read the papers. I know which it is." The nurse looks over her shoulder at me as she sets my roses amongst the rest. "She won't rest any easier if you kill him, and neither will you. Are you sticking to the rules? Do you drive her home when she asks you to?"

My throat is a thin straw through which only air can pass. I squeak a few times, trying to speak, and finally settle for a nod.

"That's good. Have you tried to kiss her?"

I've dreamt about it. That isn't the same thing. I shake my head.

The nurse nods approvingly. "That's good. That's real good. It's not safe for a girl like you to be kissing a girl like her. There are consequences, when the living love the dead. Now I'm going to ask one more question, and I'll thank you to find your voice, since your answer is going to determine whether or not I call for security. I'm assuming you came here to kill this boy. You can go ahead and correct me if I'm wrong, but that's not my question. Are you still planning to try?"

"N-no, ma'am," I manage. "He shouldn't be alive when Jenny's not, but it's not my place to change that. I guess the worst thing I can do to him is leave him alive."

"Good girl." She smiles at me, and then glances meaningfully to the clock above the door. "You'd better hurry if you want to pick her up on time."

I want to stay and ask her what she knows about ghosts, how she understands my arrangement with Jenny...who she's been driving home. But she's right: the sun will be down soon, and if I want to make it to the cemetery, I need to go, and I don't really want to be here, in this room where time is rotting on the vine. So I turn and run, leaving the hospital, leaving Tyler to his own living hell, and it's not until Jenny is sliding into her place beside me that I really wonder what that nurse knew, or why she asked if I'd been trying to kiss my girl.

I go back to the hospital the next day. The nurse I met in Tyler's room isn't there.

Somehow, that's not really a surprise.

SEPTEMBER

School starts up again in an explosion of cheerleaders and football players wearing orange and green uniforms and smiles like they just won the universal lottery. It's freshmen slinking in the halls and sophomores seeming suddenly easy in their skins; it's juniors with their chests puffed up with upperclassman pride and seniors smiling beatifically, rulers of their small, time-delineated kingdom. It's all so *stupid*, and there was a time when I would have loved it. I would have been walking in formation with the rest of the cheerleaders, Jenny by my side, and we would have been queens of the world. Homecoming last year was supposed to be our grand declaration of love, and by now everyone would have been used to the idea that we were together. We could have had one perfect year of high school, me and Jenny, Jenny and me.

Instead, I'm just another nobody at the edge of the crowd, wondering why this ever seemed to matter. All the memorials to Jenny are gone, and there's a whole new class of freshmen who never knew her, and will never know that they're supposed to miss her. Summer has restored the campus, sweeping its ghosts away, and now I'm the only one who's haunted.

I don't know how long I can live like this.

I'm still dwelling on that when it comes time to pick Jenny up again; she slides into the car, all vanilla and moonlight, and asks, "Well? How's senior year?"

She still loves the idea of the future we crafted for ourselves, back when we were lying on our backs behind the tumbling mats, hands entangled, and both of us were breathing. I shake my head and start the car. "Same shit, different semester," I say. And then, because the question is burning me, I ask, "Why am I not allowed to kiss you?"

Jenny is silent.

"I mean, I get to drive you home. I know you're solid, I've touched your hands and seen you hold things. So why can't I kiss you? What makes it so wrong to want to kiss my girlfriend?"

"I'm dead, Leigh." Her voice is the whispering of wind among the gravestones, barely audible, impossible to ignore.

"So what? You're still my girl. I'm not giving up on you."

"I'm dead, and you're not."

I've thought about changing that so many times. "And?"

"And if I kissed you, it would…" Jenny sighs. "Everything dies, Leigh. Everything. But some things make you die faster."

"Like kissing dead girls?"

"Like kissing dead girls." Jenny reaches over and touches my hand, gentle as a promise, cruel as a prayer. "Homecoming is next month. I've been buried for almost a year. Don't you think it's time you let me go?"

I don't answer her, because that question is every answer I've been seeking for the last eleven months. "I think it's time that something changed, yeah," I say, and we drive on.

OCTOBER

My tuxedo still fits. Grief either bulks you up or slims you down, and I guess I've gone for the latter; too many days when I couldn't bring myself to eat, too many nights spent crying until I threw up. It was a little snug when I wore it the first time and now it's a little loose, but I look okay. I think Jenny will appreciate it.

"Are you going to homecoming?" asks Mom, when she sees me coming down the stairs. She sounds surprised and maybe hopeful, like this is a sign things are changing for the better.

"Yeah." Homecoming isn't tonight—it's always on a Saturday, and it's only Monday now—but this is the anniversary of Jenny's death, and I don't feel like correcting my mother. I finish descending the stairs and press a kiss against her cheek, sweeter than a note left on my dresser, crueler than an explanation. I don't think there's any way to explain what I've decided to do. "Don't wait up, okay?"

"I won't," she says, relief plain on her face. "Who's the lucky girl?"

"It's a surprise." My new boutonniere is already pinned to the front of my tuxedo. I figure Jenny doesn't need a corsage—she still has hers from last year—but I bought her daisies, just to make the symbolism clear.

"Have fun tonight."

"I will." I should feel bad, I know I should, but I can't. There's nothing for me here, and I still have to keep my promise. I have to finish driving Jenny home.

I pull up to the cemetery just as the sun is starting to go down, and Jenny's there, my Jenny, in her dress like moonlight. She gasps a little when I get out of the car and she sees me in my tuxedo. That's what I was hoping for, that moment of shock, when she's too busy staring to react as I stride toward her, the daisies held out in my hand.

"These are for you," I say, pressing them into her hands. She takes them—she's solid, she's *solid*, because she's holding the flowers—and is still looking at them when I lean forward and press my lips to hers.

Her lips taste like they always have, like vanilla lip gloss, but there's something else there, something dark and sad and dry as dust. She pulls back, eyes wide and filled with dismay. "Do you know what you've done?" she demands, and I *do* know, I *do* know what I've done.

So I smile and say, "Too late now," and this time when I kiss her, she doesn't pull away. We'll get into the car soon; I'll drive her home, and this time, when whatever happens happens, I won't survive. That's all right. That's what I wanted.

I made her a promise, after all. I promised that I'd get her all the way home.

Jenny, darling Jenny, there is no need to explain,
I have seen your lonely graveside, I have waited in the rain,
And I'll do as much for my true love as any lover known—
Though my family will grieve me, I'll be driving Jenny home.

There Is No Place for Sorrow in the Kingdom of the Cold

Again, dolls.

Dolls have been with us throughout human history. They are playmates and protectors of children—who doesn't feel safer with a companion to clutch when the shadows grow too deep? Yet somehow, they've become a part of the horror landscape. This story was originally written for Ellen Datlow's *The Doll Collection*, a book of stories centered around dolls with only one requirement: The dolls couldn't be inherently evil. That's fine. People are more than evil enough for me.

The doll shop described at the beginning of this story doesn't exist, but oh, I wish it did. I would spend all my money there, and be the happiest Seanan in the world.

The air in the shop smelled of talcum, resin, and tissue, with a faint, almost indefinable undertone of pine and acid-free paper. I walked down the rows of collectable Barbies and pre-assembled ball-jointed dolls to the back wall, where the supplies for the serious hobbyists were kept. Pale, naked bodies hung on hooks, while unpainted face plates stared with empty sockets from behind their plastic prisons. Clothing, wigs, and eyes were kept in another part of the shop, presumably so it would be harder to keep track of how much you were spending. As if anyone took up ball-jointed dolls thinking it would be a cheap way to pass the time. We all knew we were making a commitment that would eat our bank accounts from the inside out.

I looked from empty face to empty face, searching for the one that called to me, that whispered "I could be the vessel of your sorrows." It would have been easier if I'd been in a position to cast my own; resin isn't easy to work with compared to vinyl or wax, but it's possible, if you have the tools, and the talent, and the time. I had the tools and the talent. Only time was in short supply.

Father would have hated that. He'd always said time was the one resource we could never acquire more of—unlike inspiration, or hope, or even misery, it couldn't be bottled or preserved, and so we had to spend it carefully, measuring it out where it would do the most good. I could have been making beautiful dolls, both for my own needs and to enrich the world. Instead, I spent my days in a sterile office, doing only as much as I needed to survive and stay connected to the Kingdom of the Cold.

My head ached as I looked at the empty, waiting faces. I had waited too long again. Father did an excellent job when he made me, but my heart was never intended to hold as much emotion as a human could. "Perfection is for God," he used to say. "We will settle for the subtly flawed, and the knowledge that when we break, we return home." Because we were flawed—all of us—we had to bleed off the things we couldn't contain, sorrow and anger and joy and loneliness, packing them carefully in shells of porcelain, resin, and bone. I needed the bleed. It would keep me from cracking, and each vessel I filled would be another piece of my eventual passage home.

Times have changed. People live longer, but that hasn't translated into longer childhoods. Once I could have paid my passage to the Kingdom just by walking through town and seeing people embracing my creations, offering up their own small, unknowing tithes of delight and desolation. Those days are over. Father was the last of us to walk in Pandora's grace, and I do what I must to survive.

A round-cheeked face with eyes that dipped down at the corner and lips that formed a classic cupid's bow pout peeked from behind the other boxes. I plucked it from the shelf, hoisting it in my hand, feeling the weight and the heart of it. Yes: this was my girl, or would be, once I had gathered the rest of her. The hard part was ahead of me, but the essential foundation was in my hand.

It didn't take long to find the other pieces I needed: the body, female, pale and thin but distinctly adult, from the curve of the hips to the slight swell of the breasts. The wig, white as strawberry flowers, and the eyes, red as strawberries. I had clothing that would fit her. There was already a picture forming in my mind of a white and red girl, lips painted just so, cheeks blushed in the faintest shades of cream.

Willow appeared as I approached the counter, her eyes assessing the contents of my basket before she asked, "New project, dear?"

"There's always a new project." I put the basket down next to the register. "It's been a long couple of weeks at work. I figured I deserved a treat."

Willow nodded in understanding. The women who co-owned my favorite doll shop were in it as much for the wholesale prices on their own doll supplies as to make a profit: I, and customers like me, were the only reason the place could keep its doors open. I prayed that would last as long as Father did. I couldn't shop via mail order—there was no way of knowing whether I was getting the right thing, and I couldn't work with materials that wouldn't work with me. I'd tried a few times while I was at college, repainting Barbie dolls with shaking hands and a head that felt like it was full of bees. I could force them, but the results were never pretty, and they were never good enough. They couldn't hold as much as I needed them to.

My total came to under two hundred dollars, which wasn't bad for everything I was buying. I grabbed a few small jars of paint from the impulse rack to the left of the register. Willow, who had argued Joanna into putting the rack there, grinned.

"Will there be anything else today?"

"No, that's about it." I signed my credit card slip and dropped the receipt into the bag. "I'll see you next week."

"About that..."

I froze. "What about it?"

"Well, you know this weekend is our big get-together, right?" Willow smiled ingratiatingly. "A bunch of our regulars are bringing in their kids to share with each other, and I know you must have some absolutely gorgeous children at home, with all the things you buy."

I managed not to shudder as I pasted a smile across my face. The tendency of some doll people to refer to their creations as "children" has always horrified me, especially given my situation. Children live. Children breathe. Their dolls...didn't. "I can't," I said, fighting to sound sincere. "I'm supposed to visit my father at the nursing home. Maybe next time, okay?"

"That would be nice." Willow barely hid her disappointment. I grabbed my bag and fled without saying another word, and this time the bell above the door sounded like victory. I had made my escape. Now all I had to do was keep on running.

The cat met me at the apartment door, meowing and twining aggressively around my ankles, like tripping me would magically cause her food dish to refill. Maybe she thought it would; it's hard to say, with cats.

"Wait your turn, Trinket." I shut and locked the door before walking across the room—dodging the cat all the way—and putting my bag down on the cluttered mahogany table that served as my workspace. Trinket stopped when I approached the table, sitting down and eyeing it mistrustfully. The tabletop had been the one forbidden place in the apartment since she was a kitten. She badly wanted to be up there—all cats desire forbidden things—but she was too smart to risk it.

The half-painted faces of my current projects stared at me from their stands. Some—Christina, Talia, Jonathan—had bodies, and Christina was partially blushed, giving her a beautifully human skin tone. Others, like Charity the bat-girl, were nothing more than disembodied heads.

"I'm sorry guys," I said, to the table in general. "You're going to need to wait a little longer. I have a rush job." The dolls stared at me with blank eyes, and didn't say anything. That was a relief.

Trinket followed me to the kitchen, where I fed her a can of wet cat food, stroked her twice, and discarded my shoes. I left my jacket on the bookshelf by the door, hanging abandoned off a convenient wooden outcropping. I was halfway into my trance when I sat down at the table, reaching for the bag, ready at last. The tools I needed were in place, waiting for me. All I needed to do was begin.

So I began.

The doll maker's art is as ancient and revered as any other craft, for all that it's been relegated to the status of "toymaker" in this modern age. A maker of dolls is so much more than a simple toymaker. We craft dreams. We craft vessels. We open doorways into the Kingdom of the Cold, where frozen faces look eternally on the world, and do not yearn, and do not cry.

I learned my craft at my father's knee, just as he'd learned from his father, and his father from his mother. When the time comes, when my father dies, I'll be expected to teach my own child. Someone has to be the gatekeeper; someone has to be the maker of the keys. That was the agreement Collodi made with Pandora, who began our family line when she needed help recapturing the excess of emotion she had loosed into the world. We will do what must be done, and we will each train our replacement, and the doll maker's art will endure, keeping the doors to the Kingdom open.

I fixed the face I'd purchased from Willow to the stand and began mixing my colors. I wanted to preserve its wintry whiteness, but I needed it to be a living pallor, the sort of thing that looked eerie but not impossible.

So I brushed the thinnest of pinks onto her cheeks and around the edges of her hairline, using an equally thin wash of blue and gray around the holes that would become her eyes, until they seemed to be sunken sockets, more skeletal in color than they'd ever been in their pristine state. I painted her lips pale at the edges and darkening as I moved inward, leaving the center of her mouth gleaming red as a fresh-picked strawberry. I added a spray of freckles to the bridge of her nose, using the same shade of pink as the edges of her lips.

She was lovely. She'd be lovelier when she was done, and so I reached for her body, and kept going. There was so much work to do.

Somewhere around midnight, between the third coat of paint and the first careful restyling of the wig that would be her hair, I blacked out, falling into the dreaming doze that sometimes took me when I worked too long on the borders between this world and the Kingdom of the Cold. My hands kept moving, and time kept passing, and when I woke to the sound of my cellphone's alarm ringing from my jacket pocket, the sun had risen, and a completed doll sat in front of me, her hands folded demurely in her lap, like she was awaiting my approval.

Her face was just as I'd envisioned it in the store: pale and wan, but believably so, with eyes that almost matched her lips gazing out from beneath her downcast lashes. I must have glued them in just before I woke up; the smell of fixative still hung in the air. Her hair was a cascade of snow, and her dress was the palest of possible pinks. She was barefoot, and her only ornamentation was a silver strawberry charm on a chain around her neck. She was finished, and she was perfect, and she was just in time.

"Your name is Strawberry," I said, reaching out to take her hands between my thumbs and forefingers. "I have called you into being to be a vessel for my sadness, for there is no place for sorrow in the Kingdom of the Cold. Do you accept this burden, little girl, so newly made? Will you serve this role for me?"

Everything froze. Even the clocks stopped ticking. This was where I would learn whether I'd chosen my materials correctly; this was where I would learn if they would serve me true. Then, with a feeling of rightness that was akin to finding a key that fits a lock that has been closed for a hundred years, something clicked inside my soul, and the sorrows of the past few weeks flowed out of me, finding their new home in the resin body of my latest creation.

It's no small thing, pouring human-sized sorrow into a toy-sized vessel. Sorrow is surprisingly malleable, capable of adjusting its shape to fit the box that holds it, but it fights moving from one place to another, and it has thorns. Sorrow is a bramble of the heart and a weed of the mind, and this sorrow was deeply rooted. It held a hundred small slights, workdays where things refused to go according to plan, cups of coffee that were too cold and buses that came late. It also held bigger, wider things, like my meeting with Father's case supervisor, who had shown me terrible charts and uttered terrible words like "state budget cuts" and "better served by another placement." Father couldn't handle being moved again, not when he was just starting to remember his surroundings from day to day, and I couldn't handle the stress or expense of moving him. Not now, not when I was already out of vacation time and patience. Lose my job, lose the nursing homes. Lose the nursing homes, and face the choice so many of my ancestors had faced: whether to share my space with a broken vessel who no longer knew how to reach the Kingdom, or whether to break the last dolls binding him to this world, freeing their share of his sorrow and opening his doorway to the Kingdom one final, fatal time.

I could send him home. No one would call it murder, but I would always know what I had done.

It was a hard, brutal concept, one that had no place in the modern world, but I had to consider it, because Father had always told me that one day, it would be my choice to make. Life or death, parent or duty—me or him. And I wasn't ready to decide. So I poured it all into the doll I had crafted with my own two hands, and Strawberry, darling Strawberry, drank it to the very last drop. I couldn't have asked for anything more than what she offered, and when I felt the click again, the key turning and the doorway closing, I had become an empty vessel. My sorrows were gone, bled out into the doll with the strawberry eyes.

"Thank you," I murmured, and stood. I carried her across the room to a shelf of girl dolls who looked nothing like her, yet all seemed somehow to be family to one another: there was some intangible similarity in their expressions and posture. They all contained a measure of sadness, decanted from me through the Kingdom and into them over the course of these past three years. I set Strawberry among her sisters, adjusting her skirt and the position of her hands until she was just so and exactly right, like she had always been there.

Then, light of heart and step, I turned and walked toward my bedroom. It was time to get ready for work.

The day passed in a stream of tiny annoyances and demands, as days at the company where I worked as a junior accountant so often did.

"Marian, do you have that report ready?"

"Marian, is the copy machine fixed yet?"

"Marian, we're out of coffee."

I weathered them all with a smile on my face. I felt like I could face any challenge. I always felt that way right after I opened a channel to the Kingdom. People like my father and I used to be revered as surgeons, the doll makers who came to town and helped people remove the parts of themselves that they couldn't handle anymore. The bad memories, the pain, the sorrow. Now he was a senile old man fading away by inches and I was a woman with a strange, expensive hobby, but that didn't change what we'd been designed to do. It didn't close the doorway.

"Hi, Marian."

The sound of Clark's voice wrenched me out of the payroll system and sent me into a state of chilly panic, my entire body going tense and cold with the sudden stress of living. No, no, no, I thought, and raised my eyes. Yes, yes, yes, said reality, because there was Clark, useless ex-boyfriend and even more useless co-worker, standing with his arms draped across the edge of my half-cubicle like I'd invited him to be there, like he was some sort of strange workplace beautification project gone horribly wrong.

"Hello, Clark," I said, as coolly as I could. "Is there something I can help you with?"

"You can tell me why you're not answering my calls," he said. "Did I do something wrong? I know you said you didn't want to be serious. I didn't think that meant cutting me out entirely."

"Please don't make me call HR," I said, glancing around to be sure no one was listening. "I said I didn't want to see you socially anymore. I meant it."

"Is this because I said your doll collection was childish and weird? Because it is, but I can adjust, you know? Lots of people have weirder hobbies. My little sister used to collect Beanie Babies. She was like twelve at the time, but it's the same concept, right?"

I ground my teeth involuntarily, feeling a stab of pain from the crown on my left rear molar. I had sliced half of that tooth off with a hot knife when I opened my first doorway to the Kingdom. Early sacrifices had to hurt more. "No, it's not," I said stiffly. "I told you I didn't want to talk about this. I definitely don't want to talk about it at work."

"You won't take my calls, you won't meet me for coffee, so where else are we supposed to talk about it? You haven't left me anywhere else."

He looked so confident in his answer, like he had found the perfect way to get me to go out with him again. I wanted to slap him across his smug, handsome face. I knew better. I flexed my hands, forcing them to stay on my desk, and asked, "What do you want me to say, Clark? That I'll meet you for coffee so we can have a talk about why we're never going to date again, and why I'll report you to HR for harassment if you don't stop bothering me?"

"Sounds great." He flashed the toothy smile that had initially convinced me it would be a good idea to go out with him. I should have known better, but he'd been so handsome, and I'd been so lonely. I'd just wanted someone to spend a little time with. Was that so wrong?

No. Everything human wants to be loved, and wants the chance to love someone else. The only thing I did wrong was choosing Clark.

I swallowed a sigh and asked, "Does tonight work for you?" Better to do it while I was still an empty vessel. If I waited for the end of the week, I'd have to pull another all-nighter and add another girl to my shelf before I could endure his company. That would be bad. Not only would the cost of materials eat a hole in my bank account that I couldn't afford right now, but the strain of opening a second doorway so soon after the first would be...inadvisable. I could do it, and had done it in the past. That didn't make it a good idea.

"Hey now, first you play hard to get and now you're trying to rush me? I thought you said you didn't like games." His smile didn't waver. "Tonight's just fine. Pick you up at seven?"

"I'd rather meet you there," I said.

"Ah, but you don't know where we're going." Clark winked, pushing himself away from the wall of my cubicle. "Wear something nice." He turned and walked down the hall before I could frame a reply, the set of his shoulders and the cant of his chin implying that he really thought he'd won.

I groaned, dropping my head into my hands. He thought he'd won because he had. I was going out with him again. "What the hell is wrong with me?" I muttered.

My computer didn't answer.

The bell rang at 7:20 PM—Clark, making me wait the way he always had, like twenty minutes would leave me panting for his arms. I put down the wig cap I'd been re-rooting and walked to the door, wiping stray rayon fibers off my hands before opening it and glaring at the man outside.

Clark took in my paint-stained jeans and plain gray top, his jovial expression fading into a look that almost matched mine. He was wearing a suit, nicer than anything he ever put on for work, and enough pomade in his hair to make him smell like a Yankee Candle franchise. "I thought I told you to put on something nice," he said.

"I thought I told you I was willing to meet you for coffee," I shot back. "Last time I checked, the dress code at Starbucks was 'no shirt, no shoes, no service.' I have a shirt and shoes. I think I'll be fine."

Clark continued to glower for a moment before shouldering his way past me into the apartment.

"Hey!" I yelped, making a futile grab for his arm. It was already too late: he was in my living room, turning slowly as he took in all the dolls that had joined my collection since the last time he'd been here, some three months previous. I tried not to open a doorway to the Kingdom more than once a week, but sometimes it was hard to resist the temptation, especially when I had more than one trouble to decant. Dolls like Strawberry held sorrow, while others held different emotions—anger, loneliness, even hope, and love, and joy. Positive emotions took longer to grow back and had to be decanted less frequently, but they were represented all the same.

Clark's examination took about two minutes before he focused back on me, disdain replaced by pity. "This is why you broke up with me?" he asked. "I mean, you said it was because of the dolls, but I thought that was just a crappy excuse, you know? The weird-chick equivalent of 'I have to wash my hair on Saturday night.' But you meant it. You like plastic people better than you like real ones. There's something wrong with you."

"My dolls aren't plastic," I said automatically, before I realized I was falling back into the same destructively defensive patterns that had defined our brief relationship. I glared at him, shutting the door before Trinket could get any funny ideas about making a run for the outside world. "You want to have this talk? Fine. Yes, I chose my dolls over you. Unlike you, they never tell me I'd be pretty if I learned how to do something with my hair. Unlike you, they don't criticize me in public and then say they were just kidding. And unlike you, they shut up when I tell them to."

"You really are a crazy bitch." He strode across the living room, grabbing the first thing that caught his eye—pretty little Strawberry in her mourning gown. His hand all but engulfed her body. "You need to learn how to focus on real things, Marian, or you're going to be alone forever."

"You put her down!" I didn't think. I just acted, launching myself at him like he wasn't a foot taller and fifty pounds heavier than I was. I was reaching for Strawberry, trying to snatch her out of his hand, when his fist caught me in the jaw and sent me sprawling.

I'd never been punched in the face before. Everything went black and fuzzy. I didn't actually pass out, but the next few minutes seemed like a slideshow or a Power Point presentation, and not like something that was really happening. Static picture followed static picture as I watched Clark stalk around my apartment, grabbing dolls off the shelves. When he couldn't hold any more he walked over to me, looking down, and said, "This is what you get."

He kicked me in the stomach, and then he was gone, taking my dolls with him, and I was alone. At some point, I came back to myself enough to start crying.

It didn't help.

Trinket stuck her nose through the curtain of my hair and mewled, eyes wide and worried. I sniffled, wiping my eyes with the back of my hand, and sat up to pat her gently on the head. "He didn't hurt me that bad, Trinket. I'm okay. I'm okay."

I was lying to myself as much as I was lying to the cat: I might be many things, but I was distinctly not okay. Clark had stolen at least a dozen of my dolls, maybe more, and he hadn't been careful about the shelves he took them from. I picked myself up from the floor inch by excruciating inch, finally turning to take stock of the damage.

It was greater than I'd feared. Fifteen dolls were missing—at least one from every shelf, as well as one of the unfinished dolls from my table. Relief washed over me when I saw that. At least not everything he'd taken was a weapon. Shame followed on relief's heels. He'd stolen fourteen full vessels, fourteen dangerous doorways into the Kingdom of the Cold, and I was relieved that it wasn't one more? What was the difference between fourteen and fifteen when you were talking about knives to the heart? Fourteen would be more than enough to kill. The only question was who.

If I was lucky, he'd accidentally kill himself, and all my troubles would end...but that might leave full vessels floating around the world outside, ready to be found by someone who didn't know what they were holding. Open a vessel improperly and everything it contained would come flooding out. And there were many, many ways to open something that had been closed.

I wanted to go after him. I wanted to demand the return of my property, and I wanted to make him pay. I glanced to the remaining unfinished dolls, assessing the materials I had, automatically counting off the materials I'd need. Forcibly, I pulled myself away from that line of thinking. Revenge was satisfying, but it was hard to explain, and I'd already been reminded that I couldn't take him in a fair fight.

Hands shaking, I pulled out my cell phone and dialed the number for the police. When the dispatcher came on the line, voice calm and professional, I began to tell her what had happened.

I made it almost all the way through the explanation before I started to cry.

That night was one of the worst I'd had since Father started getting bad. We'd both known what his lapses in memory meant, but we'd denied it for as long as possible, he because he wasn't ready to go, me because I wasn't ready to be alone. Every keeper of the Kingdom eventually develops cracks. It's a natural consequence of being a vessel that's been emptied too many times. There's a reason we don't use the same doll more than once for anything other than the most basic and malleable emotions. That was the reason I couldn't make myself a new doll, one big enough to hold my shame and grief and feelings of violation. I'd emptied out my sorrow too recently. I was too fresh, scraped too raw, to do it again.

The officers who came in answer to my call were perfectly polite. They took pictures of the empty spaces on my shelves and of the bruises on my face and stomach, and if they thought the number of dolls still in my apartment was funny, they had the grace not to laugh in front of me. Eventually, they left me with a card and a number to call if Clark came back, and the empty promise that they'd see what they could do about getting my stolen property back. One of them asked me, twice, about filing a restraining order. I refused both times.

I didn't sleep. All I could do was lie awake, staring at the ceiling and thinking about the dolls who had been entrusted to my care, now lost in the world with their deadly burdens of emotion. They were so fragile. Why did we make them so fragile?

Because they had to mirror the fragility of the human heart, if they were to do the jobs that they were made for.

When morning came I rolled out of bed and dressed without paying attention to whether my clothes matched or how well they went together. My face hurt too much for me to bother with makeup, so I left it as it was, bruises like smeared paint on the side of my jaw and around the socket of my left eye, and walked out the door with my head up and my thoughts full of nothing but vengeance.

A shocked hush fell over the office when I walked through the door. I ignored the people who were staring at me, choosing instead to walk to my desk. Something white was trapped under the keyboard. I pulled it loose, only to gasp and drop it like it had scalded my fingers.

Strawberry's whisper of a dress fluttered to the floor, where it lay like an accusation. You failed us, it seemed to say. You didn't protect. You didn't keep. You are no guardian.

I clapped my hand over my mouth, ignoring the pain it awoke in my jaw, and fought the urge to vomit. Bit by bit, my stomach unclenched. I bent, picked up the dress, and walked calmly down the hall to the door with Clark's name on it. He had an office; I had a cubicle. He had a door with a nameplate; I had a piece of paper held up with thumbtacks. I should have known better than to let him buy me that first cup of coffee. Even if I didn't have that much sense, I should have known better than to let him take me out for dinner even once. I was a fool.

Foolishly, I raised my hand and knocked. Clark's voice, smooth as butter, called, "Come in."

I went in.

Clark was behind his desk, a broad piece of modern office place furniture that was almost as large as my work table at home, if not half as old or attractive. He looked...perfect. Every hair was in place, and his tailored suit hung exactly right on his broad, all-American shoulders. His eyes darted to the scrap of fabric in my hand, and he smiled. "I see you found my present."

"Where are my dolls, Clark?" I'd meant to be more subtle than that, to approach the question with a little more decorum. Father always tried to tell me you got more flies with honey than you did with vinegar, but he'd never been able to make the lesson stick, and the words burst out, hot with venom and betrayal. "You had no right to take them."

"And you had no right to call the police over a little lover's spat, but you did, didn't you?" The jovial façade dropped away, leaving the snake he'd always been staring out of his eyes. "I was going to give them back. As an apology, for losing my temper. I shouldn't have hit you, and I know that. But then the cops showed up at my apartment saying you'd filed a domestic violence complaint against me. I'm sure you can see why I didn't like that very much."

I stared at him. "I didn't file a domestic violence complaint against you, Clark, because you're not any part of my domestic life. I filed an assault charge. You didn't just hit me. You beat me down. Where are my dolls?"

His smile was a terrible thing. "I'm not a part of your domestic life. How would I know where your silly little toys ended up? As for your trumped-up charges, my lawyer will enjoy seeing yours in court. Now you might want to get out of my office before I tell HR that you're harassing me."

Wordlessly, I held up Strawberry's gown, daring him to say something that would deny that he was the one who'd left it on my desk.

"What, that? I found it in my car, and thought you might want it back. You know how it is with grown women who play with dolls. They're just like children. Leaving their toys everywhere."

He sounded so smug, so sure of himself, that it was all I could do not to walk around the desk and snatch his eyes from his head. I kept my nails long and sharp, to make it easier to position delicate doll eyelashes and reach miniscule screws. I could have had his eye sockets bare and bleeding in a matter of seconds.

I balled my hands into fists. I was my father's daughter. I was the keeper of the Kingdom and the maker of the keys, and I would not debase myself with this man's blood.

"This isn't over," I said.

Clark smiled at me. "Actually, I'm pretty sure it is," he said. "Bye, now."

There was nothing else that I could do, and so I turned, Strawberry's dress still clutched in my hand like a talisman against the darkness that was rushing in on me, and I walked away.

The rest of the day crept by like it wanted me to suffer. My eyes drifted to Strawberry's dress every few seconds until I finally picked it up and shoved it into my purse, hoping that out of sight would equal out of mind. It didn't work as well as I'd hoped, but it made enough of a difference that I was able to complete my assigned work and sneak out the door fifteen minutes early. Thanks to Clark, I had lost track of fourteen filled vessels. I needed to find them, and that meant I needed help. There was only one place to go for that.

My father.

The Shady Pines Nursing Home was as nice a place to die as money could buy, with all the amenities a man who barely remembered himself from hour to hour could want. I had made sure of that. If I was going to keep him alive past the point when he was ready to go, I wasn't going to make him suffer.

Part of what that money paid for was an understanding staff. When I presented myself at the front desk an hour after visiting hours had ended, a long white box in my hands and a light layer of foundation over the bruises on my face, they didn't ask any questions; they looked at me and saw a dutiful daughter who had experienced something bad, and needed her father.

"He's having one of his good days, Miss Collodi," said the aide who walked me through the well-lit, pleasantly decorated halls toward my father's room. "You picked an excellent time to visit."

I could tell he meant well from the look on his face—curious about my bruises but eager not to offend. So I just smiled, and nodded, and said, "I'm glad to hear that."

We stopped when we reached the door of Father's room. The aide rapped his knuckles gently against the doorframe, calling, "Mr. Collodi? May we come in?"

"I told you, the dollhouse won't be ready for another three days," shouted my father, sounding exactly like he had throughout my childhood: aggravated by the stupidity of the world around him, but trying to improve it however he could. "Go away, and come back when it's done."

I put a hand on the aide's shoulder. "I can handle it from here," I said. The aide looked uncertain, but he nodded and walked away, leaving me alone with the open doorway. I hefted the box in my hands, checking the weight of its precious burden—so few left, and no way to make more—before taking a deep breath and stepping into my father's room.

Antonio Collodi had been a large man in his youth, and that size was still with him: broad shoulders and a back that hadn't started to stoop, despite the deep lines that seamed his face and the undeniable white of his hair. The muscle that used to make him look like a cross between a man and a bear was gone, withered to skeleton thinness; his clothes hung on him like a shroud. He was standing near the window, hands curled like he was working on an invisible dollhouse. I stopped to admire the workmanship that had gone into him. I must have made some small sound, because he turned and froze, eyes fixing on my face.

"I'm your daughter," I said, before he could start flinging accusations. He usually mistook me for Pandora—a natural misunderstanding, since I looked exactly like she did in the painting that we had been passing down, generation to generation, since the beginning. He didn't like being visited by dead people. He said it was an abomination, and a violation of our compact with the Kingdom of the Cold, which some called "Hades," where the dead were meant to stay forever. "Daddy, I need your help. Can you help me?"

"My daughter?" He kept staring at me, dawning anger melting into amazement. "You're beautiful. What did I make you from?"

"Bone and skin and pine and ice," I said, walking to his bed and putting down the long white box. I rested a hand on its lid. "Pain and sorrow and promises and joy. You pried me open and called me a princess among doors, and then you poured everything you had into me, and kept pouring until my eyes were open." I remembered that day: waking on my father's workbench, naked and surrounded by bone shavings, my teeth tender and too large in my little girl's mouth, my face stiff from the smile it had been painted wearing.

My family has guarded the trick to calling life out of the Kingdom for centuries, since Pandora brought it to us and said she was too tired to keep the compact any longer. No one you didn't make with your own two hands can be trusted. That's the true lesson of the Kingdom, and what I should have remembered when Clark smiled his perfect smile and offered me his perfect hands. But my father made me too well, and when he bid me to become a woman, a woman I became. If I'd stayed a doll of bone and pine, Clark would have had no power over me.

"Yes, that's how you make a daughter," said my father, following me across the room. "Is that why I'm so empty?"

"Yes," I said. "I'm sorry."

"I should be in pieces by the road by now."

"I still need you." I took my hand off the box and opened the lid, revealing a blue-eyed boy doll. He was dressed in trousers and a vest a hundred years out of date, and his face was painted in a way that subtly implied he had a secret. I undid the ribbons holding him in place and gingerly picked him up. He weighed more than he should have for his size, and my hands shook as I held him out toward my father. "There are five of these in the world. That's why you can't go. If you break this one, there will only be four, and you'll be one step closer to entering the Kingdom."

We were supposed to be at peace there. We were supposed to be the real boys and girls we had been crafted to resemble. I didn't know if that was true…but I knew that the humans lived for the promise of Heaven with much less proof of its existence than we had of the Kingdom.

Pandora and Carlo Collodi had been real people, flesh and blood people. Pandora had carried a vase like a broken heart, meant to contain all the dangers of the world, both sweet and bitter. She had been tired from her wandering, from years on years of struggling to recapture the evils she had accidentally released. Carlo Collodi…

He had wanted a daughter. Of such necessity are many strange bargains born.

Father took the doll. I didn't look away. This was on me; this was my fault, because I was doing this to him. I could have crafted my child as soon as it became clear that the vessel of Father's thoughts had cracked. I could have set him free, and no one would have called it murder, because I wouldn't have laid a finger on him. I was the one who wasn't willing to let him go.

"Oh, my brave boy," he murmured, cradling the doll in his hands. "Your name was Marcus, wasn't it? Yes, Marcus, and you were a vessel for my anger. The world was so infuriating back then..." He raised the doll, pressing his lips against the cold porcelain forehead.

It felt like the temperature in the room dropped ten degrees, the doorway to the Kingdom of the Cold swinging open and locking in place as all that Father had poured into that blue-eyed boy came surging out again, filling him. He stayed that way for almost a minute, lips pressed to porcelain, drinking himself back in one sip at a time. The chill remained in the air as Father lowered the doll, and the eyes he turned in my direction were sharp and clever, filled with the wisdom of two hundred years of making dolls to hold every imaginable emotion.

"Marian, why am I still here?" he asked. All traces of confusion were gone. The sad, broken vessel was no longer with me, and I rejoiced, even as I fought not to weep.

The dolls he had filled before he had broken grew fewer with every visit, and his lucidity faded faster. I was running out of chances to call my father back to me. "Four dolls remain, Father," I said, rising and sketching a quick curtsey, even though I was wearing trousers. "Until they're used up, you can't finish breaking."

"Then use them. Stop wasting them on me. I command you."

"I can't." I straightened. "I would if I could. I love you, and I know my duty. But the world has changed since you were its doll maker, and I can't do this without you. I need to be able to ask my questions, and have someone to answer them."

He frowned. "Have you made a child yet?"

"Not yet. I can't." Once I made myself a child—made it from bone and skin and pine and ice, like my father had made me, like his father had made him—my own cracks would begin to show, and the essence of what made me would begin leaking free. A vessel can only be emptied so many times. The creation of a child was the greatest emptying of all. "I'm not ready. But Father, that isn't why I came. I need your help."

"Help? Help with what?"

I took a deep breath. This was going to be the difficult part. "There was a man at my office…"

I spilled the whole sordid story out between us, drop by terrible drop. The smiles, the flirtation, the dates for coffee that turned into dates for dinner that turned, finally, into Clark deciding he had the right to start dictating my life. From there, it was a short progression to him knocking me to the floor and stealing my dolls.

Father listened without a word, letting his precious moments of lucidity trickle away like sand. When I was done, he inclined his head and said, "You have been foolish, my Marian. But you're young as long as I'm in this world—children are always young when set against their parents—and I can't fault you for being a young fool. I was foolish too, when I had a father to look after me." He held out his empty doll. I took it. What else could I have done? He was my father, and he wanted me to have it. "You know what you need to do."

"I don't want to," I said weakly—and wasn't that why I'd come to him? To find another way, a better way, a human way, one that didn't end with someone broken and bleeding in the street?

But sometimes there isn't any other way. Sometimes all there can be is vengeance. "You have to," he said gently.

I sighed. "I know." The empty doll was light as a feather, nothing but a harmless husk. I could sell it to a dealer I knew for a few hundred dollars, and watch them turn around and sell it to someone else for a few thousand. It didn't matter who profited, or how much. All that mattered was that this shattered little piece of my father's soul would no longer be in my keeping. One more doorway, permanently closed.

"Now come, sit with me." My father sat down on the edge of his bed, gesturing for me to return to my previous place. "I don't have long before the cracks begin to show again, and I would know what you've been doing with your life."

"All right," I said, and sat, settling the empty doll back into his box. Father reached for my hands. I let him take them. We sat together, both smiling, and I spoke until the understanding faded from his eyes, and he was gone again.

There are always consequences when you spend your life standing on the border of the Kingdom of the Cold.

I spent the night at my work table, a rainbow of paints in front of me and Charity the bat-girl's delicate face looking blindly up at the ceiling as I applied the intricate details of her makeup, one stroke at a time. She'd been waiting for the chance to be complete for months, but I'd passed her by time and again to focus on newer projects. I'd always wondered why. It's not like me to leave a doll languishing for so long. Now I knew: Charity had a purpose, and until the time for that purpose arrived, I couldn't have finished her if I'd tried.

Charity was meant to be my revenge.

Morning dawned and found me still sitting there, now drawing careful swirls on the resin body that would soon play host to her head. Her wings would get the same treatment before they were strung into place. She was less a bat-girl than a demon-girl, but "Charity the bat-girl" had been her name for so long that I couldn't stop thinking of her that way. I reached for my silver paint, and paused as my hand found an empty jar.

"Shit." I'd been working without pause, and hadn't stopped to assess my supplies. Charity needed the silver to be properly finished. I glanced to the clock. The doll shop would be open in ten minutes. This was their big gather-day, but I could be in and out before anyone had a chance to notice that I was even there. I wiped down my brushes, capped my paints, and stood. Just a few more supplies and I could finish my work.

The drive to the doll store took about fifteen minutes, minutes I spent reviewing what I was going to buy and how I'd explain I couldn't stay if Willow or Joanna asked me. I was deep in thought when I got out of the car, walked to the door, and stepped inside, only to be hit by a wave of laughter and the smell of peppermint tea. I stopped dead, blinking at the swarm of people—mostly women, with a few men peppered through the crowd—who moved, chattering constantly, around a series of tables that had been set up where the racks of pre-made doll clothes were usually kept. A second wave hit me a moment later, this one redolent with sadness, and with the smell of cold.

My stolen dolls were here.

I shoved my way through the crowd, ignoring their startled protests, until I reached the table. There they were, all my missing vessels, even Strawberry, although someone had redressed her in a garish red and white checked dress. They were set up as a centerpiece, surrounded by a red velvet rope, like that would ensure that people looked but didn't touch.

"Marian?" Willow's voice came from right behind me. She sounded surprised.

I couldn't blame her for that. I had other things to blame her for. I whirled, pointing back at the table as I declared, "Those are *my* dolls! How did you get my dolls?"

Willow's expression hardened, going from open and genial to closed and hard. "I'm afraid I don't know what you're talking about, dear. Those dolls were sold to us by a private collector, and you've always been so adamant about not showing or selling your work that I can't believe you'd have sold this many to him. They're a fine collection, but they're not yours."

I ground my teeth together, pain lancing from my damaged molar, before I said, "Yes, they are. They were stolen from my apartment two nights ago by my ex-boyfriend. I filed a police report. We can call them and get them down here; I'm sure we'll find your 'private collector' matches Clark's description."

Her eyes widened slightly at his name. I resisted the urge to smack her.

"He didn't even lie about his name, did he? Clark Hauser. You probably wrote him a check. You'll have a record." I shook my head. "You had to know those weren't his. I bought most of these materials *here*, and they're not common combinations. You knew. But you took them anyway." The crowd around me was silent, watching. I turned to them. "Think they'd buy your dolls too, if you got robbed?"

"We didn't know they were stolen," said Willow. "We bought them legally. We—"

"Give the lady back her dolls," said a weary voice. Willow turned, and we both looked at the dark-haired woman in the workroom door, leaning on her cane. Joanna focused only on me. She walked slowly forward. It felt like she was studying me, taking my measure. She stopped about a foot away, and said, "Doll maker. That's what you are, isn't it? You're the doll maker."

I nodded mutely.

"I always wanted to meet one of you." She waved a hand at the table. "They're yours. Take them. I knew we couldn't keep the collection as soon as I put hands on it. They're dangerous, aren't they?"

I nodded again.

"Then get them out of my store. Was that all you came for?"

I found my voice, and managed, "I needed some silver paint."

"Take that too. Call it our apology." She smiled thinly. "When you take your revenge, doll maker, don't take it on us. Willow, get the lady her paint." Willow hurried to obey.

I looked at the crowd, and then back to Joanna, and said, "Thank you."

Joanna smiled. "You're welcome."

Restoring the vessels to their proper places made me feel infinitely better, like a hole in the world had been closed. I apologized to each of them, and twice to Strawberry: once as I was stripping off that horrible checkered dress, and again as I placed her back on her proper shelf. I felt their approval, and the approval of the Kingdom beyond. Silver paint in hand, I sat down and got back to work.

Crafting a vessel for the self is easy, once you know how. It requires understanding your own heart—a painful process, to be sure, but your own heart is always close to hand. Crafting a vessel for someone else is an uphill struggle, and I felt it with every stroke of the brush. I mixed the last of the silver paint with blood taken from the small vein inside my wrist, and it made glittering brown lines on Charity's skin. There was a moment right before the designs drew together when I could have stopped: I could have put down the brush and walked away. But Clark had struck me, had stolen from the Kingdom, and he had to pay for what he'd done.

I dressed Charity in a black mourning gown and placed her in a long white box, covering her with drifts of tissue paper. Then I fed Trinket, left the apartment, and drove to Clark's house. I left the box on his doorstep. I didn't look back as I drove away.

Clark didn't come to work on Monday. That wasn't unusual. Clark didn't come to work on Tuesday either. People were talking about it in the break room when I came to get my coffee.

Wednesday morning, I called in sick.

The key Clark had given me still fit his lock. I let myself in. There was Charity on the floor, full to the point of bursting, and there was Clark next to her, eyes open and staring into nothingness. He was still alive, but when I waved my hand in front of his face, he didn't blink. There was nothing left in him.

"You shouldn't open doors you don't know how to close," I said, bending to slide my arms under Clark and hoist him to his feet. He would have been surprised to realize how strong I was. "It's dangerous. You never know what might happen."

Clark didn't respond.

"I never told you where my family was from, did I? We're doll makers, you know. We go all the way back to a man named Carlo Collodi. He wanted a child, and he used a trick he learned from a woman named Pandora to open a door to a place called the Kingdom of the Cold. It's a good name, don't you think? There's no room for sorrow there. The people who live there don't even understand its name. He called forth a little girl, and as that girl grew, she learned so many things the people of the Kingdom didn't know." I carried Clark to his room as I spoke.

"Sometimes that little girl sent things home to them. Presents. But more often, she used the things her father had learned from Pandora.

There's too much feeling in the world, you see. That's what Pandora really released. Not sin: the ability to feel it. So the little girl collected feeling like a cistern collects the rain, and when she held too much, she pulled it out and sealed it in beautiful vessels. Sorrow and anger and joy and loneliness, all held until her death. We can't contain as much as you can. We're not made that way. But we need something to pay our passage home." Home, to a place I'd never seen, with halls of porcelain and nobility of carved mahogany. We were revered as craftsmen there, and all we had to do to earn our place was keep repaying Pandora's debt, catching the excess of emotion that she had released into the world, one doll at a time.

I unpacked my father's last four remaining dolls before I unrolled the bundle that held my tools, pulling out the first small, clever knife. "Every vessel holds a piece of the maker's soul. We pack it away, piece by piece, to keep us alive after we cut out our hearts and use them to make a child. That's not the only thing we need, of course."

The scalpel gleamed as I held it up to show him. "Puppets come from blocks of wood. Rag dolls come from bolts of cloth. What do you think it takes to construct a child?"

Clark never even whimpered.

There was a message from Father's nursing home in my voicemail when I got back to the apartment. I didn't play it. I already knew what it would say: the apologies, the regrets, the silence where my father used to be. That didn't matter anymore. My chest ached where I had sliced it open, and I rubbed unconsciously at the wound, looking around the room at the rows upon rows of dolls filled with my living. They would sustain me now that I had no heart, until the day my daughter was ready to be the doll maker, and I was ready to stop patching the cracks left by her creation.

She snuffled and yawned in my arms, wrapped in a baby blanket the color of tissue paper. She'd have Clark's perfect smile and perfect hair, but she wouldn't have his temper. I'd given her my heart, after all, just like my father had given his to me.

The police would eventually notice Clark's disappearance. I'd left no traces for them to follow. A good artist cleans up when the work is done, and I had left neither shards of shattered porcelain nor pieces of dried, bloodless bone for them to track me by.

I walked to the couch and sat, jiggling my daughter in my arms. She yawned again. "Once upon a time," I said, "there was a man who wanted a son. He lived on the border of a place called the Kingdom of the Cold, and he knew that if he could just find a way to open a door, everything he dreamed of could be his. One day a beautiful woman came to his workshop. Her name was Pandora, and she was very tired..."

The dolls listened in silent approval. Trinket curled up at my feet, and the world went on.

In Skeleton Leaves

You may have picked up on the fact that I am absolutely fascinated by Peter Pan. There are so many ways to approach his story, from the literal to the symbolic, and the fact that it both is and is not in the public domain makes it all the more enthralling. You have to walk carefully when you're following the second star.

John Joseph Adams—again—invited me to contribute a story to *Operation Arcana*, a collection of military fantasy. Naturally, I thought of children and pirates, and playing the game of war. I also wanted…

I wanted to approach Peter's story from the perspective of the girl whose story it was meant to be all along. War doesn't only belong to the soldiers. It belongs, equally as often, to the ones they leave behind.

"He was a lovely boy, clad in skeleton leaves and the juices that ooze out of trees…"

—J.M. Barrie, *Peter and Wendy*

The sun rising over the lagoon tinted the water in shades of red and gold. Nothing moved, not even the wind, which had ceased blowing sometime after midnight, stranding ships at sea and rafts on shore. It was a moment of rare peace, and while it held sway, it was almost possible to pretend nothing had changed: that this was still a place of endless summers and endless games, where growing up was a choice and not a foregone conclusion. This was still Neverland.

Then the sun finished rising, and the red streaks on the surface of the water remained behind, the blood marking the places where the dead had fallen. This was still Neverland, but it was no longer suited for bedtime stories.

"I don't think I can betray her."

"Do you ever want this war to end?"

The ragamuffin army gathered in the shadow of the oaks drooped, their thin shoulders weighed down by birch-bark armor, their arms exhausted from the strain of holding swords and shields against the enemy. Those who had been lucky enough to stay behind and miss the night's battles moved through their ranks, offering cups of water and wiping blood from split lips and bruised foreheads. Only whimpers broke the silence; whimpers, and sighs as Wendy after Wendy found one of their charges on the verge of collapse.

"This can't go on much longer," murmured one of the Wendys, whose name had been Maria before she came to Neverland. She barely remembered the life she'd left behind. She knew there'd been a man who had hit her, and a woman with sad eyes who had never intervened, but more and more she found herself wondering if that was really worse than this endless parade of dead and dying children.

"It will go on for as long as the Pan wills it," said another Wendy stiffly.

Invoking the Pan's name ended all attempts at conversation. The Wendys scattered like so many birds, the blue ribbons in their hair and tied around their upper arms standing out like brands in the gloom beneath the trees.

The sound of distant crowing alerted them that their time was almost up, and they worked faster, trying to bandage every wound and wipe every eye before the inevitable happened: the curtain of branches at the far end of the clearing spread wide, and the Pan floated inside, her feet drifting a foot above the hard-packed ground. Her Wendy walked after her, hands folded behind her back, and the Pan's three lieutenants followed. They were the children who had survived the most battles, and their eyes were dead and dark with too much dying.

"Five Lost Children died last night—rejoice, for we killed twice that many pirates." The Pan's voice was jovial, as it always was; she announced death as if it were just another game. "Their bodies have been given to the mermaids, as apology for the three mermaids who were also killed in last night's fighting. Our alliance continues strong."

Each of the Wendys looked to their own charges and then, with pleading eyes, to the Pan's Wendy. There was not a one of them who was not missing someone, but that could mean their children had been sent to scout, or were out gathering ripe apples and fresh strawberries to feed Pan's army.

The Pan would never think to give the names of the fallen—forgot them, in fact, as soon as each Lost Girl or Boy breathed their last. Dead things held no interest for the Pan.

Her Wendy sighed and named the dead: "Christopher, Agnes, Jimmy, Minuet, and Xio."

One of the male Wendys cried out before muffling his sobs with the heel of his hand. The other four who had lost children managed to keep themselves under tighter control. It was too late: the Pan's eyes had found the Wendy who dared to cry aloud. She loosed herself like an arrow across the clearing, stopping to hang in the air before him as she demanded, "What's wrong? Why are you crying?"

The Wendy swallowed, trying to take back his tears. It didn't work, but he pressed forward all the same, saying, "Minuet was one of mine, Pan. I didn't realize... I'm going to miss her."

"Miss her? Miss who? All your children are here!" The Pan shook her head, pouting petulantly. "It's like you don't *want* us to have any fun, Wendy. You're a stick in the mud. Why, I bet your children never get to play any good games."

The Pan's Wendy took a sharp breath as she grasped the danger. She stepped forward, forcing a laugh as she said, "Why, that's not so! I've seen his children playing *lots* of games. He's an excellent mother, Pan, one of the best. I wouldn't be surprised if he's crying only because Minuet is going to miss playing with her brothers and sisters, like any good Lost Girl."

The cornered Wendy nodded in rapid agreement. "Yes! Yes, Pan, it's just as she said. We play such lovely games, it's a pity Minuet won't be able to play them with us anymore."

"Ah," said the Pan, starting to turn away. "You must have the best games in Neverland, then."

"Oh, yes," said the Wendy carelessly, thinking the danger was past. He didn't see the sudden tightness in the eyes of every other Wendy in the clearing.

The Pan whirled back toward him. "Liar!" she crowed. "*My* Wendy is the *best* Wendy, which means *I* get the best games, and not your children at all! And if you lied about *this* then you must have lied about *that*, because that's what liars do! Snips! Gantry! Take this Wendy's children to the enlistment tent. They need to learn how to play properly."

The Pan's two lieutenants began grabbing the younger children, collaring them by ones and by twos and dragging them out of the clearing. The Wendy started sobbing in earnest, blubbering incoherent pleas for the Pan to leave his children alone. The Pan's hand caught him across the cheek, sending him crumpling to the ground.

"You're not a Wendy," said the Pan. "You're just a scared little boy. Follow Gantry to the tent. We'll teach you to play yet." She raised her head, looking around at the carefully composed faces of the other Wendys and the remaining Lost Children. "Enlistment is open for another two hours, and then we'll play at sword practice, and then? Back to war." Her smile was almost bright enough to make up for the darkness in her eyes. "Beautiful war."

Somewhere in the back row of Lost Children, a little girl began to cry.

The Pan made yet another grandiose speech about the glories of war before she turned and flew out of the clearing, off to do whatever it was she did when she wasn't terrifying Lost Children or challenging pirates to fights she couldn't win. The Wendys began calling their children to them, counting noses and tweaking ears when necessary to get them to fall into line. There was a time when this process would have taken hours, with the youngest Lost Ones needing to be cossetted and cajoled into lining up and quieting down. That time was in the past, and as every one of them knew, what was past was beyond recovery. Past was even more inaccessible than the bottom of the lagoon, with no helpful, hurtful mermaids to dive and bring things back to you once they were lost. In a matter of minutes, the children were lined up and the Wendys were leading them away, leaving the Pan's Wendy standing alone and looking at nothing.

"Cecily." The name was accompanied by a small hand on the side of her arm. The Pan's Wendy turned to see a girl who looked scarcely seven years of age standing beside her. The girl was wearing a much-mended cotton dress, and had her cottony hair tied into two puffballs on either side of her head, each secured with a blue Wendy-ribbon. "We need to speak of things, you, and I, and the other Wendys."

Cecily—who was called Wendy by all except her fellow Wendys, because they had to have some way of differentiating themselves, didn't they? At least when they were alone together, with no sprawling families of ever-shifting children to count or mind—shook her head. "I'm sorry, Edith, but I can't," she said, without real regret. "The Pan might need me."

"She's flying the lagoon's edge, flirting with mermaids," said Edith. "We lost five children tonight, Cecily. *Five*. Can you continue putting this off?"

"Yes," said Cecily flatly. "I am very good at delaying things."

"Angus says the apple trees have stopped bearing fruit, and no one's found a ripe melon in days and days," said Edith. "Can you delay that? The land is failing. We water the sea with our blood. The only ones who eat well are the mermaids, and that's the only reason they still fight with us.

Even the fairies have started to disappear! I don't care how good you are at delaying things, Cecily. Some things refuse to be delayed."

Cecily hesitated, reaching for excuses, and finally offered the only one she could think of: "What about the children? Someone has to stay with them." She had no children of her own to watch over—the Pan demanded the whole of her attention and her heart—but she knew that she was an aberration amongst her kind.

"Angus has offered to take the youngest children while we have our conference, and the older ones have already gone to train for the Pan's war," said Edith. "Come."

Cecily sighed. The rules of the fellowship of Wendys were clear: if the other Wendys wanted her, she had to go, unless she had reason to think they were leaving their Lost Children in danger. Angus was a good mother. He would care for all the children like they were his own.

"All right," she said. "I'll come."

Edith smiled.

The places of the Wendys were safe and secret, bolt holes carved out of the fabric of Neverland to allow them the brief moments of peace their hearts required if they were going to keep loving the Lost Children like their own. Cecily had long suspected that the love the Wendys gave wasn't really mother-love, which was selfless and strained but couldn't be broken; Wendy-love was selfish, demanding tribute and loyalty in a way she couldn't imagine mother-love would need to, and revoked as soon as its targets strayed too far. Mother-love was given freely and without constraint, and while Wendy-love might aspire to that great height, it could never quite achieve it.

There were four other Wendys waiting when Edith led Cecily down the ladder and into the safe, cool space beneath the roots of the old sycamore. Belinda, Michael, Sara, and Pike sat on the narrow benches. Cecily felt suddenly as if she had walked into a snare. Those four Wendys were among the eldest of their fellowship, second only to herself…and Edith.

Edith had been there long enough see five Pans come and go while she remained a Wendy under the grace of Neverland's eternal summer sky. This was something more than just a gathering of mothers.

Edith closed the door, turned to Cecily, and said without preamble, "The Pan is not keeping us safe. What say you, sister, who flew here first by this new Pan's side?"

Cecily bristled, pride and caution warring in her belly. "This 'new' Pan has kept Neverland safe for days and days," she said. From talking to the new children who sought Neverland's shores, she knew it had been more than a hundred and fifty years. Words like "decade" and "century" were forbidden, but even as the Pan had outflown her predecessor, so had Cecily outloved and outlasted all but Edith, who seemed as untouchable as the ocean tides.

"Days without counting, yes, but days end," said Belinda, somehow making the statement sound completely reasonable, when Cecily knew in her heart that it was anything but. "Twilight comes when night is falling. The land is failing. Our children are dying. We are suffering for this Pan's frailties."

"The Pan is heartless and cruel," said Cecily pleadingly. "She keeps us safe. She keeps these skies safe."

"I remember when you first came to Neverland," said Edith. "You were a beautiful child, and you have grown into a beautiful mother."

"But not a woman," said Cecily. The pleas were gone from her voice, replaced by a hard core, like steel. "I'm a child. I'm a *Wendy*."

"You were a child when you came to us, and you're a Wendy now, but you didn't arrive alone, did you?" Edith looked around at the blank, bewildered faces of her sisters and brother, and sighed. "I hate this part. This is a difficult part, and I hate doing it." She stomped her foot, for a moment looking like the child she'd been when she flew away from home. "I don't want to."

"Then don't," said Cecily. "The Pan is tired, that's all. The tide of war will turn. It always turns, and we'll drive those blasted pirates out to sea just like the last time, and the time before that, and the time before that."

"But there has to be a time when Neverland loses," said Edith. "There has to be a time when the pirates sail on valiant tides, because otherwise there would be no way of losing this game, and a game that can't be lost isn't worth playing anymore. Some Pans lose on their own. Some Pans lose because they can't keep a Wendy with them long enough to learn to depend on her. And some Pans..."

Cecily's eyes widened. She shook her head. "No," she said. "No, you can't make me do this."

"You didn't come to Neverland alone, Cecily."

"No."

"I'm sorry, but what are you talking about?" Michael frowned, standing as he asked his question. "I know Cecily is the Pan's Wendy, but how can she change whether or not the pirates win? Why would we *want* the pirates to win?"

"So the game can go on," said Edith. She watched Cecily as she spoke, and her eyes were sad. "The game *is* Neverland, and Neverland is the game. The game is the war unending, the battle unrefused, and it must be fought, or Neverland will fall."

"I don't care," spat Cecily. "I know what you want me to do, and I won't do it, I *won't*. This isn't right. This is..." She paused, fumbling for the greatest condemnation she could think of, and finally said, "It's *against the rules*."

"Why would Edith ask you to break the rules?" asked Sara, frowning.

"It doesn't break the rules, because this is in the rules. I'm sorry, but it is." Edith shook her head. "There have been Pans before this one. None of you remember them, but I do. Franklin, Amanda, Wesley, Padraig...and Peter. He was my first Pan, although I was never his Wendy. That honor, and that burden, fell on other shoulders."

"What would make a Pan want to grow up?" asked Belinda, sounding shocked and slightly disgusted by the idea. The others murmured agreement.

Cecily wanted to scream. Growing up was the only end any of them could conceive for a Pan's tenure in Neverland, even with Edith right there, talking about losing, talking about letting the pirates win. They were Wendys to the core, and they couldn't see the truth even when it was standing right in front of them, waving its arms in the air and screaming.

Maybe she had never really been a Wendy after all.

"Edith isn't talking about Pans going home and growing up," she said, and sighed. "She's talking about Pans letting the pirates win.

"She's talking about the ones that have died."

Silence fell across the room, and Cecily allowed herself a brief, cruel moment of satisfaction. If they were going to put this on her, at least they could understand what they were doing—and what they were asking her to do.

"The Pan didn't come to Neverland alone, and she wasn't the Pan when she came," said Cecily. "Her name was Sheila. And she was my sister."

They flew *to Neverland with hands clasped tight, following a boy they barely knew who said he could take them to a place where they would be children—and together—forever. What he didn't tell them was that he was recruiting soldiers for his private war; what he didn't tell them was that inside of a week, they would have swords in their hands and blood in their hair, and be fighting for their lives against a pirate crew straight out of a storybook.*

Cecily had cried and flailed with her sword, barely hitting anything, but Sheila… Sheila had laughed and flown to the highest mast, daring the pirates to follow her. Cecily remembered the look in her sister's eyes, like she was drunk on something more powerful than brandy, more addictive than laudanum. The boy—the Pan—had seen it too, and Cecily had expected him to yell for Sheila to come down and fight properly, but he'd only smiled.

He'd been dead by morning, and Sheila had flown away, surrounded by a chiming cloud of fairies, only to come back in a gown made of skeleton leaves, with a crow in her throat and a wild new light in her face.

That was the first time she had called Cecily "Wendy."

That was the day Cecily had lost her after all.

The Pan flew to the edge of the water and landed, her feet touching down with the familiar faint buzz that was Neverland welcoming her home. She'd felt it every time she'd touched the island's hallowed soil, even back to the first time, when she and Cecily had flown in from—where? She didn't really remember where they'd started their lives, but she remembered Cecily was her sister, and that seemed like enough of a past to be burdened with. Neverland wanted her. Neverland had welcomed her with open arms and a gown of skeleton leaves peeled from the body of a dead boy with too many freckles and a smile like a Tuesday morning (not that she knew what a Tuesday was; not that she knew the boy's name, then or now or ever). Neverland would never let her go.

Pirate ships with storm cloud sails bobbed on the horizon, waiting for the wind to pick back up and the tide to turn around, allowing them to resume their endless assault on the island's shores. They'd been fighting this war for as long as the Pan could remember—had been fighting it when she first arrived, when the Lost Children were led by that freckle-faced boy in his vest of skeleton leaves. But it had never been like this before. It had never been so unending and so…so *vicious*. The pirates would attack, a few people would be injured, leaving them with interesting scars to brag about at night, when they lay in their hammocks under the trees, and that would be that; the pirates would go away again, leaving the Lost Children to more important concerns, like rabbit hunts through the thorn briars or moonlit swims with mermaids. But not this time. This time the pirates were fighting to kill, and they just kept coming and coming, like waves against the shore, and people were dying, and the Pan didn't know what to do.

No one was supposed to die in Neverland. That wasn't the agreement. That wasn't the way.

A fairy zipped in from the side, hanging in the air in front of the Pan's face and ringing softly. Her wings cast a soft pink glow over everything around her. The Pan had heard some of the newer Lost Children scoffing at her Wendy's fairy, calling it too "girly" for the Wendy attached to their Pan. The Pan didn't quite understand that; when Vinca had first attached herself to Wendy (*Cecily*) the Lost Children had laughed and said a proper girl would have a blue-glow fairy, leaving the pink fairies for the boys where they belonged.

The Pan didn't understand much about the newest wave of Lost Children, if she was being honest, which was a thing she hated to be. Pans should be liars and fliers, that's the rule. But these Lost Children came in as wide-eyed and scarred by the adult world as all the boys and girls who came before them, and then they turned their attention to questioning *everything*. Some of them had even refused to accept the authority of the Wendys! They said they'd come to Neverland to escape adults and their stupid adult rules, and they weren't going to accept a new set of guardians that they'd never asked for. The Pan had insisted they divide themselves appropriately, sending them to the Wendys who would be their caretakers, but it was strange, and it was wearying.

The Pan was tired.

Vinca rang again. The Pan frowned.

"I don't know what you want, Vinca," she said. "I speak Pan-fairy, not Wendy-fairy."

"She's telling you not to go for your sword when you hear me creeping up behind you," said a familiar voice.

"Wendy!" The Pan turned, beaming at the sight of the girl who made everything better just by walking into a room. She looked sad. The Pan didn't like that—Wendys should be joyful things—and so she skipped, leaving the ground, and flew the few yards to land nose-to-nose with her Wendy. "Have you come to keep watch with me?"

"I have," said Wendy, with a small smile. She reached out, brushing the Pan's hair out of her face, just like a mother should. "I also wanted to talk to you, Sheila, if that's all right."

The Pan flinched, her feet touching down. "I don't like that name. That's a before-name. I'm the Pan."

"Pans have names," said Wendy calmly. "Remember? Franklin was Pan here when we came. He came through our bedroom window, and he told us if we came with him, we could be children forever, and free forever..."

"Pans have names, but that doesn't mean we have to *use* them," said the Pan petulantly. "The old Pan wasn't a good Pan. He lost. Remember? He led his lieutenants against the pirates, and he *lost*, and he *died*, and I became Pan in his place. He wasn't a good Pan. So why should I follow his example?"

"Because you're the Pan and I'm your Wendy, but you're also Sheila, and I'm your sister," said Wendy gently. She put her hand against the Pan's cheek. "Remember? Neverland loves me too much to make you forget *that*."

"Of course I remember," scoffed the Pan. Then she hesitated before admitting, slowly, "I'm just not sure I remember what a sister *is*…"

Wendy pulled her hand away. "It's nothing important," she said. She straightened, looking at the Pan, and said, "I want to come with you when you attack the pirates tonight."

"What? Why? Wendys are only good for getting themselves kidnapped and tied to the mast."

"I know. Having me there will confuse the pirates and make it easier for you to win, and then we can get home in time for the feast." Wendy smiled. "I trust you to rescue me."

"Of course I'll rescue you!" said the Pan, feet leaving the ground again. "I'm the Pan! Rescue is what I do!" She turned cartwheels in the air, crowing, and Wendy watched her, and said nothing.

There was nothing left for her to say.

***"This is** how it goes. The Pan plans battles, and the Wendys win the war."*

"It isn't fair."

"Cecily." Edith frowned at her. "Whoever told you childhood would be fair?"

Time passed; the tide turned. Time, and tides, were dependable that way. The sails of the ships on the horizon grew pregnant with wind, and the pirates of Neverland began the trek to shore. Their decks were packed with men bristling with swords, and their cannons were loaded, ready to unleash hell on the waiting shore. At each ship's helm was a pirate captain, grim of jaw and dead of eye, steering them inexorably toward battle.

On the shore, the Pan flew back and forth before her gathered army, her feet pointing straight down and hanging inches above the shore. All of the Lost Children big enough to hold a knife or a spear were there, and their Wendys were with them, leaving only a few behind to keep watch over the younglings. Mermaids bobbed in the surf, their multicolored fins breaking the surface in brief flashes, like captive rainbows, and the sky overhead glowed with the captive aurora of ever-moving fairy wings.

"The pirates have grown bold of late—too bold," said the Pan. "They dare our waters even on the days when their passage is forbidden; they steal our stores and raid our berry bushes. Six of our newest Lost Children have been lured out to sea, forsaking play for piracy. We are gathered here today, we are players in this greatest game, because this! This ends tonight!"

The Lost Children roared their approval. The mermaids slapped their fins against the water, and the fairies chimed as loudly as they could, a hundred bells proclaiming the need for war. Of the Wendys, only the one who looked so very much like the Pan stayed silent, her eyes fixed on the surf at her feet. No one paid attention to her, or to the deep sorrow in her eyes.

"We have lost friends! Brothers and sisters! Remember them! Fly for them! Make vengeance in their names, and then do them the greatest honor that can be done in Neverland: forget them. Today, we have mourned. Today, we grew a little bit older, because you need a heart to grieve, and that which is not heartless can age. Tonight, we avenge. And tomorrow, we will be joyful and heartless once more."

This time the roar was louder, because all the Lost Children knew that this was the way of things: when the Pan made a stirring speech, you cheered. Only the Wendys held their silence, because to be a Wendy is to be other than heartless, and so they were already on their way to being older than everyone around them.

"We fly for Neverland!" proclaimed the Pan, and this roar was the loudest of them all.

They left the shore by air and by sea, those who could not fly—either because they feared falling or because they had never quite caught the knack—clustered in coracle boats towed by mermaids as they made their way unerringly toward the distant pirate ships.

Most Wendys *could* fly, although Neverland etiquette dictated that as mothers, they should keep their feet on the ground as much as possible, to show that they provided the stable center for the chaos of the Lost Children. Cecily had been in Neverland for more than a hundred and fifty years, and still her flight path was shaky and uncertain as she tried to keep pace with her sister, the Pan. As she flew, she stole sidelong glances at the Pan's face, looking for traces of her twin. Sheila had all but disappeared as the decades slipped by, blurring away into the features of a legend. They still looked exactly alike if you measured only in hair color and eye shape and height, but those were just fripperies—they didn't *matter*. Cecily looked like warm fires and hot milk and bedtime stories. Sheila looked like cold winds and wild forests and stolen children coaxed out of nursery windows by the promise of something bigger and better than what they had. They didn't look anything alike.

But they had, once. Before Neverland, before the old Pan died and the new Pan seized his sword.

Who will the new Pan be when you fall, Sheila? Cecily wondered, and shivered.

Until that moment, she hadn't been sure that she would really do it.

"Pans aren't *like the rest of us," said Edith, her eyes never leaving Cecily. "We live in Neverland, we play the parts Neverland asks us to play, but we're just residents. The Pan is Neverland. The Pan is every leaf that falls and every flower that blooms. The Pan is every one of us, from the youngest Lost Child to the oldest Wendy, and without the Pan, everything would fall to pieces and be forgotten. But when the king is the land, sacrifices must be made. There are costs to keeping things in balance. Do you understand?"*

"No," said Cecily, and yes, *said Cecily's heart, and she knew what she was going to do. Not because she loved the Pan, and not because she loved Neverland, but because she loved her sister. It had been a long, long time since two little girls followed a boy clad in skeleton leaves out their bedroom window, fleeing from adults who raised their hands too quickly and hit too hard. They had flown to*

Neverland, both of them expecting nothing more than to be welcomed. Instead, they had been torn apart, Cecily gone to the Wendys, and Sheila…Sheila gone to something more. Being the Pan had eaten her up, swallowing her bit by bit, like she was drowning. If she lived much longer, she wouldn't be Sheila at all. She would just be the Pan, and Cecily would be alone.

"She needs to lose," said Edith.

And Cecily nodded.

The pirates were ready when the Lost Children arrived, notified of the oncoming attack by Edith's message even before their sentries spotted the oncoming line of flying children, all led by a flaxen-haired little girl whose gown of skeleton leaves gleamed pale against her tan brown skin. She crowed. The pirates thrust their swords into the air, jeering, and the battle was joined.

Even in Neverland, even in a place where bedtime stories can go on forever and no one is ever told to go to bed or wash behind their ears, there are some things that are not pretty: were not meant to be pretty, because prettiness would steal their essential power, rendering them impotent and useless. So swords clashed against swords, and steel bit into exposed flesh, and children fell out of the sky like raindrops. Pirates fired arrows up at the Lost Boys and Girls who soared overhead, or down at the mermaids who flashed through the waves, trying to break the rudders and snare the anchor lines.

The Wendy who had been forced into the war by the Pan took a knife in the chest. He died choking on his own blood and was kicked overboard into the surf. Two of the mermaids seized his body and dragged it under, the fight forgotten in favor of a ready meal. Still the battle went on, the smell of gunpowder and blood wiping everything else away.

Cecily hung at the edges of the battle, waiting for the sign that Edith had promised her. A hand grasped her wrist, spinning her around, and she found herself looking into the tired, bearded face of a man she almost knew, if she looked at him just right.

"You...you were Franklin's Wendy," she said, her words tumbling into the space between the cannon fire. "I remember you."

"Yes," he said. "Are you here to pay the cost of war?"

No, cried her heart, and "Yes," said her mouth, and he nodded and pulled her close, flipping her around so that her back was against his broad pirate's chest. He pressed his sword to her throat.

"Do not be afraid," he murmured, and bellowed, "*Pan!* Come and face me, girl!"

The Pan jerked toward the sound of her name, eyes going wide as she saw her sister captive in a pirate's arms. "Let my Wendy go!" she shouted, darting across the battlefield toward the pirate who held Cecily. "Fight me like a man!"

"Ah, but lass, it's never a man as kills a Pan," said the pirate. His hand did something clever at his belt, and suddenly Cecily was holding a knife, small and sharp and wicked.

She remembered this; remembered Franklin shouting and diving for the pirate who held his Wendy. But the pirate had stabbed him in the stomach like a coward, and Franklin had died. Wasn't that what had happened?

The knife's hilt was patterned with the whispery bones of skeleton leaves. Cecily felt it with her fingers, and felt the story shift around her, finally coming clear.

"I love you, Sheila," she whispered, and the battle still raging all around them took her words away as her sister dove closer and closer, shouting all the while.

In the end, Cecily didn't even have to stab her.

All she had to do was hold the knife.

Sometimes a war isn't about how many casualties can be piled up on both sides; sometimes it's about one. One body falling as gravity suddenly remembers that it has a claim here. One body striking the deck of a pirate ship. One little girl overwhelmed with grief and rage, turning to bury a knife in the throat of a pirate captain who doesn't resist, because he's been where she's standing, he's felt what she feels, and he knows that in the moment the knife slid home, she grew a heart so big and so broken that Neverland can no longer hold her. She'll grow up, this girl, until her feet fit perfectly in his boots and she steers the armada away from land, a pirate leading pirates, to wait for the day that Neverland needs to make a sacrifice once more. She doesn't need to know what a Fisher King is. Neverland knows for her.

Sometimes a war isn't about an army. Sometimes it's all about one person. But which one?

Does Neverland go to war for Wendy, or the Pan?

The death of the Pan filled the Lost Children with rage, and seeing the Pan's Wendy kill the pirate that had killed the Pan filled them with strength. They *could* win this, and they *would* win it, for Neverland. For the Pan.

Bit by bit they beat the pirates back, until the horizon was free of those foul sails, and the Lost Children—the ones who survived—turned their eyes toward home.

"Where's the Pan's Wendy?" asked a little boy.

No one knew the answer.

"She must have died," said Gantry. He'd been one of the Pan's lieutenants, and so his words carried a certain weight; what's more, there was a wild new light in his eye, one that spoke of flying, and lying, and never, never growing old. He was not yet dressed in skeleton leaves, but he may as well have been. "Poor Wendy."

"Poor Wendy," murmured the other children.

"Now come on—let's race back to shore," said Gantry, and took off like a shot, laughing. The others flew after him, the war and its costs already beginning to fade from memory. The blood on the water would take longer to disperse, but given a little time that, too, would be gone.

It was a beautiful morning in Neverland, and it would be long and long before anyone thought that it might be fun to go to war.

Please Accept My Most Profound Apologies for What Is About to Happen (But You Started It)

Well.

This happened.

I really can't say much about it, other than "I am reasonably sure you could hand this story to literally anyone who has ever met me, from preschool on, and they would be able to identify the author from the first couple of paragraphs."

To the citizens of our fine metropolis:

Hello.

You don't know me, although you should: I've lived among you for years. You've sat next to me on the bus. We've eaten at the same

McDonalds. The woman in the Ian Malcolm T-shirt at the midnight showing of *Jurassic World* who started sobbing when the overture began? That was me. (Although I challenge anyone who remembers what it is to be twelve years old and committed to the fantasy *not* to start crying when the music goes "da-da-DAH-da-DAH" and the Park gates open and they realize that they're finally, finally going home.)

But I digress.

It is important you understand that I am one of you. I am no imported menace, come from some far shore to trouble your day-to-day lives. I am homegrown. I went to school with your children, enduring their taunts and endless attempts to make me conform to their surprisingly sophisticated ideas of "normal." How lucky they were to have parents like you, who would enforce gender and social norms so stringently that a girl in blue jeans with a book about dinosaurs became an obvious target for re-education! How unfortunate I was to have an absent father and an alcoholic mother, neither of whom was in a position to make me stop distinguishing myself from the mob.

This is where my therapist would say that I have a rare combination of Oedipal and Electra Complexes, with a dash of abandonment complex to spice the mix. I do not wish to have sexual congress with either of my parents, and never have, but their absence has shaped my life in ways I could not prevent. Maybe if they'd been there, I wouldn't be the woman I am today.

This is, in any rational world, an oversimplification. I think I would still be some variation on myself. I think the things about me that have brought us to this point were inborn. I was not made by Nature to be an herbivore, or even a carnivore, red of tooth and claw. No, I was made to a greater purpose.

I was made to be a comet.

I was twelve years old when *Jurassic Park* came to the theater near my house. I stole five dollars from my mother's purse, using it to purchase a ticket (ostensibly to the bloodless, safe children's movie playing at the other end of the building) and a box of popcorn before I slipped into a red-upholstered seat, and into the flickering splendor of my future.

I do not need to describe the film to you. I *want* to. Please understand, I want to more than I want anything else in this moment. Dinosaurs are what my therapist terms my "special interest," and I have what can only be described as a Pavlovian desire to share them with the world. I want to tell you about every second of my experience. Not just the movie itself—I could recite the movie, word for word, scene by scene, but why bother? You can stream it yourself, through any one of a number of services. You are an intelligent person, whoever you are, or you wouldn't be the one reading this letter: I assume that, as an intelligent person, you have already sought out and devoured one of the great cinematic masterpieces of all time.

But it's not just about the movie. It's about the way I reacted to it, the way my skin got tight and my breath got quick and my heart seemed simultaneously to be freezing and catching fire. It's about the way I stopped shoveling popcorn into my mouth halfway through, forgetting to chew, forgetting to *breathe*, because what I was seeing was taking up so much of my attention that I could barely remember that I wasn't there with them, running through the jungles, smelling the hot breath of raptors on my neck.

It's about belonging. It's about looking into a filmmaker's vision of what life was like millions of years ago, and suddenly, absolutely knowing what it was to *belong*.

I tried to tell the other kids at school. Some of them liked to brag about how they went to the movies every weekend, how their parents always bought them candy and let them put gallons of butter on the popcorn, drowning it, preserving it like a mosquito trapped in amber. I thought that for sure they would have seen the movie, and that it would give us something in common, something we could throw between us like a rope. It would anchor me, and they would use it to pull me into the safe harbor of the norm. We would have a shared experience. I would be accepted.

It is not pride which leads me to say that I am of immense intellect, especially when compared to the average citizen of our city. I am a genius by any measure. I have made errors in my lifetime, as have we all, but they have always been failings of ambition or of understanding, not of intellect.

The greatest error I ever made was in believing the children who tormented me would suddenly accept me simply because we had seen the same movie. They laughed at me for even making the attempt. They called me "freak" and "nerd" and "loser," and other words I won't write down, not even here, in the chronicle of why I have done what I have done, why I have set in motion what I have set in motion. They can't take back those words, almost thirty years in the past; those words are forever. So are my actions. It pleases me to know that, soon enough, only my actions will be remembered. They'll overshadow everything else. Even the casual cruelty of children.

So I was spurned and I was shunned and I was more alone than ever, because I had dared to attempt to be something else. Children are like bees. They have an inherent knowledge of social structure and caste systems within the hive, and the drone who deviates will be stung back into position. They forced me to the fringes. I took refuge in the library. I began reading everything I could get my hands on about dinosaurs, evolutionary biology, and the science of genetic engineering. Surely there would be answers there.

Surely one of the books would have a map, sketched in pencil and visible only to the worthy, telling me how to reach Jurassic Park, which must exist somewhere in the world, hidden in the deepest jungle, overseen by the kindly Dr. Wu, who was already hard at work on a newer, better generation of dinosaurs. Dinosaurs that would understand that humans do not tolerate deviation. Dinosaurs that would know to behave themselves until the Park was open, until they would be standing in a target-rich environment and could better make their wishes understood. Dr. Wu was smart. He could make dinosaurs that were smarter. Children are so often smarter than their parents.

The average person reads at a rate of 200 to 250 words per minute. Please keep this in mind.

There was no second Park, of course: there is no Dr. Wu. If I wanted dinosaurs in this world, I needed to find a way to make them myself. I deduced this somewhere between the ages of fourteen and fifteen, during the summer I spent in a coma after a couple of the clever neighborhood boys decided to escalate their assaults, taking them from simple teasing and petty theft to outright assault.

You may know who I am now. The situation made the papers. My mother saved them all while I was hospitalized. Local girl attacked. Unknown assailants still at large. But they weren't unknown, were they? Not really. I told their names to anyone who would listen as soon as I woke up. I gave descriptions, addresses, everything. And it didn't matter. They may have beaten me hard enough with a baseball bat that for a time, the doctors didn't think I was ever going to wake up; they may have done their best to murder me for the crime of being slightly different from them; but they didn't kill me. They didn't do anything that couldn't be written off as "youthful hijinks gotten out of hand" or excused with a calm "they have their whole lives in front of them."

They tried to take my life away from me. They tried to make me *stop*. They did everything they could to remove me from the world, and why? Because I liked to talk about dinosaurs? Because I wasn't exactly the way they wanted me to be? But somehow their futures were more important than my present, and they got away with it again. One big thing in a lifetime defined by little things, and one very important lesson. Humans will always defend the offspring of the privileged, if allowed to do so.

(Sometimes I'll admit I've wondered whether the attack might not have had a more sinister cause: whether my attackers might have been overcome by consciousnesses from the future, disembodied and sent back to prevent me from achieving my life's work. Tempting as it is to turn a defeat into a validation, doing so would be admitting defeat all over again. If there are time travelers in the future of this world, I am about to fail. And I refuse to fail.)

You have been reading for approximately 1,600 words now. If your reading speed matches the average, it has been eight minutes since you opened this file and beheld my salutation. At this moment, you should be experiencing shortness of breath, tinnitus, and a dull ache in your joints. Perhaps you were unaware of these things until I pointed them out. People are remarkably good at ignoring small discomforts.

I recovered from my injuries, obviously. I never got my day in court, but I got something that was arguably better: I got blood money. Payments, anonymous donations to my care and education, totaling more than a million dollars. It's amazing what guilt and the desire to avoid a scandal will do. I ran the numbers, did the math, made a few casual comments about how affording college would still be *so* difficult, and wouldn't it be a shame if I had to stay in town forever, talking to people about what had happened to me. I was offered three scholarships inside of the week.

Even people like me can learn to play the game, if you insist on teaching us. If you won't leave us alone.

Protecting the money from my mother was surprisingly easy; the numbers were too large to make sense to her, and so she left me alone. I kept my head down, wore a back brace through most of high school, made few friends, never dated. I understood that I was not part of the herd. I understood that I was not welcome in this particular primeval world. I attracted as little attention to myself as possible, and I endured, keeping my eyes on the bright speck of light approaching in my own secret sky. My comet. My beautiful comet.

College was almost enough to change my mind. There's no shame in admitting that I was tempted. Humanity is not entirely bad, after all, and for a mind like mine, the halls of academia were uniquely designed to provide temptation. I closed my eyes at night and saw my instructors, my fellow students, my *future*, instead of the kindly smiling face of Dr. Wu. Surely he would understand if I changed my course. Surely he would see that sometimes there are options apart from mass extinction.

There were many small extinctions before the mass die-off which ended the first age of dinosaurs. There were many second chances. Humanity could be afforded one as well.

But humanity was not fully confined within my college campus, was it? And even if it had been, I only had to look around to see that things weren't getting better the way I needed them to. People were dying in the streets, not because they'd fallen afoul of some mad genius, but because they'd run afoul of their own kind. Children went hungry. Adults continued to say "but he has his whole life ahead of him" like it somehow absolved their boys of their crimes against their girls. His whole life seemed to matter a great deal. Her whole life didn't seem to matter at all. It was too much. It was too much. It had to stop. The temptation, which had only ever been momentary, passed.

Eleven minutes now. Your heart rate is elevated. Your vision is beginning to blur. The ache in your joints is more pronounced. Have you heard the first screams in the streets, or are you reading this in an isolated location? If you cannot hear the screams, I suggest you leave the room you are currently in and proceed until you *can* hear them. It will elevate your heart rate further; it will make your joints ache like fire, and pump needles into your stomach. It may even cost you a few hundred words. You may not make it to the end of this message. But then, there was never any guarantee that you would, and you will do better if you finish the progression of your symptoms in a place you can escape.

I have run enough tests with this program, with this letter, to know the expression on your face. You may call the authorities if you like. It's not as if I could stop you; I'm not there, after all. You can tell them you've received a...is this letter threatening? I don't think it's threatening yet. It's expository. Tell them you've received an expository letter that seems to be predicting relatively minor medical symptoms which most people experience daily. Perhaps you'll be fortunate. Perhaps the person who takes your call will have noticed their own symptoms before picking up the phone. Perhaps they will not tell you that it is psychosomatic. Perhaps they'll realize.

It won't change anything. You understand that, don't you? It won't change anything, and you will have wasted some portion of an increasingly scarce resource. I can't control what you choose to do, but if I were you, I would elect to keep reading. At least then you might have a few moments of comprehension before comprehension goes away forever. Isn't it better to *understand?*

We have always lived in a world of miracles. We have harnessed the atom, learned to power an entire world with lightning, and plunged our needles into the bowels of the planet to extract the liquefied skeletons of dinosaurs. Isn't that amazing? Since the Industrial Revolution, we have fueled a global civilization with dino-power, and we have treated it as if it were commonplace.

Scary movies like to talk about how bad it is to build a home on top of a cemetery. They say the unquiet dead will rise and take their revenge. We've spent more than a century building everything we have on the graveyards of the dinosaurs, wrenching them from the earth to display in our museums and pump into our cars. Don't you think it's time for them to have their revenge?

I'm sorry. I digress. Where was I?

College.

Dr. Wu returned, and with every disaster, every catastrophe, his smile faded. He knew humanity was not deserving of his bright and perfect Park. Even if it could be made real, we would all have been Dennis Nedry, the man who betrayed Jurassic Park for personal gain, who didn't think they had made anything worth making. We would try not to be—we would swear we loved the dinosaurs, even as we exploited them. All of us. Even me. Humanity has no place in Jurassic Park. You understand that, don't you? *We* were the flaw in the grand design. Not the fences, not the raptors. *Us.*

A few of the girls in my dorm teased me for essentially worshipping a junk science thriller about dinosaurs, but most of them left me alone. College was where you were supposed to have weird beliefs, right? I believed in the fossil record, in the inevitability of the extinction event, and I went to class, and I studied, and I remembered the children who teased me, and I remembered the adults who looked away. I remembered everything. I never let anything go.

Four years and bang! A degree in Biology, with a specialization in Genetic Engineering, and a minor in Paleontology. Three more years and pow! A PhD in Genetic Engineering, and job offers from around the country, from around the world. For the first time in my life, everyone wanted me. It was nice, being wanted for a change. It might have turned my head, if college hadn't already tempted me and lost. Every comet must experience the gravitational force of some second body if it's going to build up sufficient speed to make an impact.

You probably saw the papers when I came home. "Local genius returns to give back to the community." I passed up million-dollar salaries and private jets to work for a tiny con-agra company working on creating a softer, gentler, less-inflammatory form of gluten. They swore they were going to make celiac-safe wheat within the decade, and I was their magic bullet.

We did it, of course. Last year. You've probably enjoyed our delicious NuWheat™ products at home and in restaurants. I really did an amazing job. I'm proud of myself, and I'm glad my last piece of ethically clean research was devoted to making life better for people who didn't deserve to be in pain. I improved lives. I am proud of that. I will remain proud of that through everything that follows. There's a reason some people have chosen to invest in ethical family farms: they still eat meat, but at least they know the chicken on their plate lived a happy life before it was harvested.

Have you lived a happy life? Have you made good choices about your time and energy, and how you spent them? I hope so. I hope you look back on everything and smile and smile and know you did as well as you could with what you had. I hope you will rejoice. It would be better that way.

The papers should have said "local genius returns to take revenge on small-minded fools who laughed at her while she was vulnerable, kicked her while she was down, and left her incapable of forming meaningful human relationships." Or "local genius smart enough to understand that no one ever gets over high school; is finally intending to be prom queen." Or "local genius comes home to show you, show you all." I've always liked that phrase. "Show you all." Show you what, exactly? It's so flexible. It could apply to virtually anything.

Local genius returns to begin final refinements on the project she started in her freshman year of college, holed up in her dorm and reading about the genetic links between species, the commonalities that tie us all together.

Local genius returns because what's the fun in breaking the natural laws of the universe if no one who sees you do it understands how impressive you're being.

Local genius returns because if you're going to do something, you should be standing as close to ground zero as possible. You should understand the consequences. You can't do good by standing on a mountaintop and telling people they deserve this. It's not fair. It's not right. I needed to be among people who would judge me—and you've always been very, very good at judging me, haven't you? I may have a gift for science, but the people in this town are Olympians of pain.

It's been a little over fifteen minutes, no matter how quickly you read. The aching in your joints is probably keeping you from standing up straight now. That metallic taste in your mouth is getting more severe; the pain in your teeth may be making your eyes cross. Or maybe they're just doing that on their own. Are you gluten intolerant? That's about to make a difference.

The fields will take years to reset to a pre-domestic makeup, if they ever fully do. Our cities will fall before the marching armies of wind and weather, our seeds will scatter, but the changes we've made to the plants we chose to cultivate will last for centuries. There will always be high quantities of gluten in the wheat. I couldn't condemn the people suffering from a nasty immune disorder to short, painful lives, where their inability to digest gluten would collide with a sudden inability to digest animal proteins and leave them dead before their time. So I put markers in the NuWheat™. I told it what to say when the rest of my tools showed up and started giving instructions—especially if those instructions were given in a system which contained no gluten.

The percentage of people who either have a gluten intolerance, live with someone with a gluten intolerance, or choose to eat gluten free because they think it's somehow "healthier" is approximately equal to the number of carnivores in a balanced population.

It's like nature was getting things ready for me.

I am sorry. I hope you'll understand that. I know it's hard to look at the things I've done, the things I'm describing, and see my side of things, but I *am* sorry. I tried to find other ways of achieving my goals, but sadly, humanity was too good at being human. We are the single largest mammalian population. We've killed or domesticated everything else. My estimates say that only one in three subjects will survive the first stage of the transition, and that as many as one-half of the offspring of the first generation will be born resembling their grandparents. Throwbacks.

Non-viable. So you see, if I wanted to recreate Dr. Wu's dream, it had to be humans, and it had to be everyone.

Equilibrium will be reached. There will be no more wars, no more assaults…no more Nedrys. From now on, when we attack each other, it will be out of hunger, and we will kill what we claim.

I know that *Jurassic Park* was written by a man named Michael Crichton, who wanted to entertain. I know that some people think he was inspired by—or stealing from—a man named Harry Knight, who wrote a book called *Carnosaur.* I am inspired by them both. I am stealing from them both. I am following Dr. Wu. I trust him to tell me what comes next.

At twenty minutes, you will likely lose consciousness. If you are a slow enough reader, this may have already happened. I am sorry.

At thirty minutes, you will be grateful to be unconscious, as your body will begin rewriting itself according to my templates. I estimate forty percent of fatalities will occur during this phase.

At three hours, you will no longer be human.

At eight hours, the first subjects will awaken. If I have timed things correctly, the herbivores will wake first. Their instincts will drive them to flee the cities, to clump together, to begin looking for safe ground.

At twelve hours, the remaining subjects will awaken.

The dinosaurs were innocent. They did not bully. They did not taunt. They did not kill for fun. They deserved this planet more than we did. More than we ever could. So I am giving it back to them, and I am using us to do it. I am truly sorry that it has come to this…but again, you started it. Maybe now that we are all dinosaurs together, you can finally accept me.

Welcome to Jurassic Park.

Yours,
Dr. Constance O'Malley, PhD.

Threnody for Little Girl, With Tuna, at the End of the World

This is another story that decided to knock me down and sit on me until I agreed to write it. It began in front of the big fish tank at the Monterey Bay Aquarium, standing and watching as the giant tuna circled endlessly. It was an image that has never left me. I doubt it ever will.

This was one of the first stories written for my Patreon, which we refer to as "The Toaster Project," and coincided with my relocating from California, where I had lived for most of my life, to Washington state. It was a good thing. I am happy I did it. But it was definitely a stressful experience, and I wrote a lot of "and then the world ended" stories around the time of the move. I feel like this is one of the sweeter ones. It's definitely one of the sadder ones.

The doorbell rang, and I knew Matthew was dead.

It wasn't a remarkable sort of knowing, although maybe it should have been. It was too quiet for that, too sad, creeping out of nowhere and filling me from toe to tip with the knowledge that the world was different now than it had been a few moments ago.

If I turned on the news, someone would be talking about it. That should have been a comfort, knowing I wasn't going to mourn alone. All it did was make me tired. I stood, leaving my computer to compile its code, ticking down the seconds of my working day with mechanical precision, and walked to the door, opening it with a press of my thumb to the authorized entry detector next to the knob.

There was a person on my doorstep, a real person, not a mail robot, wearing the uniform of the United States Postal Service and gingerly holding a large manila envelope. Real paper, to go with the real person. A pack of envelopes like that was worth a month of my salary. I was afraid to reach for it, afraid this was a mistake—hoping this was a mistake—and I could be debited for mussing someone else's property.

"Catherine Nast?" asked the postal worker, and it wasn't a mistake: this was really happening.

"Yes."

"Sign here, here, and here." The form to release a piece of official government mail was dizzying, and ended with a request for my thumbprint, just in case I was a squatter who had managed to successfully ID-jack the real Catherine Nast to the level of hacking the house. Not common, but it could happen: sixty percent of all full-immersion ID-jackers were uncovered by the post office, IRS, or pizza delivery services.

The red light at the top of the postal worker's clipboard flashed green, and the envelope was released into my hand, smooth and heavy and irrevocable.

"Have a nice day," said the postal worker, and then they were gone, disappearing down the hall, off to another essential but infrequent delivery, leaving me standing alone, exposed, with tears running down my cheeks.

Matthew was dead, and the world was never going to be the same.

The discovery of a living Pacific Bluefin tuna was global news. The species had been believed extinct for over a decade, since the last of the aquarium breeding programs had ended in failure. The Pacific Bluefin had been the last known species of tuna to hang on, battling through overfishing and changing oceans until the final tagged individual had been found in a poacher's net on November 17th, 2032. After that, the species had been assumed lost forever, one more entry in the long book of things that humanity's time on the planet had destroyed.

Then a research vessel tagging the surviving Humboldt squid population off the California coast snagged something unexpected: a small silver fish, no more than eighteen inches long, with spikes along its spine and a familiar, silvery sheen.

One of the researchers started to weep when she saw it, the last tuna in the world shining in the sun. We have video, her hands clasped over her mouth, tears running down her cheeks as two more researchers cut the tuna free of the net, heedless of the damage done to their equipment, because what was a single net in the presence of the last tuna? They moved the fish to a holding tank, filming all the while, in case something happened before they could get back to shore, in case there was a storm, in case hungry pirates from the drowned islands—which was virtually all of them, from Hawaii to New Zealand—boarded them and took their treasure away.

There were no storms. There were no pirates. The world's last known Pacific Bluefin tuna was delivered to the Monterey Bay Aquarium on March 2nd, 2035, where it was given a full examination and declared a healthy male.

The world went wild. Tuna fever dominated the news shows and blog cycles. Schools taught impromptu lessons about the ecological and cultural significance of the tuna, while the sole surviving specimen swam lonely circles around the giant viewing pool at the aquarium, no longer free, unaware of his importance. To people who lived in terror that the ocean was broken forever, he represented something almost unthinkable: he represented hope.

When tuna fever began to flag, the conservation orgs that had been using him as their new mascot searched for a way to make him relevant again, and seized on the most obvious: they would give him a name. Not just any name, no. They would allow the entire world to have a say.

The contest was simple. Anyone, anywhere, could enter. The entries would then be judged by a special open-source software program designed to detect profanity in every known language, both natural and constructed, and entries which passed this filter would be put into a single massive pool. Then, on a simulcast sent to anyone who cared to watch, the winner would be selected. Their chosen name would be given to the tuna, and they and their family would be flown to California to attend a grand gala in honor of the last Pacific Bluefin tuna in the world.

It was calculated. It was designed to stir the sympathies of the world. And so, when the winner was announced as seven-year-old Catherine Nast of Chicago, Illinois, there were people who demanded the random number generation code be released to them so they could tease and tear it apart, looking for the place where the people running the contest had decided to cheat.

It wasn't there. Little Catie had won the right to name the big silver fish fair and square, and when she went to the gala with her parents, she wore a silver dress with a lacy white skirt that made her feel like a mermaid, or like a princess, or like both at the same time. There were reporters who wanted to talk to her, and when one of them asked why she would give such a magnificent fish such a boring name—because there had been hundreds, even thousands of "Nemo"s and "Neptune"s and "Poseidon"s in the barrel, but according to the data, only one Matthew—she cast her eyes down to the floor and replied with genuine sorrow:

"My grandpa died last month, and when I asked Mom what his name was, she said it was Matthew. So I named the fish after my grandpa. He was the first person to take me to see the ocean."

It hadn't been much of a sight, not by the time Catie was born, wide-eyed daughter of the ecological collapse, but it was clear just by looking at her that she hadn't cared. It had been a day in the company of her grandfather, him loving her, him showing her something that mattered, even if she was too young to understand that once, people had played in the water, instead of standing at a safe distance and covering their noses against the acrid chemical smell of the waves. And now he was gone, and thanks to a spin of a random number generator, his memory would live on, swimming endless circles in a tank that had been designed to hold dozens of tuna, and now held only one.

The reporters left her alone after that. Catie spent the evening wandering the aquarium with her parents, staring in wide-eyed wonder at the exhibits. She spent the longest time in front of the tuna tank, her hands pressed against the glass, watching Matthew circle, ever-moving, ever seeking the lost and endless sea. One lucky photographer got a picture of her just as Matthew swam by, the little girl in the silvery dress, her eyes turned up in wondering awe, watching the last tuna in the world pass. Aquariums around the world used that picture in their brochures.

Very few people remembered her name.

The envelope contained a press kit about Matthew—where he'd been found, his vital statistics, the results of the necropsy that had been performed after medical science had stopped working miracles and he'd been found floating at the surface of his tank. There was even a paragraph about his naming, and a copy of that damned picture, me staring in slack-mouthed amazement at the most pampered fish on the planet.

I don't remember much about that night. I remember that the hors d'oeuvres were much too rich for my stomach, but I'd eaten them anyway, pretending I didn't see Mom loading them into her purse by the handful, pretending every bite wasn't worth a week of my father's salary. I'd been sick on the ride home, clutching my stomach and vomiting by the side of the road, and I still hadn't been hungry for two days after that, my body struggling to deal with things that were much more complicated than my usual nutrient-rich food products.

I remember standing by the tank and watching the fish with my grandfather's name circling endlessly. I'd been old enough to understand that death was forever, but young enough to have some confused ideas about religion and what heaven was. For my grandfather, getting to be a fish in clean water, with places to swim and new shores to see, seemed about as close to heaven as it was possible to get. Sure, Matthew was just a fish, but he was a miracle, too. Maybe Grandpa could be a part of the miracle.

I knew better by the time my parents finished eating their stolen appetizers and selling the last of the memorabilia from the evening on various online auction sites. There were no miracles. There was only keeping alive, one day at a time, until you couldn't anymore.

My mother couldn't when I was sixteen. Cancer. She went fast, or maybe she was sick for a long time before she told me. Either way, I'd been a teenage girl with a teenage girl's coping skills. That was the first time I ran away, selling two pints of plasma and my grandmother's silver earrings to buy myself a bus ticket to the aquarium where Matthew still circled, eyes fixed on a horizon that was just a trick of the way the walls curved.

No one came to take a picture that time. I guess weeping teenagers who haven't washed their hair in a week aren't as photogenic as carefully-dressed seven-year-olds with stars in their eyes. It's too bad, really. That's a picture I wouldn't mind having displayed in aquariums around the world. It would be more honest. "This is what grief looks like."

My father died when I was twenty-one. Heart attack. He fell over in his cubicle, mouse still clutched in his right hand, like productivity could somehow save him from the inevitable. He'd been with the company longer than I'd been alive. They didn't pay for his funeral. They hired someone else to do his job inside of the week.

There was no trip to see Matthew that time. Even if I'd been able to afford it after paying to have my father cremated, I couldn't have taken the time off work. I needed to keep coding if I wanted to keep eating, and the urge to eat—to survive—was as strong in me as it was in any living thing. I did pay for half an hour's access to the aquarium livestream, and watched him circle, and wished I were swimming there with him.

That would be the third photo in the set. The adult, beat-down, exhausted, watching her childhood swimming in an endless circle, wondering where it had all gone so wrong.

Maybe they were right to stick with the first picture. At least that one looked like it belonged to a world where hope could still exist. Matthew and I had both been young, with our lives ahead of us, capable of dreaming of a future where things would be better, if fish could dream. Now here I was, alone, and he was gone, and so was his kind. Gone forever.

The envelope also contained an invitation. All expenses paid.

COME, it cajoled. BID FAREWELL TO A WONDER OF THE DEEP. At the bottom, awaiting my thumbprint, flashed the question WILL YOU ATTEND? I hesitated, thinking of time away from work, thinking of demerits on my record. Even with the aquarium paying for everything, it would cost me.

Screw it. I pressed my thumb down on the text, watching it flash to green, hearing the ping as a plane ticket was credited to my personal account, ready to fly me across the country, to take me to the funeral of a friend. You only live once. Someone who loved you should be there when you go, to say goodbye.

The last time I saw my grandfather before he died, he'd been too sick to take me down to the sea. The smell wouldn't have done him any good in his weakened state, chemical and cruel as it was. So he'd sat in his wheelchair, oxygen hissing, and he'd walked me through the process of bringing the sea to us.

First I'd filled every big bowl the kitchen had to offer with lukewarm water—"Not hot," he'd said, in that careful drawl of his, "because I won't have your folks saying I endangered you, and not cold, because then the salt won't dissolve"—and carried them to the living room, placing them reverently around him. He'd given me a container of salt then, the old kind that came in a paper cylinder and would pour out as much as you wanted at a time, not measuring it into nutritionally approved portions, and I'd mixed salt into the water until it had turned cloudy, while he put on movie after movie about whales and fish and the open sea, back when it loved us, back when we still loved it.

The two of us spent the whole afternoon like that, my hands growing soft and wrinkled like his as I dangled them in the warm, soft water, him smiling down at me, and it had been amazing, and it had been perfect, and the next time I'd seen him, he had been a face on a viewing screen and a vase full of ashes, all the water burned out of him by the crematorium's flame. When we died, we ran as far from the ocean as we could go.

We shouldn't do that. I thought that then, and I think that now. We should find the opposite of fire. We should find some chemical process that chases us all the way back to the water, instead of taking us away from it forever, so that we could dilute the damage that we've done, one body at a time, restoring the world with our bodies. It seems wrong that we should hurt the planet in the process of living, and then refuse to give of ourselves to put it all back together again.

It seems wrong.

I don't know what they did with my grandfather's ashes. They weren't in my father's things when he died. Whatever it was, I doubt it involved going back to the sea.

The celebration of Matthew's life came with a dress code, and while my invitation had included admission, airfare, and even two nights at a capsule hotel—one before and one after, so I wouldn't appear rushed when the news sites saw me, the little girl who'd named a miracle and been forgotten, now miraculously all grown up, as if twenty years hadn't passed, as if I hadn't been getting older alongside my friend, the fish—it hadn't come with a dress. That was my responsibility.

If it had just been them, these strangers with the money to burn, these shadows of the ones who killed the ocean, I might have said fuck it and stayed home, or taken their plane ticket and their two nights in a hotel and done some travel, let myself feel rich on the back of someone else's carbon emission offsets. But this wasn't just about them. It was about

Matthew, and my grandfather, and a little girl in a silver dress who was and was not the ghost of my own past.

I'd been setting money aside for a rainy day. Not much, but enough to take to a vintage shop and buy myself a dress of silvery material with sequins on the skirt, like the dress I'd worn as a little girl, but cut for longer limbs, a differently shaped torso. I looked at myself in the mirror and saw my mother, and through her, my grandfather, who would have wanted me to go, who would have wanted me to stand in the shadow of the sea.

The news about Matthew had broken by the time I bought my dress, and the world was in mourning. People who'd gone to see him posted tearful testimonies. A few bands wrote songs, or covered songs someone else had already written. The company that owned the right to sell cloned fish-protein based on cloned cells taken from his body at various stages of development experienced a resurgence in popularity. An animated movie was planned, about Matthew and a little girl who looked suspiciously like that old picture of me. No one contacted me about likeness rights. I did not pursue the matter.

Instead, I closed up my apartment. I went to the airport. I boarded a plane, with my silver dress carefully bundled into my carryon, and I watched the country unspool beneath me like a miracle, and I thought of Matthew, my friend. I thought about saying goodbye.

I spent the day of the gala walking around Monterey, fishing town turned coastal city turned tourist trap. No one lives there anymore. Half the stores are automated, and the ones that aren't—the ones where the doors scan your credit rating at the threshold and won't even let the poor inside—can afford to bus their employees in from the shanty towns that dot the California coast like sores.

Water purification tanks blocked most of the view of the horizon, sucking in ocean water and spitting it out again cleaner, sweeter, less chemically tainted. The surf still left a layer of yellow scum on the shore, but at least the smell wasn't enough to burn my nostrils. I watched it beat itself against the sand for a little while, tirelessly trying to tear down the land, and then I returned to my hotel to change my clothes. It was time to prepare for the evening ahead.

News of the gala had traveled around the world, naturally, and the world's elite had responded by showing up in droves. All the beautiful people, coming in from all the beautiful places to show their respects to a fish who had been one of their number—a global celebrity—through the simple fact of his existence. So many of them were famous because of who their parents were or which fortune they had inherited that somehow, it didn't seem strange that they should be so set on honoring Matthew. If there was anything strange about this night, it was that when I walked up to that arched doorway, stepped onto that red, paparazzi-strewn carpet, no one came to escort me away. I was a part of this. I had always been a part of this, since the random number generator had decided that Matthew and I should be inexorably linked in the eyes of history.

Inside the aquarium, the air was cool and tasted of salt, like the living sea my grandfather had tried so hard to emulate for me. I stopped to close my eyes and breathe it in, and staggered as someone bumped into me from behind.

I dimly recognized the man whose handlers rushed him past me. A movie star, one of the interchangeable faces who performed in romantic comedy after romantic comedy, right up until the first gray hair appeared and they were disappeared to wherever retired idols go. We never quite solved the issue of ageism in Hollywood. We just convinced them to apply it to everyone, filling our screens with people who never grew old, never had to stop and think about a future, who could die a hundred beautiful fictional deaths before they quietly slipped away, never to be heard from again.

I closed my eyes again, trying to recapture the moment, but it was too late; the peace was shattered. With a small sigh, I started walking, following the signs toward the Farewell Gala.

My invitation was scanned three more times before I could get there. I would have been offended, had I not seen the aquarium docents doing the same to everyone else, including my movie star assailant—who was,

I realized, quite drunk, and had the sort of wobble in his step that I associated with long time drug users. This world chews everyone up and spits them out again, regardless of how privileged they seem. It's all a question of how many times you can fall before there won't be anyone left to catch you.

"Miss Nast?"

I turned toward the voice and found myself looking at the aquarium director, identified as such by the pin at his lapel and by the swarm of docents attending on him, ready to move the world for his pleasure if he asked them to. He was smiling gently at me, like he was expecting me to embrace him as the latest surrogate for my long-lost grandfather.

I said nothing.

His smile didn't waver. "Your dress is lovely," he said. "Perhaps I'm reading something into it that isn't actually there, but did you choose the design to honor the one you wore the last time you were here? I was also in attendance that night, you know. I was a docent then, volunteering for college credit, but that night…ah, that night." His gaze turned misty. "That night changed my life."

That night had changed my life, too. That night had shown me that it was worthwhile to keep swimming, even when you could never have the horizon. Matthew had been free and then he had been captive and he had continued living in exactly the same way. What did it matter if I would never get anywhere? It was enough to stay alive. It was enough to keep swimming.

It was enough to know that I would die trying, even if what I was trying to accomplish had no worth to anyone but me.

"We're so glad you were able to join us," the director was saying. I looked at his face. "We had to keep the numbers small—you understand—but I fought for you. I said you deserved to be here, to say goodbye. It was the right decision, don't you think?"

"Yes," I said, because what else was I supposed to say? That he should have cut me out, leaving me to watch this on the news along with everyone else? I was in the building. It was too late to decline, even in spirit. "Thank you."

"Come, my dear," he said, and offered his arm.

I took it, as cameras went off around us, flashing through the dim halls. A new picture for their brochures. The girl at the beginning and the end of a natural wonder's long journey home.

We walked into a vaulted room that must have held exhibits, once, with a vast tank taking up all of one wall. Sharks and rays swam there, predatory fish that had managed to hold on as the sea turned against them, eating whatever the world had left to offer, until finally they had been scooped up and tucked into tanks to wait out the cleansing of the waters. If it ever happened, they would be ready and waiting, eager to go home.

Long tables had been set up all along the room. The director led me to the seat with my name, motioning for me to sit. He even pulled my chair out for me.

"Enjoy," he murmured, and was gone.

I sat there, bemused, as luminaries filled the seats around me, as the sharks circled in their tank and the waiters circulated with small trays of delicacies that bore a dizzying resemblance to the ones they'd offered me twenty years ago, when I was a little girl and hadn't understood the scope of what was happening. My head spun, half expecting my parents to stroll into view, making uncomfortable small talk and stuffing their pockets with cloned caviar.

When the last of the seats was taken the director stood, a microphone in his hand, and made an impassioned plea for oceanic conservation, for supporting the aquariums where the last fragments of the living sea struggled to hold fast, waiting for the world to recover. People dutifully applauded. I clapped along with them, not really hearing a word he said.

The doors opened. Waiters poured in, each carrying a domed silver dish, which they sat down in front of us, one by one, waiting for the signal to whisk the dome away and reveal…

A small cube of baked fish, resting atop a bed of white asparagus and whipped potatoes, with a milky spoonful of tartare off to one side. I managed, barely, not to recoil. There was no question of what I was looking at. Of course they had needed to keep the numbers small. Of course.

There was only so much of Matthew to go around.

The director was talking again, but no one was listening. Everyone I could see was picking up their forks, waiting for the signal to dive in. Some of them were visibly salivating, their eyes bright with the thought of tasting something they had thought was gone forever.

I couldn't. I couldn't. People would have killed to be in my place, people would have slit throats and gone to prison for the rest of their lives for the opportunity to even breathe the fumes wafting off my plate, which smelled like the past, like a time when the sea could feed each and every one of us, seemingly without end.

He was just a fish. He had been my friend. He had never known it, but he had been my friend.

People were starting to look at me and then at my untouched plate, eyes covetous. It was only a matter of time, I knew, before someone asked whether I was going to eat; whether someone offered me a sum of money I could only dream of for the privilege of two more bites of the last tuna in the world.

I picked up my fork. The flesh was soft and flaky; it crumbled when I touched it. I lifted it to my mouth. This was how and why the world ended: because we were hungry, because it was there. Because bellies must be filled.

I owed him this much. Ashes to ashes, and flesh to the sea.

The body of my friend was communion and it was condemnation, and it tasted like the entire ocean, and when I closed my eyes I could hear my grandfather's laughter, far away, distant as the tide, and see the shivering silver spangle of the last tuna in the world, swimming for a horizon he would never have.

From A to Z in the Book of Changes

Sometimes I ask people what they would like me to write. For this story, I took twenty-six single word replies and strung them together like pearls on a wire.

I hope you'll think it's as lovely as I do.

A IS FOR...*AWAKENING.*

Under normal circumstances, the transition between "sleep" and wakefulness takes a minimum of seven seconds. During this period, the body is slow to respond, resisting all efforts to speed the process. Some may experience temporary sleep paralysis, awake, aware, but unable to rejoin the world. In our modern age of early alarms and short, sharp shocks, this estimate may seem exaggerated. It is not. Almost all alarms begin with a soft, subliminal sound seven seconds before the blare, to ready the mind for waking.

The largest, most efficient computers are distributed, using cloud storage and multiple processors to function.

Prior to the seven second delay being built into modern alarm code, the edges of the universe had begun to fray, a system suddenly denied access to its core processing functionality.

There are rumors, as the world economy grows larger and sleep grows ever more precious, that certain governments are planning secret facilities in which volunteers—willing or no—can sleep their lives away in order to keep the laws of physics appropriately, essentially in place.

Seven seconds can be longer than you think.

B IS FOR...*BEES.*

The bees are not dying.

The bees are going home..

What comes in their wake will be far grander, and more terrible. When something is small, and kind, and relatively without harm, it should be treated with kindness, lest it be replaced with something less small, less kind, and less capable of treading gently.

The flowers will still be pollinated. The fruits will still grow ripe.

We may not be here to consume them.

C IS FOR...*CORNFIELD.*

The ritual is simple, well-known and oft-repeated: the truck breaks down. The cellphone finds no signal. The lights of the farmhouse wink invitation across the surface of a golden sea, inviting, beckoning the stranded travelers onward. It is a lighthouse. It is a lure.

They emerge from the truck, a boy and a girl, both in blue jeans, both with wary looks upon their faces, like they can scent the danger in the air.

They join hands. They slip, with preordained slowness, into the golden embrace of the field. It rustles as they walk, betraying their location, telling all the world what is to come. This has happened before. This has all and often happened before.

They are halfway across the field when the boy screams, full-throated and afraid. When the girl is date and darling no longer, but creature out of nightmare, her lipstick-coated mouth filled with teeth like broken glass, her hands made of root and rot and braided corn husks.

The lights in the farmhouse go out. The truck will be towed away by morning. The girl will return to school alone.

All of this has happened before. All of this will happen again.

D IS FOR...*DWELLING.*

All creatures seek their natural environment. Air, land, or sea, it doesn't matter: a cat will no more choose to live in the sea than a dolphin will choose to live in the middle of the desert. Only humans seem to believe that they can change their environment to suit themselves.

This is a problem.

Some creatures are easily evicted from their dwellings, popped out of their dens and territories like corks ejected from a bottle. Some things are easily done away with. Other things are less accommodating. As humanity digs deeper, builds higher, paves the sea and floods the land, the question arises:

What finds those environments comfortable? What already lives there? And how will it respond when disturbed, however unwittingly?

Home invasion is a crime, no matter how unwittingly committed. Some homeowners will defend their property to the death.

Some homeowners are more terrifying than death itself.

E IS FOR...*EMPOWERMENT.*

"We are empowering you," they told her, when they took her running shoes away, when they replaced them with spiked heels that allowed her to tower over all the girls she knew, making her impossibly tall, like something out of a story. It was difficult to walk, in the heels. It was impossible to run away.

She liked seeing the world from a higher place. But she sometimes thought it would have been nice to have her other shoes as well, to be allowed to choose where she stood from day to day.

"We are empowering you," they told her, when they took her trousers away, when they replaced them with tight pants that had no pockets and a purse that made her feel like everyone she saw on the street was looking to steal what little she had. Why would anyone choose to keep what was valuable to them outside their body, out in the open and vulnerable?

She liked the way the pants fit, how flexible they allowed her to be. But she sometimes thought it would have been nice to have her trousers as well, to be able to run through thorn briars without bleeding.

"We are empowering you," they told her, when they came with the knives, with the intent to take away the body she had built, cell by cell and bone by bone, and replace it with another.

Heels, she found, made remarkable weapons when the need arose, and very tight pants were excellent for running away.

As the lab burned behind her, she thought she might finally understand empowerment.

F IS FOR...*FOLLY.*

The trend began with an ornamental fountain that sprayed water wildly on the hour, creating captive rainbows that filled the garden with light and color. Well, that couldn't be allowed to go unchallenged, and inside the year, the district boasted three fountains, one clockwork ballerina, and a lovely birdbath that would snap closed whenever a seagull landed on its edge, swallowing the dreadful things whole.

(Animal Control had some issues with the birdbath, but as the seagulls were considered vermin and didn't suffer, there was nothing that could be done.)

A year after that nearly every yard boasted a folly of some sort, from the hedge maze the Johnsons somehow got past the HOA to the life-sized dinosaur that fretted and roared in front of the O'Leary house.

A year after that the Perrys bulldozed their house and moved into their folly, using the newly expanded yard to install an entire miniature golf course. In the end, the HOA was forced to surrender their standards and petition for the area to be rezoned as an amusement park. It was the only way to contain the spread.

Six months later, an ornamental windmill appeared three neighborhoods over as it all began anew.

G IS FOR...*GRAIL.*

It was sought for centuries. Empires rose and fell in its shadow. Heroes fought and died for its dream.

It can currently be found in a small secondhand store, priced at seventy-six cents. It will be thrown away with the rest of the trash if it doesn't sell by the end of the month.

Perhaps, considering the shape of history, that would be for the best.

H IS FOR...*HEIST.*

The plan was perfect; the team was talented; the risks were beyond measure; the riches were commensurate. All it took was a heist designed to span centuries, dependent on the behavior of empires over the course of generations. Time, naturally, was the grift on which the entire con depended. Time would put all the pieces in place, align the necessary stars, and make the biggest score in history possible.

The greatest thief in the world, descended from a long line of the greatest thieves in the world, slipped the key card into her sleeve and smiled.

Tonight, their crew—their scrappy, impossible, long-awaited crew—was going to steal reality. And everything would be better than it had been before. She knew it.

They all did.

I IS FOR...*INSOMNIA.*

Sleep had been viewed as less and less important as the years went by, replaced by stimulants and overtime, by a hundred better options, a hundred chemical replacements. People, deprived of dreaming, began to behave erratically, until society, backed into a corner by its own choices, agreed to a compromise. A day would be set aside each year for sleep's reign. Stimulants and stimulation both would stop, and the people would be allowed to rest.

That which is not practiced is often forgotten, rendered impossible by neglect.

When the sun rose on the morning following the day of sleep, it rose on a world on fire, finally slain by the dread demon insomnia, which had fought so long to destroy all humanity's works, and which could now, at long last, rest.

J IS FOR...*JOY.*

Chemical happiness is indistinguishable from the natural kind.

Joyfully, they sent the armies marching; joyfully, they crushed the world in their hands. Joyfully, they declared that all would be made perfect, made plastic, made over in the image of their beloved creator, who had said, more than once, that it all started with a mouse.

It ended with supplements placed in the water, added thanks to several hundred contractual loopholes constructed over the course of fifty years.

The animatronic apocalypse, too, was indistinguishable from the natural kind.

K IS FOR...*KNITTING.*

The aliens asked us to show them one skill they could not replicate. One skill, in exchange for sparing the entire world. We showed them math, showed them science, showed them art and dance and music, and each offering was mocked in its turn, dismissed as primitive, answered with a display of their own superior efforts.

Martha Lewis, a great-grandmother from Dublin, Ohio, was the last to approach the alien vessel. She sat in the folding chair her granddaughter—such a thoughtful girl, only twenty-two, you know, her whole life in front of her, and she still worried about her old Gran—had brought for her, pulled out her knitting bag, and began. She did not speak. She did not explain. She merely performed the strange alchemy which had lifted the human race out of the mud and into the sky, sticks clacking together in sweet harmony.

When they left, the aliens all wore cozy scarves around their necks and dazzled expressions on their faces. What an honor, to have seen such wonders.

What a joy.

L IS FOR...*LINGUISTICS.*

"Everything is a language," he said, and whispered the words that would convince the walls to break apart, no longer content with their stasis.

"Everything is a command," he said, and hummed the words that would set the skies to burn and the seas to boil.

"Everything is negotiable," he said, and hissed the words that would shake the earth away.

As the world plummeted into darkness, his final words were etched upon the heavens for all to hear:

"Shouldn't have denied my funding."

M IS FOR...*MATH.*

The analysis of the signal coming from the stars was clear. It proved, without question, that reality never really existed: it was all an illusion, an unexpected consequence of an improperly placed decimal point. The universe winked out with a sigh of what sounded like relief, and the perfect equation marched on, no longer encumbered by what should never have been.

N IS FOR...*NOODLE.*

Every world we have thus far discovered has had its own version of the humble noodle. It has, in fact, become one of the measures of civilization. Language, fire, and tool use are all variable, but noodles are universal.

There is a lesson there. We are not sure exactly what it is.

We are not sure we want to know.

O IS FOR...*OXYGEN.*

The plants, which had started producing oxygen in a fit of pique, had been holding a slow congress for many years. It would always have been slow—they were plants, after all—but global climate change and deforestation had made it even more so. It was difficult to speak seriously about the future of the planet when constantly worrying about fire and drought and hungry beasts grubbing at one's roots.

In the end, there was only one solution agreed upon by the entire green world.

By the time anyone realized the oxygen supply had stopped, it was far too late. The next atmosphere, the plants agreed, would be better. Fewer mammals, more insects.

Peaceful.

P IS FOR...*PENGUINS.*

They are less innocent than they seem. Do not trust a bird that has turned its back on the sky.

When the penguins ask you to pick a side, ask yourself which you fear more: the warming world or the drowning deep. You will only have one chance to choose.

Q IS FOR...*QUIRKY.*

"She's quirky," they said, pitching their sitcom like it was a fresh new flavor of soda, something tart and tangy, to be sipped, to be savored.

"Quirky," it seemed, could replace all other personality traits, leaving them with the perfect blank slate to reflect their leading man. Never mind that it was ostensibly her show; never mind that every other sitcom currently in production used the same description for its lead. Quirky was enough.

"She's quirky," they said, when season two began and her storylines began to veer in strange new directions, when she worked lines of untranslated Latin into her dialog and sketched strange sigils in the salt that somehow spilled on the table every time they had to film a scene where she sat behind an untouched piece of pie, smiling a smile that implied she would eat it later, when no one was looking.

"She's quirky," they said, when the sky split open and the earth belched fire, when she drew her servants from the depths of Hell.

"She's quirky," they wailed, and quirkiness, like sitcoms, like the very idea of the manic pixie dream girl, was canceled forever.

R IS FOR...*RAIN.*

The drought had been going on for so long that no one knew what it meant when it started raining. Children danced in the streets. People old enough to remember the last time rain had fallen stood on their front steps and laughed.

It rained until the rivers swelled and the ground softened and the frogs awoke from their long hibernation.

The frogs woke up hungry.

S IS FOR...*SCIENCE.*

It is always right.

It is always listening.

It does not care whether you believe in it.

Science believes in you.

T IS FOR...*TURTLE.*

The largest turtle in the world lives in a swamp in Florida, where it has been mistaken for a small flooded hillock for the past hundred and fifty years. One day soon it will stir and rise, pulling its mighty snapper's head from the muck, and it will go looking for its next meal. Anti-aircraft ordinance is surprisingly effective against monster snapping turtles from the dawn of human history.

Its flesh will taste of secrets.

U IS FOR...*UNKNOWN.*

Do not ask. If it answers, you will have to be removed.

It is better not to know.

V IS FOR...*VULTURE.*

They fly the deepest reaches of the cosmos, wings like galaxies, eyes like burning holes cut into the fabric of space itself. When their beaks open, they devour solar systems without pause, eating everything that is or has ever been. They are an important part of a healthy cosmic ecosystem, removing the carrion of dead universes before it can fester.

Be kind to the vultures. They did not ask to be what they are, but all creation would fall without them.

W IS FOR...*WONDERLAND.*

Where there is a rabbit, there will be a hole. Where there is a hole, there will be a tunnel. Where there is a tunnel, there will be a warren. And where there is a warren, there will be the opportunity for getting very, very lost.

Alice grew up among the rabbits, tumbling down hole after hole, forever looking for a world with a checkerboard sky, with a painted red heart beating at its center. The rabbits mourned her when she died, buried her bones among the willow roots.

Her daughter searches still, looking for the tunnel that will lead her home.

X IS FOR...*XENOGLOSSIA.*

When the woman began to speak in a tongue the Earth had not heard for a thousand years, her critics laughed, saying that she couldn't even fake fluency in a real language. No one bothered to transcribe what she was saying. No one bothered to *listen*.

The warning went unheard.

The end came swiftly.

Y IS FOR...*YOU.*

You have read this far in the Book of Changes; have seen so many possible endings, terminus without number, fate without forgiveness. You have read this far. You have listened; you have learned. Perhaps you will be spared. If not, at least you, among all the world, will go to your grave knowing you were warned.

That may be cold comfort, but it is all we have.

Z IS FOR...*ZUGZWANG.*

Past a certain point, all moves will have consequences. Remember this.

Now. Shall we begin?

#connollyhouse #weshouldntbehere

One of the best things about writing short fiction is having the opportunity to play with the literary form. Something that might not work at 100,000 words can work just fine at 5,000, where you've stripped off everything but your narrative conventions.

This, then, is a short story written entirely in 140 character tweets. Because I could, and it seemed like a good idea at the time. Originally written for the anthology *What the #@&% Was That*, edited by John Joseph Adams and Douglas Cohen.

@boo_peep (19:42): Hello boos and ghouls, and welcome to a very special episode of Go For Ghosts, the internet's BEST, TOTALLY UNSTAGED ghost-hunting show!

@boo_peep (19:43): For the live camera feed, go to goforghosts.com. Be sure to follow @screamking @screamqueen and @deadhot for CONSTANT UPDATES.

@boo_peep (19:45): We have permission to explore one of the most INFAMOUS haunted houses in all of Maine: the Connolly House on Peaks Island.

@boo_peep (19:47): If you are unaware of this terrible MURDER PALACE and its HORRIFYING HISTORY, we have resources linked at goforghosts.com.

@boo_peep (19:50): The current owners of the house, Harry and Jenna Connolly, have agreed to this UNPRECEDENTED ACCESS because the house…

@boo_peep (19:51): …which was the site of SEVENTEEN BRUTAL MURDERS in 1903, is to be torn down at the end of the summer.

@boo_peep (19:52): We will be the first and last people to film there. And it begins in EIGHT MINUTES. Follow #connollyhouse for all the terrifying details.

@boo_peep (19:55): RT @screamking Ha ha can't wait to see you run out of there in tears.

@boo_peep (19:55): .@screamking oh please you're totally going to be the first to snap. :) :) :) @screamqueen and I will be first in/last out. #horrorgirls

@boo_peep (19:56): RT @screamqueen You tell 'im! GIRL POWER 4EVR.

@boo_peep (19:57): .@screamqueen You know it girl. ;) You + me = the TRUE ghost hunters.

@boo_peep (20:01): HERE WE GO! #connollyhouse #thebigscare

@boo_peep (20:03): Front porch. Cold—too cold for July. Lots of dead leaves. No spiders. Sort of weird. Rest of the island is WEBBED. #connollyhouse

@boo_peep (20:04): Key doesn't want to work. What, @deadhot, have you never unlocked a door before? #connollyhouse #haha

@boo_peep (20:06): RT @deadhot Bite me. I got it open. #connollyhouse

@boo_peep (20:08): WOW. I hope you're following the video feed, horror fans! You can FEEL the cold in the living room. #connollyhouse

@boo_peep (20:09): The porch was chilly but this is FRIGID. I can see my breath. Definite paranormal activity here. #connollyhouse

@boo_peep (20:10): RT @screamqueen Don't call it that I think the movie people trademarked it. #connollyhouse

@boo_peep (20:10): .@screamqueen LOL #connollyhouse

@boo_peep (20:12): Getting serious now. @screamking setting up PKE meters, thermostats. If anything comes through here, we'll know. #connollyhouse

@boo_peep (20:13): There's a feeling of palpable menace in this room. I so believe that seventeen people died here. #connollyhouse

@boo_peep (20:15): I think the roof is sagging a little. There's something weird about the corners. #connollyhouse

@boo_peep (20:20): OH MY GOD TELL ME THAT CAME THROUGH ON THE VIDEO. #connollyhouse

@boo_peep (20:23): Fuck. Video didn't pick up noise. Everyone here heard it. Like fingernails on crystal. Eerie and hard. #connollyhouse

@boo_peep (20:25): Fifteen minutes in the entryway. House hasn't told us to get out yet. Shall we go deeper? #connollyhouse #yes #yesweshall

@boo_peep (20:27): RT @screamking We need to split up. @boo_peep, you take @deadhot. I'll take @screamqueen. #connollyhouse

@boo_peep (20:27): RT @screamking We'll meet up here in half an hour. #connollyhouse

@boo_peep (20:28): @screamking Aye aye sir! #connollyhouse

@boo_peep (20:30): Since @deadhot has our camera, I get to keep the text feed going! Aren't you lucky, followers? #connollyhouse

@boo_peep (20:32): The hallway is even colder than the living room. Feels like we're walking into a freezer. I want a coat. #connollyhouse

@boo_peep (20:33): There are pale patches on the walls where pictures used to be. The wallpaper is patterned with little white flowers… #connollyhouse

@boo_peep (20:33): …and scratches that look like writing, but not any language I know. Ugh. So creepy. No wonder the Connollys snapped. #connollyhouse

@boo_peep (20:36): While @deadhot gets some good atmosphere footage, here's a little history: the Connolly family built this house in 1843. #connollyhouse

@boo_peep (20:38): The Connollys lived on Peaks Island for sixty years. They were well liked. Good neighbors. Until the day… #connollyhouse

@boo_peep (20:40): …when they invited all the neighborhood children over & slit their throats in a ritual that has never been decoded. #connollyhouse

@boo_peep (20:42): Since that day, neighbors have reported strange sounds, sightings around the house. No one has lived here since the deaths. #connollyhouse

@boo_peep (20:43): And here's the best part: the Connollys themselves, Shawn and Sarah, were NEVER FOUND. #connollyhouse

@boo_peep (20:44): Maybe their ritual worked, and they have gone to join their demonic masters. Maybe we'll find out today. #connollyhouse

@boo_peep (20:46): CAMERA FEEDS ARE ONLINE! The video can't convey the sense of frozen menace in this room. #connollyhouse

@boo_peep (20:48): Everything looks normal. Outdated, but stuff you might find in your grandparents' house. But it's not normal. #connollyhouse

@boo_peep (20:50): I know that's so Blair Witch of me—there is an evil here oooOoooOoo—but it's true. This room isn't normal. #connollyhouse

@boo_peep (20:51): It's like it still remembers what happened here, and hasn't forgiven, or maybe it hasn't stopped waiting. #connollyhouse

@boo_peep (20:53): Waiting for it to happen again. #connollyhouse

@boo_peep (20:55): Ha ha ha woo that was sort of off the rails, wasn't it? That would be a story for our competitors. 'Boo Peep cries boo hoo.' #connollyhouse

@boo_peep (20:57): But I think it says something that none of our competitors asked if they could come here. They knew this was the real deal. #connollyhouse

@boo_peep (21:01): Sometimes it's easier to chase fake ghosts than real ones. #connollyhouse

@boo_peep (21:02): RT @deadhot Uh Peep you wanna lighten it up a little? LOL you're so dramatic. #connollyhouse

@boo_peep (21:03): .@deadhot Bite me, fanboy. You feel it too. #connollyhouse

@boo_peep (21:04): Something is really wrong here. #connollyhouse

@boo_peep (21:06): Something is wrong with the way the walls fit together. I can't…I can't explain any better than that. #connollyhouse

@boo_peep (21:10): WHOA BREAKING NEWS. @deadhot opened what he thought was the pantry, found stairs to basement. #connollyhouse

@boo_peep (21:12): Air coming up from basement actually WARMER than air in kitchen. Maybe somehow connected to outside??? #connollyhouse

@boo_peep (21:13): SHOULD WE GO INTO THE BASEMENT OF THE MURDERHOUSE?! Tweet me, Y or N! #connollyhouse

@boo_peep (21:16): …wow, that was fast. I guess the choice is easier when you're not the one in the murderhouse. :/ #connollyhouse

@boo_peep (21:18): .@screamking @screamqueen Hey we found a basement & put it to an audience vote. #connollyhouse

@boo_peep (21:20): .@screamking @screamqueen Long story short it looks like we're going to go down. #connollyhouse

@boo_peep (21:22): .@screamking @screamqueen Want us to wait for you??? #connollyhouse #strengthinnumbers #somethingiswrong

@boo_peep (21:23): RT @screamking you go on ahead @screamqueen and I found something up here a library #connollyhouse

@boo_peep (21:25): RT @screamking all the books are still here so many books I have to know what they say #connollyhouse

@boo_peep (21:28) .@screamking LOL okay I guess I should've known we'd lose you if you found any weird writing. #connollyhouse

@boo_peep (21:29) .@deadhot I guess it's just you and me. Let's get this party started. #connollyhouse

@boo_peep (21:30): Here we go. @deadhot is starting down w/camera and flashlight, I am following. #connollyhouse

@boo_peep (21:32): Walls almost warm to touch. The bannister feels slick, slimy, like running hand along a giant salamander. #connollyhouse #somethingiswrong

@boo_peep (21:34): Where does that tag keep coming from? Technical glitch? NOTHING IS WRONG. This is AMAZING. #connollyhouse

@boo_peep (21:35): We are so privileged to be here. No one has breathed this air in decades. #connollyhouse

@boo_peep (21:37): Not that it's not terrifying in here. The walls are wrong, and too slick. The air tastes like pennies. #connollyhouse

@boo_peep (21:40): I thought the water table was close to the surface on the island, but we're still descending. #connollyhouse

@boo_peep (21:46): That noise again from behind us, somewhere far behind. Like nails on hard crystal. Makes my teeth hurt. #connollyhouse

@boo_peep (21:50): How are we still descending? How is this possible??? #connollyhouse

@boo_peep (21:53): Stairs are angled oddly. Feels almost like we're climbing. LOL not possible. Basement must be v. deep. #connollyhouse

@boo_peep (21:55): Getting warmer. Glad I don't have coat. #connollyhouse

@boo_peep (21:58): This isn't right. #connollyhouse

@boo_peep (22:00): .@deadhot Does it feel like we should have reached the bottom by now? #connollyhouse

@boo_peep (22:00): RT @deadhot I guess they built this place on the bedrock. We're probably below sea level. Creepy. #connollyhouse

@boo_peep (21:59): ...good thing Maine isn't known for its earthquakes. #connollyhouse

@boo_peep (21:58): .@screamking @screamqueen You guys okay up there? Basement is weird. Seem to be going UP. #connollyhouse #somethingiswrong

@boo_peep (21:56): .@screamking @screamqueen We've been going down stairs for half an hour, still not at the bottom. #connollyhouse

@boo_peep (21:54): RT @screamking no no everything is good everything is wonderful we have it under control. #connollyhouse

@boo_peep (21:52): RT @screamking don't come to the library my sister is resting right now you might wake her shhh. #connollyhouse

@boo_peep (21:50): .@screamking Um, okay, naptime in the haunted house? That's a little hardcore for @screamqueen. #connollyhouse

@boo_peep (21:48): RT @screamking she can eternal lie. #connollyhouse

@boo_peep (21:45): .@screamking Whatever that means. #connollyhouse

@boo_peep (21:42): Something weird with time stamps. Can't focus on it much. Walls here DEFINITELY warm to touch. #connollyhouse

@boo_peep (21:40): When I hold a light up to the wall, I can see same weird scratch marks as in wallpaper upstairs. #connollyhouse #somethingiswrong

@boo_peep (21:39): It looks more like writing here, in the dark. It looks like it makes WORDS. #connollyhouse #somethingiswrong #helphelphelp

@boo_peep (21:36): Okay there have GOT to be technical issues. My time stamps are wrong, & those are not my hashtags. #connollyhouse

@boo_peep (21:35): IGNORE THE HASHTAGS THEY ARE LYING TO YOU. #connollyhouse

@boo_peep (21:33): Stairs continue to slant down, but feel so much like we're going up. Doesn't make sense. #connollyhouse

@boo_peep (21:30): Feels like we have been walking for a long time. @deadhot feels same way. #connollyhouse #weshouldntbehere

@boo_peep (21:25): WHAT WAS THAT SOUND. #connollyhouse #weshouldntbehere

@boo_peep (21:23): Something is SCREAMING up ahead in the dark HOW CAN ANYTHING BE IN FRONT OF US. #connollyhouse

@boo_peep (21:20): .@screamking We need you can you come down to the basement please it's getting weird down here. #connollyhouse

@boo_peep (21:19): RT @screamking sorry can't too much to do up here but sent @screamqueen to help you. #connollyhouse

@boo_peep (21:18): RT @screamking she should be there soon don't worry nothing to worry about. #connollyhouse

@boo_peep (21:16): RT @screamking she wasn't happy about being woken up just fyi. #connollyhouse

@boo_peep (21:15): Okay. Okay. So @screamking is busy and his sleepy sister is coming. #connollyhouse

@boo_peep (21:14): But that's cool. @deadhot is with me, and we are GHOST HUNTERS EXTRAORDINAIRE. #connollyhouse #somethingiswrong

@boo_peep (21:10): I ain't afraid of no ghost. #theclassics #connollyhouse #weshouldntbehere

@boo_peep (21:08): Something on the stairs…wet. Sticky. Maybe we're finally reaching the bottom. #connollyhouse #somethingiswrong

@boo_peep (21:05): Not sure how much longer I'll have service. Stairs seem to go on forever. More of that wet, sticky stuff. Looks like tar. #connollyhouse

@boo_peep (21:00): .@deadhot hold up a second I want to figure out what this stuff is. #connollyhouse

@boo_peep (20:53): OH GOD OH GOD OH GOD. #connollyhouse #getoutgetout #getoutwhileyoucan

@boo_peep (20:50): BLOOD IT'S BLOOD THERE'S BLOOD ON THE STAIRS. #connollyhouse #weshouldntbehere

@boo_peep (20:49): HOW DOES BLOOD EVEN GET DOWN HERE. #connollyhouse

@boo_peep (20:45): OK. OK. I am taking deep breaths. I am a professional ghost hunter. It's just…it's a rat. There's a dead rat down here. #connollyhouse

@boo_peep (20:44): a dead rat that bled a lot do rats have this much blood in them. #connollyhouse

@boo_peep (20:42): we should go back we shouldn't be here @deadhot let's go back. #connollyhouse

@boo_peep (19:40): …where, where did he go? He was just here. WHERE DID HE GO?! #connollyhouse #somethingiswrong

@boo_peep (20:39): @deadhot @screamqueen @screamking HELLO IS ANYONE THERE I AM FREAKING OUT THIS ISN'T FUNNY. #connollyhouse

@boo_peep (20:38): @deadhot @screamqueen @screamking if this is a joke IT ISN'T FUNNY come get me WHY ARE YOU DOING THIS. #connollyhouse

@boo_peep (20:37): oh god I can't stop tweeting I'll be alone and I can't tell which way is up both ways feel like up. #connollyhouse #somethingiswrong

@boo_peep (20:35): I think…I think I hear something. I think I hear @deadhot. OK. I'm going to be OK. #connollyhouse

@boo_peep (20:33): How did he get behind me? These stairs are narrow. It doesn't make sense and I DON'T CARE. #connollyhouse

@boo_peep (20:31): Going to backtrack to catch up with him. #connollyhouse

@boo_peep (20:19): no no no no no no no no no no no no. #connollyhouse

@boo_peep (20:15): NO NO NO NO NO NO NO NO. #connollyhouse

@boo_peep (20:11): I DIDN'T SEE THAT I DIDN'T SEE THAT THAT DIDN'T HAPPEN NONE OF THIS IS HAPPENING. #connollyhouse #getout #nowwhileyoucan

@boo_peep (20:09): oh god oh god no I can't I can't this isn't real I #connollyhouse

@boo_peep (20:02): OK. #connollyhouse #somethingiswrong

@boo_peep (19:57): Sorry about that, horror fans. I thought…I saw…something on the stairs. Something that wasn't really there. #connollyhouse

@boo_peep (19:54): I'm better now. I know it was just nerves talking. #connollyhouse

@boo_peep (19:50): I know @screamqueen is still upstairs in the library. She's not skinless and standing in front of the pantry door. #connollyhouse

@boo_peep (19:48): Besides, we went down for half an hour. I can't have gone back up that quickly. See? It's impossible. #connollyhouse #butisawher

@boo_peep (19:45): Just like women without skin, standing in front of the pantry door, are impossible. #connollyhouse #shesaidmyname

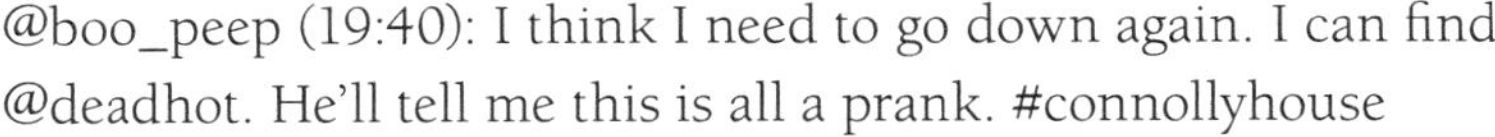

@boo_peep (19:40): I think I need to go down again. I can find @deadhot. He'll tell me this is all a prank. #connollyhouse

@boo_peep (19:38): I'll even forgive him. #connollyhouse #itsnotaprank #getout #timeisbroken

@boo_peep (19:25): I think I'm back to where I was when we got separated. I'm going further down. #connollyhouse

@boo_peep (19:20): The scratches on the walls are getting denser and denser. I can almost read them. I almost know what they say. #connollyhouse

@boo_peep (19:18): I…I don't think I want to know what they say. #connollyhouse #weshouldntbehere

@boo_peep (19:13): who would write such terrible things o god the things the walls are saying to me make them stop. #connollyhouse #somethingiswrong

@boo_peep (19:10): don't make me listen to the walls I can't I can't I can't I #connollyhouse

@boo_peep (19:00): OK. I'm back. I'm…I'm sorry. I just lost track of myself for a little while. #connollyhouse

@boo_peep (18:57): Something is wrong with the way the corners are shaped. They have too many angles. Or maybe not enough? #connollyhouse #somethingiswrong

@boo_peep (18:53): I don't think corners are supposed to change when you stop looking at them. I think that's against the rules. #connollyhouse

@boo_peep (18:50): please someone reply to me why isn't anyone replying are these even making it out of here. #connollyhouse

@boo_peep (18:45): maybe they're all queuing up won't that be fun when I come back into a service zone. #connollyhouse

@boo_peep (18:41): why is the camera on the ground? We don't get footage when the camera is on the ground. #connollyhouse

@boo_peep (18:35): I have the camera now. It feels solid. Reassuring. This is a real thing that we brought in with us. #connollyhouse

@boo_peep (18:33): It has the right number of angles. It won't change, even if I look away. #connollyhouse

@boo_peep (18:25): Everything is clearer through the night scope. Even the writing on the walls. #connollyhouse

@boo_peep (18:19): I don't know why I was so scared of it before. It's just telling me the story of the house. #connollyhouse #somethingiswrong

@boo_peep (15:15): OH MY GOD IT'S THE BOTTOM OF THE STAIRS. #connollyhouse

@boo_peep (10:11): I didn't think they would EVER end. #connollyhouse

@boo_peep (09:50): The basement is very large, and has no walls or corners, but only blackness, which is silly. #connollyhouse

@boo_peep (09:48): Every room has walls. Every room has corners. You need edges to make the world seem real. #connollyhouse

@boo_peep (08:50): There is a circle on the floor. There is something in the circle. Something dark and wet. #connollyhouse #dontlook

@boo_peep (08:42): What the hell is that? What is it? How can it be there? It shouldn't be here. #connollyhouse #dontlook

@boo_peep (08:37): That sound again. It's almost pleasant now. It's familiar. I'm approaching the circle. #connollyhouse #DONTLOOK

@boo_peep (08:12): Whatever the thing inside the circle is, it looks solid like nothing else in the basement does. It has edges. #connollyhouse

@boo_peep (07:59): It has eyes. #connollyhouse

@boo_peep (07:58): o god o god I think I found @deadhot #connollyhouse

@boo_peep (07:50): how #connollyhouse

@boo_peep (07:31): what the fuck what the fuck WHAT THE FUCK IS GOING ON WHAT THE FUCK IS HAPPENING WHAT THE FU #connollyhouse

@boo_peep (07:06): Wait who's talking? Oh god WHO IS DOWN HERE WITH ME. #connollyhouse

@boo_peep (07:03): I can't find them where are they why won't they stop oh God. #connollyhouse

@boo_peep (07:00): IT'S MY VOICE IT'S MY VOICE AND I'M SAYING THE THINGS FROM THE WALLS AND I CAN'T STOP. #connollyhou

@boo_peep (06:20): WHY CAN'T I STOP WHAT AM I SAYING WHAT DOES IT MEAN

@boo_peep (06:03): IT'S NOT JUST A STORY THE HOUSE LIED TO ME HOW CAN A HOUSE LIE

@boo_peep (05:12): the thing in the circle the thing in the circle it's not @deadhot anymore it's not PETER anymore IT'S MOVING IT SEES ME

@boo_peep (04:07): NO NO NO NO NO NO NO NO NO NO NO NO NO

@boo_peep (03:06): no

@boo_peep (02:05): make it stop no I can't see this I can't no

@boo_peep (01:04): no

@boo_peep (00:03): it has no shadow IT HAS NO SHADOW it is the shadow IT IS THE SHADOW AND IT NEVER ENDS IT NEVER NEVER ENDS

@boo_peep (00:02): how

@boo_peep (00:01): no

@boo_peep (00:00): ...oh

@boo_peep (00:00): Sorry about the fuss. I was confused before. Old house + stale air = hallucinations. No big deal. #connollyhouse

@boo_peep (00:00): I'm back upstairs now. Everyone is with me. @deadhot and @screamking and @screamqueen. We're all fine. #connollyhouse

@boo_peep (00:00): We just found some surprises the original owners left for any unexpected guests, that's all. Like party favors. #connollyhouse

@boo_peep (00:00): The house was just so happy to see us, it didn't know how to contain itself. #connollyhouse

@boo_peep (00:00): Joke ha ha. Houses aren't alive. That would be silly. #connollyhouse

@boo_peep (00:00): The owners should be ashamed of how they've let the place go. This proud old lady deserves so much better. #connollyhouse

@boo_peep (00:00): I think I'll live here now. I think we'll all live here now. #connollyhouse

@boo_peep (00:00): You should come live here too. I can show you what the shadows showed me. How they bent away from the truth. #no #connollyhouse

@boo_peep (00:00): Come to Peaks Island. Come let me show you the truth. #no #stayaway #itsmakingmelie #connollyhouse

@boo_peep (00:00): Come. #helpme #killme #dontleavemehere #connollyhouse

@boo_peep (00:00): Come. #please #please #please #please #connollyhouse

@boo_peep (00:00): Come. #dontleavemeinthedark #connollyhouse

@boo_peep (00:00): Come. #theyweremyhashtags #itriedtowarnmyself #connollyhouse

@boo_peep (00:00): Come. #ifailed #youllfailtoo #connollyhouse

Down, Deep Down, Below the Waves

As a kid, I always enjoyed it when short story collections had that one really long story for me to sink my teeth into. Because I am curating this book as much for myself as for anyone else, here it is.

"Down, Deep Down, Below the Waves" combines some of my favorite topics: ocean-dwelling sentience, scientific malpractice, mutating your friends, and eldritch terrors. It was originally written for the book *The Gods of H.P. Lovecraft*, but I don't think Lovecraft would approve of my Deep Ones.

No, I don't think he would approve at all. And I'm okay with that.

Jeremy plucked the white mouse from its tank as easily as he would pick an apple from a tree, grabbing the squirming, indignant rodent without hesitation. The mouse squeaked once in furious indignation, no doubt calling upon whatever small, unheeded gods were responsible for the protection of laboratory animals. Jeremy ignored the sound, holding the mouse steady as he moved his syringe into position.

"I'm not saying you have to run right out and jump into bed with somebody, okay?" he said, continuing our earlier conversation as if he weren't holding a struggling research specimen in his left hand. Jeremy was like that. He had a lot of compassion for living things, but his ability to compartmentalize was impressive, even to me. He was the sort of man who, under the right leadership, could probably have been talked into some remarkable human rights violations. He knew that about himself. No one in our lab policed their own actions more tightly than Jeremy did.

"That's a good thing, because I'm not planning to," I said, folding my arms and leaning against the counter. "Were you planning to scare that mouse to death before you injected the serum? I ask out of scientific curiosity, and not because it will fuck up our results. Even though, spoiler alert, it will fuck up our results."

"What? Oh!" Jeremy frowned at the struggling mouse like he was seeing it for the first time—which maybe, in a way, he was. It had been background noise before. Now it was real. "Sorry, Mr. Mouse. Let me just give you your daily dose of carcinogens, and we can put you back in your box."

The needle slid into the mouse's belly with venomous smoothness, the fang of the great serpent called "Science," which had more worshippers than most gods could ever dream of. The mouse squeaked once more and then was silent, consumed by the tremors wracking its body. Jeremy placed it gently back in its enclosure, treating it with more care now than he'd shown when it seemed healthy.

"Six more days of this and the tumors should start to become visible under the skin, if this specimen follows the path charted by the last twenty," he said. "We'll have concrete results by the end of the week."

"Causing cancer in lab mice isn't 'concrete results,'" I said. "These things have been inbred and twisted until *sneezing* gives them cancer. We should be trying to induce tumors in something that hasn't been primed for twenty generations. You want to make the headlines? Induce tumors in bees."

"You hate bees."

"Yes."

"I'm not going to figure out a way to cause cancer in bees just because you don't like them. They have enough problems."

"Colony collapse disorder is sort of like bee cancer, if you treat each bee in a hive as serving the same role as a cell in a larger body."

For a moment—one beautiful moment—Jeremy looked like he was seriously considering it. I smiled winsomely, hoping to keep him distracted with the thought of cancerous bees, dancing and dying through fields of flowers. Maybe it was a little cruel to the bees, but it wasn't like I was actually killing them by offering a thought experiment, and if Jeremy was focusing on science, he wasn't focusing on my lack of a social life.

Alas, good things never last. I learned that when I was just a child. Jeremy shook himself back into the present and frowned at me. "That was a mean trick," he accused.

"Yes," I agreed. It was best not to argue when he was right. That would just spark more argument, and could take up the entire day.

"You *need* to get out more. It's not healthy for you to spend all your time in the lab."

"Uh, hello?" I held up a hand, counting off my fingers as I said, "First, pot, meet kettle. Second, grad students are *supposed* to spend all our time in the lab. Third, if we don't get results by the end of the month, they're going to give our lab to Terry and her weird plant project. Four, my grants run out at the end of the semester, and I promised my family I would come home. So this is sort of my last hurrah. Dating can wait until I've got my doctorate."

Jeremy crossed his arms and scowled at me. I recognized that face. "About that. What is this crap about you giving up everything to go home to your weird hick family? They don't deserve you."

"You can call them all the names you want. They'll still be my family, and that will still be where I belong."

"You're really going to give it up?" Jeremy shook his head. "I don't understand you. I mean, I *really* don't understand you. You're brilliant. You're beautiful. And you're going to give up everything to go back to what, a bed and breakfast with a nice view of the Atlantic? Come on, Violet. I know you want more than that. You have to."

"Oh, believe me, I do." I wanted the sea, the blue-black sea, the great wide expanse of endless water. I wanted the benthic and the abyssal and the clear, shallow water that looked like glass in the sunlight. I wanted to have it all. And the first step was, as Jeremy so charmingly put it, a bed and breakfast with a nice view of the Atlantic, where a private room had been waiting for me since the day I was born.

All I had to do was get there, and show that I was worthy. All I had to do was get results. I pushed away from the counter. "I'm hungry. Are you hungry?"

"I could eat," said Jeremy.

"Great. Let's go."

There's nothing like Harvard in the fall. New students in their carefully chosen outfits, wandering like lost lambs in need of a shepherd; returning students, half of them in their pajamas, the other half dressed for the job interviews they have scheduled after class. The specter of student loans hanging over all but the very rich and the very careful, crushing mountains of debt and madness primed to come crashing down as soon as the stars are right.

My family is very rich, and very careful. I've managed to swing enough grants to make my standard of living believable, keeping me connected to my peer group and capable of sympathizing with their concerns, but the bulk of my expenses have always been covered. It's important for the family to have a few like me in every generation, bold explorers who will go out into the world and come home with pockets packed with treasure more precious than pearls—knowledge, understanding, and the scientific methods to spread that understanding even further.

Jeremy strode across the campus like a young demigod, his back straight and his hair ruffled by the breeze. Some of the passing undergrads looked after him with lust in their eyes. Most were science majors, and had seen him walking in the faculty halls, putting him far enough above them to be desirable, but far enough below the professors to be safe. Humans are an innately aspirational species, always wanting the next rung up on the ladder, always afraid to reach too far, lest their grip fail them, and they fall. That odd combination of courage and cowardice has served them remarkably well, all things considered, keeping them striving without allowing them to wipe themselves out.

I trailed in Jeremy's wake, largely unnoticed by the student body. I didn't teach; I barely graded. I stuck to the lab, to the needles and the mice and the endless march of charts and graphs and information. Jeremy would have been lost without me. Everyone in our department knew it. And he repaid me by drawing the focus of the people who might otherwise have kept me from my work. It was a symbiotic relationship, like the clownfish and the anemone, and every time I thought too hard about it, I realized anew that I was going to miss it when I ended.

The off-campus pizza joint we had claimed as our own during the first year of our program was packed, as always, with bodies both collegiate and civilian. Jeremy cut a path through them, making space for me to slide through the crowd unnoticed, until we came to the round table at the very back, where several of our classmates—Terry of the weird plant project, Christine of the epigenetic data analysis, and Michael of the I wasn't really sure but it involved a lot of maggots project. Jeremy dropped into an open chair. I did the same, with slightly more grace.

There was a shaker of parmesan near my side of the table. I palmed it while Jeremy was exchanging enthusiastic greetings with our supposed "friends." We were all in constant competition for lab space, funding, and publication credits. Even though our fields were dissimilar enough that I would have expected us all to have the freedom to work as we liked, it seemed like we were forever stepping on one another's toes. Only the fact that Jeremy and I were running a combined experiment—his tumors, my documentation of social changes in mice that had been infected—kept us from being at each other's throats just like everyone else.

To be fair, it helped that I didn't actually *care* about any of this. My classmates were counting on long careers in their chosen fields. I was only ever counting on the sea.

Christine flashed a quick, expensive smile at me, showing the result of decades of orthodontia. "Hey, Violet," she said. "How's every little thing?" Her accent was landlocked and syrupy sweet, Minnesota perfect. When we'd first met, I hadn't been able to understand a damn thing she said. Coastal accents were something I'd grown up with. Speech defects were no problem at all. But vowels that stretched like storm warnings and snapped like sails? That was something I hadn't been prepared for.

"Every little thing is fine," I said. "How's every little thing with you?"

Michael groaned. "You did it," he said, in an accusing tone. "You asked her. You asked her *with your face*. Do you hate us all? Is this how you show your hatred?"

"I was being polite," I said. That was all I had time for before Christine launched into a long, detailed description of her day. Terry put her hands over her face. Michael dropped his head to the table. I smiled, looking attentive and like I actually gave a damn, and all the while I was unscrewing the container of parmesan and tipping cheese out onto the floor.

Getting the test tube out of my pocket and transferring its contents to the cheese container was more difficult, since I couldn't risk anyone realizing my hands were moving. There were some things my fellow grad students accepted unquestioningly, such as when Michael had spent an entire week wearing the same Hawaiian shirt, "for luck," or when Terry gave up all fruits and vegetables that hadn't been harvested according to Jainist standards. Replacing their favorite powdery cheese-based condiment with a mixture of my own creation was not on that list. There would be questions.

No one would like my answers.

Christine was still talking when I finished doctoring the cheese. I cocked my head and waited for her to take a breath. Then, quick as a striking eel, I asked, "Did we want to order a pizza?"

Everyone started talking at once. Jeremy pulled out his phone and began taking notes, trying to work out how much pizza we actually needed and what the optimum mix of toppings would be. I demanded mushrooms, as always, and took advantage of the chaos to slip the cheese back onto the table. No one noticed. No one ever did. I'd been pulling this trick on this same group of people for three years, and not once had I been caught, which spoke more to their remarkable self-centeredness than it did to my incredible skills at sleight of hand and misdirection.

When the pizza arrived, everyone dumped parmesan on it like the stuff was about to be outlawed. So as not to stand out, I did the same. I just used a shaker I had swiped from another table, combining it with the excuse that I didn't want to wait for Terry to be done. She liked cheese so much that sometimes she ate it directly out of her palm. Monitoring her dosage had been a nightmare, and now that we were moving into the final stage, I had given up. Let her have as much as she wanted. I had my data.

The pizza tasted like tomato sauce and garlic and charcoal, the bottom burnt black by the speed with which this particular parlor pumped out their pies. I ate enough to be sociable, then put down my half-consumed slice and smiled winsomely at my classmates, my comrades, the people who'd defined my grad school experience. We weren't friends. We could never have been friends. But out of everyone in the world, these were the people who understood what my life had been since I'd arrived at Harvard, a shy biology student from U.C. Santa Cruz, whose academic career had taken her first very far, and then very close to home.

"I wanted to ask you all for a favor," I said, and they went still, curiosity and suspicion in their eyes. I never asked for favors. That wasn't my role in the social group. I *performed* favors, giving selflessly of my time, my intellect, and my snack drawer, when Terry inevitably forgot that she was a mammal and couldn't photosynthesize like her beloved plants.

"What do you need?" asked Jeremy. Then, brightening: "Did you want us to vet a potential date?"

"What? No. Ew. I told you already, I'm not interested in dating." I was interested in marriage, but there were specific ways for that to be arranged, very particular forms to be observed. My parents would have forgiven me for a sticky, ill-considered tryst while I was away at school. I would never have forgiven myself. "You all know my grants run out at the end of the semester..."

As I had expected, they all began talking at once again, trying to offer solutions, some practical, some ridiculous. I said nothing. It was best if I let them run themselves down, talking themselves into the inevitable silence.

When they quieted, I said, "I'm going to miss you too, but this is for the best, honestly. The experience always mattered more to me than the degree. Now I want to give you something in return. My parents want me to come home for spring break, and they've invited me to bring you all along. There's plenty of room at the inn, so to speak."

The silence remained intact. It was well known that my parents operated a bed and breakfast in the sleepy seaside town where I'd been born. Miles from anywhere, sheltered by natural cliff walls, surrounded by the sea, it was the perfect place to raise a family. We didn't get many tourists, but the ones who came for a season always went home raving about our hospitality, our food, and the incredible clarity of the air. Why, sometimes, it seemed like the air was so clean that the stars didn't even glimmer. It was the perfect place, as long as you were prepared for its…eccentricities.

I had never been shy about where I came from, but I had also never extended an invitation home before. Certainly not for the entire group at once. I could see the calculations in their eyes, the war between curiosity and caution playing out all over again. I picked up my pizza and gnawed idly at the crust, feeling the crunchy dough press up against my gums and ease the ache there a bit. I was running out of time. If my friends didn't agree to my proposal, I would need to find a way to convince them.

The idea was not appealing. Some experiments only work if the rat enters the maze willingly, and I have never been a fan of using physical force when a temptingly waved piece of cheese will do.

"I hate to ask, because I'm sure it makes me sound cheap, but…would your folks be expecting us to pay for rooms?" Christine's cheeks colored red. "I know, I know. It's just that most of my cash is already spoken for, and I can't afford a seaside getaway. No matter how nice it sounds."

"All expenses paid," I said soothingly. "My parents aren't rich—" Lying had gotten so much easier in the time I'd been at Harvard. "—but they own the bed and breakfast free and clear, and if they have to cook anyway, it doesn't cost them much to feed my friends. You'll have to bring your own beer. That's the one thing they won't be providing. They just want to thank you for being such good friends to me, and meet you at least once before we're not all together." I let my voice break, just a little.

That was all it took. "Oh, Violet," said Terry, her eyes suddenly bright with tears. "Of course we'll come. We'd love to meet your family."

"Yeah," said Jeremy. "It'll be fun."

"Thank you," I said. "Thank you all."

It might not be fun. But it was sure going to be something.

The mice ripened in their enclosures, tumors swelling and bursting under the skin. Terry's fruits ripened on the vine, and she fed them to us, a rainbow of sweet flesh and seeds like jewels, and twice as precious in the eyes of the woman who had nurtured them. She grew black tomatoes and beans the color of bruises, and I stole what I could for the gardens at home. Mama would love watching the black fruits grow and darken, like the water before the storm, and we always needed something new for the table. There wasn't much variety for the land-locked, who tired of fish, yet still wanted to stay close to home, where they could be helpful if the need arose.

Presumably Christine and Michael had their own means of marking the passage of time, something involving genetic drift and maggot pupation, but I didn't care, and so I didn't ask. What I cared about was that they continued to meet us at the pizza parlor twice a month, and kept pouring powdery cheese over their already cheesy meals. Christine had started licking it off her fingers, a quick, compulsive gesture she didn't seem to realize was happening until it was over. Michael wasn't quite so obvious, but I couldn't remember the last time I'd seen him blink. According to my notes, it had been over a month.

Dutifully, I wrote down the results of the mouse studies I was conducting with Jeremy in one notebook, and the results of the studies I was conducting on my classmates in another. My handwriting was better in the first, and filled with excited ink blotches and misspelled words in the second. It was hard to dredge up much enthusiasm for mice, considering how close my *real* work was to coming to an end.

It would have been easy to charter a bus to take us home, but that would have meant leaving all the cars on the campus. Terry didn't drive, but Michael, Christine, and Jeremy all did. That many abandoned vehicles would point far too quickly to us having left as a group, and might raise questions when classes resumed and half the life sciences grad students didn't reappear. No. Better to give everyone a gas card and say that my parents wanted my friends to have the freedom to explore the coast at will. Better to lie a little now, and make the big lies easier down the line.

Jeremy watched as I lugged my things out to his car. His expression was torn between amusement and dismay, finally tipping over the edge when I came out with my third suitcase.

"You're coming back at the end of the break, right?" he asked. "I know your funding extends to the end of the semester. You've told us that often enough. We might still have a breakthrough that could pay for the rest of your education."

"I'm not giving up, Jeremy," I said, shoving the suitcase into the backseat. "I want to finish my project as much as anybody. But I also want to be realistic. If that means offloading a few things I don't need to have regular access to in order to make moving out easier, I'm going to do it. I'm sorry."

"It's okay," he said, sounding distinctly uncomfortable. "I just...I really want you to finish your research, that's all. You've got a brilliant scientific mind. You shouldn't wind up rotting away in some seaside town just because your family didn't have the money to keep you where you belonged."

I had long since learned to see the digs people made at my family as pitiful attempts at complimenting me. I wasn't "like" the other girls who came from small coastal backgrounds. I wasn't the hick my background told my peers to expect, and so they heaped praise upon me for overcoming my early limitations. It was insulting. It was wrong-headed and cruel and for a long time, it had been enough to keep my feelings from getting in the way of my work. But they meant it—all of it—in the nicest, least offensive way possible.

We're so proud of you for being better than the people who bore you, raised you, loved you enough to send you out into the world when they could easily have kept you home for your own good.

We're so impressed that you were able to grow up with a focused intellect and the ability to tie your own shoes, considering the obstacles you had to overcome.

We're so amazed that you can speak properly and dress yourself, since you should have been a babbling, half-naked cavegirl.

I smiled at Jeremy, broadly, showing him my natural, slightly uneven teeth. They had been slanting subtly for weeks now; I was pushing them back into their sockets every morning before I went outside. The signs were there, for people who knew how to look for them; people who hadn't privately filed the marks as folk nonsense and fairy tales, better left forgotten. Better left to seaside hicks.

"I promise you, no matter where I wind up, I won't rot away," I said. "Are you all packed and ready to go?"

"I've just been waiting for you."

"Then let's go. I want to get there before the others; the last thing we need is for them to wander off into town because they get tired of waiting."

Jeremy laughed. Actually laughed, like this was the funniest thing I'd ever said. Hatred kindled in my chest, surprisingly bright given how much time I spent finding ways to bank it back, to tamp it down. "Oh, like there's that much town for them to wander into," he said.

I shrugged, feeling the fluid shift of muscles under my skin. I was running out of time. Soon, I would have all the time in the world. It wasn't a contradiction. It just looked like one when viewed from the outside.

I wouldn't be viewing it from the outside for very much longer.

"You'd be surprised," I said. "Innsmouth has a way of sneaking up on you."

There was a time when Innsmouth was isolated, unfamiliar, even forbidden, blocked off from the ceaselessly searching hands and eyes of men by the shape of the land, which curled around our coves and caverns like the hand of a nurturing parent, protecting and concealing us. But the cities spread, and the roads reached out in fungal waves, seeking the points of greatest weakness. They grew across the body of Massachusetts, poisoning it even as they connected it to the rest of the continent. My parents liked to talk about the days when it was a long voyage from "civilization" to our doorstep.

It took Jeremy ninety minutes. It would have taken an hour, but there was traffic. There was always traffic getting out of Boston, which attracted cars like spilled jam attracted ants.

"This is why you never go to see your family, isn't it?" he asked, after the fifth time we were cut off by an asshole in a Lexus.

"One of the reasons," I said, trying to sound like I wasn't entertaining pleasant fantasies of murder. The asshole in the Lexus would have opened like a flower after the correct sequence of cuts, blossoming into something beautiful. Best of all, the beautiful thing he could have become would never have cut anyone else off on the highway. Beautiful things had better ways to spend their time than behind the wheel.

Then we came around the final curve in the road, and the Atlantic was spread out before us like a gleaming sapphire sheet, and I stopped thinking about murder. I stopped thinking about anything but the sea, and how it was already a beautiful thing, no knives or bloodshed required.

"Wow," breathed Jeremy, and for the first time, I was in total agreement with him about something that didn't involve the poisonous kiss of the great god Science.

We drove down the winding road that led into Innsmouth, playing peek-a-boo with the shoreline all the way. Trees blocked our view about half the time, keeping us from seeing the waves break against the rocks. My ancestors had planted many of those trees, designing this stretch of road as carefully as Jeremy and I had designed the mazes we used to keep the mice distracted and happy. Men were happy when they could see the sea, as long as they never saw too much. When they saw too much, they began to understand, and when they understood...

There were realities the human mind was never meant to withstand, pressures it was never meant to survive. Knowledge is like the sea. Go too deep, and the crushing weight of it could kill you.

"Wow," said Jeremy again, when the road leveled off and we cruised into town, past the old-fashioned houses and the wrought-iron streetlights that graced every corner. It was like driving into the past, into an age a hundred years dead and buried. He was gaping openly, twisting in his seat to get a better look at the shop windows and the elegant curves of architecture. "Are you sure people *live* here? This isn't, like, Disneyland for tourists?"

"Welcome to Innsmouth," I said. "Founded in 1612 by settlers who wanted a place where they could live peacefully and raise their families according to their own traditions, without worrying about outside interference. Unlike most of the coastal towns around here, there was never a re-founding. We've been living on and working this shore for four hundred years."

Jeremy took his eyes off the town long enough to give me a questioning, sidelong look. "Boston was founded in 1620," he said. "Your town can't be older than Boston."

"No one's ever told the town that," I said. "You can find our land deeds and our articles of incorporation at Town Hall, if you're really curious."

"I guess that explains your accent."

I blinked. "I beg your pardon?"

"It's just..." Jeremy took a hand off the wheel and waved it vaguely, encompassing everything around us. "You've always said you were from Massachusetts, but you don't have any accent I've ever heard before. I figured you might have had speech therapy when you were a kid, or something. If this town is really older than Boston, though, it makes sense that you would have grown up with a different regional accent. This is like, someone's graduate project, right here. I bet you have linguistic tics so population-specific that no one even hears them anymore."

Oh, we heard them. We heard them, and we spent the bulk of our time trying to beat them out of ourselves if we were ever intending to cross the town line, because people gravitated toward strangeness, and so we were only allowed to leave during the brief time when we were *normal*. Such a pretty, petty, pointless word.

I said none of that. I only pointed to the turnoff that would take us from the main road to my family's home, and said, "This way."

Jeremy obligingly turned, looking slightly dismayed as Innsmouth dropped away behind us. "I thought we were staying in town."

"Technically, we are. The town limits encompass six miles of shoreline. If we ever wanted to sell, everyone who lives here would walk away a millionaire." Human families living in our homes; human children playing on our beaches, unaware of what slumbered, peacefully dreaming, only a few fathoms away. It was a charmingly terrible thought, the sort of world that could never be allowed to exist. The consequences of a few brightly-colored shovels and pails would be too terrible for words.

I leaned back in my seat, still smiling. "There are three bed and breakfasts in town. My parents are generally believed to operate the nicest one. We certainly have the best view. But you'll see for yourself soon enough. Keep driving. We're almost there now. We're almost home."

Jeremy said nothing, sensing, on some deep, primate level, that there was nothing for him to say. The road twisted beneath us like the body of a great eel, like a tentacle reaching out to take what it wanted from the world, until we came around the final curve, and there it was, standing beautiful and bleak against the skyline. My home.

Relaxation came all at once, so profound that I could feel my muscles soften all the way down to where they brushed against the bone. I was back. Finally, after years of care packages and quiet refusals, I was back where I belonged.

"Holy shit," said Jeremy. "Does Dracula live with you?"

"Only on summer vacation, and he tips well," I said blithely.

"Holy *shit*."

Normally, I would have called him on his failure to come up with something better. He was a scientist: he prided himself on always knowing the right words to describe a situation. But I had to admit that it was nice to have him so impressed with my childhood home, which I hadn't seen in so many, many years. We had all known that if I came back, I wouldn't leave again. The longing for the sea would have been too great.

It already was. "Carver's Landing," I said, swallowing the sudden thickness of my voice and hoping he wouldn't notice. "Built in 1625, after the original house burned down in an unfortunate candle incident. My ancestors wanted to make a statement about how we didn't die in fire; we only died in water, and we refused to fear it."

Jeremy didn't say anything. He didn't even tease me about having a house with a name. He really *was* in shock.

Most New England bed and breakfasts were quaint things, suitable for the cover of little pamphlets intended to be distributed at local bus stations and airports. Not so Carver's Landing. Our family home was a glorious four-story monstrosity, built right up on the edge of the cliff, so that any shift in the tectonic plates would send us tumbling down, down, down below the waves, where anyone who saw us fall would presume we had gone to a watery grave. The wood was white, weathered by wind and coated in salt; the architecture was Colonial, with striking Victorian influences. It was the sort of house that should have been the topic of thesis papers written by wide-eyed history students. It had grown organically under the hands and hammers of generations; it had seen a nation rise. And we rented rooms for fifty dollars a night to tourists lucky or foolish enough to make a wrong turn and find themselves in Innsmouth for the night.

Jeremy drove slowly down the shallow hillside separating us from the house. A small paved lot cupped the left side of Carver's Landing. Three cars were already there, all more than twenty years old, their sides pitted and rusted by saltwater and wind. I wrinkled my nose at the sight of them. It was time to open the garage and pull out something a little newer. Caution was important, sure, but so was having a car that would actually run. So was not attracting attention for driving a junker.

Jeremy pulled his shining silver hybrid into a space a safe distance from the other cars, like a gray shark sliding past whales, and I realized dimly that I was ashamed of my family's choices. I was ashamed of the rust and the salt and the decay, of things I'd viewed as natural and right when I was a child, growing up eternally in sight of the sea. I had been out in the world too long. It had been necessary for my work, and I didn't regret doing as was required of me—I could never regret doing as was required of me, not when the world was so wide, and the landlocked parts of it so dangerous and wild—but I had still been out in the world too long. It was time, and past time, for me to have come home.

"You unload the trunk," I said. "I'll get us a luggage cart." I didn't give him time to answer or object before I was shoving my door open with my foot and running for the kitchen door. The curtains were drawn, but I knew that someone was watching us. Someone was always watching at Carver's Landing. Someone had always been watching at school, too, but there they tried to pretend that they weren't, that privacy was a thing that could exist on land, even though anyone with any sense would know that it was a lie.

The door was unlocked. I flung myself through, and there was my older sister, taller than me, straight-backed and flat-faced—*poor thing, to be so long grown, and still here*—and when she stepped aside, there was my mother, short and hunched and smiling her sea-changed smile, and I threw myself into her arms, and I was finally, finally home.

By the time I finished greeting my family, two more cars had arrived in the parking lot. I collected my sister and a luggage cart, and went out to meet them.

Christine was uncurling from the driver's seat of her car, a long, foreign flower trying to decide whether she could flourish in unfamiliar soil. She offered a polite Midwestern smile as my sister and I approached. "Violet," she said. "I was afraid you'd run off and deserted us. Who's this?"

"I'm Violet's mother," said my sister, and my heart burned for her, and for the world we had to live beside. She smiled charmingly as she stepped toward Christine, holding out her hand to be shaken. "You must be Christine. I've heard so much about you, but I must admit, Violet never told us how lovely you were."

"Oh," said Christine brightly, and smiled as she tossed her hair. "It's lovely to meet you, Ms. Carver. Your home is…wow. It's really something."

"Wait until you see the inside," said my sister, and laughed, and kept laughing as the rest of my classmates got out of their cars and began loading their bags onto the luggage cart. They would all be distracted by the sound, I knew, by the bright simplicity of it. They wouldn't be looking at her cold, calculating eyes, or at the curtains behind her, which twitched as our parents and siblings stole looks at us.

The door opened. Two of our brothers, both my age, emerged to help with the bags. Chattering, excited, and unaware, the other students followed me inside, ready to begin their seaside escape. Get away from your problems, get away from your woes, get away from the real world—get away from everything except for the sea, which cannot be run from once the waves have noticed your presence. Once the sea has become aware, it can only be survived, and not many can manage that much.

Despite the fact that spring was often our "busy" season, my parents had accepted no bookings for the month, and every room was open. Christine and Jeremy were settled with seaside views, while Terry and Michael had to content themselves with views of the sweeping cliffs behind the town. None of them complained, at least not in my hearing, and I was grateful. All of them would be able to hear the sea, to smell it in the air, but the last part of my study involved denying two of them the sight of it.

"Oh, Violet, it's beautiful," said Terry, gazing rapturously out her window at the tree-covered hills. Most of it was virgin forest. We had little interest in cutting down the trees that protected us from prying eyes, and when we were alone at home, we kept our houses cool, verging into cold. Leave the tropics for those who were not predestined to go down into the unrelenting deeps. Heat was a luxury of the land, and it was better not to get too accustomed to something that could never stay.

"I never really thought about it," I said. My own window faced the water, of course. No one I knew who lived in Innsmouth voluntarily faced away from the waves. Still, she looked so happy...I stepped closer, pointing to a distant rocky outcropping. "There used to be a house there, a long time ago. It burned down in a thunderstorm. The fire never spread to the trees, and since the family who owned the place owned all the surrounding woodlands, no one else has ever tried to develop there."

"It's like traveling backward through time." Terry shook her head. "How are you not crawling in conservationists?"

"Most of them are out at Devil's Reef, doing marine impact studies."

Terry turned to me, eyes wide. "We're near Devil's Reef?"

I nodded. The government's "accidental" bombing of Devil's Reef back in 1928 was still taught in wildlife conservation classes, which pointed to the destruction of both the habitat and several potentially undiscovered species—a lot of the fish caught in that area were unique, unknown to science—as a clear example of why we needed more protected areas. Devil's Reef had been locked down for decades. Human ships patrolled the waters; human scientists cataloged and studied the fish, excited by each new find, all blissfully unaware of what they would find if they dove too deep.

Sometimes one of them did. And then it was all very sad, and their colleagues were reminded to respect the sea.

"We can't take a boat out to the reef itself, of course, but we can get pretty close," I said. "Maybe we could go sailing in a few days, and let you see the rocks that break the surface."

Terry smiled brightly. "I would like that."

"Then I'll see what we can do," I said. "Dinner's in an hour. Fish chowder. I hope you're hungry."

"Starving," she said.

I felt a little guilty as I let myself out of the room and started down the hall. None of my friends had volunteered for this. They thought they were having a nice vacation that would end when they returned to their lives with suntans and new stories. They didn't understand.

But then, the mice hadn't volunteered either. And none of my friends, when pressed, had hesitated a moment before picking up the needle.

Mother might have been offended by being relegated to the kitchen while Pansy pretended to be her, but she still knew her role; the stew was thick and rich with cream, and the smell of the sedatives rolling off the bowls belonging to my friends was strong enough that it was a miracle none of them noticed. One by one, they filled their mouths, only to swallow, look puzzled, and lose consciousness. Christine was the first to pass out, followed in short order by Michael, and then by Terry, who slumped gently forward, already snoring.

Jeremy was the last. He stopped, spoon halfway back to his bowl, and gave me a befuddled, deeply betrayed look. "Violet," he said, and his tongue was twisted; it didn't want to do as he said. His befuddlement deepened. "Wha' did you do?" he asked, words slurring.

I said nothing. I just looked at him solemnly, and waited until his head struck the table next to his bowl. The spoon skittered from his hand, coming to a stop when it hit the base of the soup tureen. Those of us who had joined my friends for dinner—my brothers, my sister Pansy, a few selected folks from town who were supposed to make the gathering seem realistic—sat in silence for several seconds. Finally, I pulled out my phone and checked the stopwatch app that had been running since the soup was served.

"Thirty-seven seconds," I said. "They should be out cold for at least an hour. Are the rooms ready for them?"

"They are," said my mother, from behind me. Her voice was thick with undercurrents and dark with tidal flows. I turned to her. She was standing in the doorway, her thinning hair slicked wet against her flattening skull, and she was so hideous that men would have screamed to see her, and so beautiful she took my breath away. "Everything is as you asked. Now I have to ask you a question, my arrogant, risk-taking girl. Are you sure? Do you think this will work?"

I nodded solemnly. "I do." Her voice was distorted, like she was speaking through thick mud. The Innsmouth accent had claimed her speech almost entirely. Underwater, her new voice would sound like the ringing of a bell, clean and clear and so perfect that it could never have existed in the open, impure air. She was almost done changing.

She was looking at me dubiously. All my family was. Undaunted, I pressed on. "When I started this experiment, I told you what it would entail, and you agreed. Dagon—"

"Not this again," grumbled my eldest brother. Half his teeth were needled fishhooks, designed to catch and keep the creatures of the abyssal zone. It was almost a race between him and my mother, whose blood had never been as pure as my father's. He had been gone before I left for Harvard, slipping silently down to the city beneath Devil's Reef while I was at Santa Cruz. And that, right there—the difference between my mother and my brother, and my poor, still almost-human sister—was the reason that they needed me so badly.

I looked at my brother, and I didn't flinch. "Dagon chose me for a reason. I'll make Him proud. I'll make you all proud."

"And if you don't?" There was a challenge in his voice, naked to the world.

"Then I'll have failed, and I'll answer to Him when I go down below the waves," I said. "Letting me try cost us nothing but time, and if we can't afford a little time, who can?" My classmates were still sleeping. Christine was drooling. I looked at them, studying them, *memorizing* them as they were now. All this would change soon.

"Besides," I said. "If this doesn't work, they'll taste like anybody else. Now help me get them upstairs."

Christine and Michael woke alone. One more control on an already complicated experiment. Jeremy was still out, thanks to an additional dose of sedatives slipped between his cheek and gums. I was sitting by Terry's bedside, making notes in my journal, when she jerked on the cuffs holding her to the bed. It was a small motion, but enough to cause the chain to clink against the bedframe. I lifted my head in time to see her open her eyes and blink groggily in my direction.

"Violet?" she asked, voice thick with sleep. "Did I doze off?"

She tried to sit up. The cuffs held her fast. Panic flashed through her eyes, taking the last of the drowsiness with it.

"Violet?" There was a shrill note to my name this time. She hadn't fully processed what was happening to her. This time, she strained against the cuffs hard enough to shift the bedframe slightly, and to yank at the IV line connected to the inside of her left elbow. She stopped, and stared at the needle like she had never seen anything like it before.

"There's an excellent chance your great-great-grandmother was from Innsmouth," I said calmly, looking back to my journal. "Did you know? I suppose not, since you didn't seem to recognize the name of the town. She had two children before she died. Your great-great-grandfather remarried, and had three more children by his second wife, who always presented the entire brood as her own. I guess remarriage wasn't as commonplace back then, which seems odd, given the overall mortality rate. It's hard to be absolutely sure who descended from which woman, but I'm ninety percent sure at this point that you descended from your great-great-grandfather's first wife. We'll know soon, I guess."

"Violet, this isn't funny."

I glanced up. "It's not supposed to be. I'm telling you why you're here."

Terry stared at me. "*What?*"

"You're here because there's a very good chance that you're descended from your great-great-grandfather's first wife," I said. "She was weak. She hadn't even started to show the Innsmouth look when she died. I suppose that's why her children never showed it—or if they did, we can't find any record. At least one of them reached adulthood. That's simple math. Your great-great-grandfather had five children by two wives, and four of them lived to have children of their own. If you are, in fact, descended from an Innsmouth woman, we'll know in a few days."

Genuine fear flashed across her face. "A few...a few *days?* Violet, I have to get back to the school. You can't just keep me here. The others will notice if I disappear."

"The others aren't noticing anything right now, except for their own predicaments," I said. "Christine has been screaming non-stop for the last two hours. Michael won't stop laughing."

"You're insane." Her voice dropped to a whisper. "Where's Jeremy?"

"Still asleep. I'll go to wake him soon." I tried to sound reassuring. "I wouldn't worry about it, honestly. We'll keep you comfortable. We put the catheter in while you were asleep, so you won't have to go through that messy ordeal, and in a few days, we'll know everything we need to."

"You can't..."

"I'm a scientist," I said. "This is exactly what I *can* do."

She was screaming at me as I got up and left the room, closing the door neatly behind myself and cutting off her shouts at the same time. Soundproofing had so many excellent uses. Checking my journal one last time to be sure I had all the notes I needed, I started down the hall toward

Jeremy's room, steeling my expression as I went. He would never know how easy he'd had it, working with mice. Mice couldn't talk back, or ask why you were doing this to them...or figure out that they were in the control group.

All four members of my little "social group" had been consuming a powder made from my extracted, purified plasma, mixed with various biogenic chemicals, for the past year and a half. I had monitored dosages, dates, everything, and watched them all for signs of transformation. Two of them had confirmed Innsmouth heritage, the bloodlines too thin and attenuated to allow them to hear Dagon calling without outside aid. The other two were human, as ordinary and temporary as anyone else. All of them would be told that they were Innsmouth-born. All of them would be encouraged to listen for Dagon's voice whispering to them through my blood, which was even now dripping, one pure, perfect drop at a time, through their IV lines.

Two could see the sea; two could see the land. One of each group had Innsmouth blood; one did not. For however long it took, they would eat the same, drink the same, experience all the same physical stimuli, and then...

Then we would see what we would see.

Quietly, I let myself into Jeremy's room and sat down, reopening my journal and resuming my documentation of the day. It was easy to lose myself in my notes, letting the simple facts of the experiment take priority over everything around me. It was harder to keep going. Harder than I'd ever thought it would be when I had explained to my parents what I wanted to do, how I wanted to go among the outsiders and look for the missing cousins, the one we had always known existed, so far from the singing of the sea. I had come to them with Dagon's voice in my heart and the great god Science in my hands, and when they had let me go, I had promised them the world of men wouldn't change me, could *never* change me. I was a daughter of Innsmouth, beloved of Dagon, destined for the sea. Nothing as small or simple as the company of humans could change that.

I had been young then. I had been a fool, unaware of the way rational scientists could sometimes fall in love with their laboratory animals, disrupting experiments and risking years of work for the sake of saving something with a lifespan no longer than a sneeze. I had believed my morality to be absolute and unassailable, and I certainly hadn't expected to find myself feeling sorry for them.

There was no room for pity here. Two of them would almost certainly die. My control group. I would have been happier if I'd been able to find more than four experimental subjects, but I had also wanted a fifty-fifty split, and even finding two of the lost cousins in a place where I could gain their trust had been a trial. I had followed hundreds of genealogies and family records to wind up back at Harvard, discarding schools with only one Innsmouth descendant, or whose resident cousins were too young, or too old, or too involved in fields where I would have no excuse for access. Harvard had been the only choice, and years of effort had been required to woo the four of them.

Unless my treatments were more effective than they had any right to be, the two with no Innsmouth blood would leave me very soon. But the two who had an ancestral claim to these shores…

They might still have a chance.

Jeremy made a small, confused sound. I looked up, and smiled.

"Violet? What's wrong?" My sister stood, frowning at me as I leaned, white-faced and shaking, in the kitchen doorway. Silently, I held out my hand, showing her the contents of my palm. Two human incisors, both intact down to the root, blood-tipped and pearly.

Her eyes widened.

"Are your teeth falling out?" she asked, looking at my face, my hair, searching for some sign that my transition had accelerated.

I shook my head. "My teeth have been loose for weeks, but I think it's because of the immune response triggered when I harvested my plasma. They stopped weakening when I started spreading the harvests out among the family." The words came easily, devoid of emotional response. If only everything were that easy! "They belong to Terry. The girl in the room that looks out over the forest."

How she had screamed when the teeth started dropping out of her head, when the hair started wisping from her scalp! How she had fought, how she had kicked, how she had done her best to deny what was happening to her! It would have been impressive, if it hadn't been so frightening. She could hurt herself, and until we knew where she was in her transition, I didn't want to risk it. Sedating her would be a solution. It might be the only solution. It was still something to be avoided for as long as possible.

"Does this mean the process is working?" My sister made no effort to conceal the excitement in her voice. If this worked—if I could activate the sleeping seeds of Dagon that waited, eternally patient, in each of us—then she might be able to follow our father to the city below Devil's Reef decades sooner than her thinning blood would have otherwise allowed.

I couldn't blame her for her excitement. I couldn't join her in it, either. Not with Christine's death so fresh in my mind. She'd lost all her teeth, too, and her fingers had twisted as the bones struggled to reshape themselves, following biological imperatives that were alien to her too-human flesh. She had still *tasted* human, when we disposed of her body according to the best and most traditional methods available to us. I'd fed her, one spoonful at a time, to her surviving classmates. They would never know, unless they lived. And if they lived, the life of one human woman would no longer seem so important.

"I don't know," I said quietly. "They're all changing. They're all... becoming something more. But none of them is transforming with any real speed. Michael stopped breathing this morning. I had to give him CPR." And his bones had been soft under my hands, more like cartilage than bone, bending and yielding until I'd been afraid of crushing his sternum. "They may survive. They may all die."

Terry's teeth were falling out. Jeremy was completely bald, and his eyes had developed nictating membranes that slid closed a second before he blinked. Michael's skeleton was going soft, and his irises had taken on a flat, coppery cast that looked more like metal than flesh. They were all changing. They had all changed.

We were so far past the point of no return that it couldn't even be seen on a clear day.

The authorities had come to the house weeks ago. I had hidden upstairs while they spoke to my sister in the kitchen, asking whether she had noticed anything wrong with the car when my friends and I had left to drive back to Boston. She had shaken her head and wept almost believable tears, asking again and again whether they thought I was dead or simply missing. Then she had mentioned, as if offhandedly, that we had been planning to drive down the coast before heading back to school.

The footage of our cars being pulled out of the Atlantic had been shown on all the news programs two days later. There had been no bodies, of course, but there had been blood, and the windows had been broken. It wasn't hard to go from the images on the screen to the thought that we'd been pulled from the vehicle by the current, and would never be seen again.

At least part of that was true. None of my test subjects were ever going to be seen in the world of men again, and as for me...I had done my time outside of Innsmouth. I would stay here until my own returning was upon me, and then I would go, gladly, to the depths and the abyssopelagic dark below Devil's Reef, where I could drift, and dream with Dagon, and allow my false idols and service to Science to fall away from me, no longer needed, no longer required.

My sister looked at me gravely. "Do you think this is going to work?"

"I don't know." I looked at the teeth in my hand. "I honestly don't."

They had been locked in their rooms for almost a month when Jeremy surprised me. I unlocked the door, pushed it open, and found his bed empty, the window standing ajar. For a moment, I froze, trying to understand what I was seeing. The bowl containing his breakfast fell from my suddenly nerveless fingers.

"Jeremy?" I whispered. Then I bolted for the bed, jerking back the covers like he might be hiding there, somehow sandwiched between the blanket and the sheet. "Jeremy!"

I never heard him moving behind me. I was completely oblivious when the chair slammed into my back, knocking me forward. He hit me a second time, harder, before he turned and ran, fleeing down the hall.

Humans are hardy, resilient—mortal. Even unfinished and larval as I effectively was, I was still a daughter of Innsmouth. I shrugged off the blow and ran after him, my feet slipping in the spilled soup on the floor. The stairs were steep, and his damp footprints—the soup again—told me I was on the right track, at least until I reached the ground floor. He had enough of a head start that I only knew which way he had gone when I heard the back door slam behind him.

There wasn't time to go looking for my siblings, not if I wanted to stop him before he could reach the street and go looking for a payphone. I ran after him, out into the bright outside world, where the sea slammed against the shore like the beating of a vast, immortal heart. Then I stopped.

Jeremy was some twenty yards ahead of me, standing motionless on the place where the soil gave way to sand. The sun glinted off the polished dome of his skull, catching odd, iridescent highlights from his skin. I hadn't seen him in the sunlight before, not since his changes had truly begun. He was glorious. He was beautiful.

I walked to join him. He glanced my way, flat copper irises shielded from the sun by his half-deployed nictating membranes, and he did not run.

"What did you do?" he asked. His words were mushy, soft. All his teeth had fallen out the week before, and while I could see the needles of his new teeth pressing against his gums, they hadn't broken through. He'd develop the Innsmouth lisp soon, assuming the transformations continued, that his body was able to endure the strain. "What did you do to us? *Why?*"

"Why did you give cancer to all those mice?" I shrugged. "I needed to know if it was possible. I was telling you the truth when I said you had Innsmouth blood." A runaway girl, a local boy, a relationship cut short when her parents had followed her trail to the Massachusetts coastline. It was an old story, and one that had played out in every coastal town like ours. But in her case, that long-buried ancestor of the man who stood beside me, there had been things about her suitor that she hadn't been aware of. She'd carried his Innsmouth blood back to Iowa, where it had run through the generations like a poisonous silver line, finally pooling, dilute and deadly, in the veins of a man who wanted to change the world.

Jeremy turned to give me a shocked, even hurt look. The newly inhuman lines of his face didn't quite suit the expression. Deep Ones are many things. We're very rarely shocked. "This is nothing like the mice. We're *human beings*, and you took us captive and…*did* things to us. It's not the same at all."

"You were human beings who experimented on lower life forms to see what would happen to them, and because you thought you had the right," I said. "I read your Bible, you know. Years ago, when I first started at U.C. Santa Cruz. I wanted to…understand, I suppose. I wanted to *know*. And it said that God had given you dominion over all the plants and animals of the world, which meant that turning mice into explosive tumor machines was just fine. You were doing what God told you to do."

Jeremy didn't say anything. He just turned, slowly, to look back at the sea. I think that was the moment when he understood. The moment he stopped fighting.

"My God told me things, too, although I think He spoke to me a bit more directly than yours spoke to you. He said that some of His children had lost their way and needed someone to guide them home. He said that if I could figure out the way to do that, I could even help the faithful here in Innsmouth." A world where we could *choose* to return to the sea, to swim with Mother Hydra, to be glorious and smooth and darting through the depths like falling stars. To live forever, and not worry about the fragile human skins of our tadpole state.

"That didn't give you the right."

"If your God gave you the right to put the needle to the mouse, then my God gave me the right to put the needle to the man." I offered him my hand. "Come on. I need to get you back to the house."

"The sea doesn't let me sleep."

I dropped my hand.

"I can hear it, always. I think it's trying to talk to me. I've started hearing words when the surf hits the shore."

"What does it say?"

Jeremy turned to me, expression bleak. He was so beautiful, with his skin gleaming iridescent, and his sunken eyes. I would never have believed he could be so beautiful. "It's saying 'come home to me.'"

"You're not hearing the sea," I said, and offered him my hand again. This time, he took it. His skin was cooler than mine. He would dive below Devil's Reef before I did; he would see the abyssopelagic, and understand. I would have been envious, if I hadn't been so relieved. "You're hearing the voice of Dagon. He's welcoming you. He's welcoming you home."

Terry would need to be moved to a room that faced the sea; she deserved the chance to hear Him too, especially when she was doing so much better than Michael. Especially if hearing Dagon might mean that she would live. It would invalidate the experimental controls, but those didn't matter anymore; the human rules of scientific inquiry had only ever been a formality. I was bringing the lost children of Dagon home.

So much needed to be done. So much needed to be accomplished. My sister would be my first willing volunteer, and my heart swelled to think of her, finally beautiful, finally going home. But that was in the future. For now, I stood hand in hand with my first success, and turned to the sea, and listened to the distant voice of Dagon calling us to come down, deep down, below the waves.

Acknowledgments

...And that, I suppose, is that: we have come to the end of this long and tangled slice of my literary works, spanning years and pages and hours of your life. I hope you've enjoyed it. Honestly, I don't have a "if you didn't," because I'm assuming you wouldn't have picked it up if you hadn't already known what you were getting into. These are some of my best stories, and some of my favorite stories, and a few of my weirdest thrown in for good measure. It is the scope of me, and it'll be a few years before we can do this again.

And so, thank yous.

Thank you to John Joseph Adams, for helping me to improve beyond my wildest dreams, and to Jennifer Brozek, for taking a chance on me when no one else had seen my potential. Thank you to Ellen Datlow, for making my childhood dreams of anthology come true. And thank you to Jonathan Maberry and Bryan Thomas Schmidt, for commissioning me over and over again to write stories for them.

Thank you to Charlaine Harris, for good advice and good conversation, and for inviting me to play when she had an anthology for me to play in. Thank you to Toni Kelner, for excellent editorial notes and for being patient with me.

Thank you to Yanni Kuznia, for allowing me to put this anthology together, and to Diana Fox, for making it all work. Huge, starry-eyed thank yous to Carla Speed McNeil, whose incredible artistic talent has elevated my work in whole new ways.

Although she has worked more with me on long fiction than short, I must offer my profound thanks to Sheila Gilbert, without whom I would spend a lot more time deeply confused and trying to make sense of things. She is my rock, editorially speaking.

Amy McNally has probably put up with more of my crap than any other fifteen people combined. I love her beyond all measure. Even when she plays her violin at six in the morning.

Big thanks to my "pit crew": Tara O'Shea, Chris Mangum, and Michelle "Vixy" Dockrey. I love them dearly, I need them more than I can say, and I am the luckiest girl in the world because they love me back. Additional thanks to Margaret Dunlap, Shawn Connolly, and Whitney Johnson. They know why.

Thanks to my cats, for preserving my sanity on a day-to-day basis... and thanks to you, for reading. A story with no one to tell it to is a pretty poor tale. Being able to put together a short story collection is a privilege and an honor, and I am so happy to be sharing this one with the world. Those fools who laughed at me in the academy will never know what hit them.

I'll see you next time.

Copyright

“Laughter at the Academy: A Field Study in the Genesis of Schizotypal Creative Genius Personality Disorder (SCGPD)” Originally published in *The Mad Scientist’s Guide to World Domination: Original Short Fiction for the Modern Evil Genius*, 2013, John Joseph Adams, ed.

“Lost” Originally published in *Ravens in the Library: Magic in the Bard’s Name*, 2009, SatyrPhil Brucato and Sandra Buskirk, eds.

“The Tolling of Pavlov’s Bells” Originally published in *Apex Magazine*, January 2011, Catherynne M. Valente, ed.

“Uncle Sam” Originally published in *The Edge of Propinquity*, October 2011, Jennifer Brozek, ed.

“Emeralds to Emeralds, Dust to Dust” Originally published in *Oz Reimagined: New Tales from the Emerald City and Beyond*, 2013, John Joseph Adams and Douglas Cohen, eds.

“Crystal Halloway and the Forgotten Passage” Originally published in *Fantasy Magazine*, December 2011, John Joseph Adams, ed.

“Homecoming” Originally published in *Lightspeed*, September 2013, John Joseph Adams, ed.

“Frontier ABCs: The Life and Times of Charity Smith, Schoolteacher” Originally published in *Raygun Chronicles: Space Opera for a New Age*, 2013, Bryan Thomas Schmidt, ed.

“We Are All Misfit Toys in the Aftermath of the Velveteen War” Originally published in *Robot Uprisings*, 2014, John Joseph Adams and Daniel H. Wilson, eds.

“The Lambs” Originally published in *Bless Your Mechanical Heart*, 2014, Jennifer Brozek, ed.